THE ONES™

HOLY SHIT! THAT'S YOUR BIG SELL RIGHT HERE?

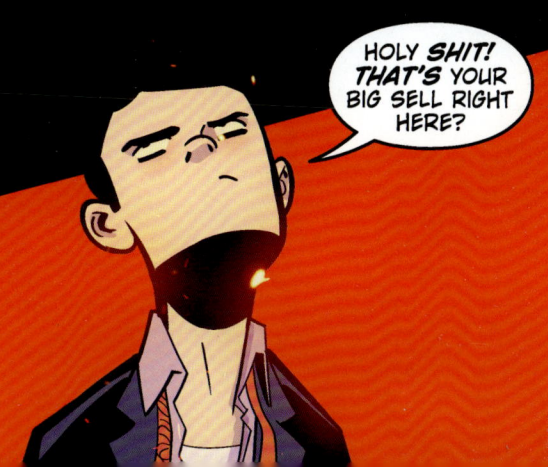

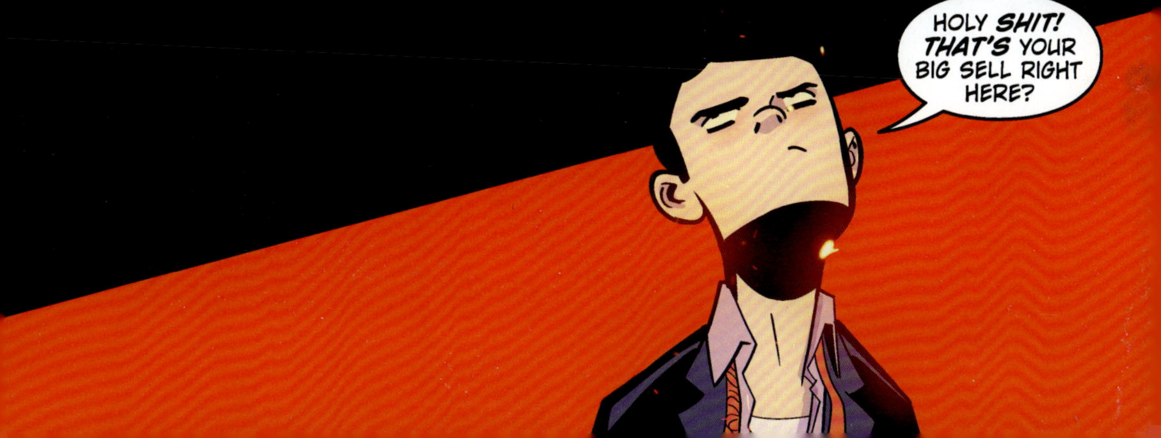

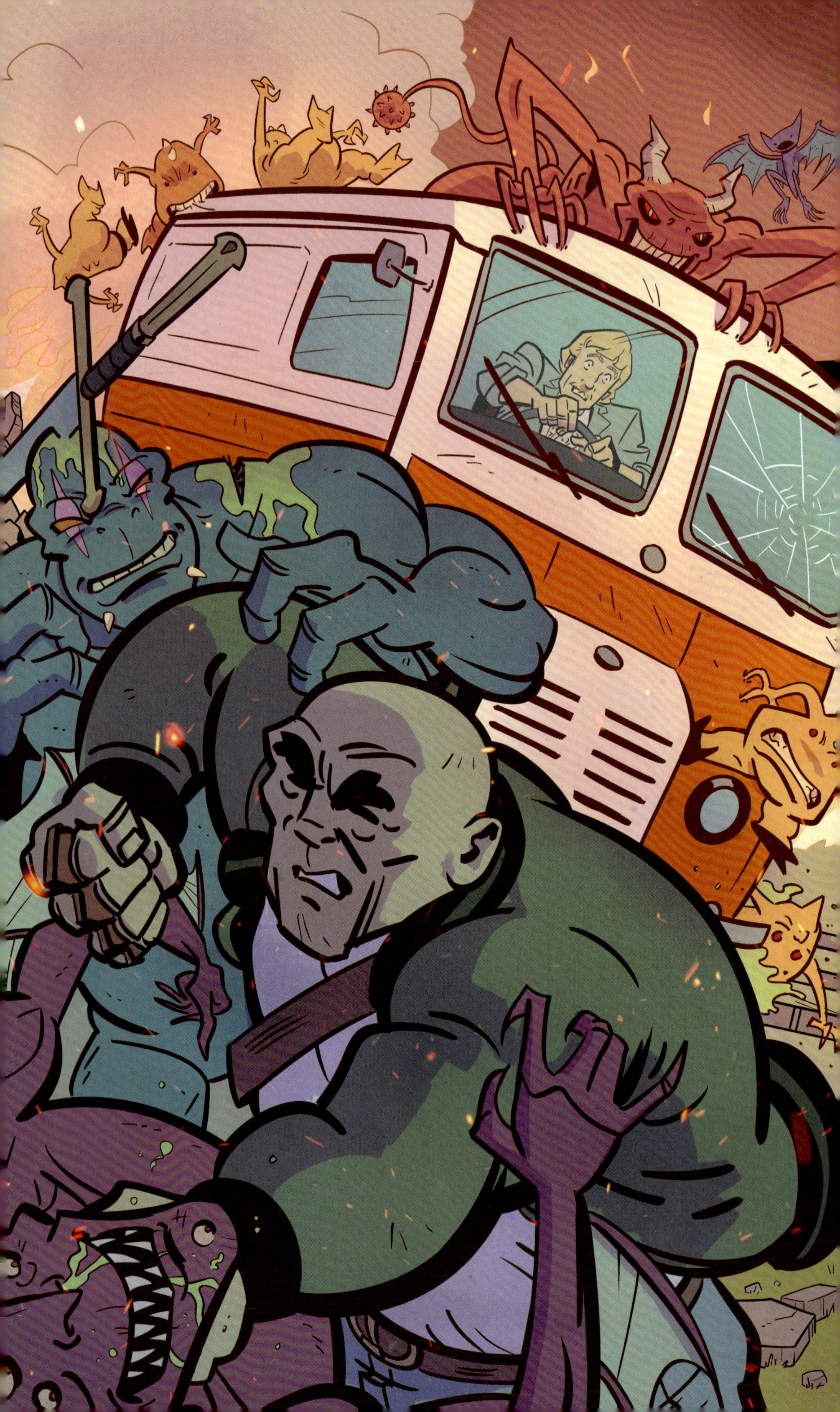

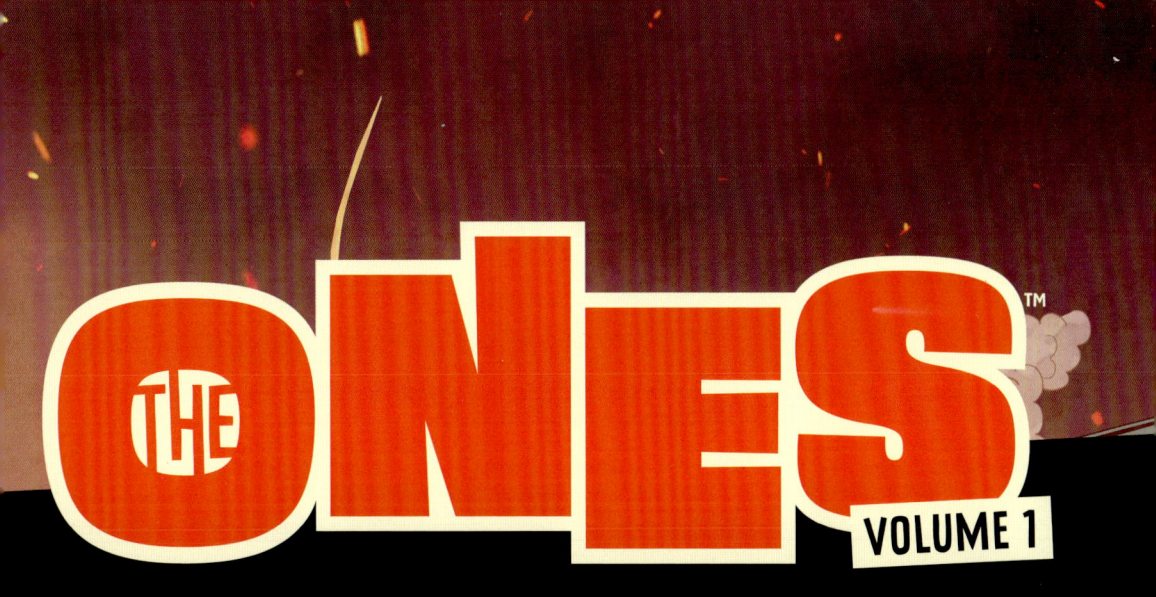

THE ONES™
VOLUME 1

CREATED BY **BRIAN MICHAEL BENDIS** AND **JACOB EDGAR**

COLORS **K. J. DÍAZ** LETTERING **JOSHUA REED**

COVER AND CHAPTER BREAKS BY **JACOB EDGAR** WITH **K. J. DÍAZ**

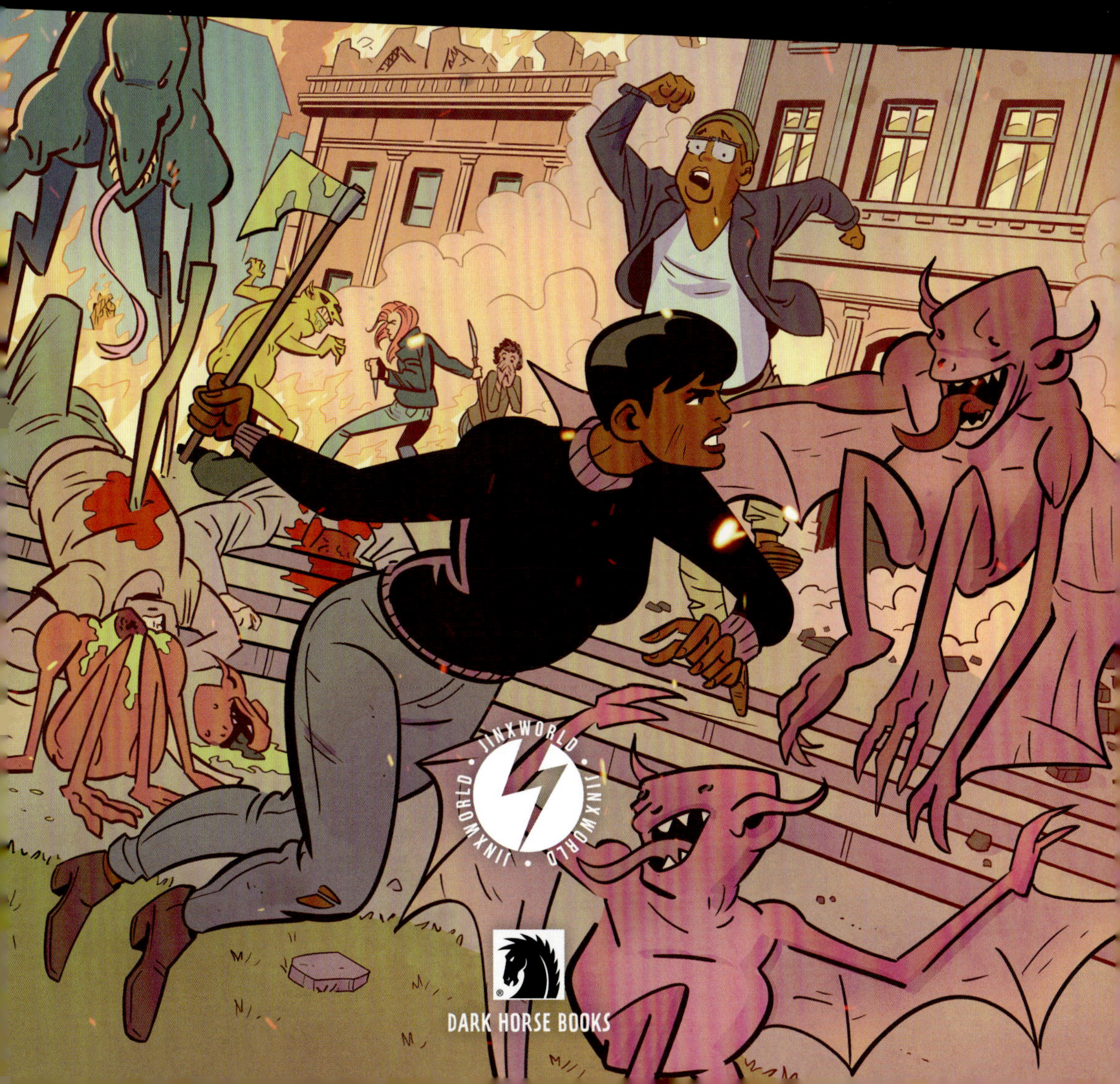
JINXWORLD
DARK HORSE BOOKS

PUBLISHER MIKE RICHARDSON **EDITOR** DANIEL CHABON
ASSISTANT EDITORS CHUCK HOWITT-LEASE AND MISHA GEHR
DESIGNER RICK DeLUCCO **DIGITAL ART TECHNICIAN** BETSY HOWITT

 Facebook.com/DarkHorseComics   Twitter.com/DarkHorseComics

To find a comics shop in your area, visit comicshoplocator.com.

THE ONES VOLUME 1™

Copyright © 2022, 2023 Jinxworld Holdings, LLC. All rights reserved. Jinxworld, its logo design, and all characters featured in or on this publication and the distinctive names and likeness thereof, and all related indicia are trademarks of Jinxworld Holdings, LLC. Dark Horse Books® and the Dark Horse logo are registered trademarks of Dark Horse Comics LLC. All rights reserved. Dark Horse is part of Embracer Group. No portion of this publication may be reproduced or transmitted, in any form or by any means, without the express written permission of Dark Horse Comics LLC. Names, characters, places, and incidents featured in this publication either are the product of the author's imagination or are used fictitiously. Any resemblance to actual persons (living or dead), events, institutions, or locales, without satiric intent, is coincidental.

This volume collects all issues of *The Ones* as well as all covers and extra content.

Published by
Dark Horse Books
A division of
Dark Horse Comics LLC
10956 SE Main Street
Milwaukie, OR 97222

DarkHorse.com

First edition: August 2023
Ebook ISBN 978-1-50672-992-3
Trade paperback ISBN 978-1-50672-991-6

10 9 8 7 6 5 4 3 2 1
Printed in China

Library of Congress Cataloging-in-Publication Data

Names: Bendis, Brian Michael, author. | Edgar, Jacob, illustrator. | Díaz,
   K. J., colorist. | Reed, Joshua (Letterer), letterer.
Title: The ones / created by Brian Michael Bendis and Jacob Edgar ; colors,
   K. J. Díaz ; lettering, Joshua Reed ; cover and chapter breaks by
   Jacob Edgar with K. J. Díaz.
Description: First edition. | Milwaukie, OR : Dark Horse Books, 2023. |
   "This volume collects all issues of The Ones as well as all covers and
   extra content." | Summary: "Every single person in every mythology that
   was told they were THE ONE are brought together for the first time to
   defeat . . . THE ONE. The actual one. The real actual one. This amazing
   new vision is brought to life by wunderkind artist and co-creator Jacob
   Edgar (Batman, Army of Darkness). Watch as he brings explosive comics
   splendor to this big new world! Think Good Omens meets Ghostbusters
   meets The Adam Project meets The Goonies meets Everything Everywhere All
   at Once meets, um, anything else you've ever liked!"-- Provided by
   publisher.
Identifiers: LCCN 2023002545 (print) | LCCN 2023002546 (ebook) | ISBN
   9781506729916 (trade paperback) | ISBN 9781506729923 (ebook)
Subjects: LCGFT: Comics (Graphic works) | Graphic novels.
Classification: LCC PN6728.O4958 B46 2023 (print) | LCC PN6728.O4958
   (ebook) | DDC 741.5/973--dc23/eng/20230127
LC record available at https://lccn.loc.gov/2023002545
LC ebook record available at https://lccn.loc.gov/2023002546

Neil Hankerson Executive Vice President • Tom Weddle Chief Financial Officer • Dale LaFountain Chief Information Officer • Tim Wiesch Vice President of Licensing • Vanessa Todd-Holmes Vice President of Production and Scheduling • Mark Bernardi Vice President of Book Trade and Digital Sales • Randy Lahrman Vice President of Product Development and Sales • Cara O'Neil Vice President of Marketing • Ken Lizzi General Counsel • Dave Marshall Editor in Chief • Davey Estrada Editorial Director • Chris Warner Senior Books Editor • Cary Grazzini Director of Specialty Projects • Lia Ribacchi Creative Director • Michael Gombos Senior Director of Licensed Publications • Kari Yadro Director of Custom Programs • Kari Torson Director of International Licensing

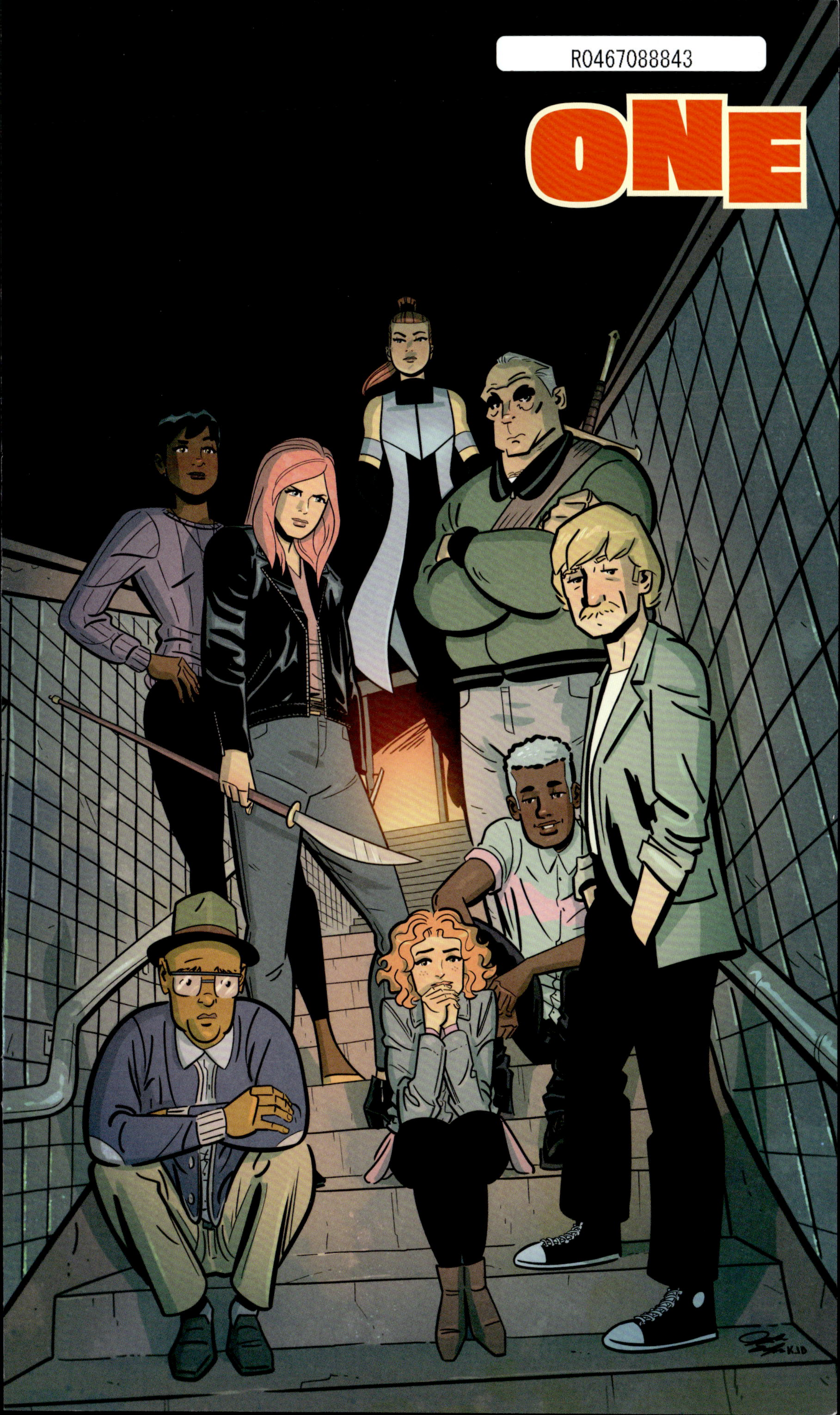
ONE

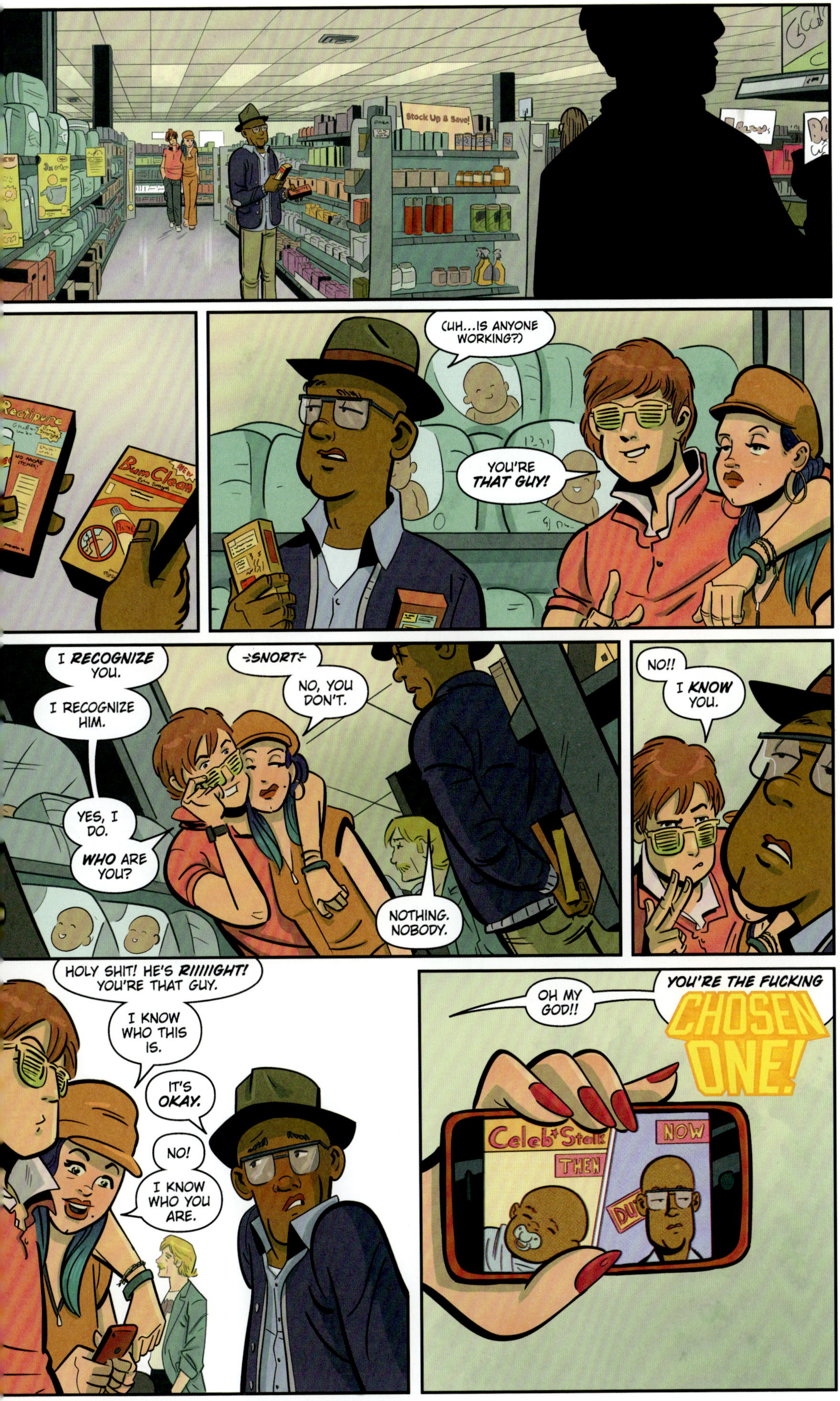
Stock Up & Save!
(UH...IS ANYONE WORKING?)
YOU'RE THAT GUY!
I RECOGNIZE YOU.
I RECOGNIZE HIM.
YES, I DO.
WHO ARE YOU?
=SNORT=
NO, YOU DON'T.
NOTHING. NOBODY.
NO!!
I KNOW YOU.
HOLY SHIT! HE'S RIIIIIGHT! YOU'RE THAT GUY.
I KNOW WHO THIS IS.
IT'S OKAY.
NO!
I KNOW WHO YOU ARE.
OH MY GOD!!
YOU'RE THE FUCKING CHOSEN ONE!
Celeb*Stalk
THEN
NOW

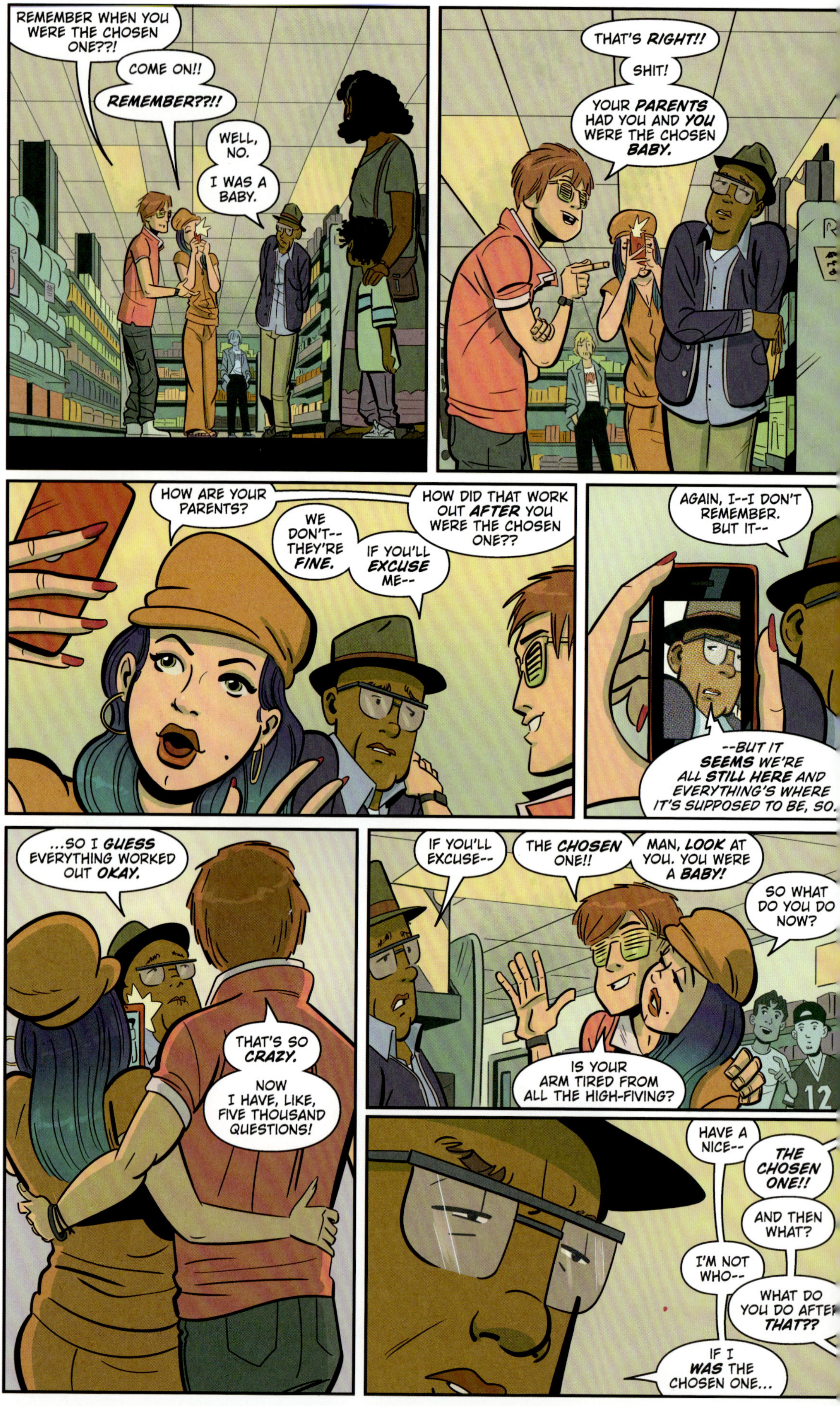
REMEMBER WHEN YOU WERE THE CHOSEN ONE??!
COME ON!!
REMEMBER??!!
WELL, NO.
I WAS A BABY.
THAT'S RIGHT!!
SHIT!
YOUR PARENTS HAD YOU AND YOU WERE THE CHOSEN BABY.
HOW ARE YOUR PARENTS?
WE DON'T-- THEY'RE FINE.
HOW DID THAT WORK OUT AFTER YOU WERE THE CHOSEN ONE??
IF YOU'LL EXCUSE ME--
AGAIN, I--I DON'T REMEMBER. BUT IT--
--BUT IT SEEMS WE'RE ALL STILL HERE AND EVERYTHING'S WHERE IT'S SUPPOSED TO BE, SO...
...SO I GUESS EVERYTHING WORKED OUT OKAY.
THAT'S SO CRAZY.
NOW I HAVE, LIKE, FIVE THOUSAND QUESTIONS!
IF YOU'LL EXCUSE--
THE CHOSEN ONE!!
MAN, LOOK AT YOU. YOU WERE A BABY!
SO WHAT DO YOU DO NOW?
IS YOUR ARM TIRED FROM ALL THE HIGH-FIVING?
HAVE A NICE--
THE CHOSEN ONE!!
AND THEN WHAT?
I'M NOT WHO--
WHAT DO YOU DO AFTER THAT??
IF I WAS THE CHOSEN ONE...

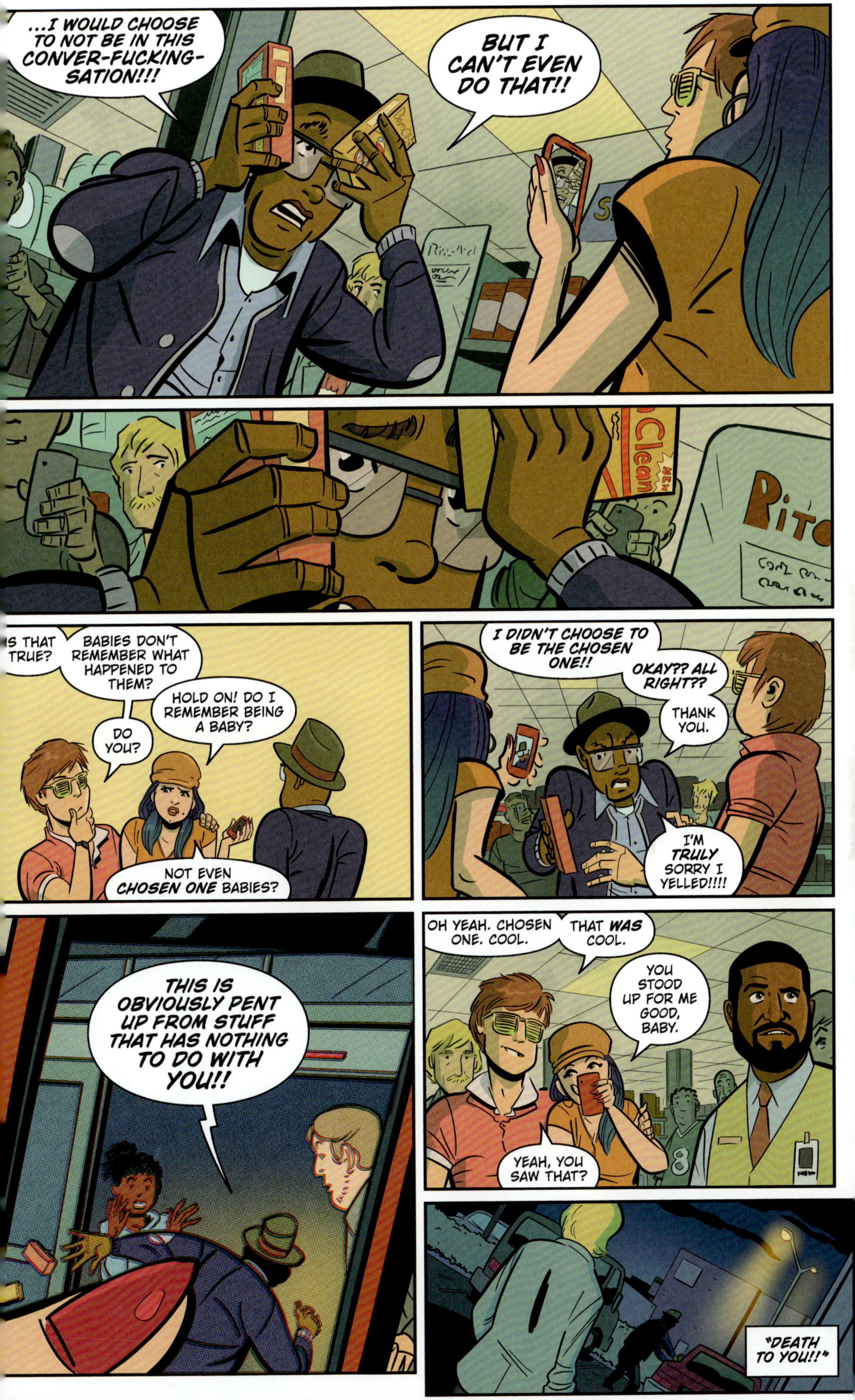
...I WOULD CHOOSE TO NOT BE IN THIS CONVER-FUCKING-SATION!!!
BUT I CAN'T EVEN DO THAT!!
S THAT TRUE?
BABIES DON'T REMEMBER WHAT HAPPENED TO THEM?
DO YOU?
HOLD ON! DO I REMEMBER BEING A BABY?
NOT EVEN CHOSEN ONE BABIES?
I DIDN'T CHOOSE TO BE THE CHOSEN ONE!!
OKAY?? ALL RIGHT??
THANK YOU.
I'M TRULY SORRY I YELLED!!!!
THIS IS OBVIOUSLY PENT UP FROM STUFF THAT HAS NOTHING TO DO WITH YOU!!
OH YEAH. CHOSEN ONE. COOL.
THAT WAS COOL.
YOU STOOD UP FOR ME GOOD, BABY.
YEAH, YOU SAW THAT?
"DEATH TO YOU!!"

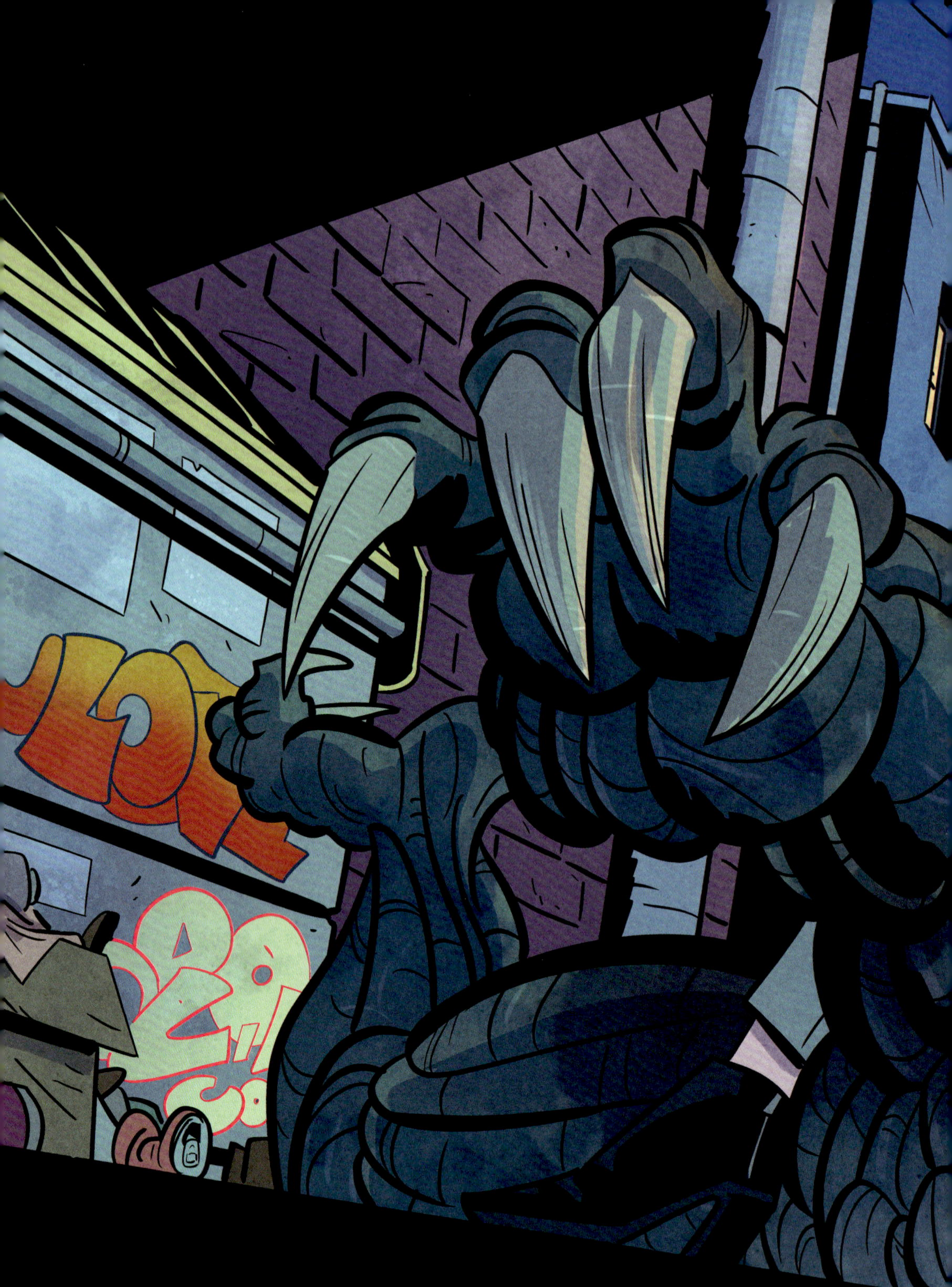

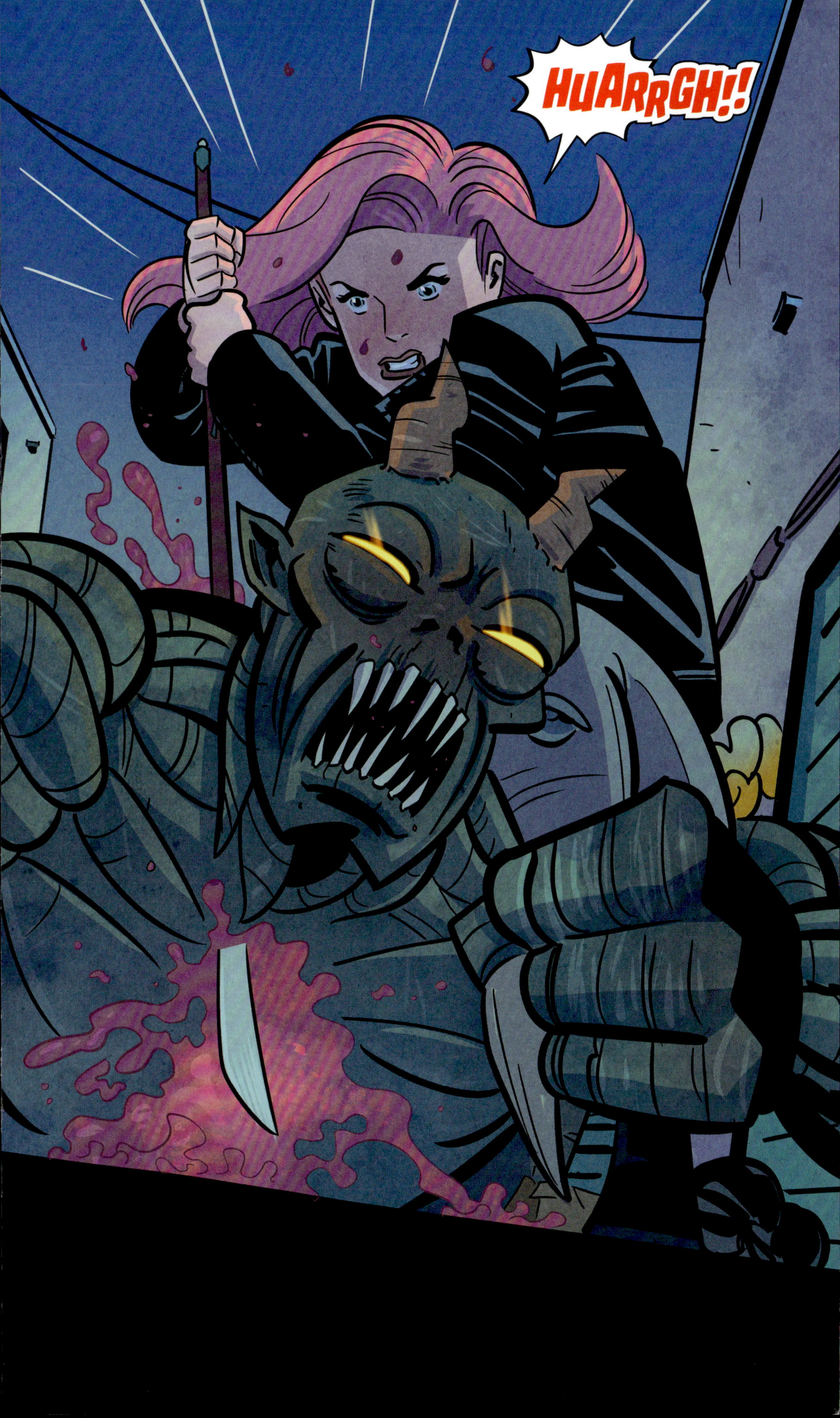
HUARRGH!!

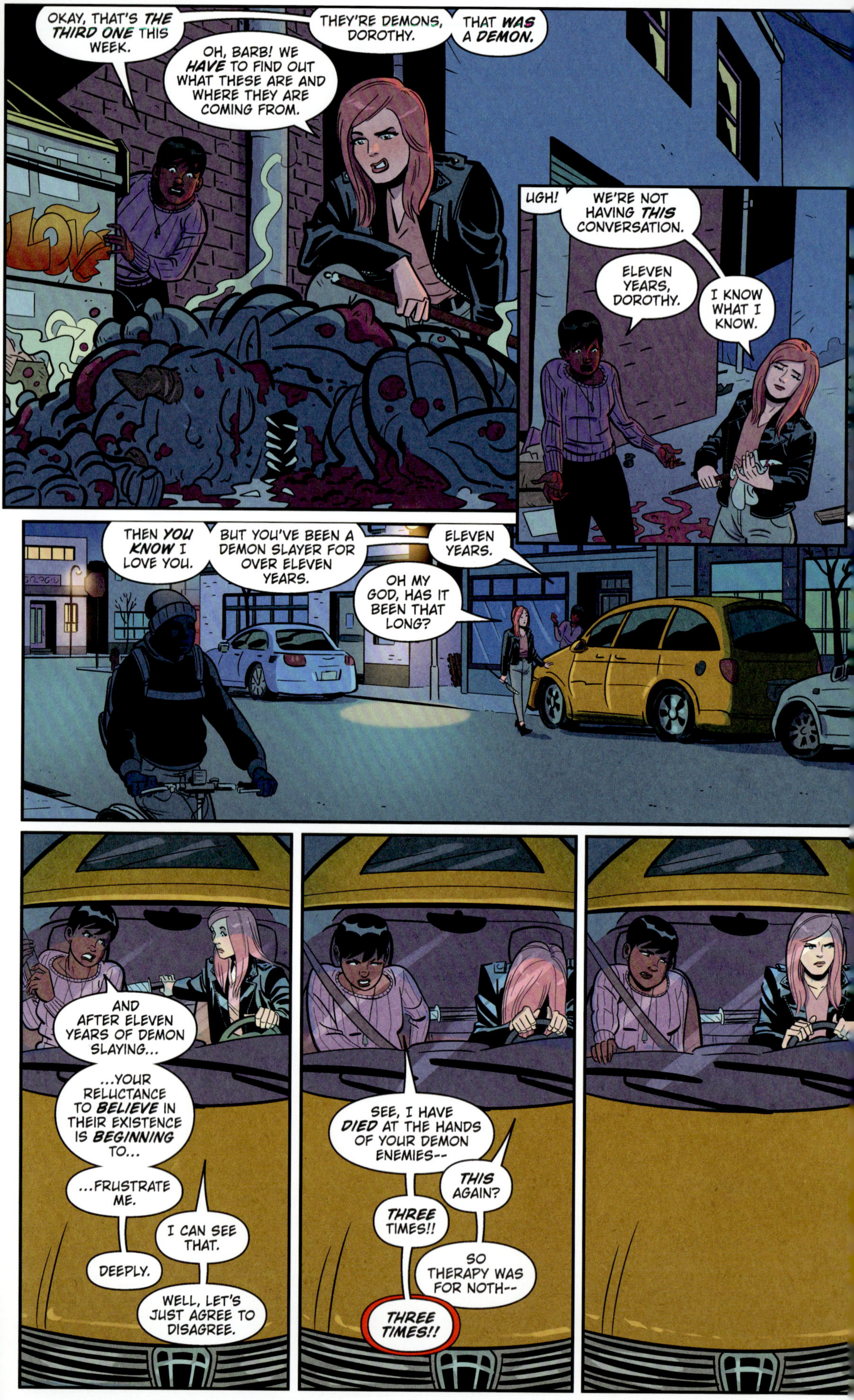

OKAY, THAT'S THE THIRD ONE THIS WEEK.
THEY'RE DEMONS, DOROTHY.
THAT WAS A DEMON.
OH, BARB! WE HAVE TO FIND OUT WHAT THESE ARE AND WHERE THEY ARE COMING FROM.
UGH!
WE'RE NOT HAVING THIS CONVERSATION.
ELEVEN YEARS, DOROTHY.
I KNOW WHAT I KNOW.
THEN YOU KNOW I LOVE YOU.
BUT YOU'VE BEEN A DEMON SLAYER FOR OVER ELEVEN YEARS.
ELEVEN YEARS.
OH MY GOD, HAS IT BEEN THAT LONG?
AND AFTER ELEVEN YEARS OF DEMON SLAYING...
...YOUR RELUCTANCE TO BELIEVE IN THEIR EXISTENCE IS BEGINNING TO...
...FRUSTRATE ME.
I CAN SEE THAT.
DEEPLY.
WELL, LET'S JUST AGREE TO DISAGREE.
SEE, I HAVE DIED AT THE HANDS OF YOUR DEMON ENEMIES--
THIS AGAIN?
THREE TIMES!!
SO THERAPY WAS FOR NOTH--
THREE TIMES!!

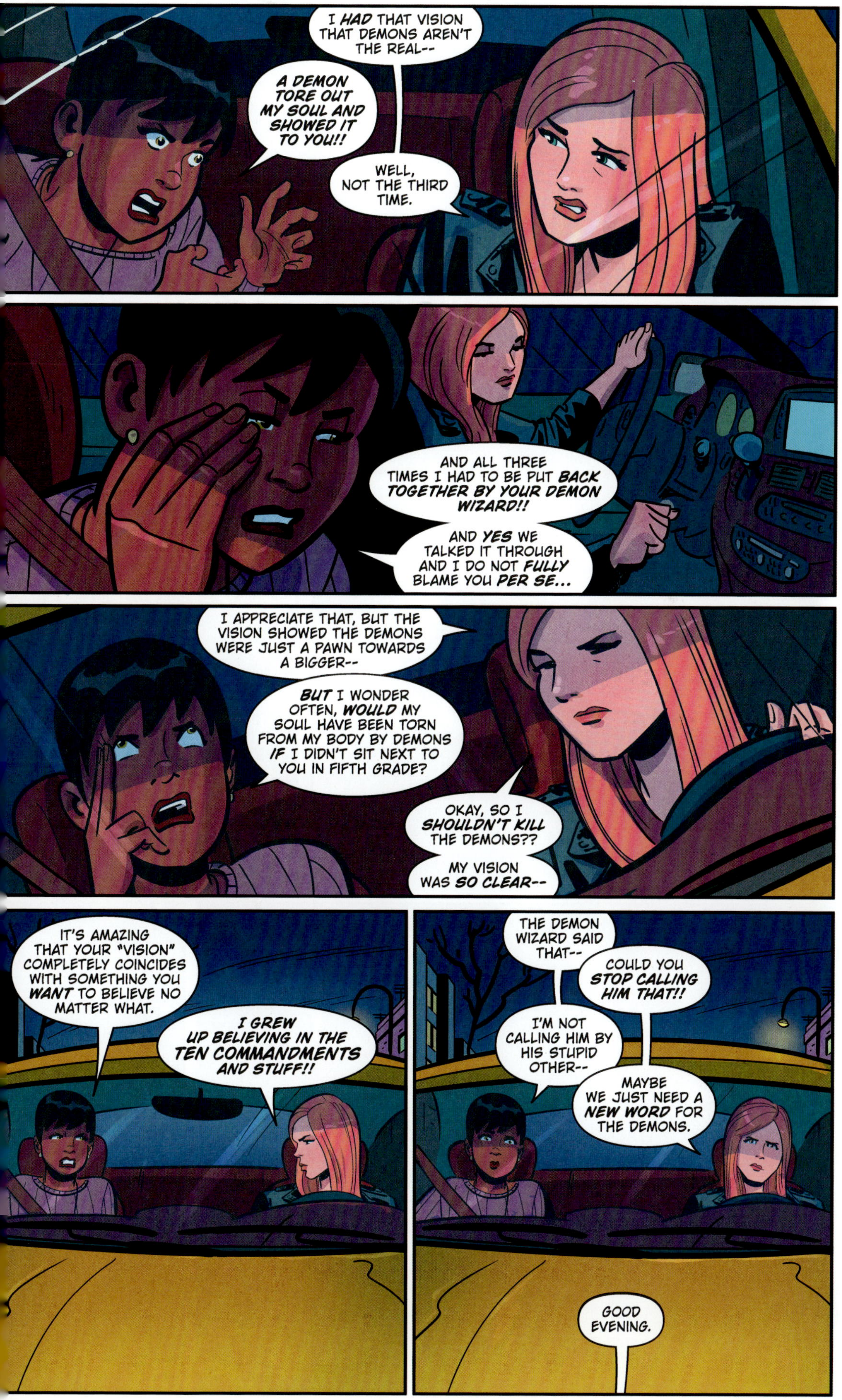
I HAD THAT VISION THAT DEMONS AREN'T THE REAL--
A DEMON TORE OUT MY SOUL AND SHOWED IT TO YOU!!
WELL, NOT THE THIRD TIME.
AND ALL THREE TIMES I HAD TO BE PUT BACK TOGETHER BY YOUR DEMON WIZARD!!
AND YES WE TALKED IT THROUGH AND I DO NOT FULLY BLAME YOU PER SE...
I APPRECIATE THAT, BUT THE VISION SHOWED THE DEMONS WERE JUST A PAWN TOWARDS A BIGGER--
BUT I WONDER OFTEN, WOULD MY SOUL HAVE BEEN TORN FROM MY BODY BY DEMONS IF I DIDN'T SIT NEXT TO YOU IN FIFTH GRADE?
OKAY, SO I SHOULDN'T KILL THE DEMONS??
MY VISION WAS SO CLEAR--
IT'S AMAZING THAT YOUR "VISION" COMPLETELY COINCIDES WITH SOMETHING YOU WANT TO BELIEVE NO MATTER WHAT.
I GREW UP BELIEVING IN THE TEN COMMANDMENTS AND STUFF!!
THE DEMON WIZARD SAID THAT--
COULD YOU STOP CALLING HIM THAT!!
I'M NOT CALLING HIM BY HIS STUPID OTHER--
MAYBE WE JUST NEED A NEW WORD FOR THE DEMONS.
GOOD EVENING.

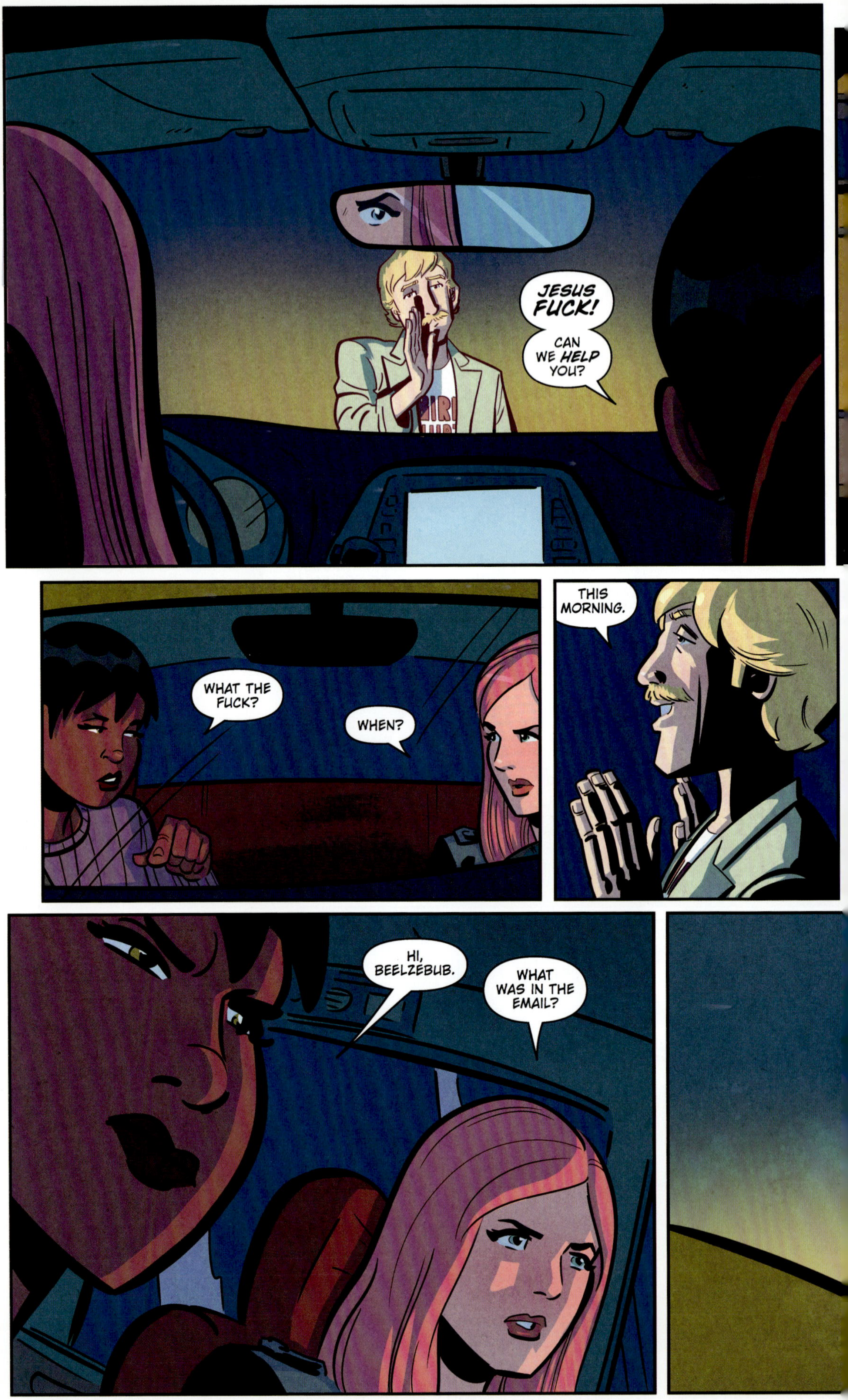
JESUS FUCK!
CAN WE HELP YOU?
WHAT THE FUCK?
WHEN?
THIS MORNING.
HI, BEELZEBUB.
WHAT WAS IN THE EMAIL?

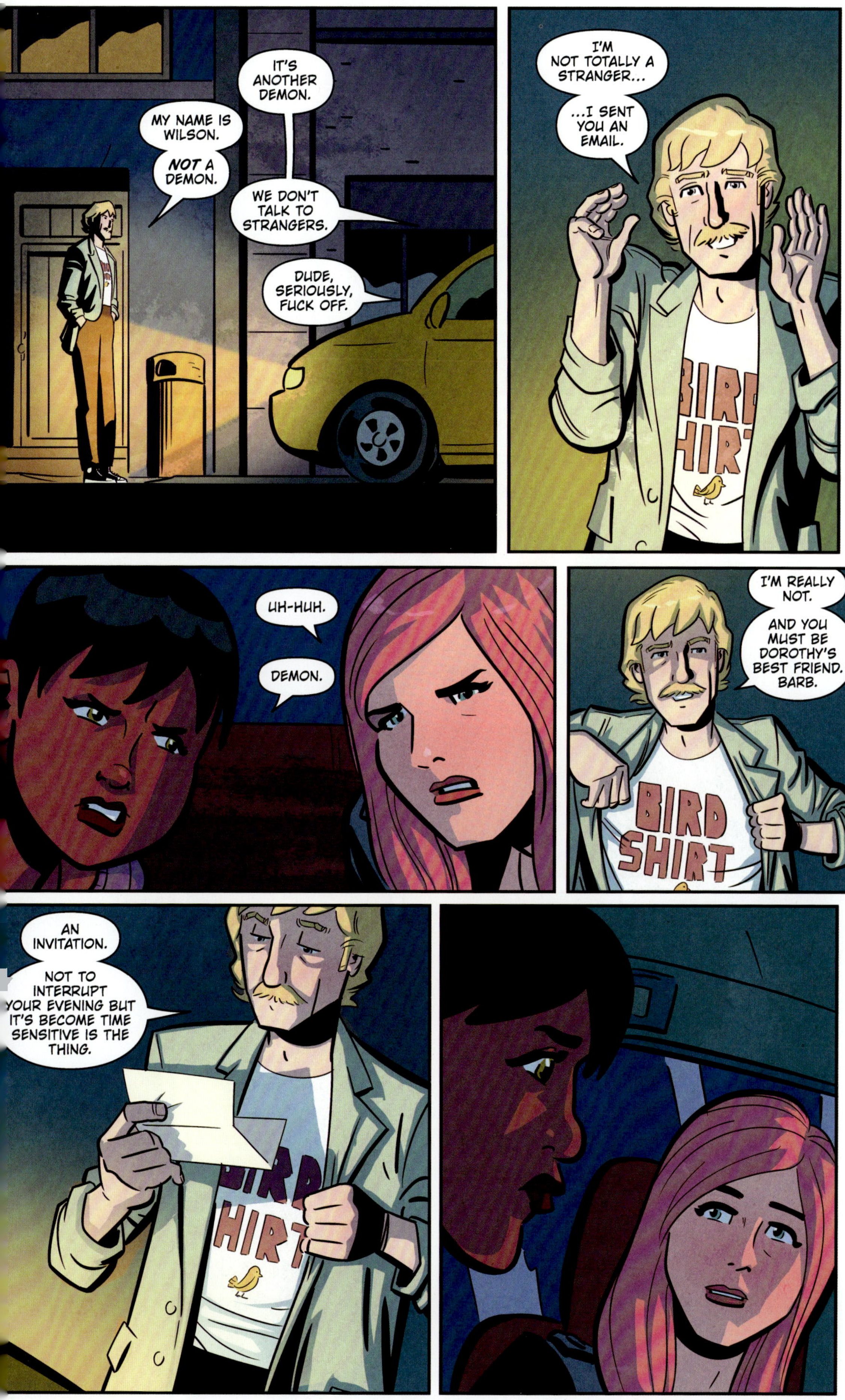
MY NAME IS WILSON.
NOT A DEMON.
IT'S ANOTHER DEMON.
WE DON'T TALK TO STRANGERS.
DUDE, SERIOUSLY, FUCK OFF.
I'M NOT TOTALLY A STRANGER...
...I SENT YOU AN EMAIL.
BIRD SHIRT
UH-HUH.
DEMON.
I'M REALLY NOT.
AND YOU MUST BE DOROTHY'S BEST FRIEND. BARB.
BIRD SHIRT
AN INVITATION.
NOT TO INTERRUPT YOUR EVENING BUT IT'S BECOME TIME SENSITIVE IS THE THING.

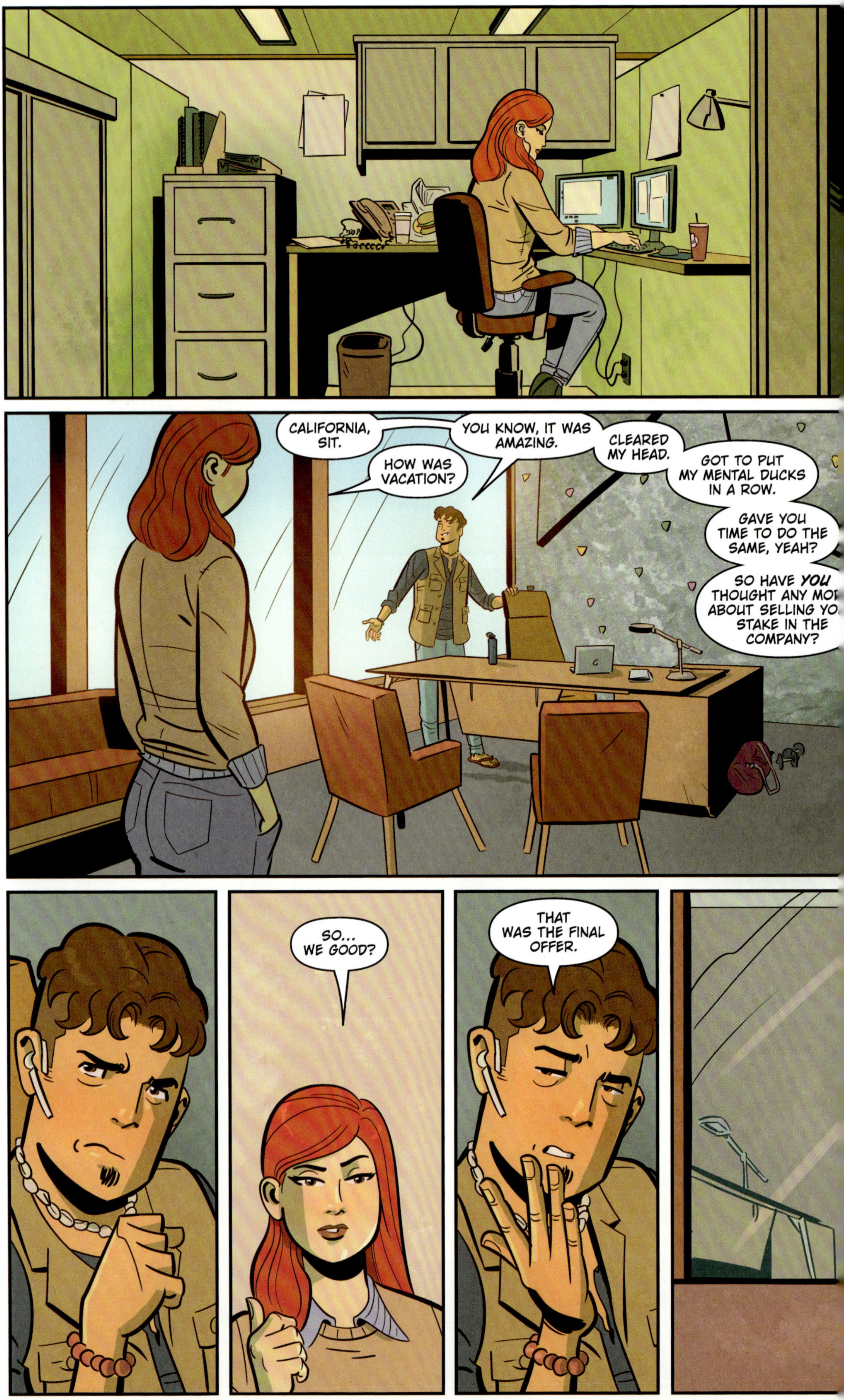
CALIFORNIA, SIT.
HOW WAS VACATION?
YOU KNOW, IT WAS AMAZING.
CLEARED MY HEAD.
GOT TO PUT MY MENTAL DUCKS IN A ROW.
GAVE YOU TIME TO DO THE SAME, YEAH?
SO HAVE *YOU* THOUGHT ANY MO
ABOUT SELLING YO
STAKE IN THE COMPANY?
SO... WE GOOD?
THAT WAS THE FINAL OFFER.

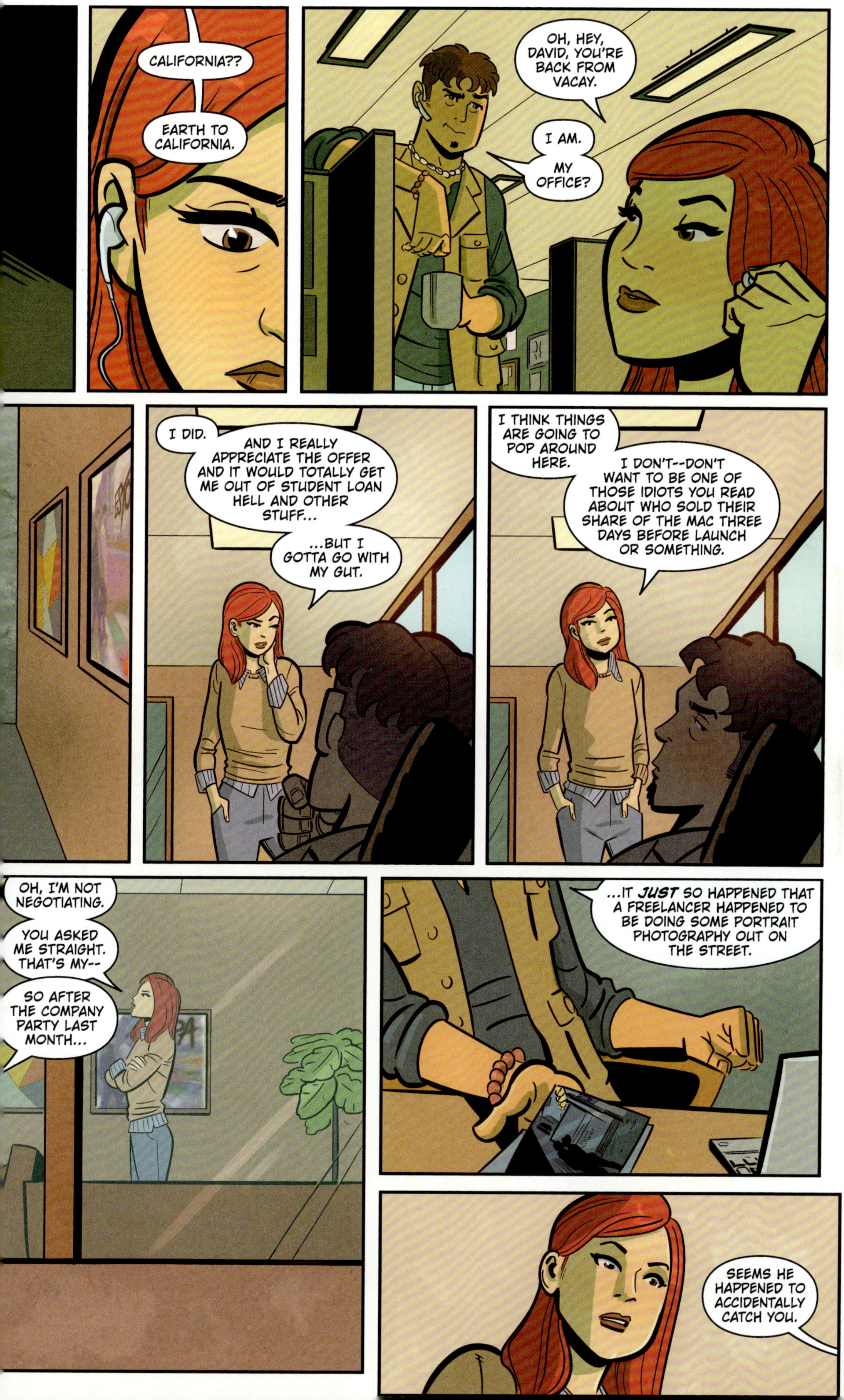
CALIFORNIA??
EARTH TO CALIFORNIA.
OH, HEY, DAVID, YOU'RE BACK FROM VACAY.
I AM.
MY OFFICE?
I DID.
AND I REALLY APPRECIATE THE OFFER AND IT WOULD TOTALLY GET ME OUT OF STUDENT LOAN HELL AND OTHER STUFF...
...BUT I GOTTA GO WITH MY GUT.
I THINK THINGS ARE GOING TO POP AROUND HERE.
I DON'T--DON'T WANT TO BE ONE OF THOSE IDIOTS YOU READ ABOUT WHO SOLD THEIR SHARE OF THE MAC THREE DAYS BEFORE LAUNCH OR SOMETHING.
OH, I'M NOT NEGOTIATING.
YOU ASKED ME STRAIGHT. THAT'S MY--
SO AFTER THE COMPANY PARTY LAST MONTH...
...IT *JUST* SO HAPPENED THAT A FREELANCER HAPPENED TO BE DOING SOME PORTRAIT PHOTOGRAPHY OUT ON THE STREET.
SEEMS HE HAPPENED TO ACCIDENTALLY CATCH YOU.

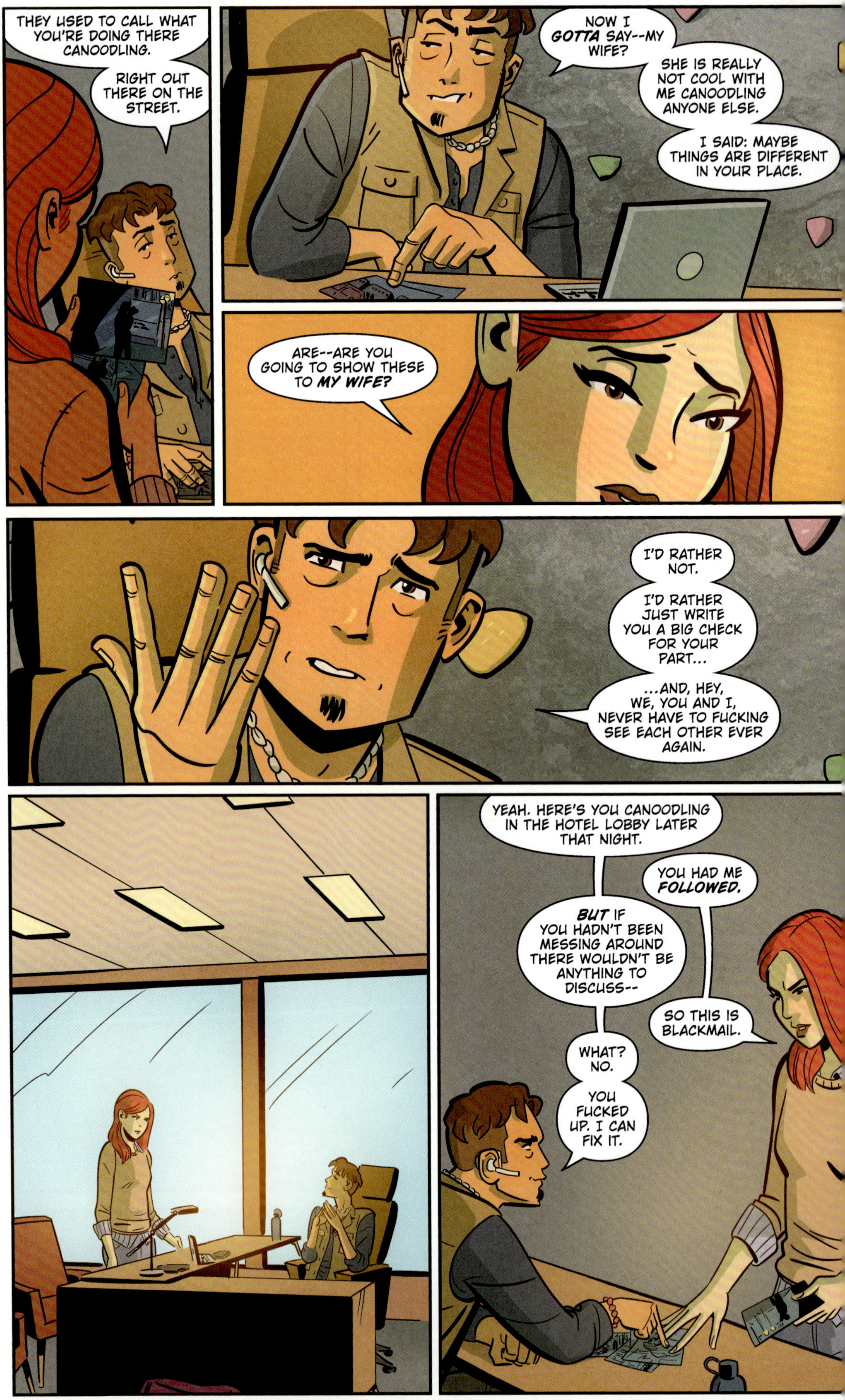
THEY USED TO CALL WHAT YOU'RE DOING THERE CANOODLING.
RIGHT OUT THERE ON THE STREET.
NOW I *GOTTA* SAY--MY WIFE?
SHE IS REALLY NOT COOL WITH ME CANOODLING ANYONE ELSE.
I SAID: MAYBE THINGS ARE DIFFERENT IN YOUR PLACE.
ARE--ARE YOU GOING TO SHOW THESE TO *MY WIFE?*
I'D RATHER NOT.
I'D RATHER JUST WRITE YOU A BIG CHECK FOR YOUR PART...
...AND, HEY, WE, YOU AND I, NEVER HAVE TO FUCKING SEE EACH OTHER EVER AGAIN.
YEAH. HERE'S YOU CANOODLING IN THE HOTEL LOBBY LATER THAT NIGHT.
YOU HAD ME *FOLLOWED.*
BUT IF YOU HADN'T BEEN MESSING AROUND THERE WOULDN'T BE ANYTHING TO DISCUSS--
SO THIS IS BLACKMAIL.
WHAT? NO.
YOU FUCKED UP. I CAN FIX IT.

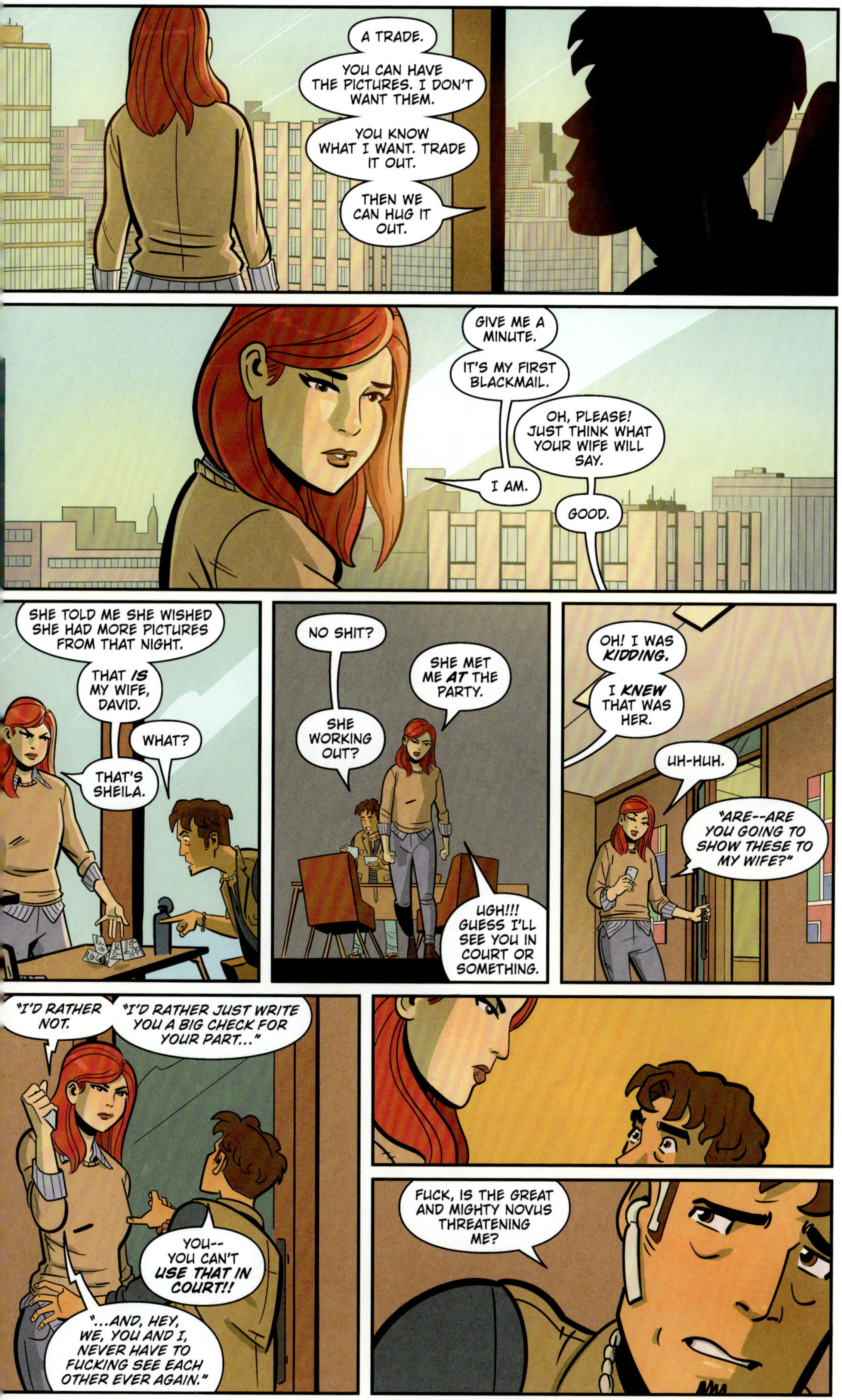
A TRADE.
YOU CAN HAVE THE PICTURES. I DON'T WANT THEM.
YOU KNOW WHAT I WANT. TRADE IT OUT.
THEN WE CAN HUG IT OUT.
GIVE ME A MINUTE.
IT'S MY FIRST BLACKMAIL.
I AM.
OH, PLEASE! JUST THINK WHAT YOUR WIFE WILL SAY.
GOOD.
SHE TOLD ME SHE WISHED SHE HAD MORE PICTURES FROM THAT NIGHT.
THAT *IS* MY WIFE, DAVID.
WHAT?
THAT'S SHEILA.
NO SHIT?
SHE WORKING OUT?
SHE MET ME *AT* THE PARTY.
UGH!!! GUESS I'LL SEE YOU IN COURT OR SOMETHING.
OH! I WAS *KIDDING.*
I *KNEW* THAT WAS HER.
UH-HUH.
"ARE--ARE YOU GOING TO SHOW THESE TO MY WIFE?"
"I'D RATHER NOT.
"I'D RATHER JUST WRITE YOU A BIG CHECK FOR YOUR PART..."
YOU-- YOU CAN'T *USE THAT IN COURT!!*
"...AND, HEY, WE, YOU AND I, NEVER HAVE TO FUCKING SEE EACH OTHER EVER AGAIN."
FUCK, IS THE GREAT AND MIGHTY NOVUS THREATENING ME?

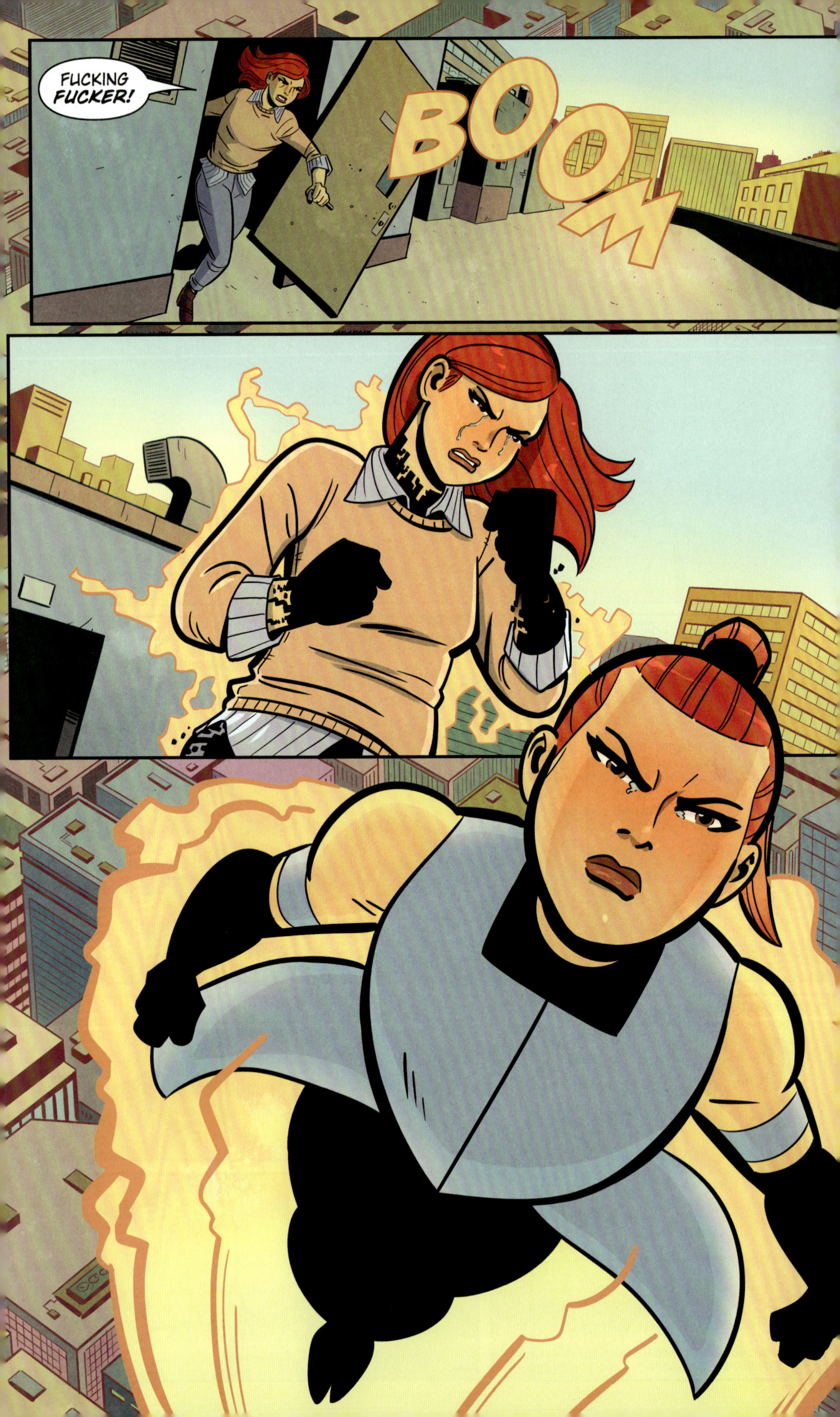
FUCKING FUCKER!
BOOM

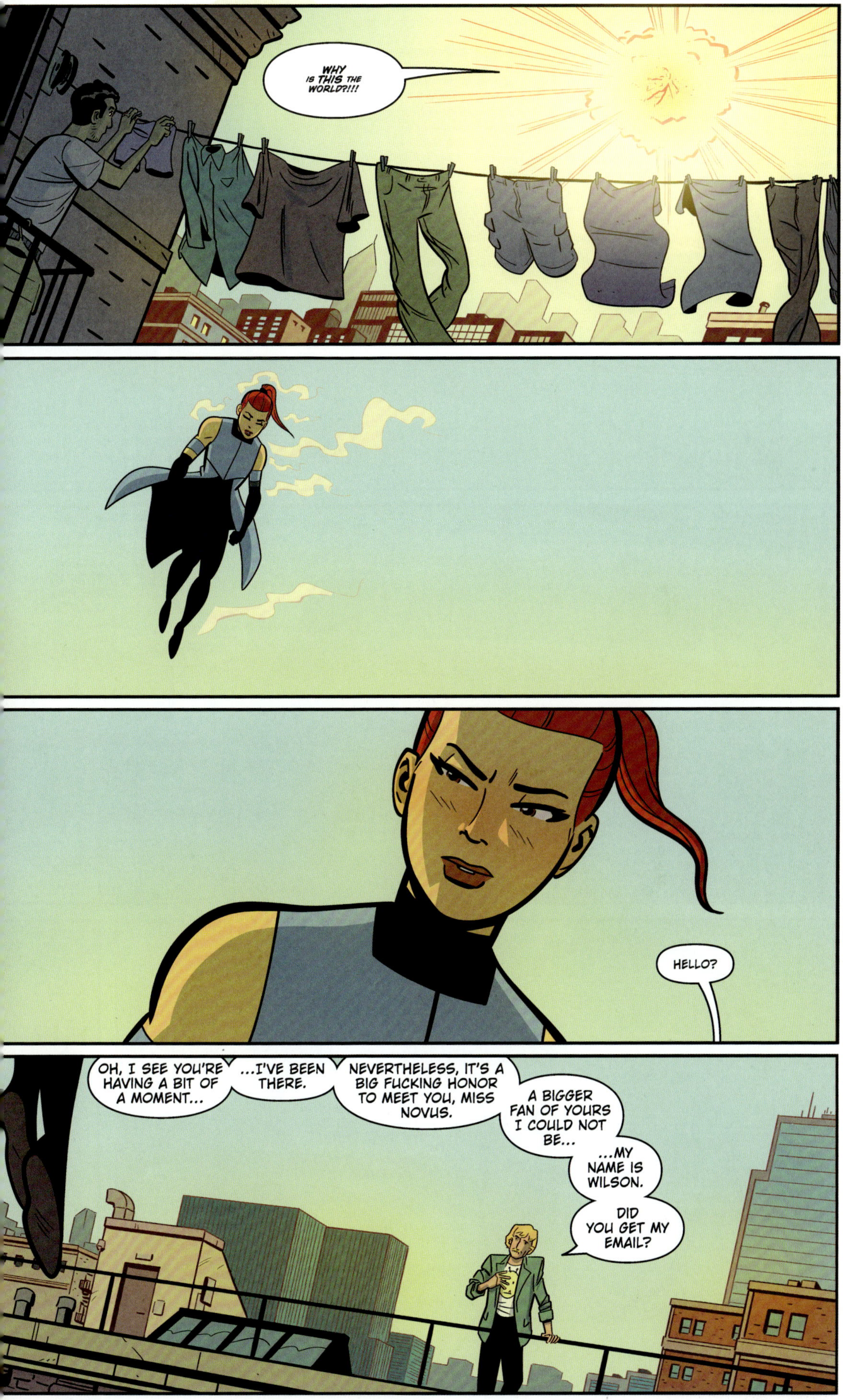
WHY IS THIS THE WORLD?!!!
HELLO?
OH, I SEE YOU'RE HAVING A BIT OF A MOMENT...
...I'VE BEEN THERE.
NEVERTHELESS, IT'S A BIG FUCKING HONOR TO MEET YOU, MISS NOVUS.
A BIGGER FAN OF YOURS I COULD NOT BE...
...MY NAME IS WILSON.
DID YOU GET MY EMAIL?

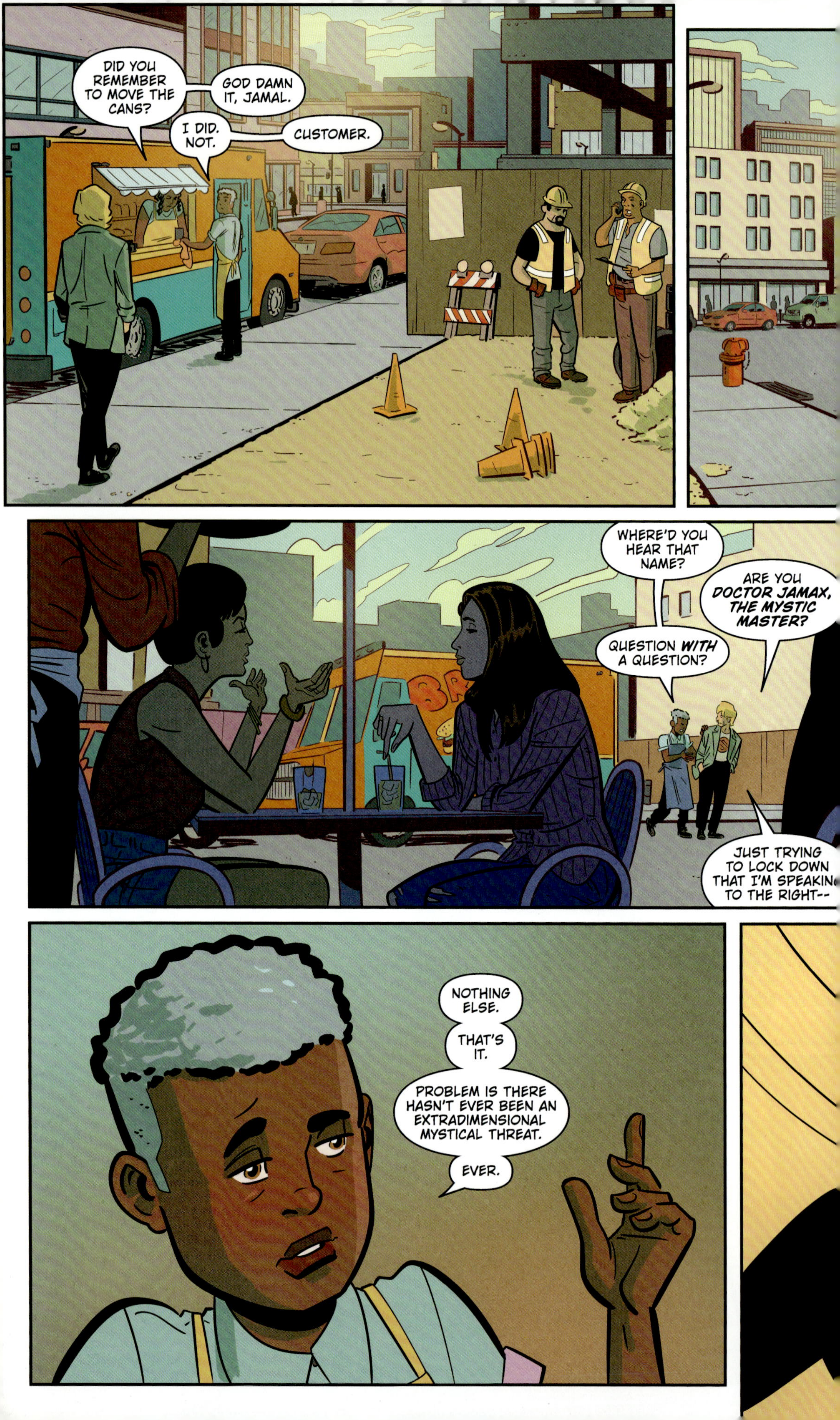
DID YOU REMEMBER TO MOVE THE CANS?
GOD DAMN IT, JAMAL.
I DID. NOT.
CUSTOMER.
WHERE'D YOU HEAR THAT NAME?
ARE YOU DOCTOR JAMAX, THE MYSTIC MASTER?
QUESTION WITH A QUESTION?
JUST TRYING TO LOCK DOWN THAT I'M SPEAKIN
TO THE RIGHT--
NOTHING ELSE.
THAT'S IT.
PROBLEM IS THERE HASN'T EVER BEEN AN EXTRADIMENSIONAL MYSTICAL THREAT.
EVER.

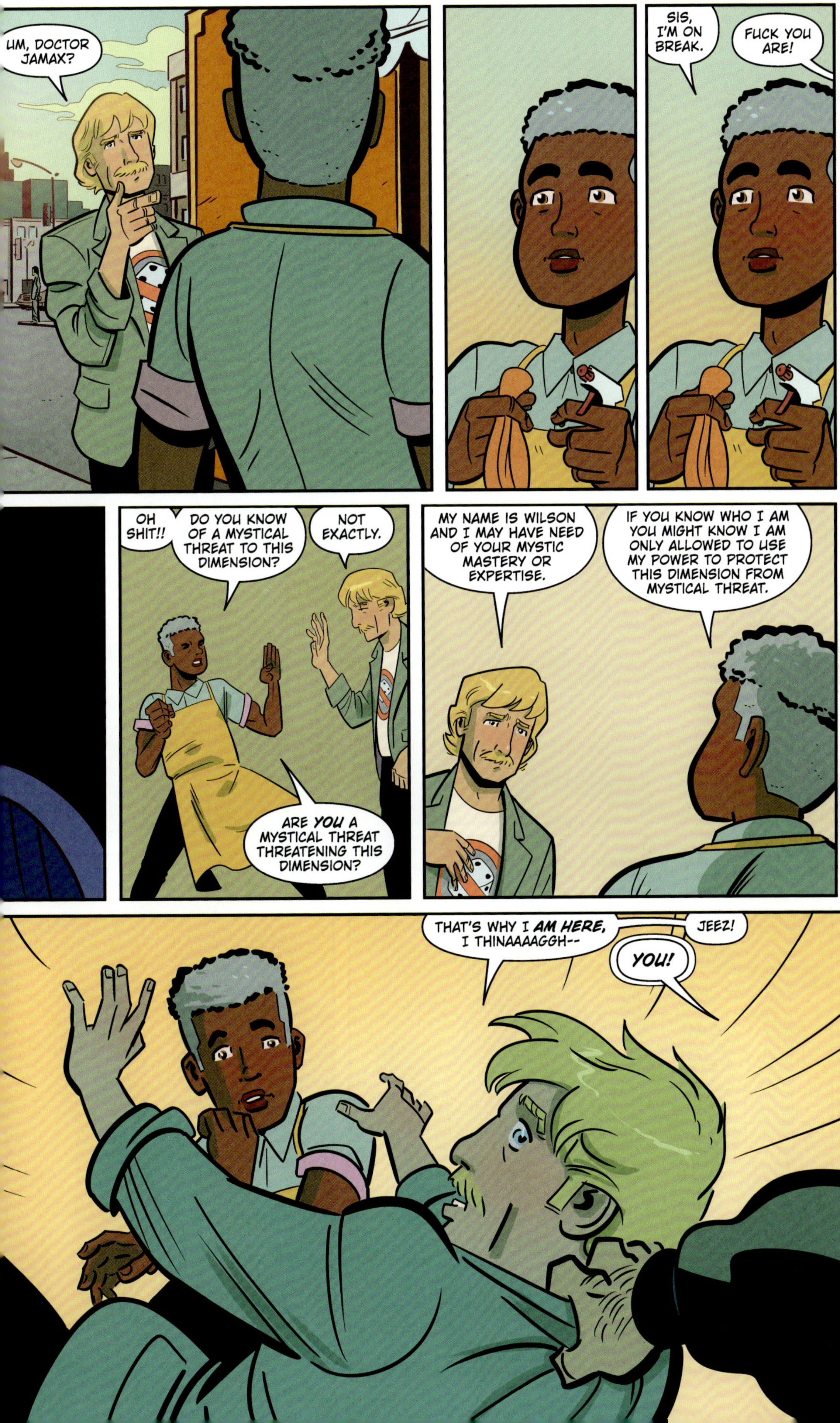
UM, DOCTOR JAMAX?
SIS, I'M ON BREAK.
FUCK YOU ARE!
OH SHIT!!
DO YOU KNOW OF A MYSTICAL THREAT TO THIS DIMENSION?
NOT EXACTLY.
ARE *YOU* A MYSTICAL THREAT THREATENING THIS DIMENSION?
MY NAME IS WILSON AND I MAY HAVE NEED OF YOUR MYSTIC MASTERY OR EXPERTISE.
IF YOU KNOW WHO I AM YOU MIGHT KNOW I AM ONLY ALLOWED TO USE MY POWER TO PROTECT THIS DIMENSION FROM MYSTICAL THREAT.
THAT'S WHY I ***AM HERE,*** I THINAAAAGGH--
JEEZ!
YOU!

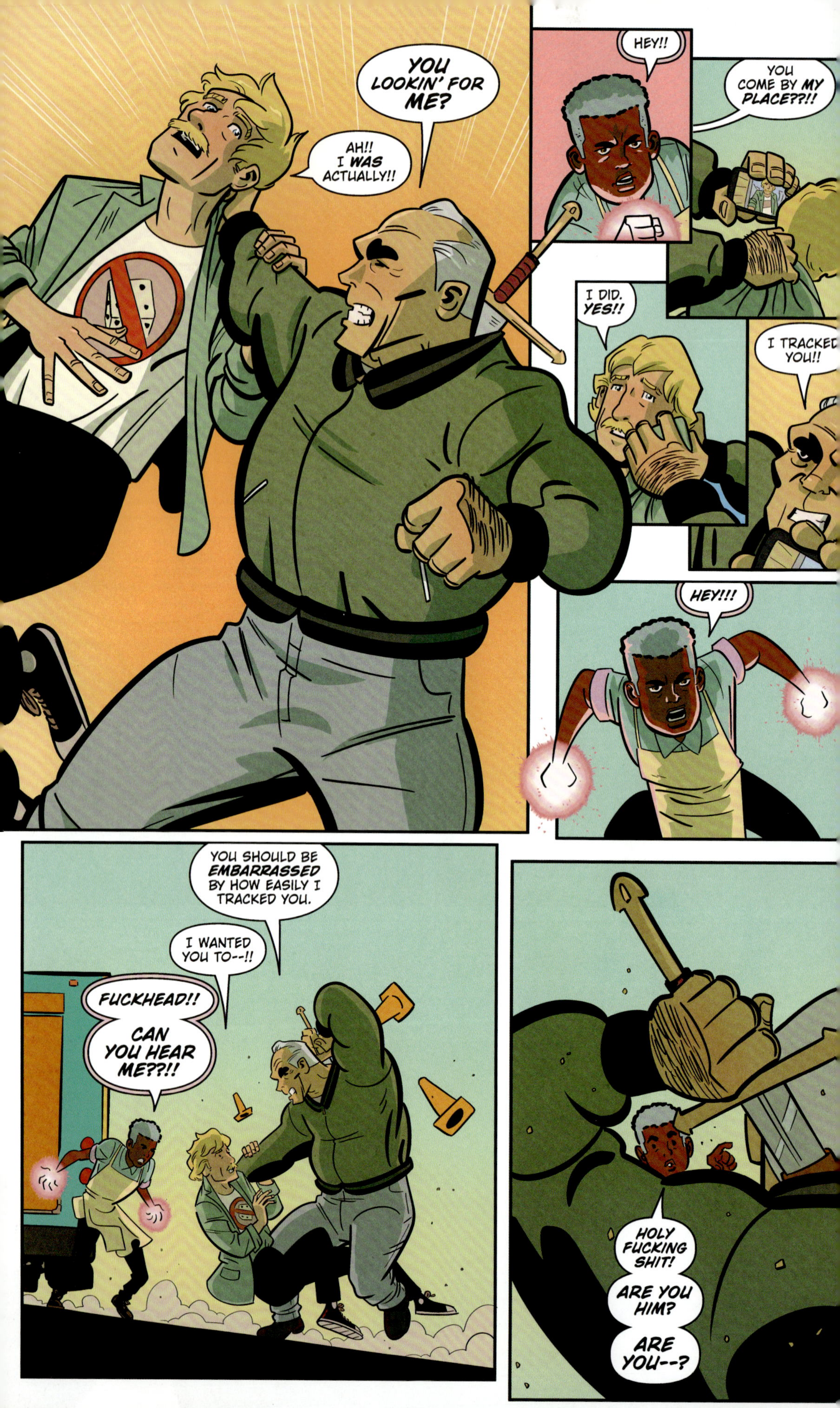

YOU LOOKIN' FOR ME?
AH!! I WAS ACTUALLY!!
HEY!!
YOU COME BY MY PLACE??!!
I DID. YES!!
I TRACKED YOU!!
HEY!!!
YOU SHOULD BE EMBARRASSED BY HOW EASILY I TRACKED YOU.
I WANTED YOU TO--!!
FUCKHEAD!!
CAN YOU HEAR ME??!!
HOLY FUCKING SHIT!
ARE YOU HIM?
ARE YOU--?

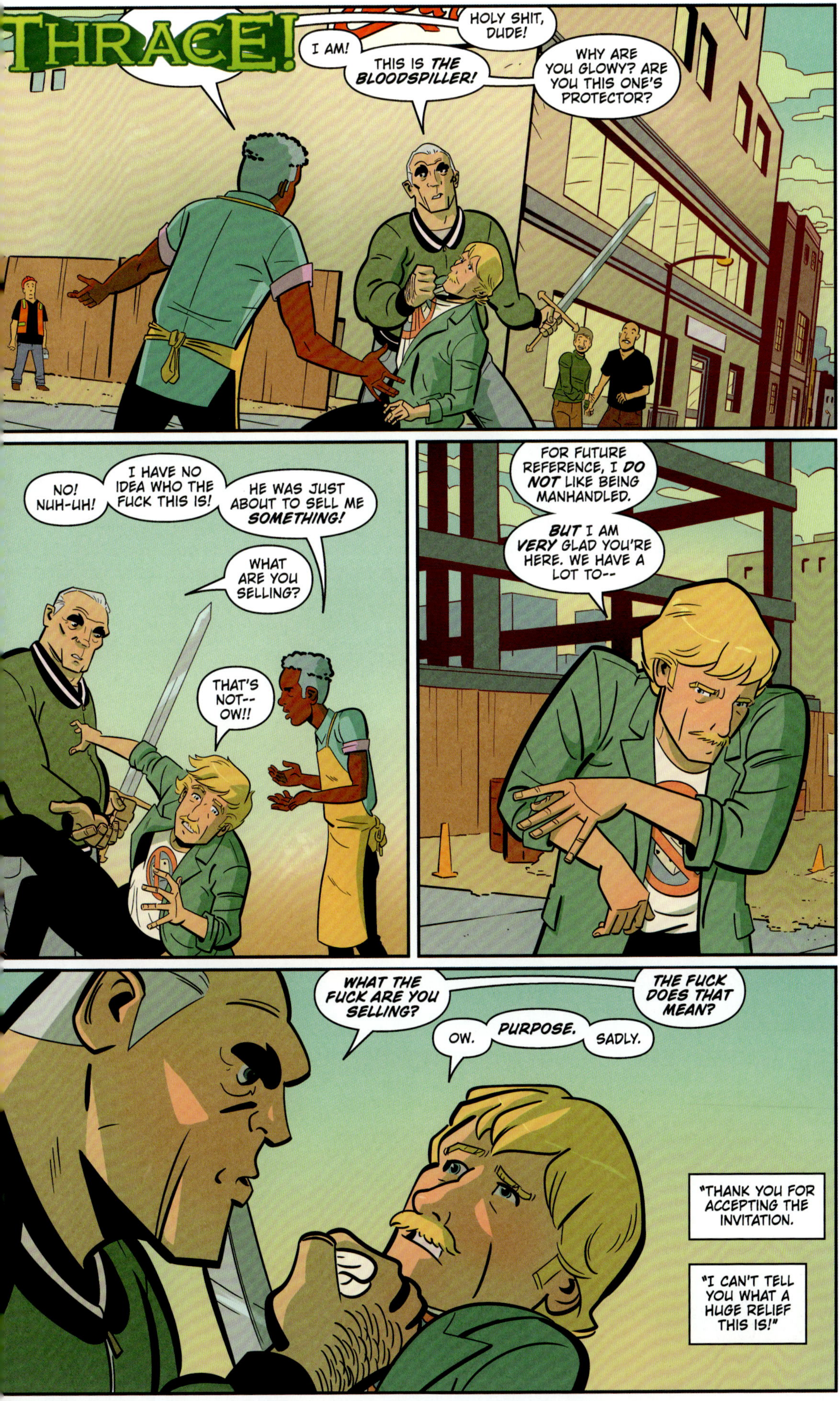
THRACE!
HOLY SHIT, DUDE!
I AM!
THIS IS THE BLOODSPILLER!
WHY ARE YOU GLOWY? ARE YOU THIS ONE'S PROTECTOR?
NO! NUH-UH!
I HAVE NO IDEA WHO THE FUCK THIS IS!
HE WAS JUST ABOUT TO SELL ME SOMETHING!
WHAT ARE YOU SELLING?
THAT'S NOT-- OW!!
FOR FUTURE REFERENCE, I DO NOT LIKE BEING MANHANDLED.
BUT I AM VERY GLAD YOU'RE HERE. WE HAVE A LOT TO--
WHAT THE FUCK ARE YOU SELLING?
OW.
PURPOSE.
SADLY.
THE FUCK DOES THAT MEAN?
"THANK YOU FOR ACCEPTING THE INVITATION.
"I CAN'T TELL YOU WHAT A HUGE RELIEF THIS IS!"

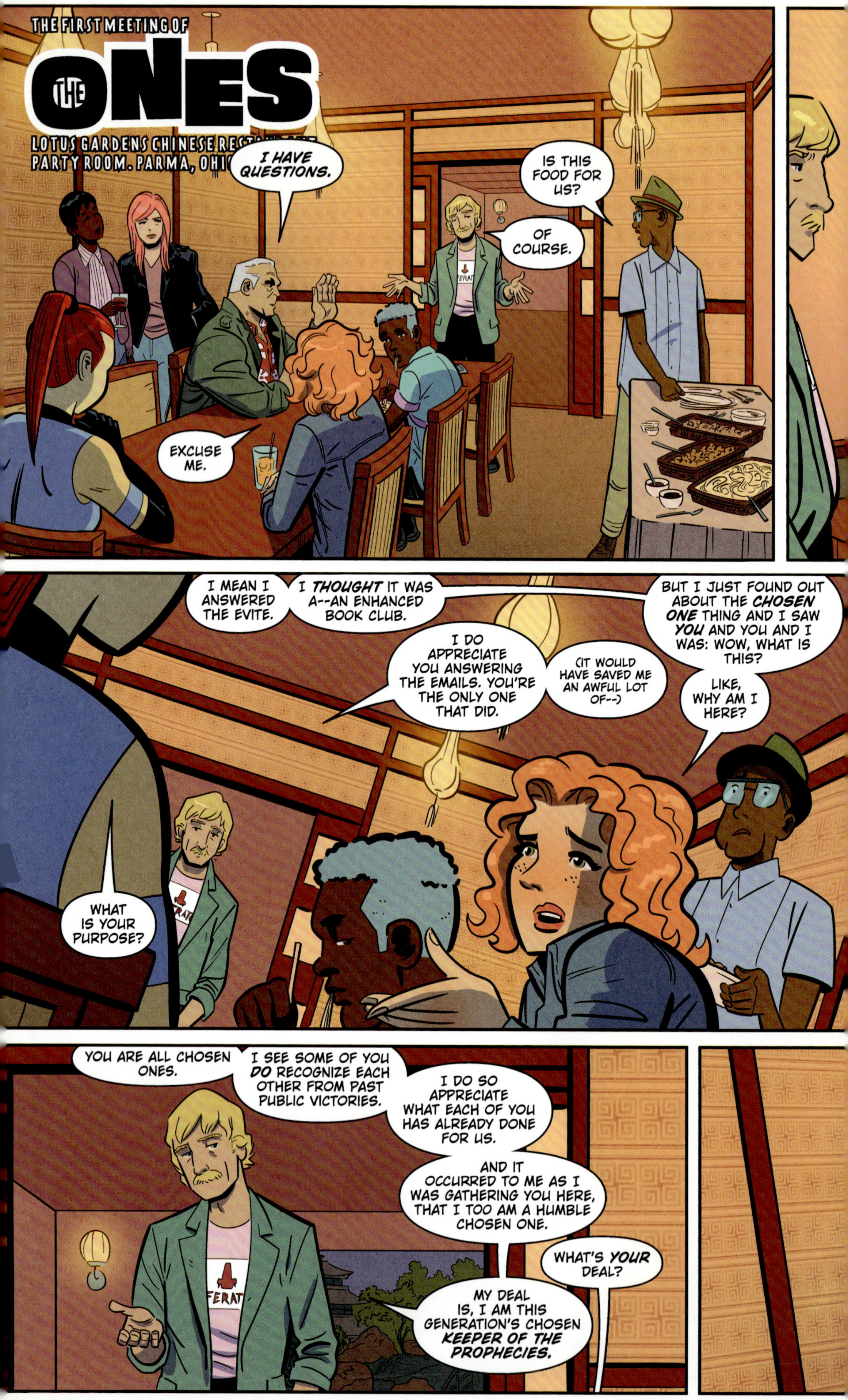
THE FIRST MEETING OF
THE ONES
LOTUS GARDENS CHINESE REST
PARTY ROOM. PARMA, OHI
I HAVE QUESTIONS.
IS THIS FOOD FOR US?
OF COURSE.
EXCUSE ME.
I MEAN I ANSWERED THE EVITE.
I *THOUGHT* IT WAS A--AN ENHANCED BOOK CLUB.
BUT I JUST FOUND OUT ABOUT THE *CHOSEN ONE* THING AND I SAW *YOU* AND YOU AND I WAS: WOW, WHAT IS THIS?
I DO APPRECIATE YOU ANSWERING THE EMAILS. YOU'RE THE ONLY ONE THAT DID.
(IT WOULD HAVE SAVED ME AN AWFUL LOT OF--)
LIKE, WHY AM I HERE?
WHAT IS YOUR PURPOSE?
YOU ARE ALL CHOSEN ONES.
I SEE SOME OF YOU *DO* RECOGNIZE EACH OTHER FROM PAST PUBLIC VICTORIES.
I DO SO APPRECIATE WHAT EACH OF YOU HAS ALREADY DONE FOR US.
AND IT OCCURRED TO ME AS I WAS GATHERING YOU HERE, THAT I TOO AM A HUMBLE CHOSEN ONE.
WHAT'S *YOUR* DEAL?
MY DEAL IS, I AM THIS GENERATION'S CHOSEN *KEEPER OF THE PROPHECIES.*

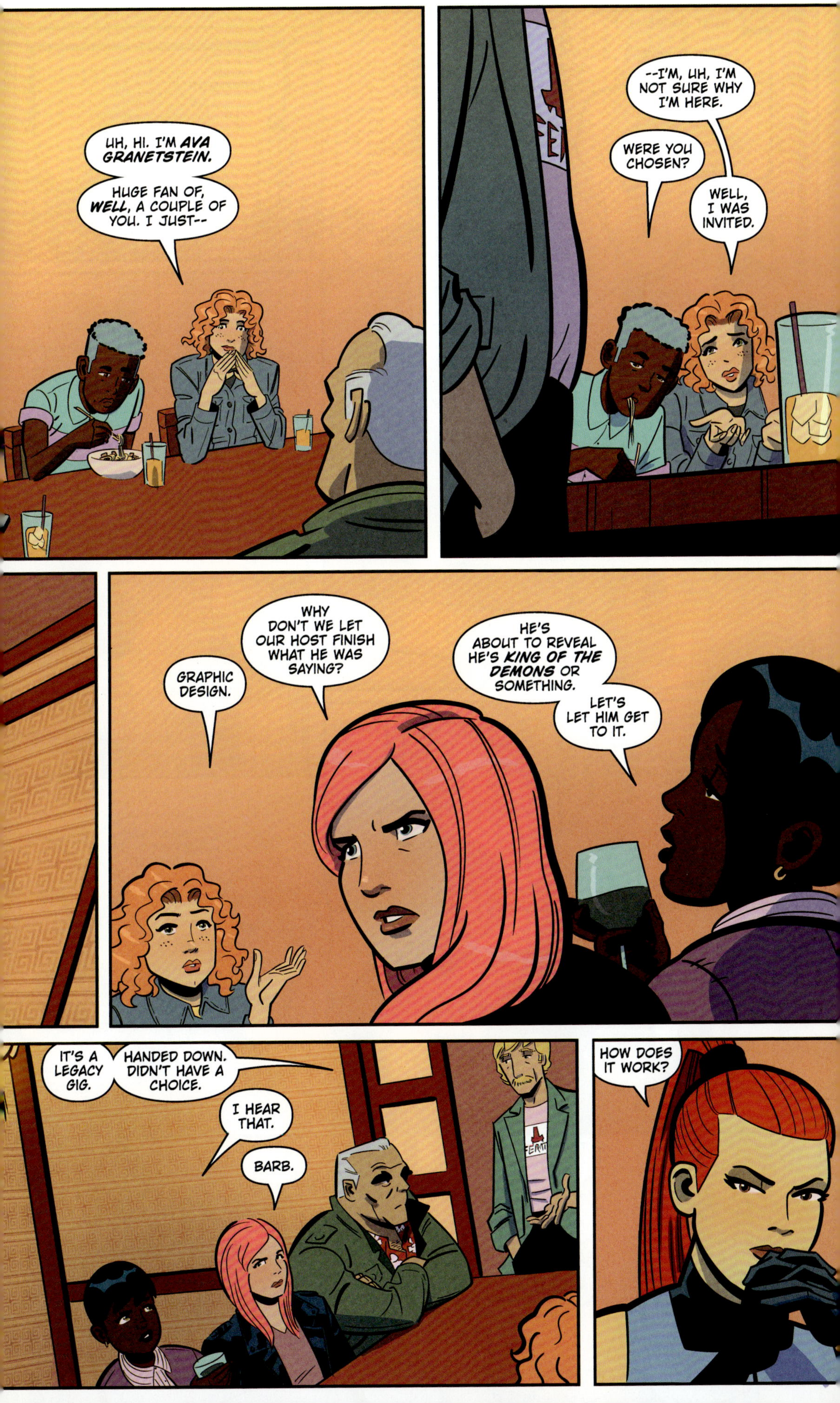
UH, HI. I'M AVA GRANETSTEIN.
HUGE FAN OF, WELL, A COUPLE OF YOU. I JUST--
--I'M, UH, I'M NOT SURE WHY I'M HERE.
WERE YOU CHOSEN?
WELL, I WAS INVITED.
GRAPHIC DESIGN.
WHY DON'T WE LET OUR HOST FINISH WHAT HE WAS SAYING?
HE'S ABOUT TO REVEAL HE'S KING OF THE DEMONS OR SOMETHING.
LET'S LET HIM GET TO IT.
IT'S A LEGACY GIG.
HANDED DOWN. DIDN'T HAVE A CHOICE.
I HEAR THAT.
BARB.
HOW DOES IT WORK?

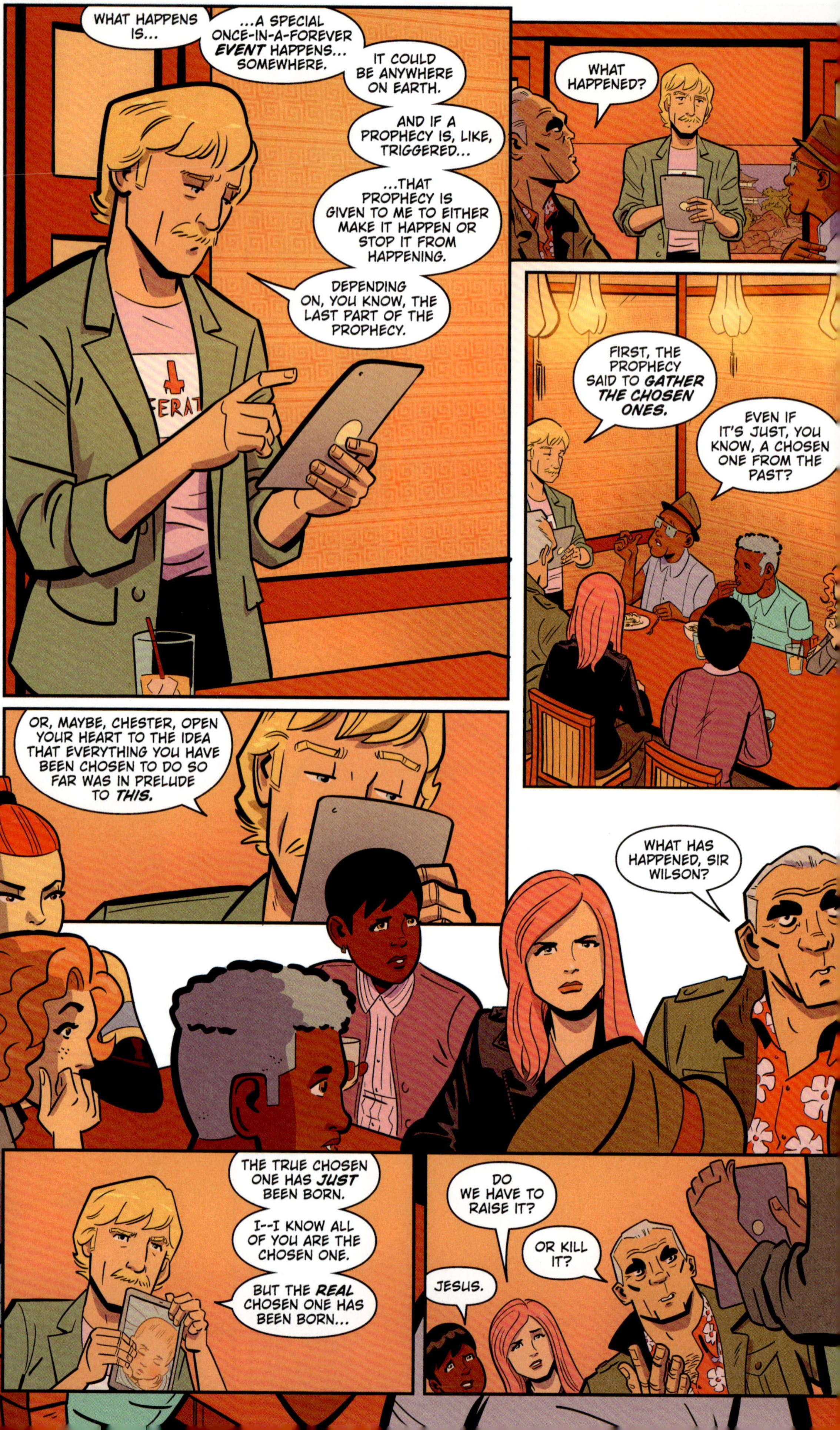
WHAT HAPPENS IS...
...A SPECIAL ONCE-IN-A-FOREVER EVENT HAPPENS... SOMEWHERE.
IT COULD BE ANYWHERE ON EARTH.
AND IF A PROPHECY IS, LIKE, TRIGGERED...
...THAT PROPHECY IS GIVEN TO ME TO EITHER MAKE IT HAPPEN OR STOP IT FROM HAPPENING.
DEPENDING ON, YOU KNOW, THE LAST PART OF THE PROPHECY.
WHAT HAPPENED?
FIRST, THE PROPHECY SAID TO GATHER THE CHOSEN ONES.
EVEN IF IT'S JUST, YOU KNOW, A CHOSEN ONE FROM THE PAST?
OR, MAYBE, CHESTER, OPEN YOUR HEART TO THE IDEA THAT EVERYTHING YOU HAVE BEEN CHOSEN TO DO SO FAR WAS IN PRELUDE TO THIS.
WHAT HAS HAPPENED, SIR WILSON?
THE TRUE CHOSEN ONE HAS JUST BEEN BORN.
I--I KNOW ALL OF YOU ARE THE CHOSEN ONE.
BUT THE REAL CHOSEN ONE HAS BEEN BORN...
DO WE HAVE TO RAISE IT?
OR KILL IT?
JESUS.

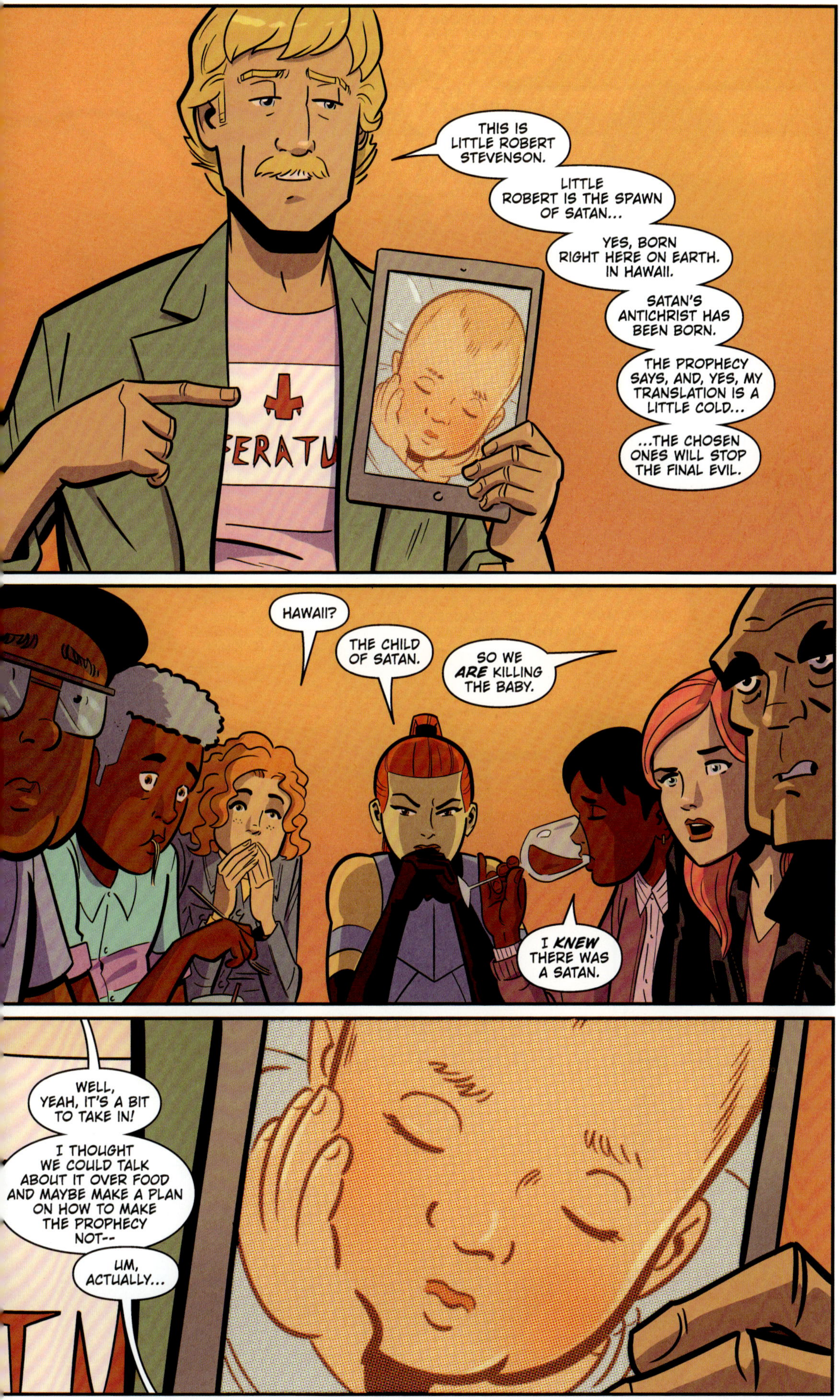
THIS IS LITTLE ROBERT STEVENSON.
LITTLE ROBERT IS THE SPAWN OF SATAN...
YES, BORN RIGHT HERE ON EARTH. IN HAWAII.
SATAN'S ANTICHRIST HAS BEEN BORN.
THE PROPHECY SAYS, AND, YES, MY TRANSLATION IS A LITTLE COLD...
...THE CHOSEN ONES WILL STOP THE FINAL EVIL.
FERATU
HAWAII?
THE CHILD OF SATAN.
SO WE ARE KILLING THE BABY.
I KNEW THERE WAS A SATAN.
WELL, YEAH, IT'S A BIT TO TAKE IN!
I THOUGHT WE COULD TALK ABOUT IT OVER FOOD AND MAYBE MAKE A PLAN ON HOW TO MAKE THE PROPHECY NOT--
UM, ACTUALLY...

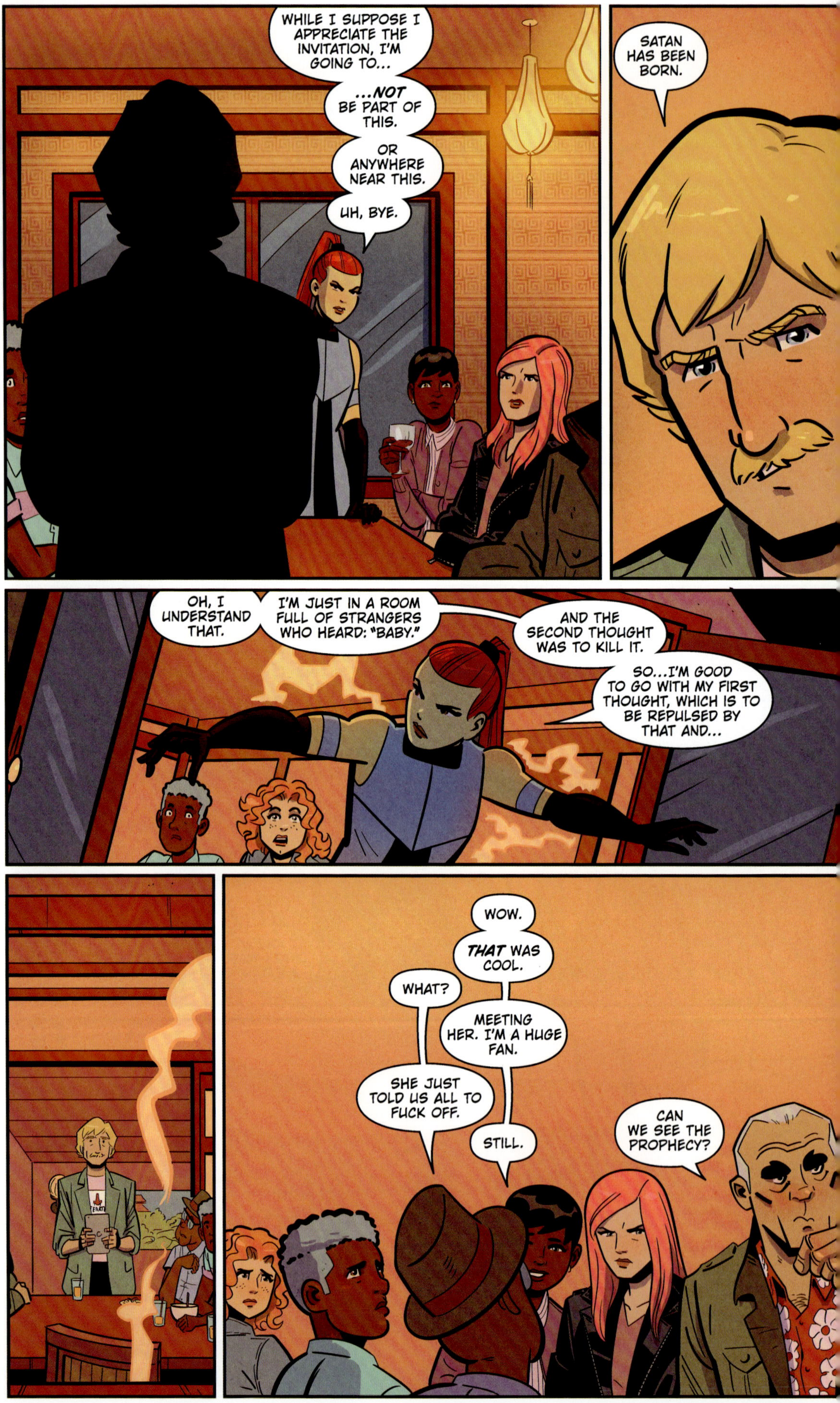
WHILE I SUPPOSE I APPRECIATE THE INVITATION, I'M GOING TO...
...NOT BE PART OF THIS.
OR ANYWHERE NEAR THIS.
UH, BYE.
SATAN HAS BEEN BORN.
OH, I UNDERSTAND THAT.
I'M JUST IN A ROOM FULL OF STRANGERS WHO HEARD: "BABY."
AND THE SECOND THOUGHT WAS TO KILL IT.
SO...I'M GOOD TO GO WITH MY FIRST THOUGHT, WHICH IS TO BE REPULSED BY THAT AND...
WOW.
THAT WAS COOL.
WHAT?
MEETING HER. I'M A HUGE FAN.
SHE JUST TOLD US ALL TO FUCK OFF.
STILL.
CAN WE SEE THE PROPHECY?

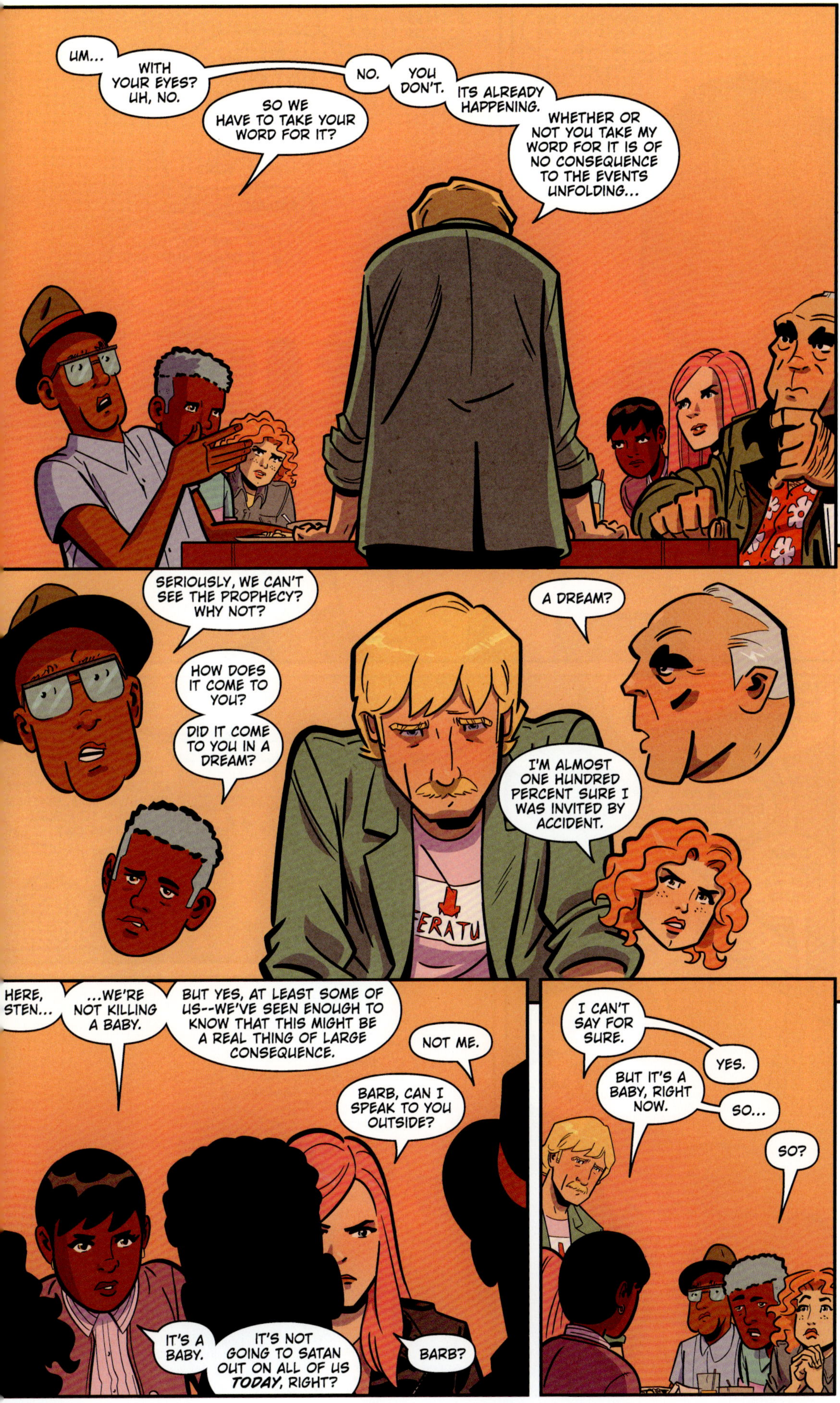
UM...
WITH YOUR EYES? UH, NO.
SO WE HAVE TO TAKE YOUR WORD FOR IT?
NO.
YOU DON'T.
ITS ALREADY HAPPENING.
WHETHER OR NOT YOU TAKE MY WORD FOR IT IS OF NO CONSEQUENCE TO THE EVENTS UNFOLDING...
SERIOUSLY, WE CAN'T SEE THE PROPHECY? WHY NOT?
HOW DOES IT COME TO YOU?
DID IT COME TO YOU IN A DREAM?
A DREAM?
I'M ALMOST ONE HUNDRED PERCENT SURE I WAS INVITED BY ACCIDENT.
ERATU
HERE, STEN...
...WE'RE NOT KILLING A BABY.
BUT YES, AT LEAST SOME OF US--WE'VE SEEN ENOUGH TO KNOW THAT THIS MIGHT BE A REAL THING OF LARGE CONSEQUENCE.
NOT ME.
BARB, CAN I SPEAK TO YOU OUTSIDE?
IT'S A BABY.
IT'S NOT GOING TO SATAN OUT ON ALL OF US *TODAY*, RIGHT?
BARB?
I CAN'T SAY FOR SURE.
YES.
BUT IT'S A BABY, RIGHT NOW.
SO...
SO?

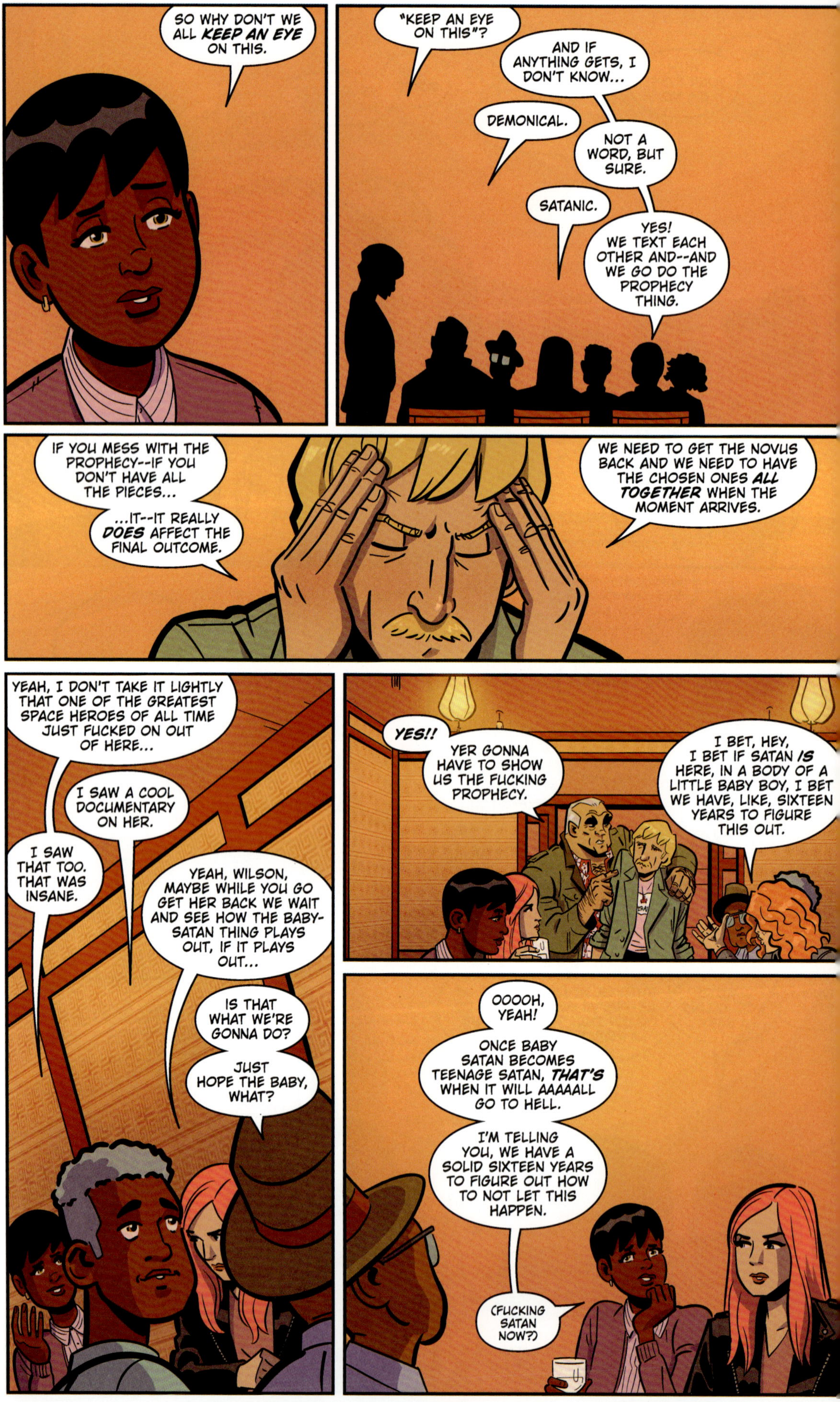
SO WHY DON'T WE ALL KEEP AN EYE ON THIS.
"KEEP AN EYE ON THIS"?
AND IF ANYTHING GETS, I DON'T KNOW...
DEMONICAL.
NOT A WORD, BUT SURE.
SATANIC.
YES! WE TEXT EACH OTHER AND--AND WE GO DO THE PROPHECY THING.
IF YOU MESS WITH THE PROPHECY--IF YOU DON'T HAVE ALL THE PIECES...
...IT--IT REALLY DOES AFFECT THE FINAL OUTCOME.
WE NEED TO GET THE NOVUS BACK AND WE NEED TO HAVE THE CHOSEN ONES ALL TOGETHER WHEN THE MOMENT ARRIVES.
YEAH, I DON'T TAKE IT LIGHTLY THAT ONE OF THE GREATEST SPACE HEROES OF ALL TIME JUST FUCKED ON OUT OF HERE...
I SAW A COOL DOCUMENTARY ON HER.
I SAW THAT TOO. THAT WAS INSANE.
YEAH, WILSON, MAYBE WHILE YOU GO GET HER BACK WE WAIT AND SEE HOW THE BABY-SATAN THING PLAYS OUT, IF IT PLAYS OUT...
IS THAT WHAT WE'RE GONNA DO?
JUST HOPE THE BABY, WHAT?
YES!!
YER GONNA HAVE TO SHOW US THE FUCKING PROPHECY.
I BET, HEY, I BET IF SATAN IS HERE, IN A BODY OF A LITTLE BABY BOY, I BET WE HAVE, LIKE, SIXTEEN YEARS TO FIGURE THIS OUT.
OOOOH, YEAH!
ONCE BABY SATAN BECOMES TEENAGE SATAN, THAT'S WHEN IT WILL AAAAALL GO TO HELL.
I'M TELLING YOU, WE HAVE A SOLID SIXTEEN YEARS TO FIGURE OUT HOW TO NOT LET THIS HAPPEN.
(FUCKING SATAN NOW?)

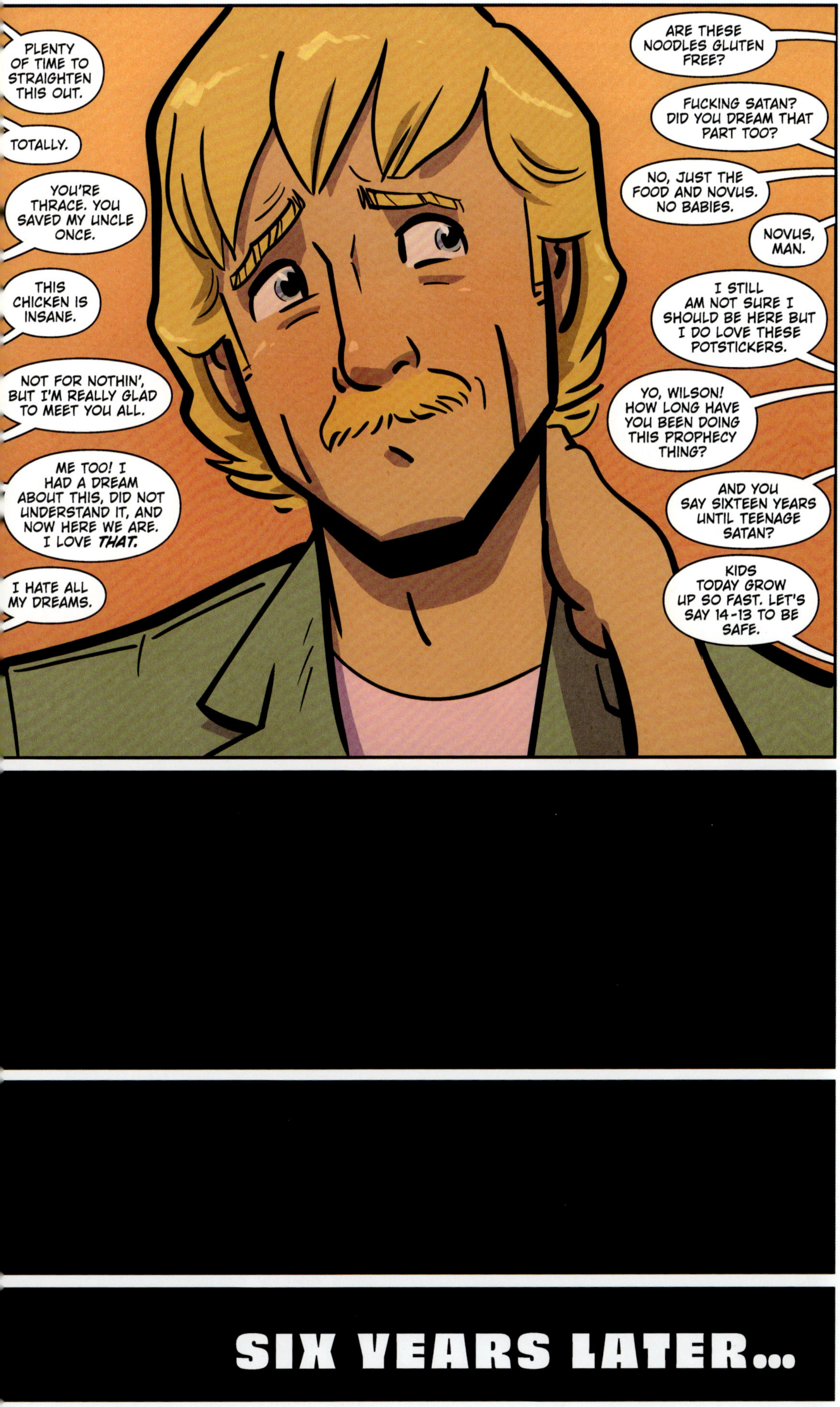
PLENTY OF TIME TO STRAIGHTEN THIS OUT.
TOTALLY.
YOU'RE THRACE. YOU SAVED MY UNCLE ONCE.
THIS CHICKEN IS INSANE.
NOT FOR NOTHIN', BUT I'M REALLY GLAD TO MEET YOU ALL.
ME TOO! I HAD A DREAM ABOUT THIS, DID NOT UNDERSTAND IT, AND NOW HERE WE ARE. I LOVE *THAT.*
I HATE ALL MY DREAMS.
ARE THESE NOODLES GLUTEN FREE?
FUCKING SATAN? DID YOU DREAM THAT PART TOO?
NO, JUST THE FOOD AND NOVUS. NO BABIES.
NOVUS, MAN.
I STILL AM NOT SURE I SHOULD BE HERE BUT I DO LOVE THESE POTSTICKERS.
YO, WILSON! HOW LONG HAVE YOU BEEN DOING THIS PROPHECY THING?
AND YOU SAY SIXTEEN YEARS UNTIL TEENAGE SATAN?
KIDS TODAY GROW UP SO FAST. LET'S SAY 14-13 TO BE SAFE.
SIX YEARS LATER...

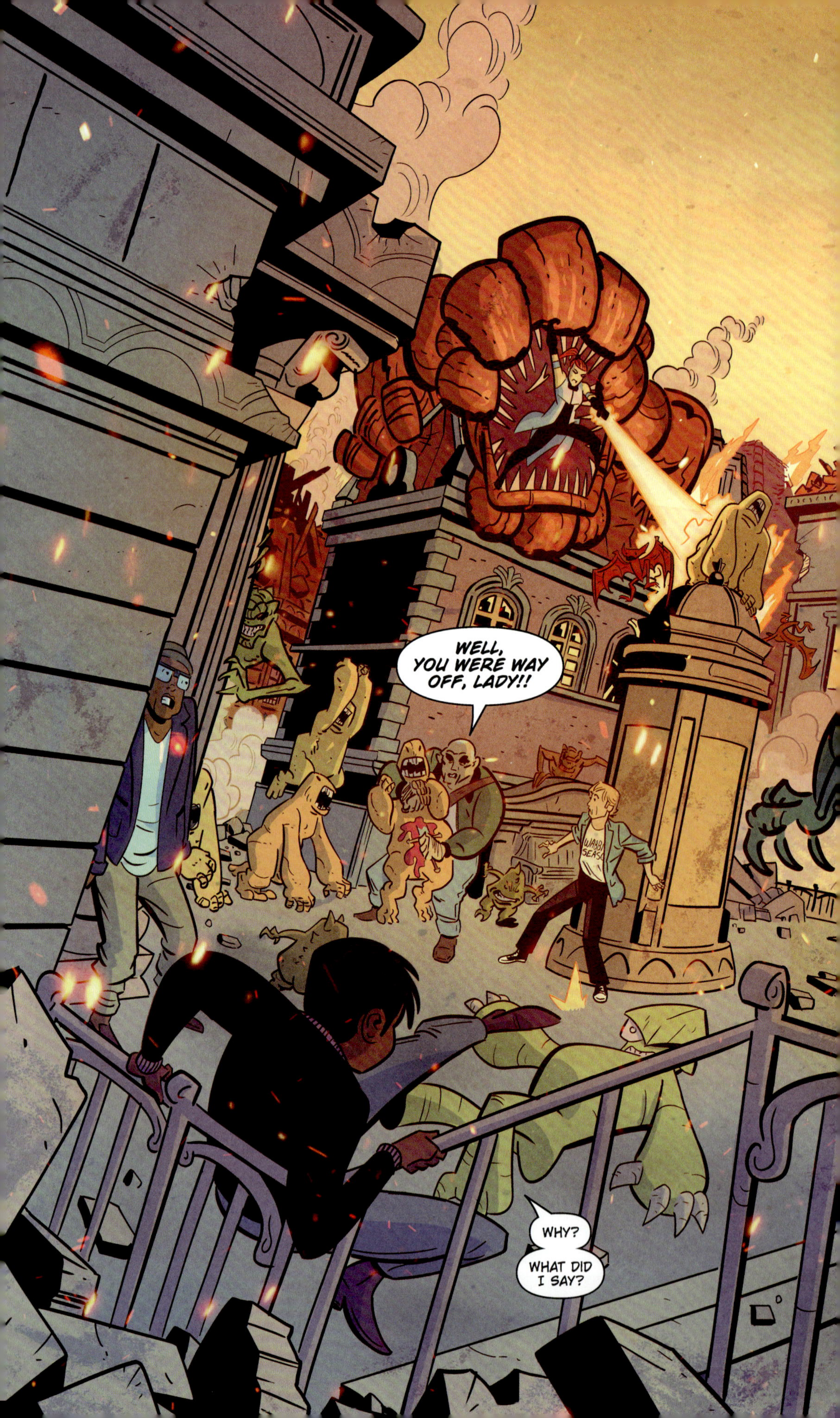
WELL, YOU WERE WAY OFF, LADY!!
WHY?
WHAT DID I SAY?

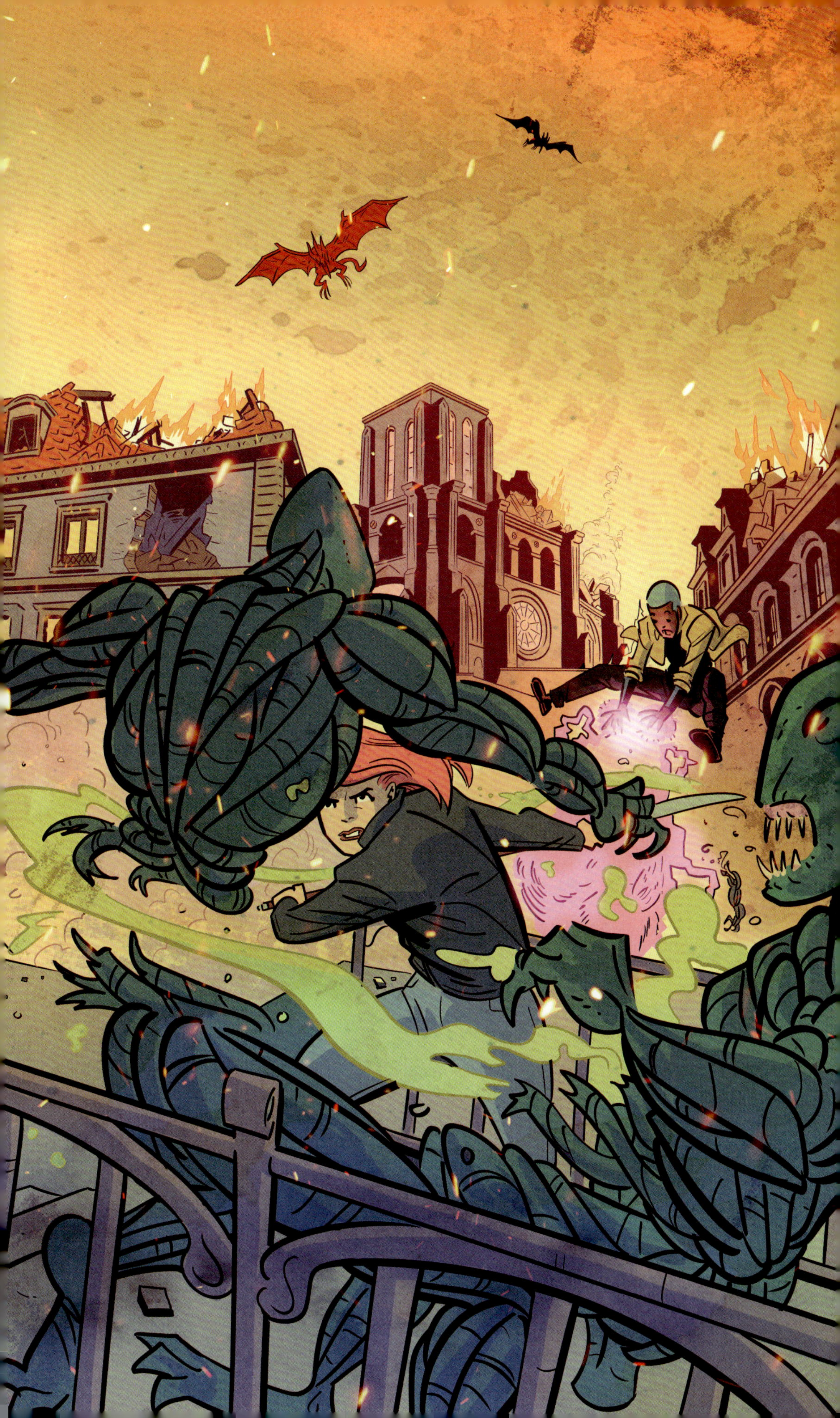

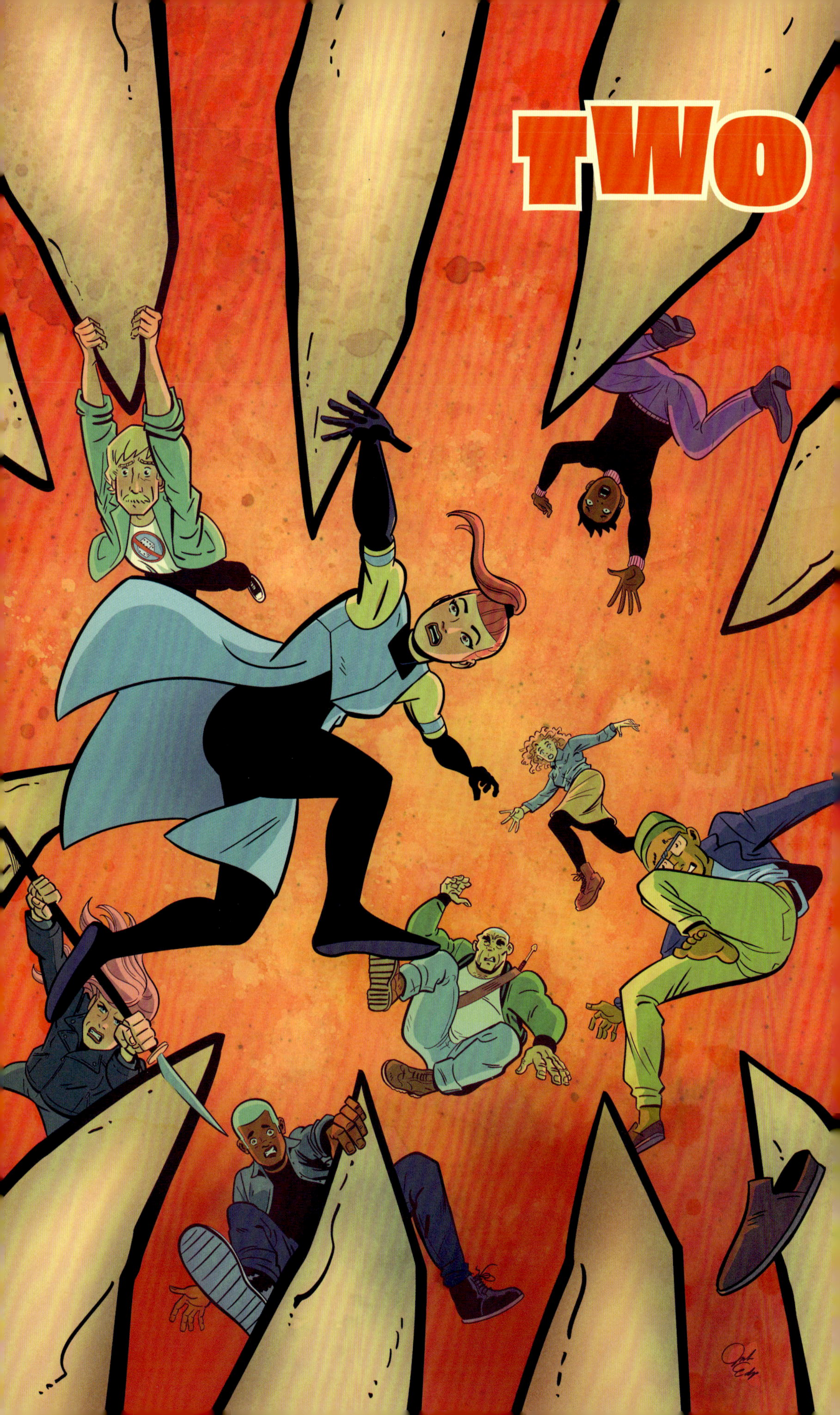
TWO

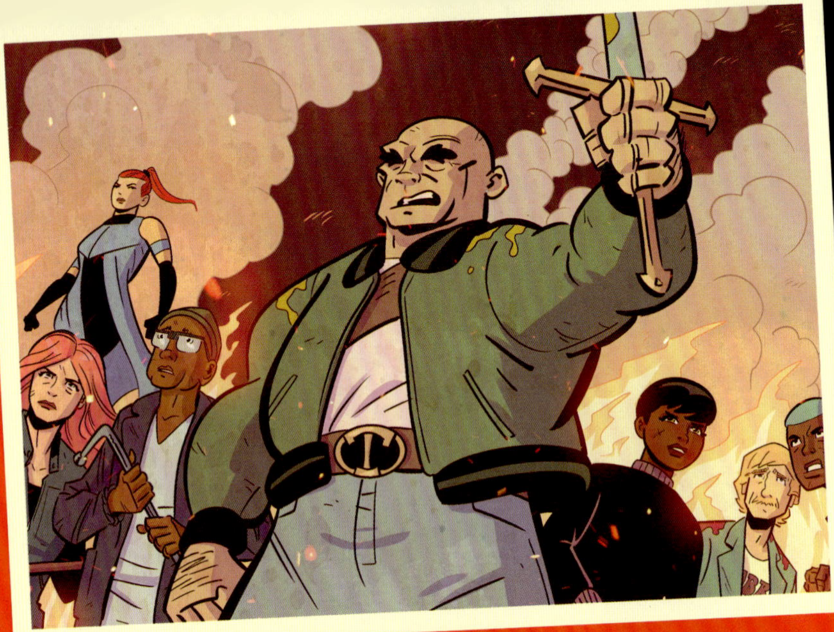

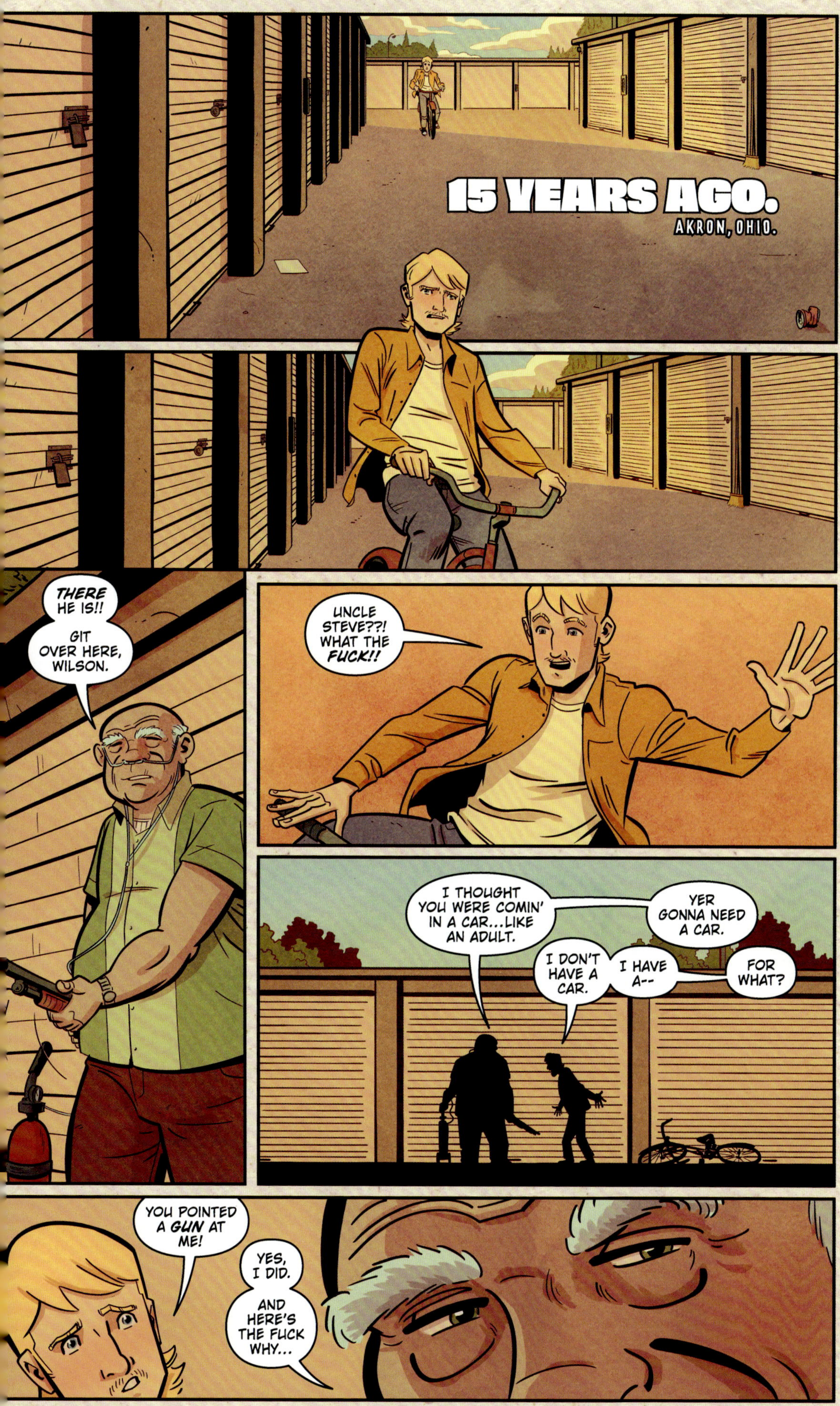
15 YEARS AGO.
AKRON, OHIO.
THERE HE IS!!
GIT OVER HERE, WILSON.
UNCLE STEVE??! WHAT THE FUCK!!
I THOUGHT YOU WERE COMIN' IN A CAR...LIKE AN ADULT.
YER GONNA NEED A CAR.
I DON'T HAVE A CAR.
I HAVE A--
FOR WHAT?
YOU POINTED A GUN AT ME!
YES, I DID.
AND HERE'S THE FUCK WHY...

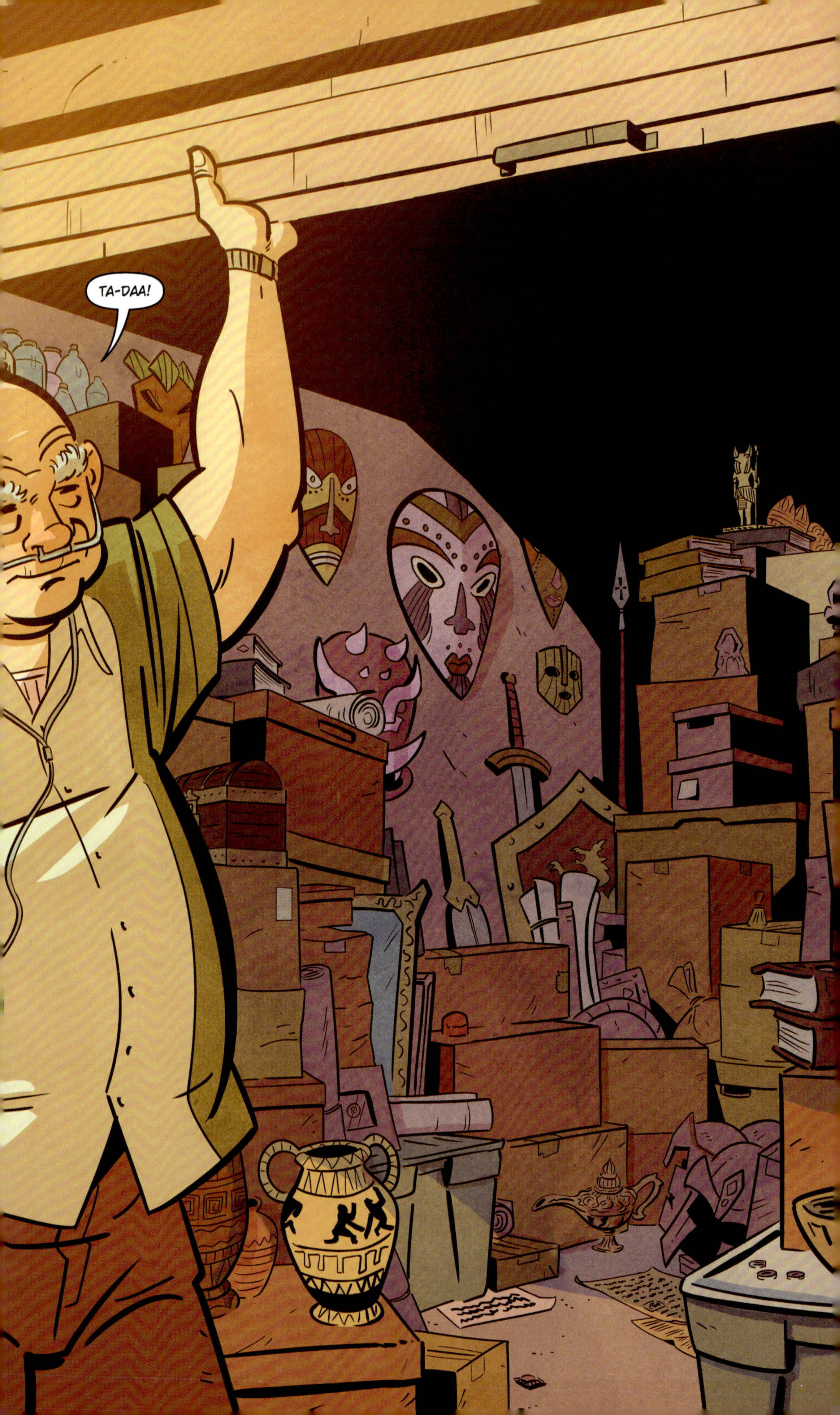
TA-DAA!

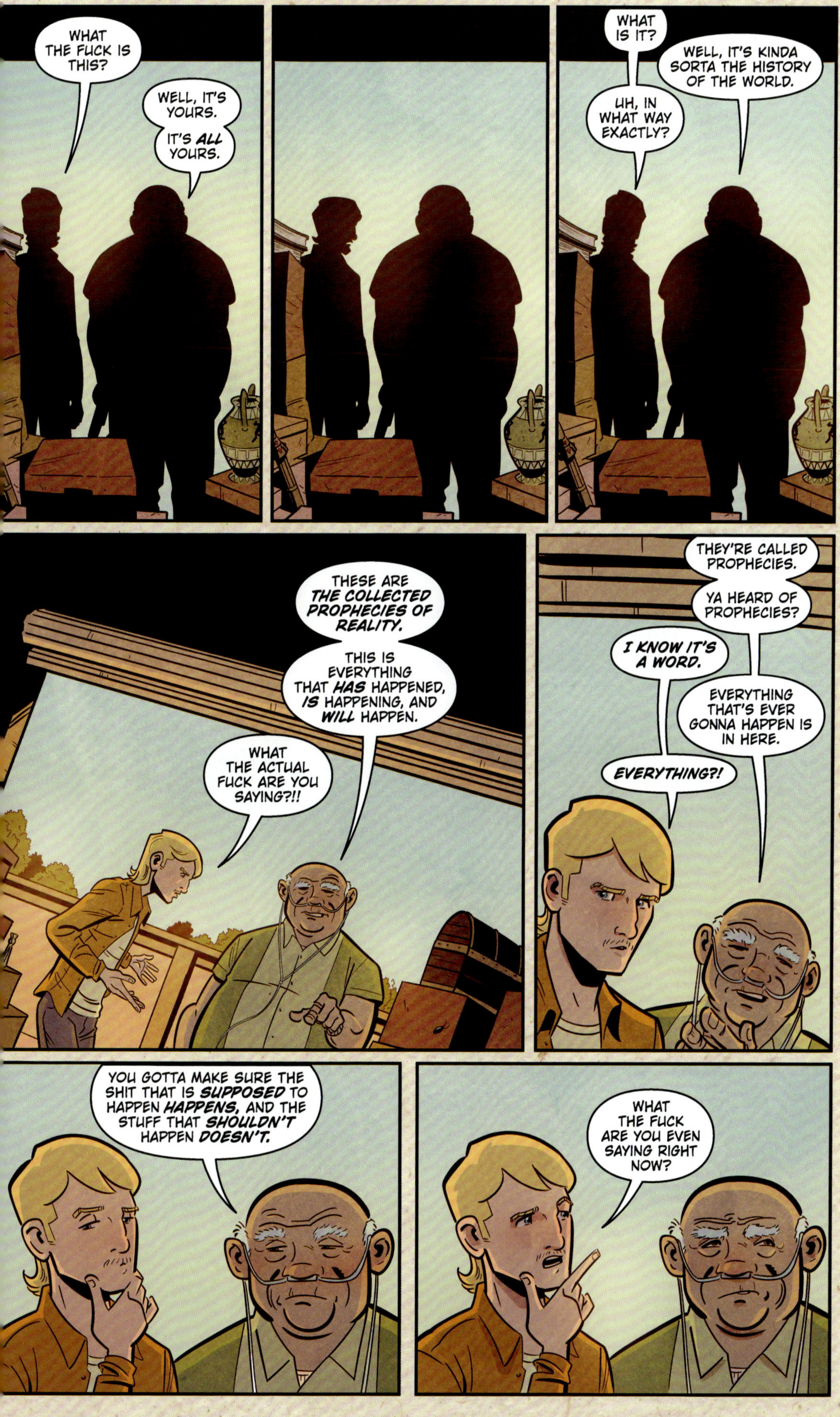

WHAT THE FUCK IS THIS?
WELL, IT'S YOURS.
IT'S *ALL* YOURS.
WHAT IS IT?
WELL, IT'S KINDA SORTA THE HISTORY OF THE WORLD.
UH, IN WHAT WAY EXACTLY?
THESE ARE *THE COLLECTED PROPHECIES OF REALITY.*
THIS IS EVERYTHING THAT *HAS* HAPPENED, *IS* HAPPENING, AND *WILL* HAPPEN.
WHAT THE ACTUAL FUCK ARE YOU SAYING?!!
THEY'RE CALLED PROPHECIES.
YA HEARD OF PROPHECIES?
I KNOW IT'S A WORD.
EVERYTHING THAT'S EVER GONNA HAPPEN IS IN HERE.
EVERYTHING?!
YOU GOTTA MAKE SURE THE SHIT THAT IS *SUPPOSED* TO HAPPEN *HAPPENS,* AND THE STUFF THAT *SHOULDN'T* HAPPEN *DOESN'T.*
WHAT THE FUCK ARE YOU EVEN SAYING RIGHT NOW?

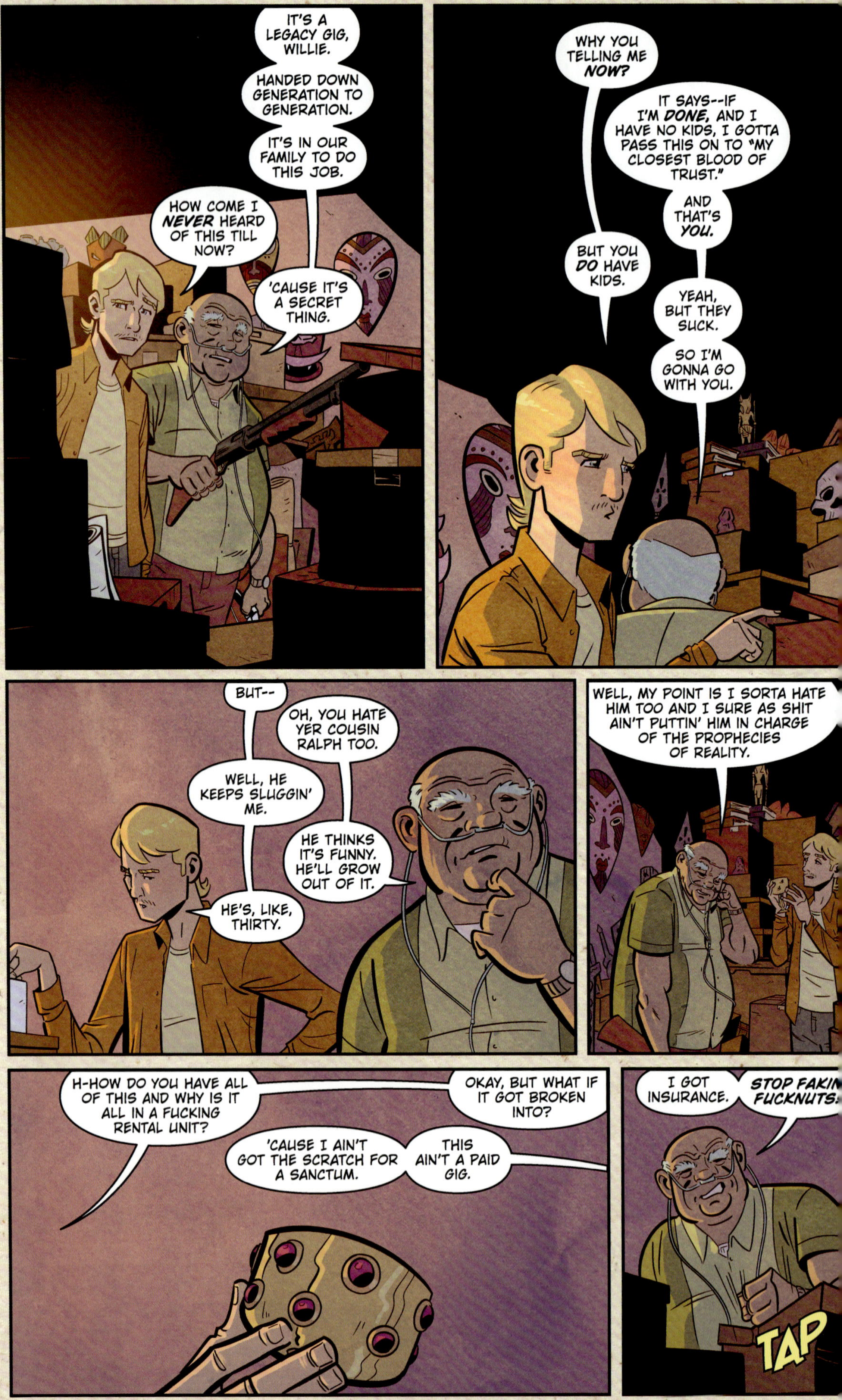
IT'S A LEGACY GIG, WILLIE.
HANDED DOWN GENERATION TO GENERATION.
IT'S IN OUR FAMILY TO DO THIS JOB.
HOW COME I NEVER HEARD OF THIS TILL NOW?
'CAUSE IT'S A SECRET THING.
WHY YOU TELLING ME NOW?
IT SAYS--IF I'M DONE, AND I HAVE NO KIDS, I GOTTA PASS THIS ON TO "MY CLOSEST BLOOD OF TRUST."
AND THAT'S YOU.
BUT YOU DO HAVE KIDS.
YEAH, BUT THEY SUCK.
SO I'M GONNA GO WITH YOU.
BUT--
OH, YOU HATE YER COUSIN RALPH TOO.
WELL, HE KEEPS SLUGGIN' ME.
HE THINKS IT'S FUNNY. HE'LL GROW OUT OF IT.
HE'S, LIKE, THIRTY.
WELL, MY POINT IS I SORTA HATE HIM TOO AND I SURE AS SHIT AIN'T PUTTIN' HIM IN CHARGE OF THE PROPHECIES OF REALITY.
H-HOW DO YOU HAVE ALL OF THIS AND WHY IS IT ALL IN A FUCKING RENTAL UNIT?
'CAUSE I AIN'T GOT THE SCRATCH FOR A SANCTUM.
THIS AIN'T A PAID GIG.
OKAY, BUT WHAT IF IT GOT BROKEN INTO?
I GOT INSURANCE.
TAP

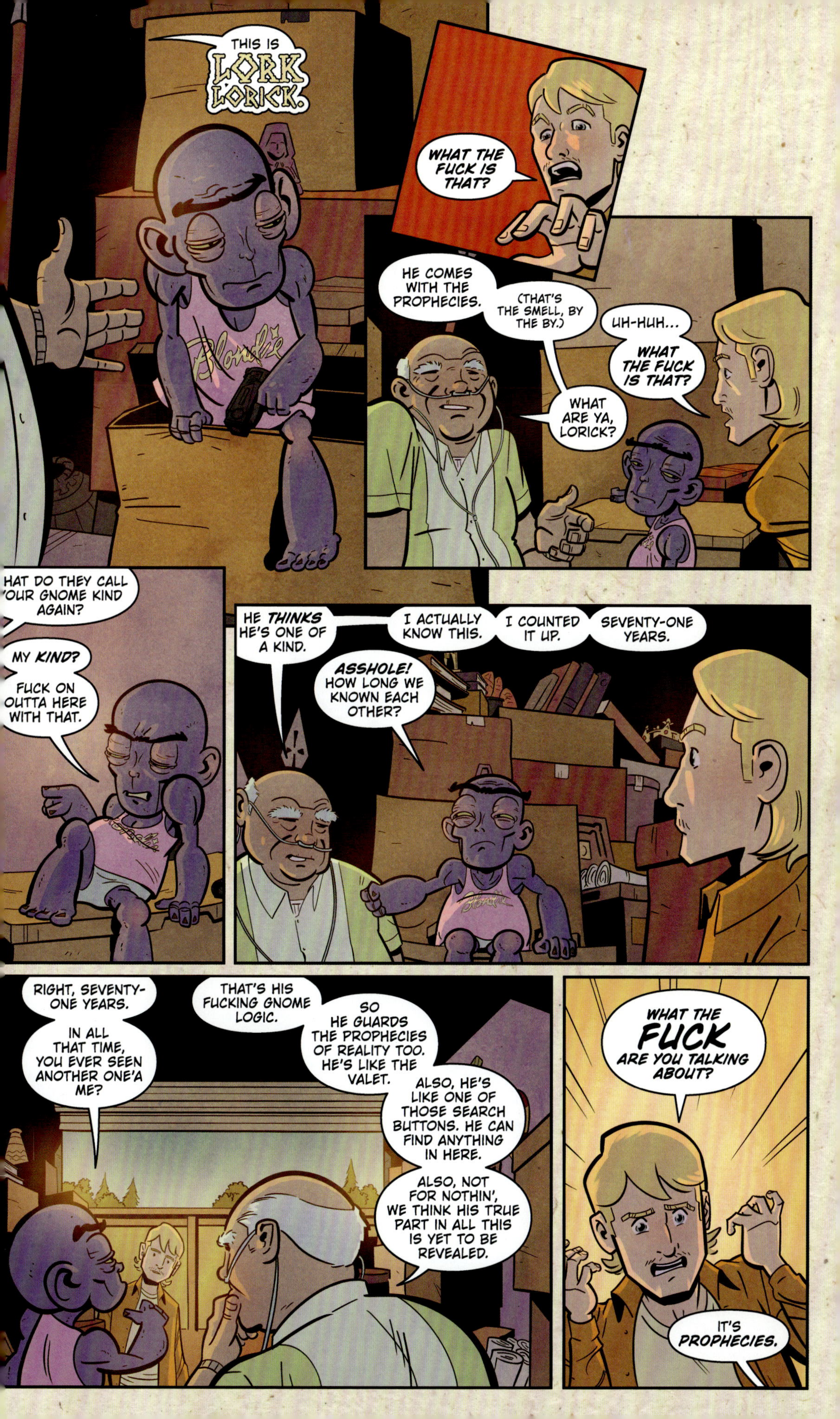

THIS IS LORK LORICK.
WHAT THE FUCK IS THAT?
HE COMES WITH THE PROPHECIES.
(THAT'S THE SMELL, BY THE BY.)
UH-HUH...
WHAT THE FUCK IS THAT?
WHAT ARE YA, LORICK?
HAT DO THEY CALL 'OUR GNOME KIND AGAIN?
MY KIND?
FUCK ON OUTTA HERE WITH THAT.
HE THINKS HE'S ONE OF A KIND.
I ACTUALLY KNOW THIS.
I COUNTED IT UP.
SEVENTY-ONE YEARS.
ASSHOLE! HOW LONG WE KNOWN EACH OTHER?
RIGHT, SEVENTY-ONE YEARS.
IN ALL THAT TIME, YOU EVER SEEN ANOTHER ONE'A ME?
THAT'S HIS FUCKING GNOME LOGIC.
SO HE GUARDS THE PROPHECIES OF REALITY TOO. HE'S LIKE THE VALET.
ALSO, HE'S LIKE ONE OF THOSE SEARCH BUTTONS. HE CAN FIND ANYTHING IN HERE.
ALSO, NOT FOR NOTHIN', WE THINK HIS TRUE PART IN ALL THIS IS YET TO BE REVEALED.
WHAT THE FUCK ARE YOU TALKING ABOUT?
IT'S PROPHECIES.

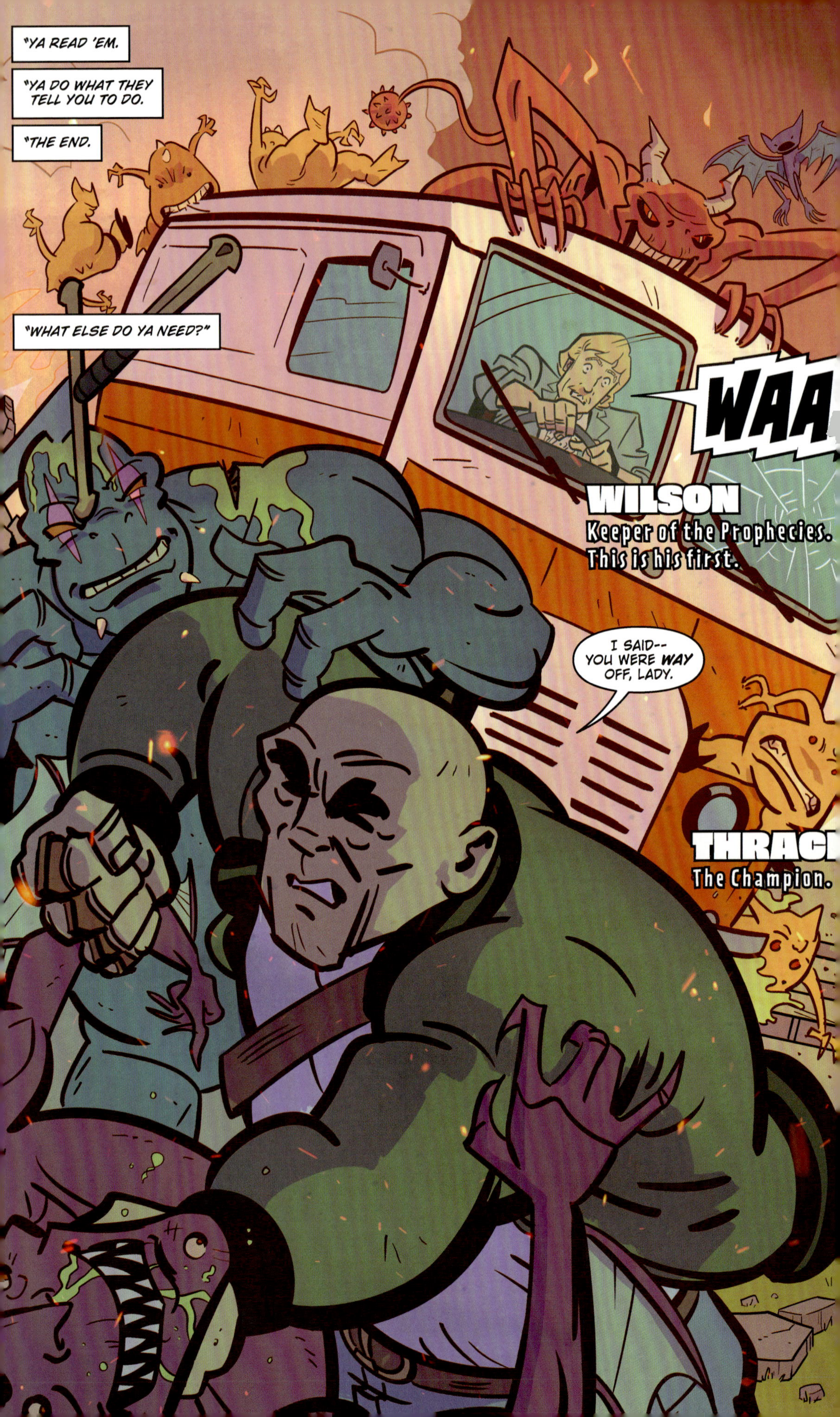
"YA READ 'EM.
"YA DO WHAT THEY TELL YOU TO DO.
"THE END.
"WHAT ELSE DO YA NEED?"
WAA
WILSON
Keeper of the Prophecies. This is his first.
I SAID-- YOU WERE WAY OFF, LADY.
THRAC
The Champion.

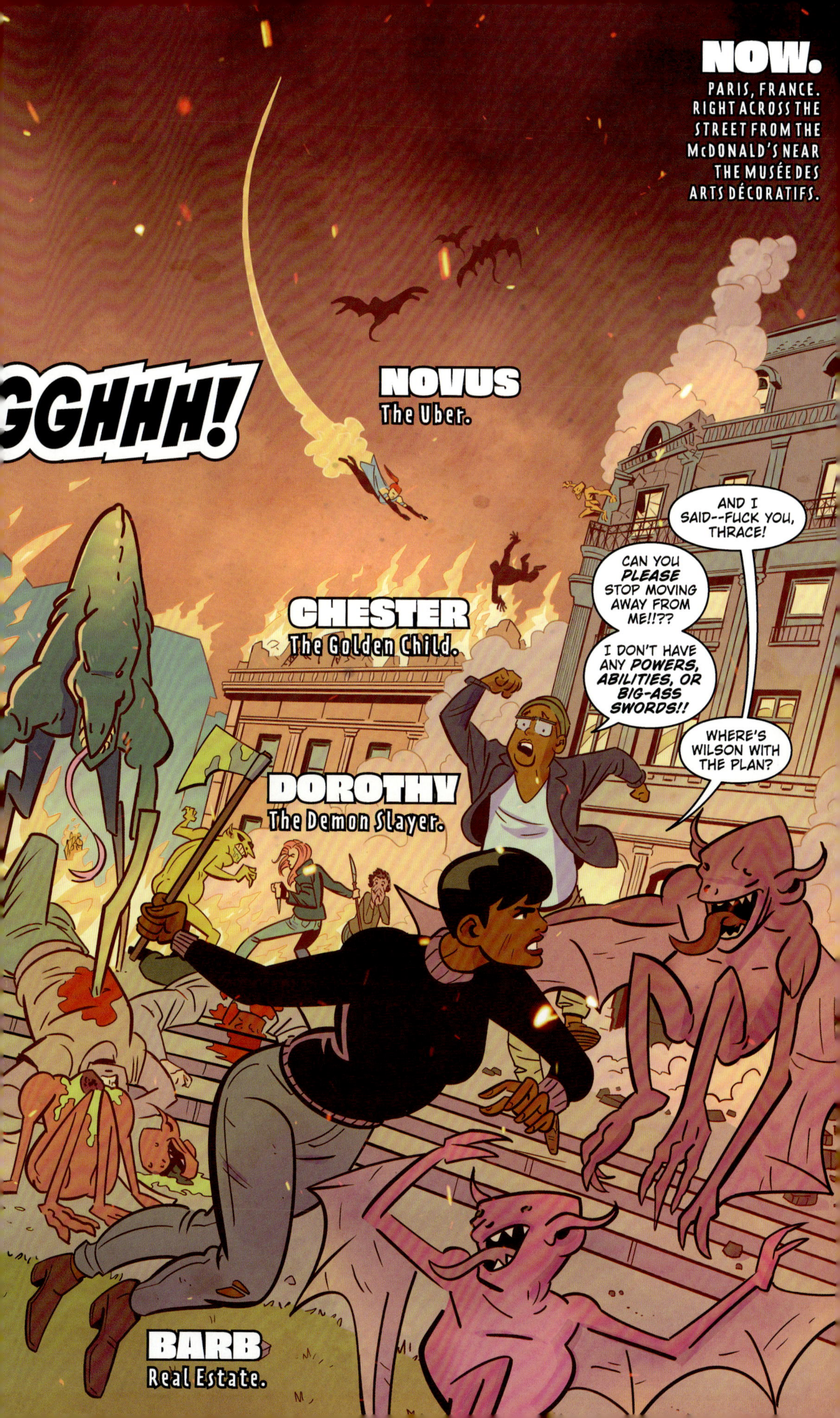
NOW.
PARIS, FRANCE. RIGHT ACROSS THE STREET FROM THE McDONALD'S NEAR THE MUSÉE DES ARTS DÉCORATIFS.
GGHHH!
NOVUS
The Uber.
CHESTER
The Golden Child.
DOROTHY
The Demon Slayer.
BARB
Real Estate.
AND I SAID--FUCK YOU, THRACE!
CAN YOU PLEASE STOP MOVING AWAY FROM ME!!??
I DON'T HAVE ANY POWERS, ABILITIES, OR BIG-ASS SWORDS!!
WHERE'S WILSON WITH THE PLAN?

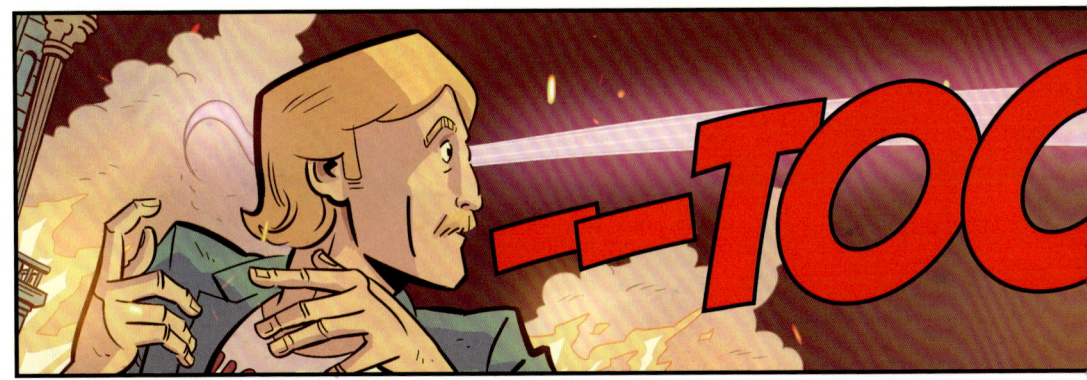

WAAAGGHH!!

SEEMS OUR BENEFACTOR IS FREAKING THE FUCK OUT!!

CRABOOM

--TOO

AIN'T NO ONE BUILT FOR *THIS* SHIT, WILSON!! THIS IS END-OF-THE-WORLD SHIT!!

THANK YOU, DOCTOR JAMAX!

HEY, LIKE I TOLD YOU, I'M NOT SUPPOSED TO BE USING MY MYSTICAL POWERS FOR SHIT LIKE THIS!!

DOCTOR JAMAX
The Mystic Master.

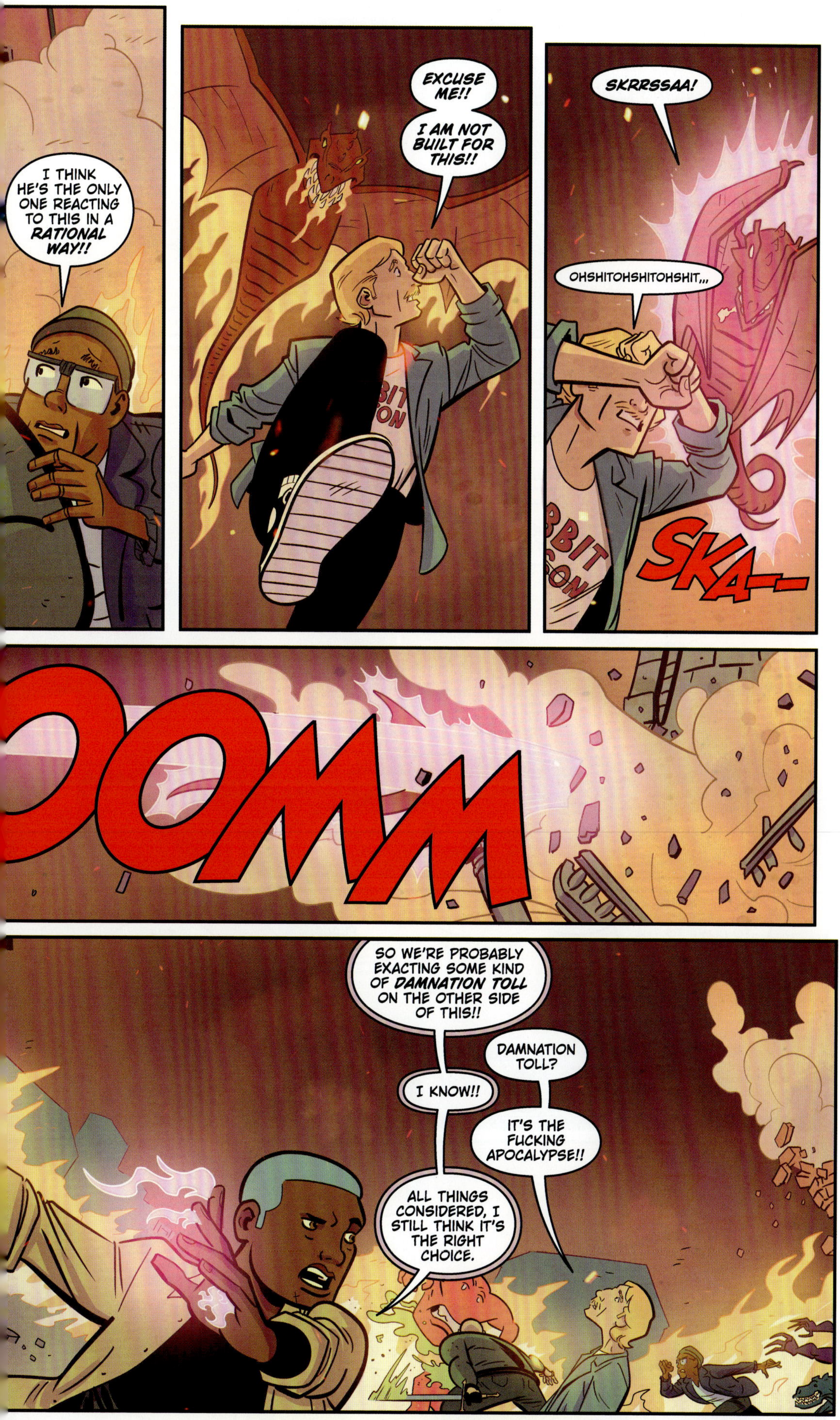
I THINK HE'S THE ONLY ONE REACTING TO THIS IN A RATIONAL WAY!!
EXCUSE ME!!
I AM NOT BUILT FOR THIS!!
SKRRSSAA!
OHSHITOHSHITOHSHIT,,,
SKA--
OOMM
SO WE'RE PROBABLY EXACTING SOME KIND OF DAMNATION TOLL ON THE OTHER SIDE OF THIS!!
I KNOW!!
DAMNATION TOLL?
IT'S THE FUCKING APOCALYPSE!!
ALL THINGS CONSIDERED, I STILL THINK IT'S THE RIGHT CHOICE.

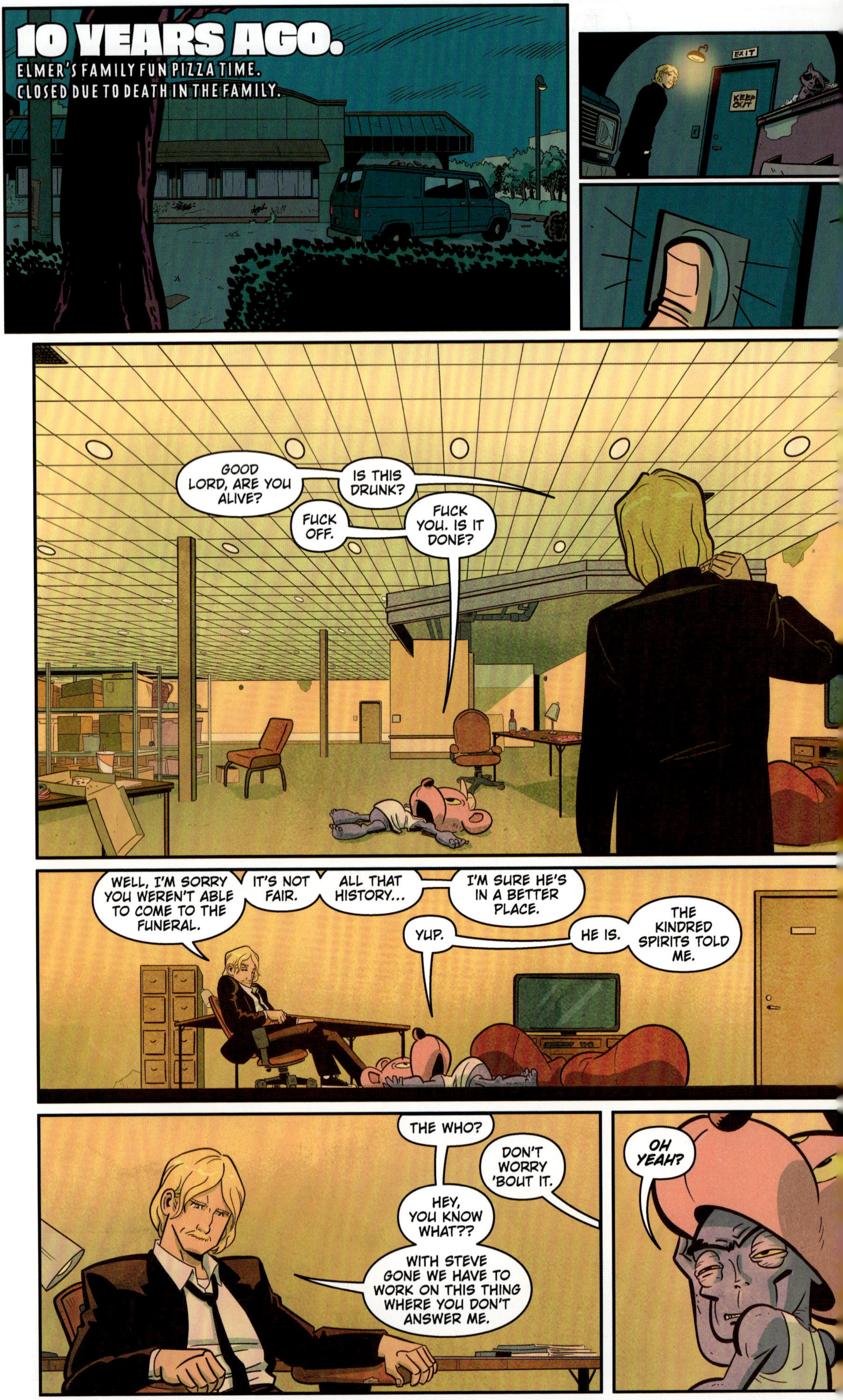
10 YEARS AGO.
ELMER'S FAMILY FUN PIZZA TIME.
CLOSED DUE TO DEATH IN THE FAMILY.
EXIT
KEEP OUT
GOOD LORD, ARE YOU ALIVE?
IS THIS DRUNK?
FUCK OFF.
FUCK YOU. IS IT DONE?
WELL, I'M SORRY YOU WEREN'T ABLE TO COME TO THE FUNERAL.
IT'S NOT FAIR.
ALL THAT HISTORY...
I'M SURE HE'S IN A BETTER PLACE.
YUP.
HE IS.
THE KINDRED SPIRITS TOLD ME.
THE WHO?
DON'T WORRY 'BOUT IT.
HEY, YOU KNOW WHAT??
WITH STEVE GONE WE HAVE TO WORK ON THIS THING WHERE YOU DON'T ANSWER ME.
OH YEAH?

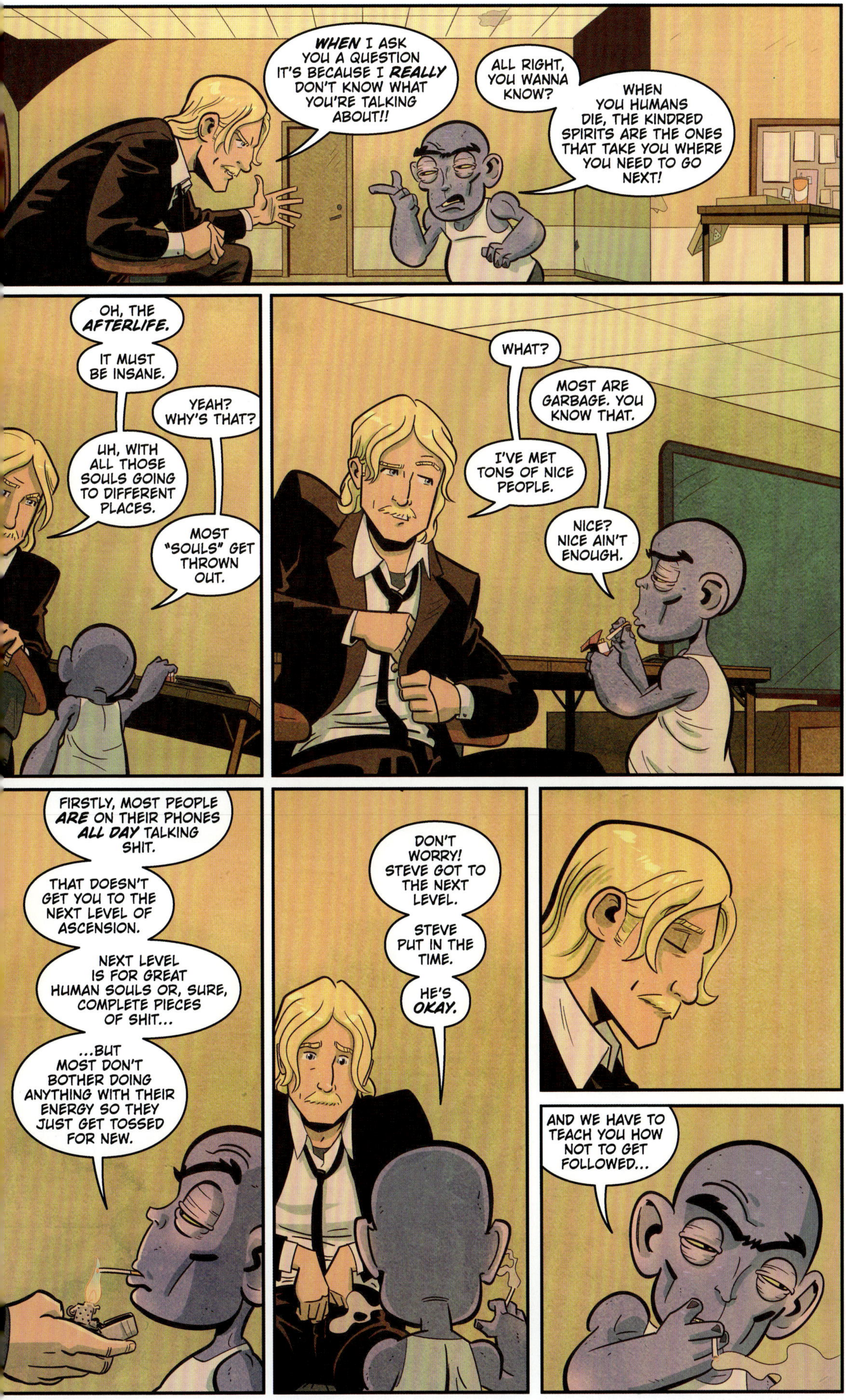
WHEN I ASK YOU A QUESTION IT'S BECAUSE I REALLY DON'T KNOW WHAT YOU'RE TALKING ABOUT!!
ALL RIGHT, YOU WANNA KNOW?
WHEN YOU HUMANS DIE, THE KINDRED SPIRITS ARE THE ONES THAT TAKE YOU WHERE YOU NEED TO GO NEXT!
OH, THE AFTERLIFE.
IT MUST BE INSANE.
YEAH? WHY'S THAT?
UH, WITH ALL THOSE SOULS GOING TO DIFFERENT PLACES.
MOST "SOULS" GET THROWN OUT.
WHAT?
MOST ARE GARBAGE. YOU KNOW THAT.
I'VE MET TONS OF NICE PEOPLE.
NICE? NICE AIN'T ENOUGH.
FIRSTLY, MOST PEOPLE ARE ON THEIR PHONES ALL DAY TALKING SHIT.
THAT DOESN'T GET YOU TO THE NEXT LEVEL OF ASCENSION.
NEXT LEVEL IS FOR GREAT HUMAN SOULS OR, SURE, COMPLETE PIECES OF SHIT...
...BUT MOST DON'T BOTHER DOING ANYTHING WITH THEIR ENERGY SO THEY JUST GET TOSSED FOR NEW.
DON'T WORRY! STEVE GOT TO THE NEXT LEVEL.
STEVE PUT IN THE TIME.
HE'S OKAY.
AND WE HAVE TO TEACH YOU HOW NOT TO GET FOLLOWED...

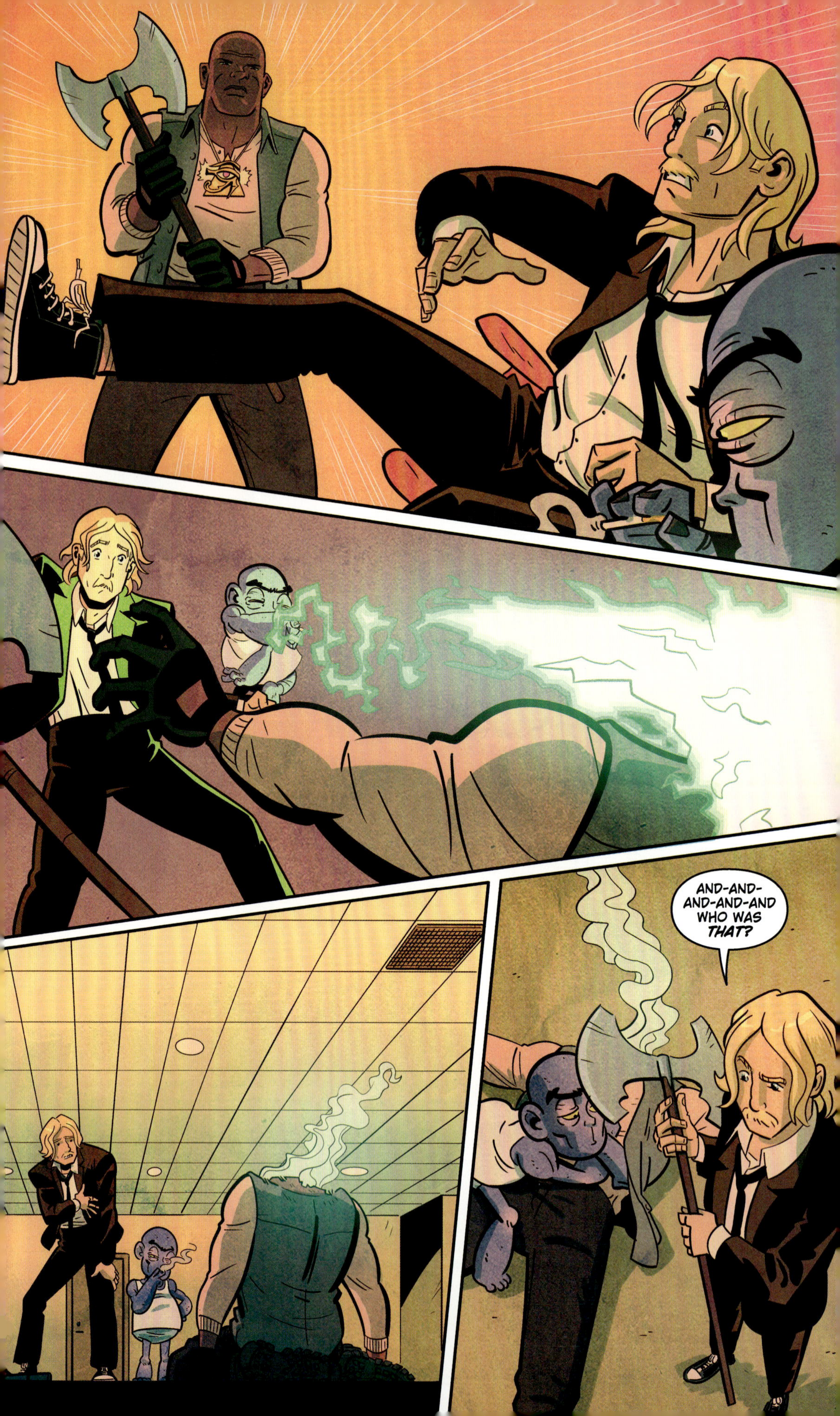
AND-AND-AND-AND-AND WHO WAS *THAT?*

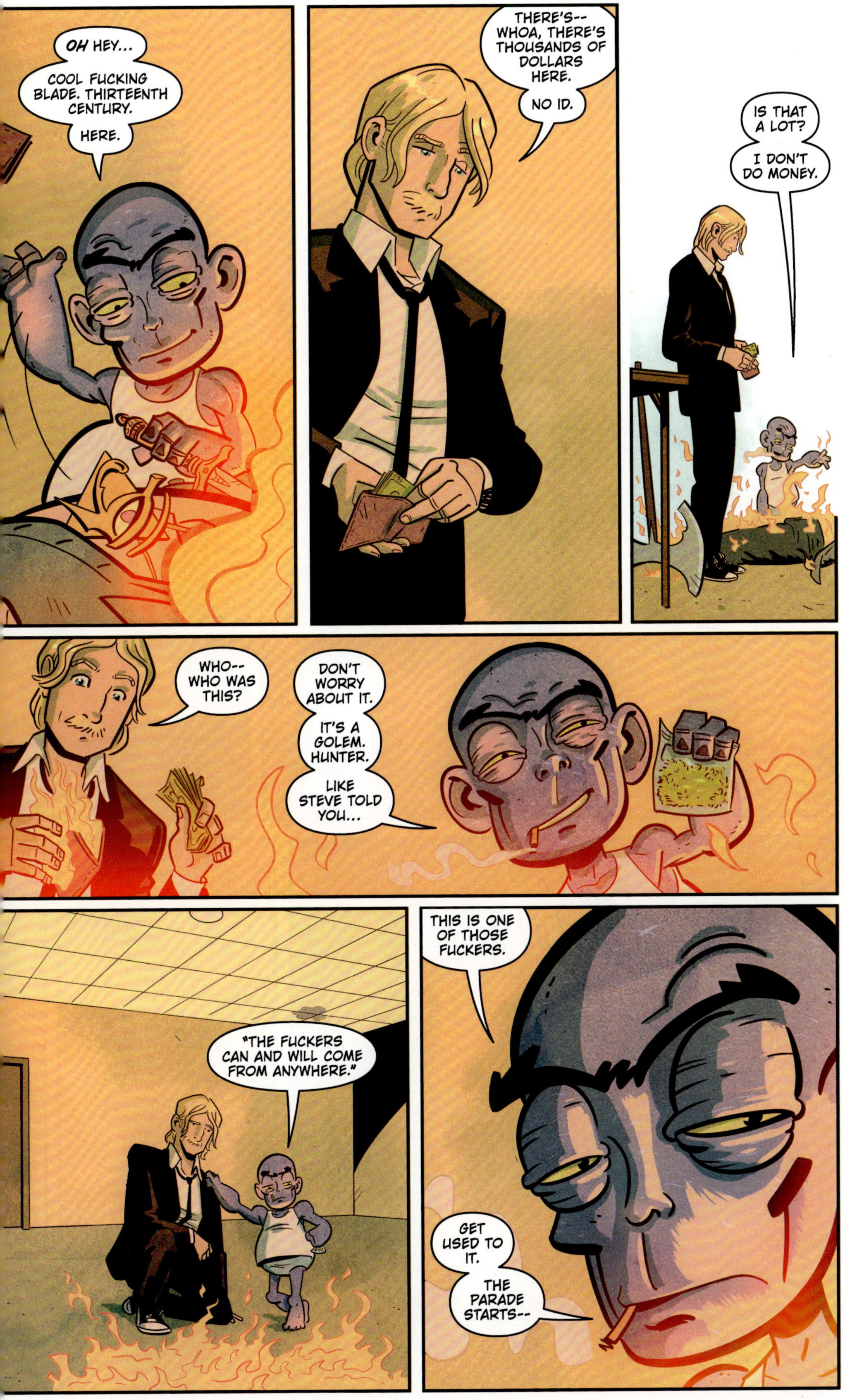
OH HEY...
COOL FUCKING BLADE. THIRTEENTH CENTURY.
HERE.
THERE'S-- WHOA, THERE'S THOUSANDS OF DOLLARS HERE.
NO ID.
IS THAT A LOT?
I DON'T DO MONEY.
WHO-- WHO WAS THIS?
DON'T WORRY ABOUT IT.
IT'S A GOLEM. HUNTER.
LIKE STEVE TOLD YOU...
"THE FUCKERS CAN AND WILL COME FROM ANYWHERE."
THIS IS ONE OF THOSE FUCKERS.
GET USED TO IT.
THE PARADE STARTS--

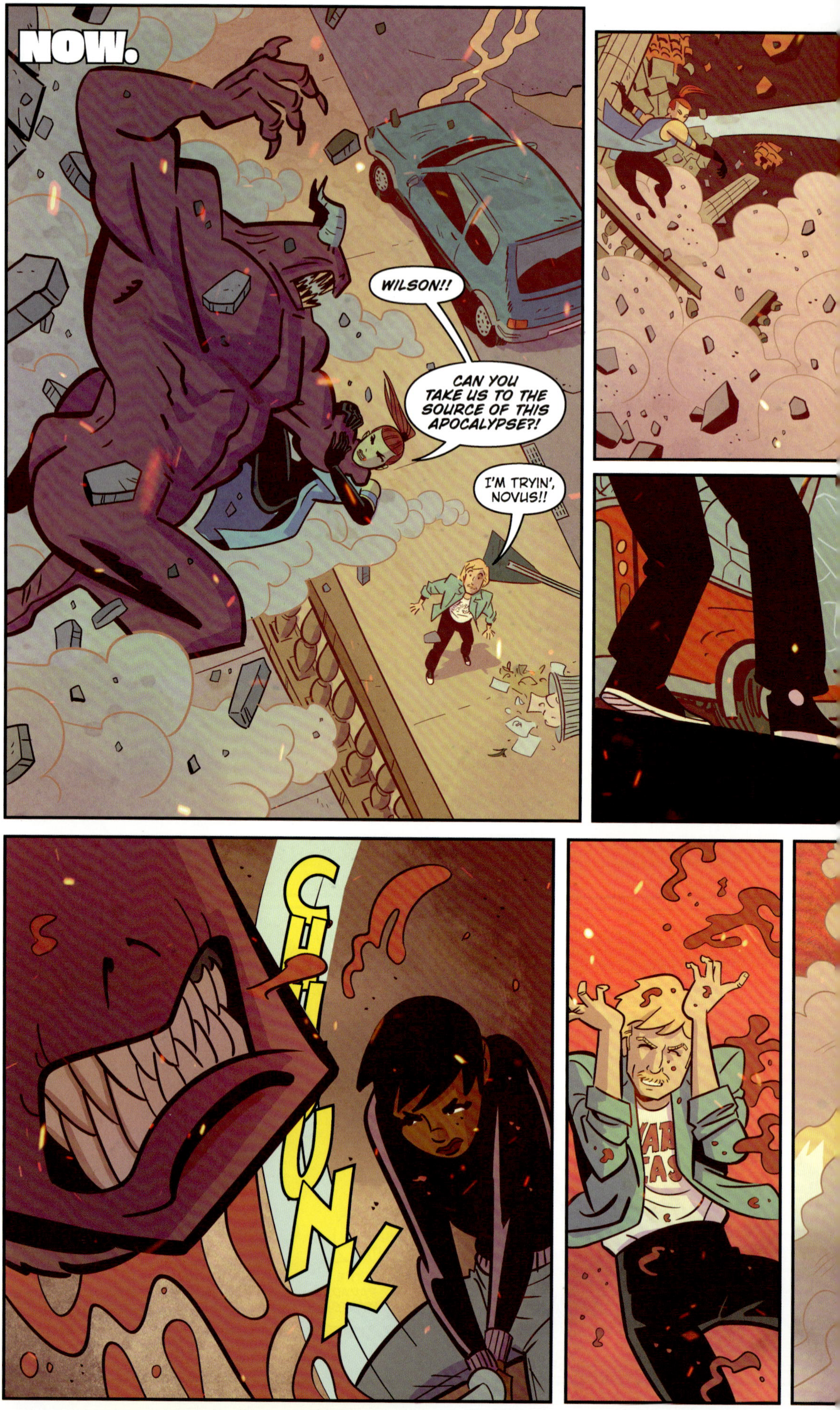
NOW.
WILSON!!
CAN YOU TAKE US TO THE SOURCE OF THIS APOCALYPSE?!
I'M TRYIN', NOVUS!!
CHUNK

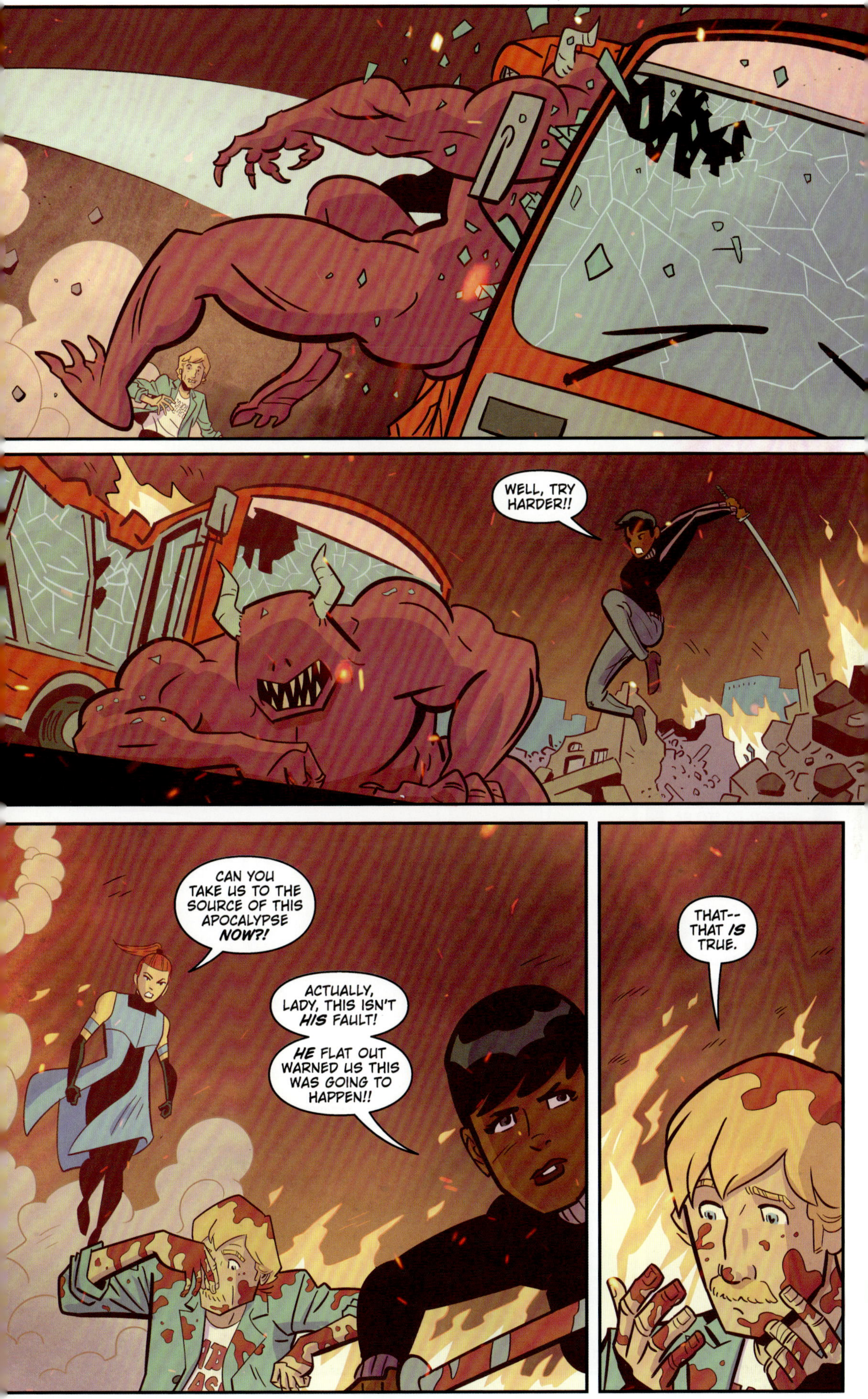
WELL, TRY HARDER!!
CAN YOU TAKE US TO THE SOURCE OF THIS APOCALYPSE NOW?!
ACTUALLY, LADY, THIS ISN'T HIS FAULT!
HE FLAT OUT WARNED US THIS WAS GOING TO HAPPEN!!
THAT-- THAT IS TRUE.

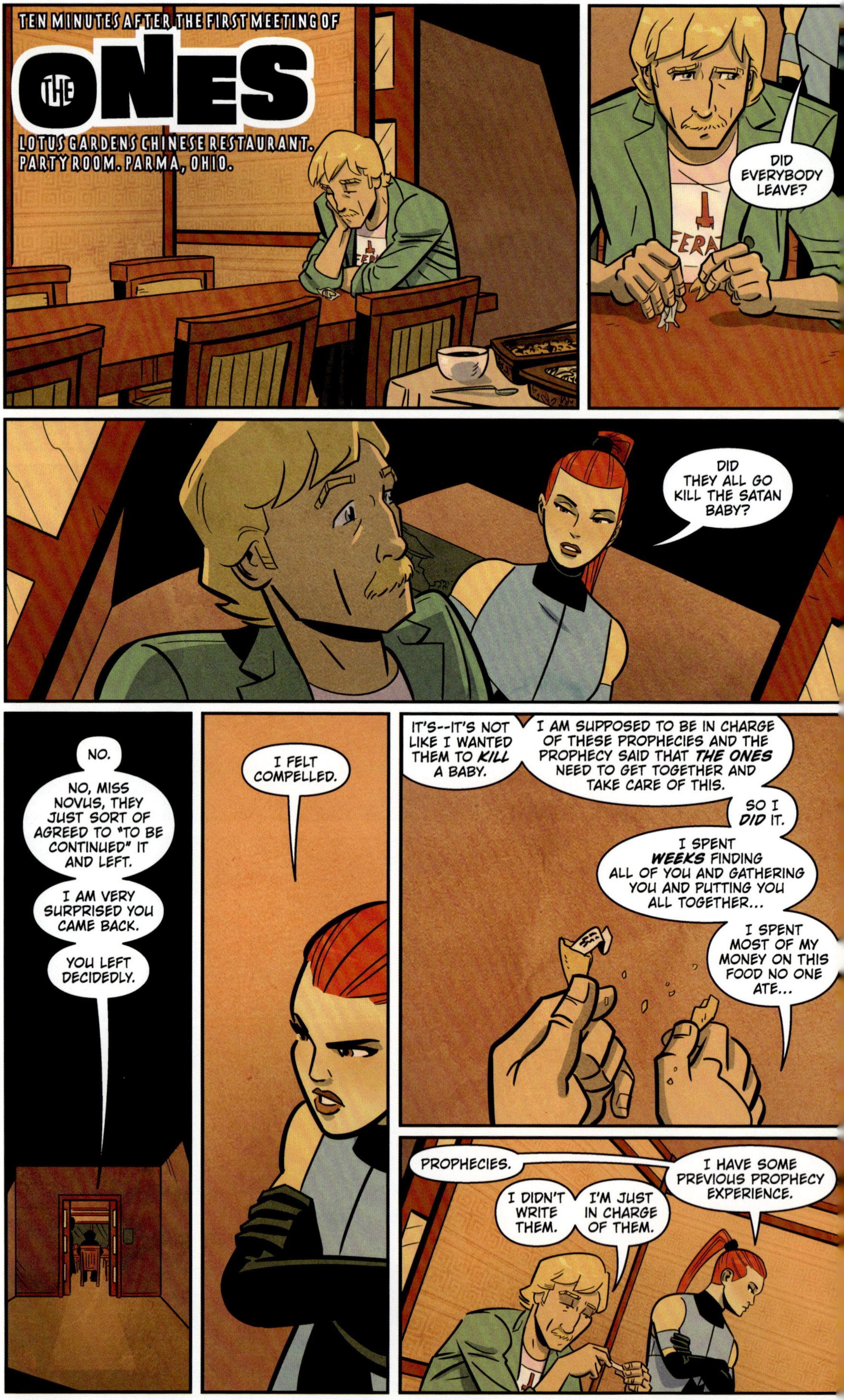
TEN MINUTES AFTER THE FIRST MEETING OF
THE ONES
LOTUS GARDENS CHINESE RESTAURANT.
PARTY ROOM. PARMA, OHIO.
DID EVERYBODY LEAVE?
DID THEY ALL GO KILL THE SATAN BABY?
NO.
NO, MISS NOVUS, THEY JUST SORT OF AGREED TO "TO BE CONTINUED" IT AND LEFT.
I AM VERY SURPRISED YOU CAME BACK.
YOU LEFT DECIDEDLY.
I FELT COMPELLED.
IT'S--IT'S NOT LIKE I WANTED THEM TO KILL A BABY.
I AM SUPPOSED TO BE IN CHARGE OF THESE PROPHECIES AND THE PROPHECY SAID THAT THE ONES NEED TO GET TOGETHER AND TAKE CARE OF THIS.
SO I DID IT.
I SPENT WEEKS FINDING ALL OF YOU AND GATHERING YOU AND PUTTING YOU ALL TOGETHER...
I SPENT MOST OF MY MONEY ON THIS FOOD NO ONE ATE...
PROPHECIES.
I DIDN'T WRITE THEM.
I'M JUST IN CHARGE OF THEM.
I HAVE SOME PREVIOUS PROPHECY EXPERIENCE.

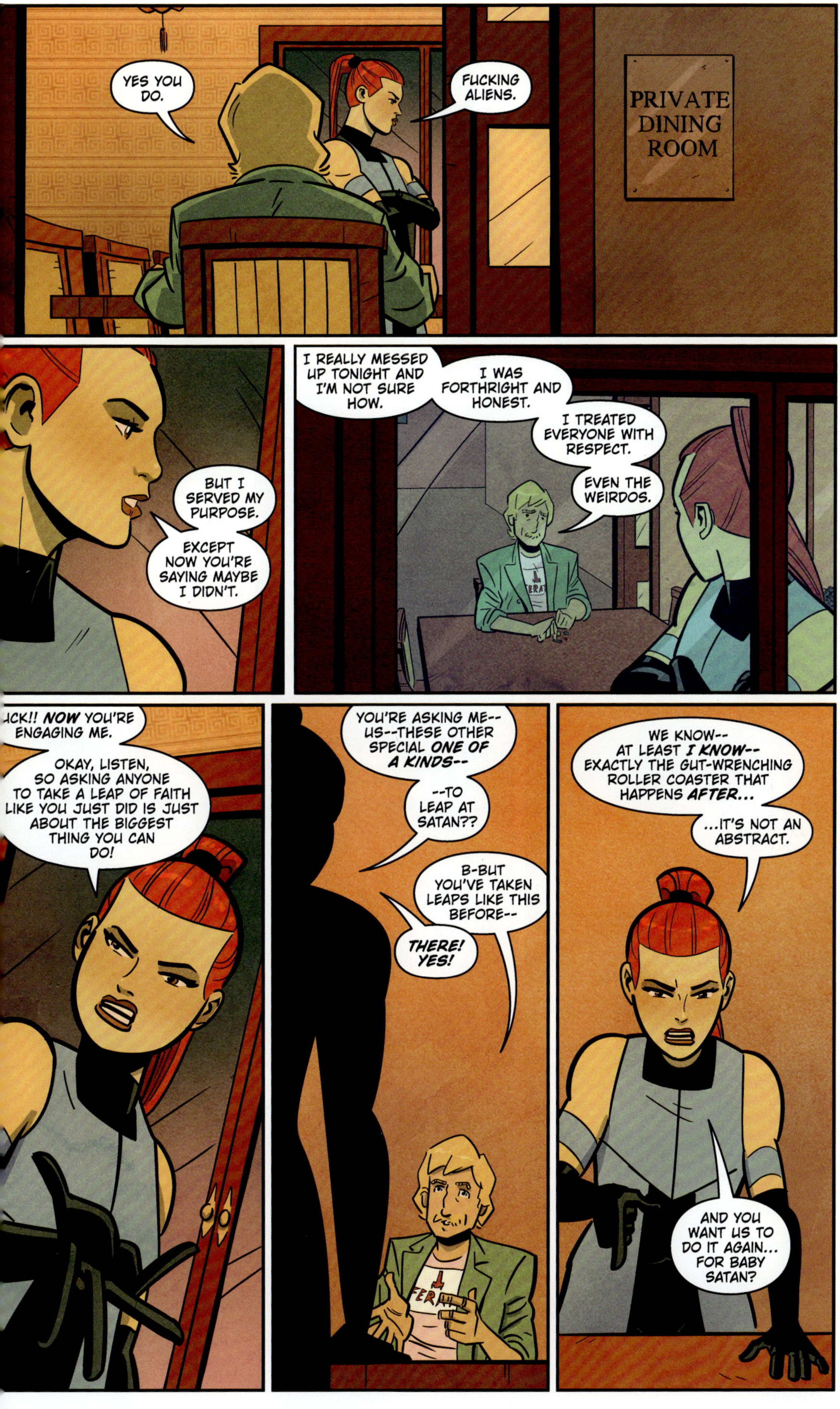
YES YOU DO.
FUCKING ALIENS.
PRIVATE DINING ROOM
BUT I SERVED MY PURPOSE.
EXCEPT NOW YOU'RE SAYING MAYBE I DIDN'T.
I REALLY MESSED UP TONIGHT AND I'M NOT SURE HOW.
I WAS FORTHRIGHT AND HONEST.
I TREATED EVERYONE WITH RESPECT.
EVEN THE WEIRDOS.
-UCK!! NOW YOU'RE ENGAGING ME.
OKAY, LISTEN, SO ASKING ANYONE TO TAKE A LEAP OF FAITH LIKE YOU JUST DID IS JUST ABOUT THE BIGGEST THING YOU CAN DO!
YOU'RE ASKING ME-- US--THESE OTHER SPECIAL ONE OF A KINDS--
--TO LEAP AT SATAN??
B-BUT YOU'VE TAKEN LEAPS LIKE THIS BEFORE--
THERE! YES!
WE KNOW-- AT LEAST I KNOW-- EXACTLY THE GUT-WRENCHING ROLLER COASTER THAT HAPPENS AFTER...
...IT'S NOT AN ABSTRACT.
AND YOU WANT US TO DO IT AGAIN... FOR BABY SATAN?

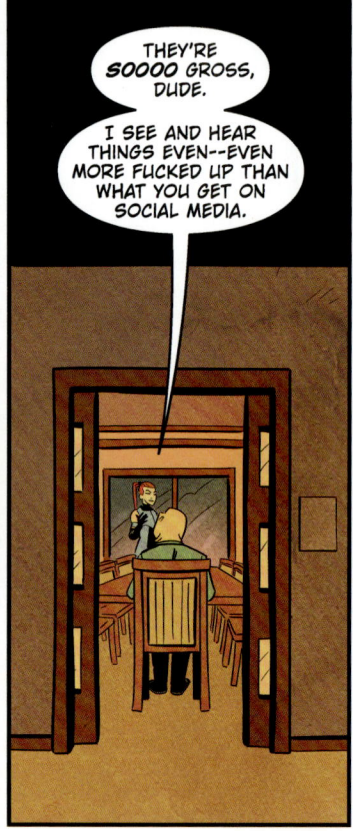

FUCKING SATAN.

WHY COULDN'T WE START WITH SOMETHING SMALL? LIKE A PLAGUE?

ACTUALLY, SATAN IS THE PART OF THIS I WAS READY FOR--

REALLY?

THAT THERE'S A *SATAN?* YEAH, UH, NOT A SURPRISE.

MY POWERS-- I GET TO SEE AND HEAR A LOT MORE OF THE WORLD THAN MOST PEOPLE...

THEY'RE *SOOOO* GROSS, DUDE.

I SEE AND HEAR THINGS EVEN--EVEN MORE FUCKED UP THAN WHAT YOU GET ON SOCIAL MEDIA.

HAVE YOU READ THE FINE PRINT OF THE BABY SATAN PROPHECY...

...BECAUSE BASED ON WHAT I HAVE SEEN, IF SATAN *IS* HERE...

...I DON'T KNOW. IT KIND OF FEELS LIKE WE ALL HAVE IT COMING.

...IF I'VE LEARNED ONE THING FROM THIS DEEP CONNECTION TO ALL MANKIND--

--PEOPLE ARE *REALLY* GROSS.

UH, WELL, I COULD GIVE IT ANOTHER LOOK OVER...

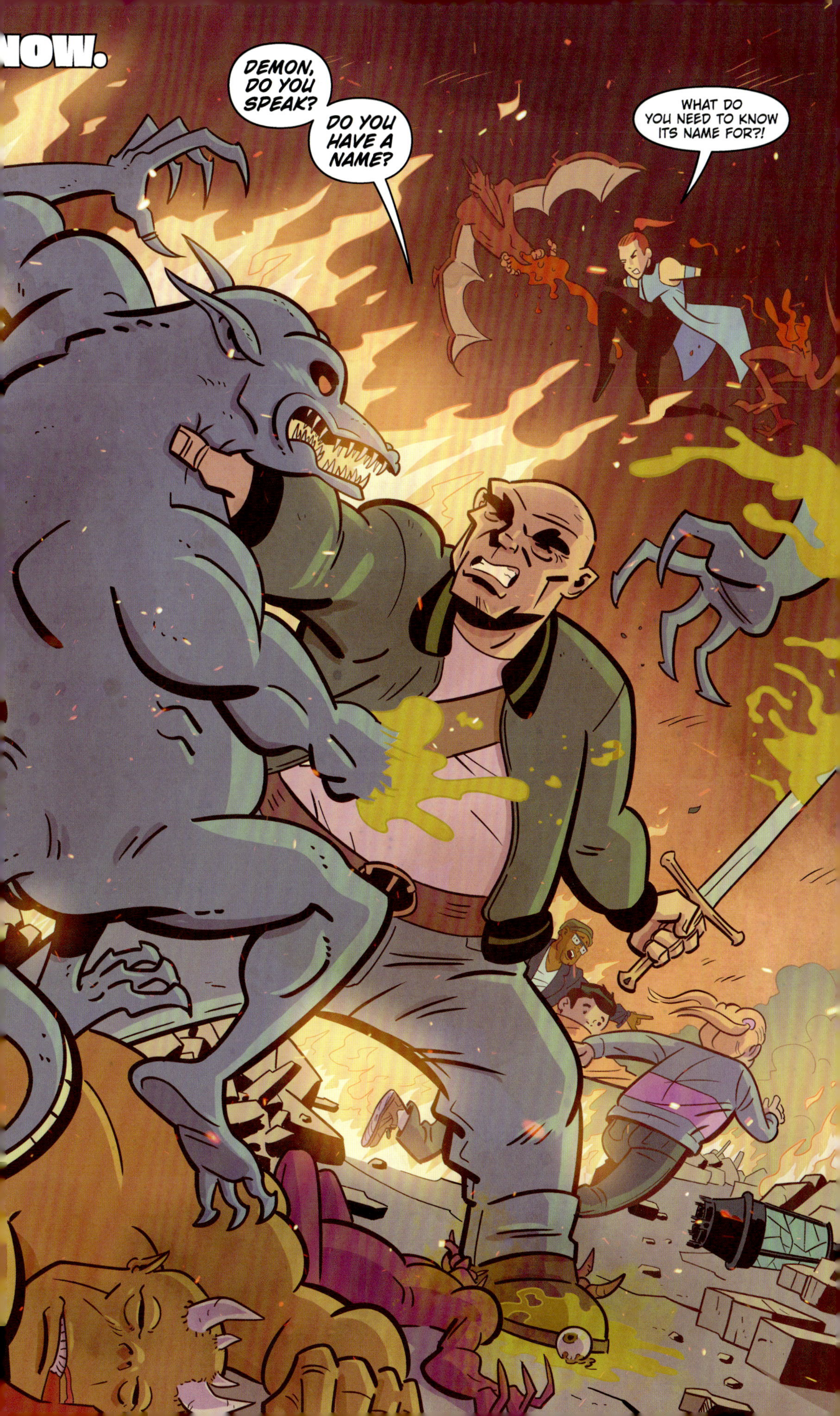
NOW.
DEMON, DO YOU SPEAK?
DO YOU HAVE A NAME?
WHAT DO YOU NEED TO KNOW ITS NAME FOR?!

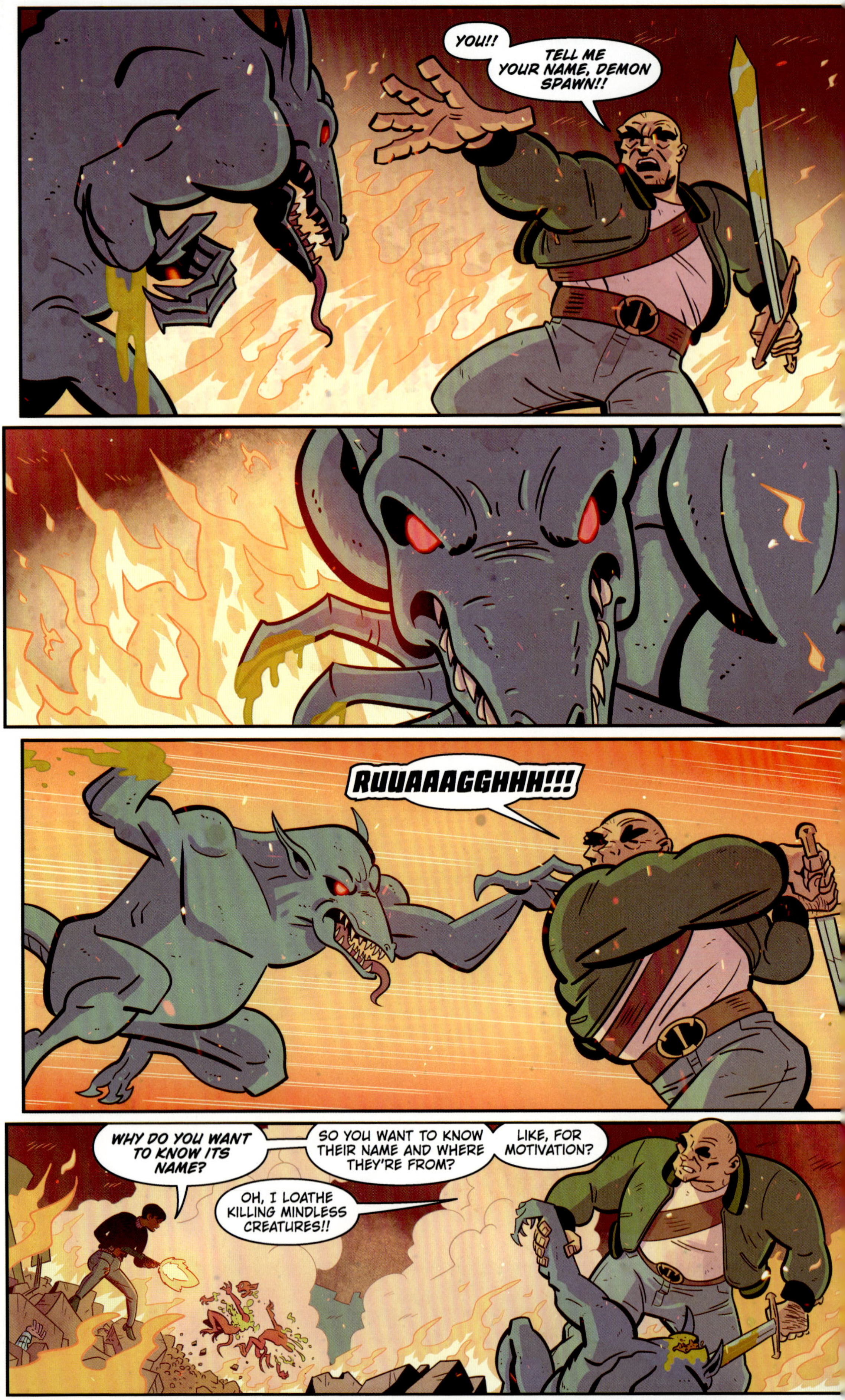
YOU!!
TELL ME YOUR NAME, DEMON SPAWN!!
RUUAAAGGHHH!!!
WHY DO YOU WANT TO KNOW ITS NAME?
SO YOU WANT TO KNOW THEIR NAME AND WHERE THEY'RE FROM?
LIKE, FOR MOTIVATION?
OH, I LOATHE KILLING MINDLESS CREATURES!!

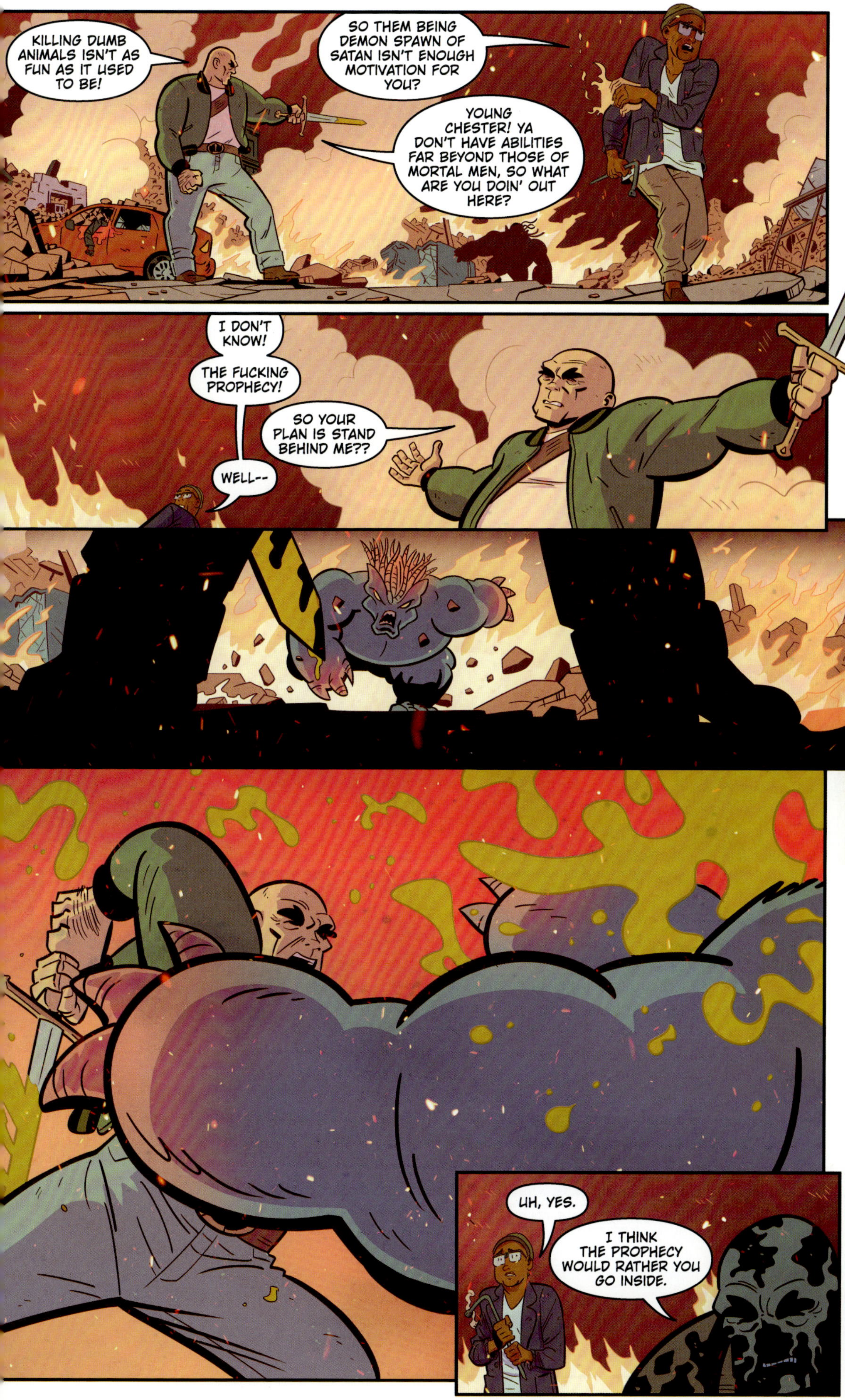
KILLING DUMB ANIMALS ISN'T AS FUN AS IT USED TO BE!
SO THEM BEING DEMON SPAWN OF SATAN ISN'T ENOUGH MOTIVATION FOR YOU?
YOUNG CHESTER! YA DON'T HAVE ABILITIES FAR BEYOND THOSE OF MORTAL MEN, SO WHAT ARE YOU DOIN' OUT HERE?
I DON'T KNOW!
THE FUCKING PROPHECY!
SO YOUR PLAN IS STAND BEHIND ME??
WELL--
UH, YES.
I THINK THE PROPHECY WOULD RATHER YOU GO INSIDE.

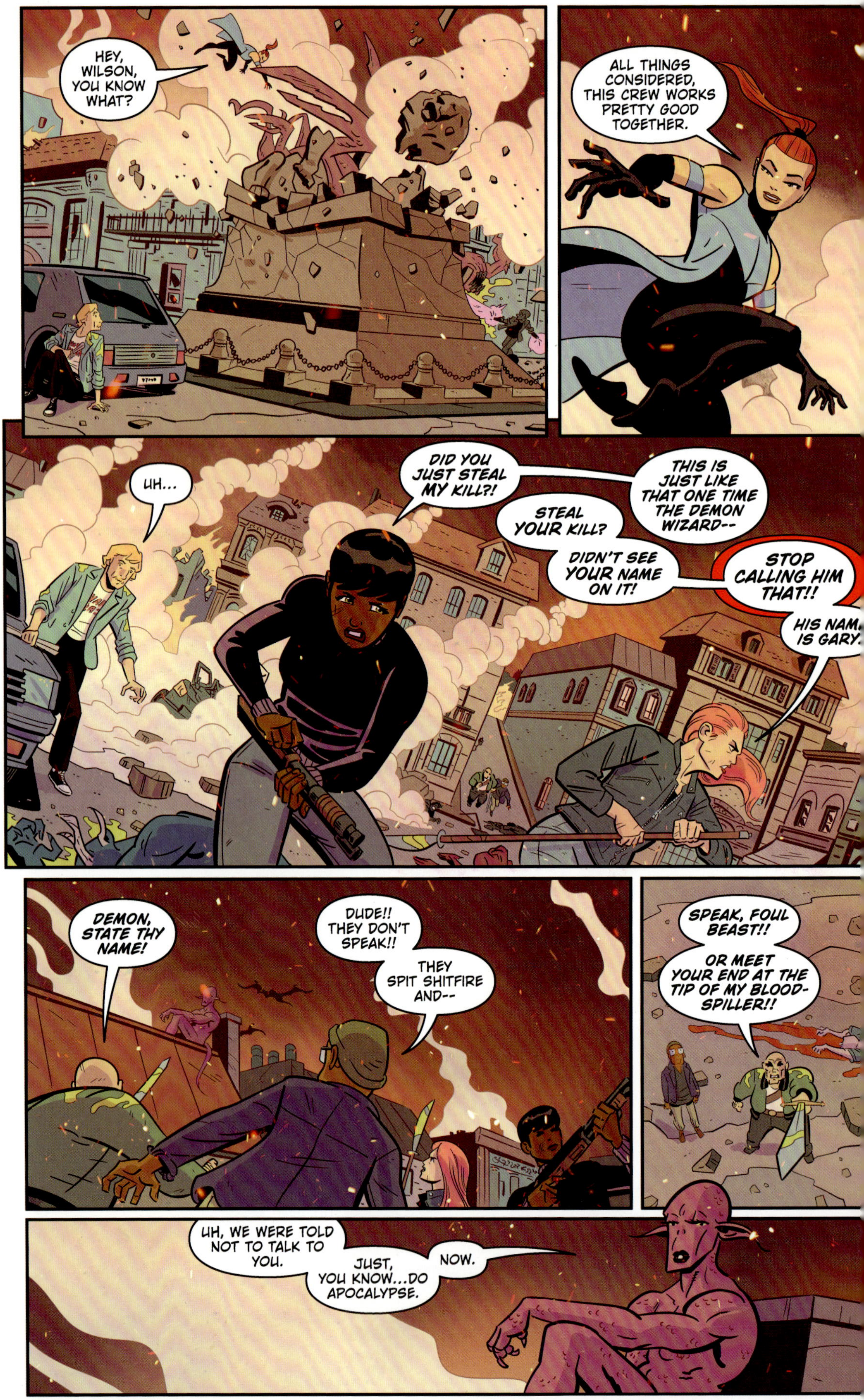
HEY, WILSON, YOU KNOW WHAT?
ALL THINGS CONSIDERED, THIS CREW WORKS PRETTY GOOD TOGETHER.
UH...
DID YOU JUST STEAL MY KILL?!
STEAL YOUR KILL?
DIDN'T SEE YOUR NAME ON IT!
THIS IS JUST LIKE THAT ONE TIME THE DEMON WIZARD--
STOP CALLING HIM THAT!!
HIS NAM IS GARY
DEMON, STATE THY NAME!
DUDE!! THEY DON'T SPEAK!!
THEY SPIT SHITFIRE AND--
SPEAK, FOUL BEAST!!
OR MEET YOUR END AT THE TIP OF MY BLOOD-SPILLER!!
UH, WE WERE TOLD NOT TO TALK TO YOU.
JUST, YOU KNOW...DO APOCALYPSE.
NOW.

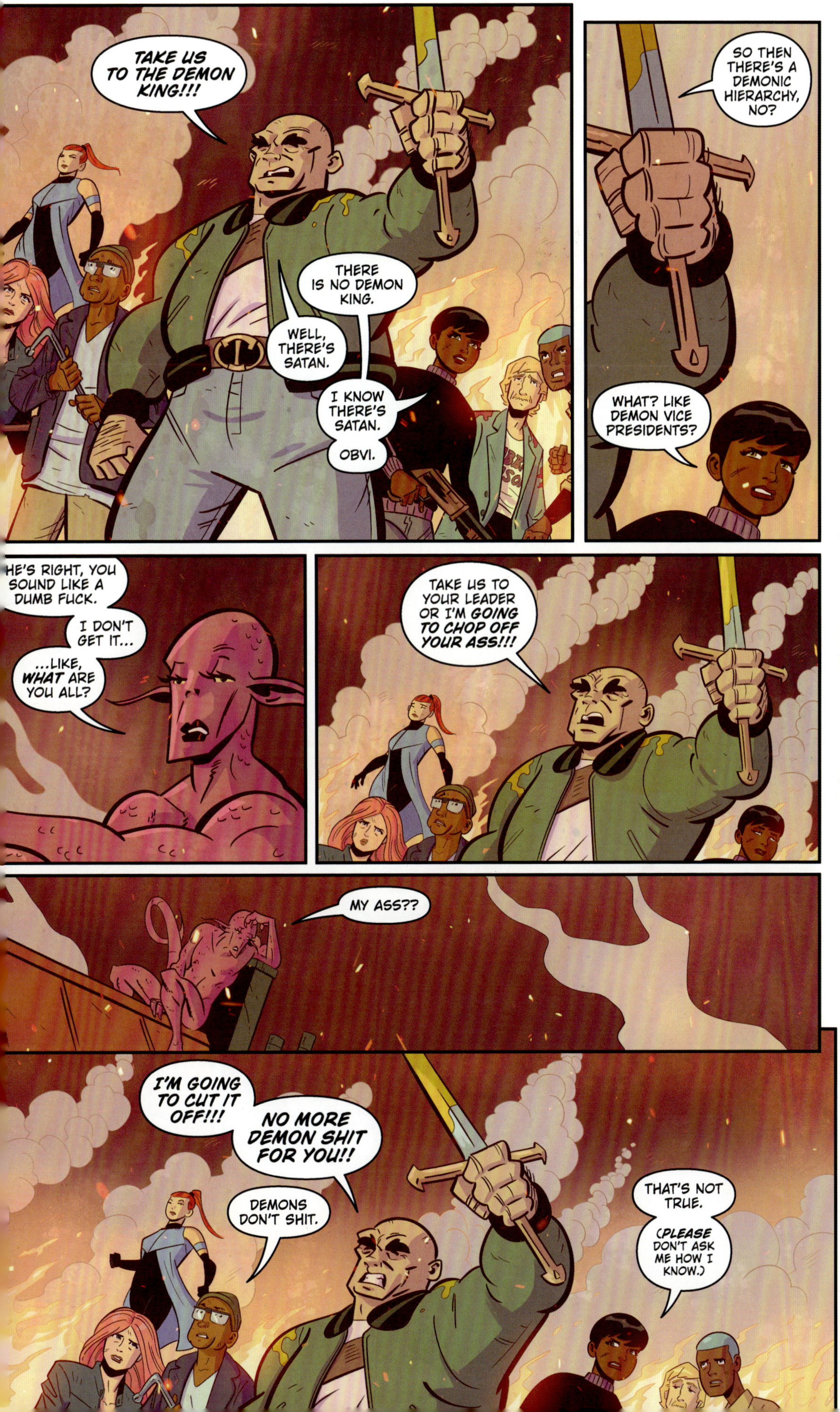
TAKE US TO THE DEMON KING!!!
THERE IS NO DEMON KING.
WELL, THERE'S SATAN.
I KNOW THERE'S SATAN.
OBVI.
SO THEN THERE'S A DEMONIC HIERARCHY, NO?
WHAT? LIKE DEMON VICE PRESIDENTS?
HE'S RIGHT, YOU SOUND LIKE A DUMB FUCK.
I DON'T GET IT...
...LIKE, WHAT ARE YOU ALL?
TAKE US TO YOUR LEADER OR I'M GOING TO CHOP OFF YOUR ASS!!!
MY ASS??
I'M GOING TO CUT IT OFF!!!
NO MORE DEMON SHIT FOR YOU!!
DEMONS DON'T SHIT.
THAT'S NOT TRUE.
(PLEASE DON'T ASK ME HOW I KNOW.)

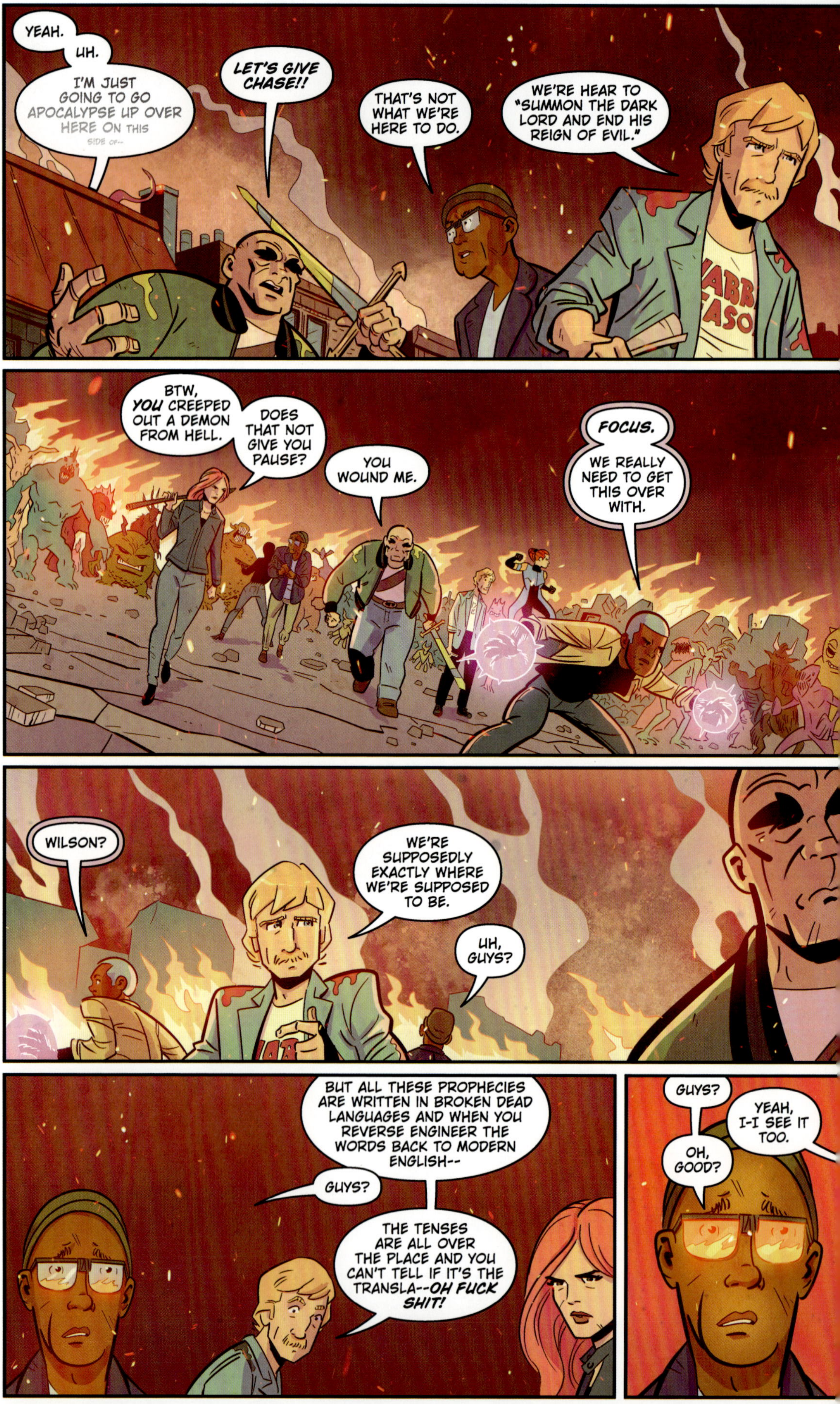
YEAH.
UH.
I'M JUST GOING TO GO APOCALYPSE UP OVER HERE ON THIS SIDE OF--
LET'S GIVE CHASE!!
THAT'S NOT WHAT WE'RE HERE TO DO.
WE'RE HEAR TO "SUMMON THE DARK LORD AND END HIS REIGN OF EVIL."
BTW, YOU CREEPED OUT A DEMON FROM HELL.
DOES THAT NOT GIVE YOU PAUSE?
YOU WOUND ME.
FOCUS.
WE REALLY NEED TO GET THIS OVER WITH.
WILSON?
WE'RE SUPPOSEDLY EXACTLY WHERE WE'RE SUPPOSED TO BE.
UH, GUYS?
BUT ALL THESE PROPHECIES ARE WRITTEN IN BROKEN DEAD LANGUAGES AND WHEN YOU REVERSE ENGINEER THE WORDS BACK TO MODERN ENGLISH--
GUYS?
THE TENSES ARE ALL OVER THE PLACE AND YOU CAN'T TELL IF IT'S THE TRANSLA--OH FUCK SHIT!
GUYS?
OH, GOOD?
YEAH, I-I SEE IT TOO.

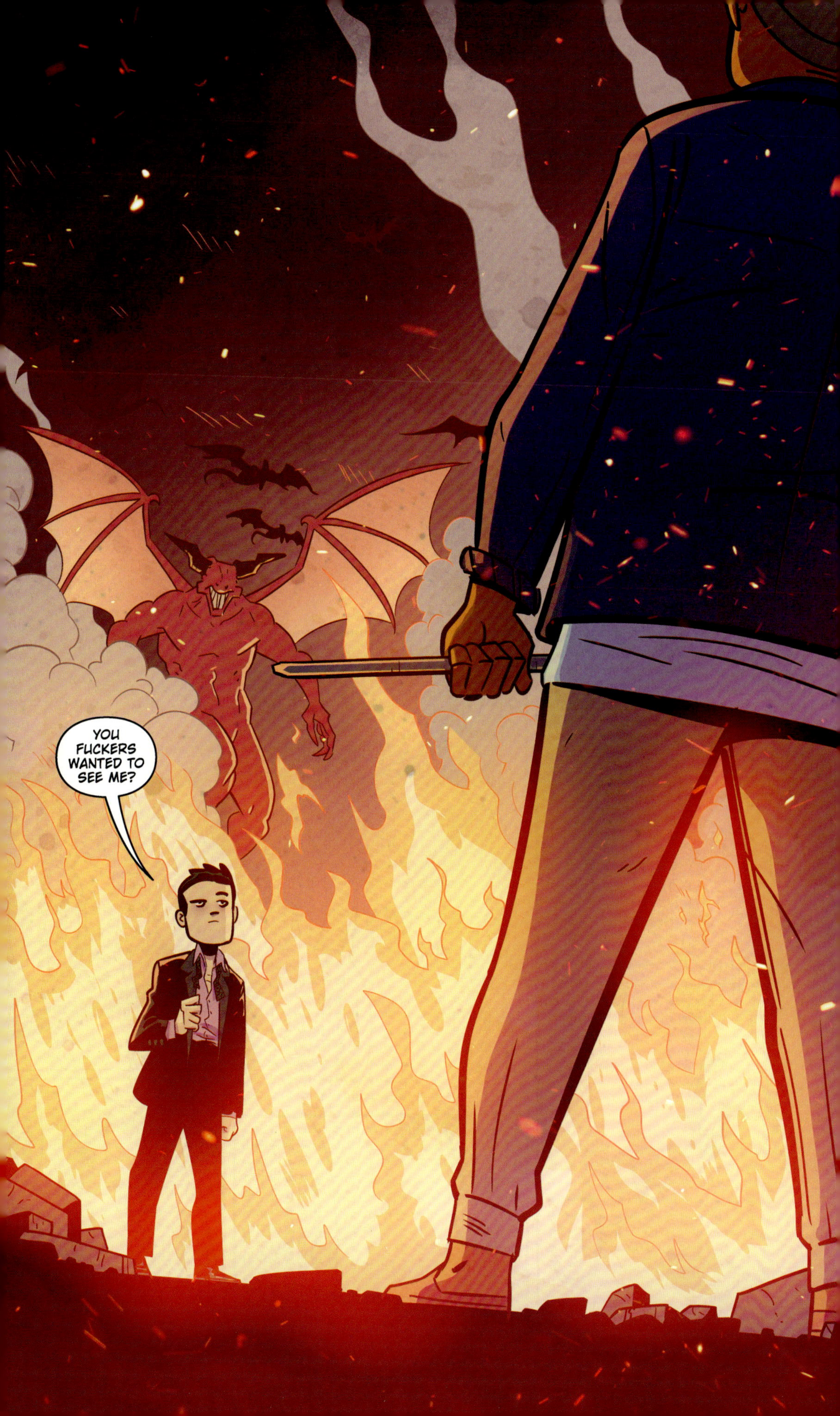
YOU FUCKERS WANTED TO SEE ME?

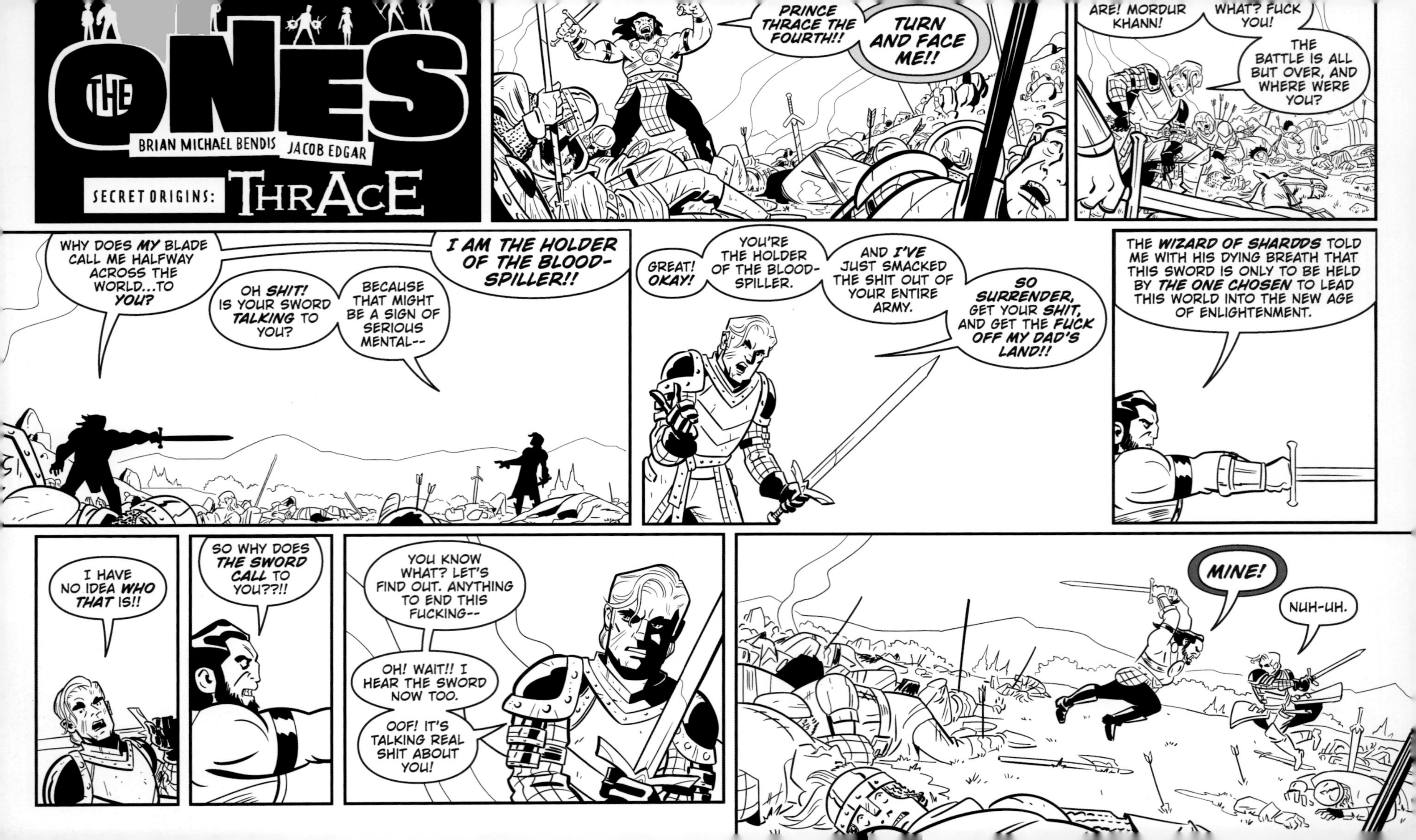
THE ONES
BRIAN MICHAEL BENDIS
JACOB EDGAR
SECRET ORIGINS: THRACE
PRINCE THRACE THE FOURTH!!
TURN AND FACE ME!!
ARE! MORDUR KHANN!
WHAT? FUCK YOU!
THE BATTLE IS ALL BUT OVER, AND WHERE WERE YOU?
WHY DOES MY BLADE CALL ME HALFWAY ACROSS THE WORLD...TO YOU?
I AM THE HOLDER OF THE BLOOD-SPILLER!!
OH SHIT! IS YOUR SWORD TALKING TO YOU?
BECAUSE THAT MIGHT BE A SIGN OF SERIOUS MENTAL--
GREAT! OKAY!
YOU'RE THE HOLDER OF THE BLOOD-SPILLER.
AND I'VE JUST SMACKED THE SHIT OUT OF YOUR ENTIRE ARMY.
SO SURRENDER, GET YOUR SHIT, AND GET THE FUCK OFF MY DAD'S LAND!!
THE WIZARD OF SHARDDS TOLD ME WITH HIS DYING BREATH THAT THIS SWORD IS ONLY TO BE HELD BY THE ONE CHOSEN TO LEAD THIS WORLD INTO THE NEW AGE OF ENLIGHTENMENT.
I HAVE NO IDEA WHO THAT IS!!
SO WHY DOES THE SWORD CALL TO YOU??!!
YOU KNOW WHAT? LET'S FIND OUT. ANYTHING TO END THIS FUCKING--
OH! WAIT!! I HEAR THE SWORD NOW TOO.
OOF! IT'S TALKING REAL SHIT ABOUT YOU!
MINE!
NUH-UH.

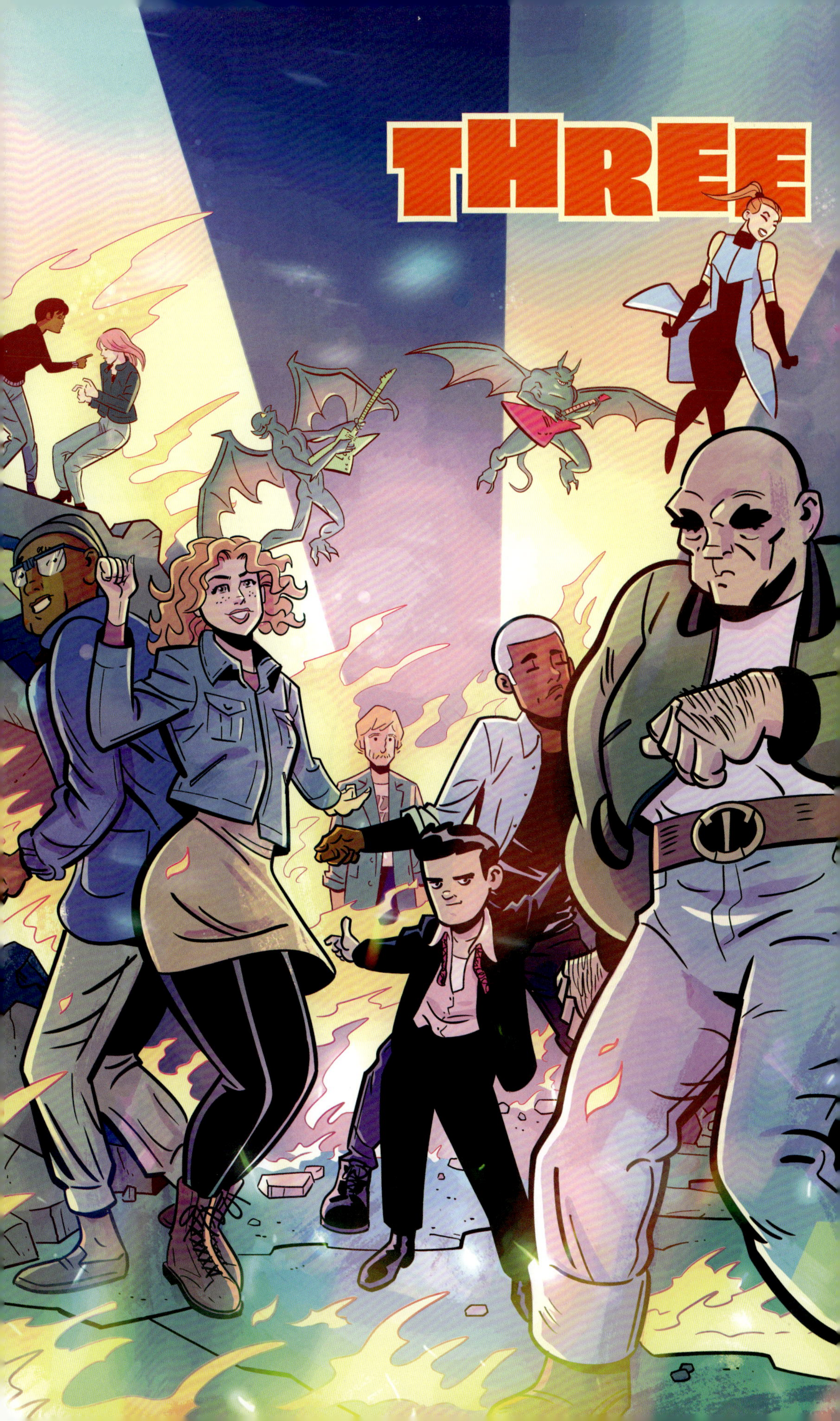
THREE

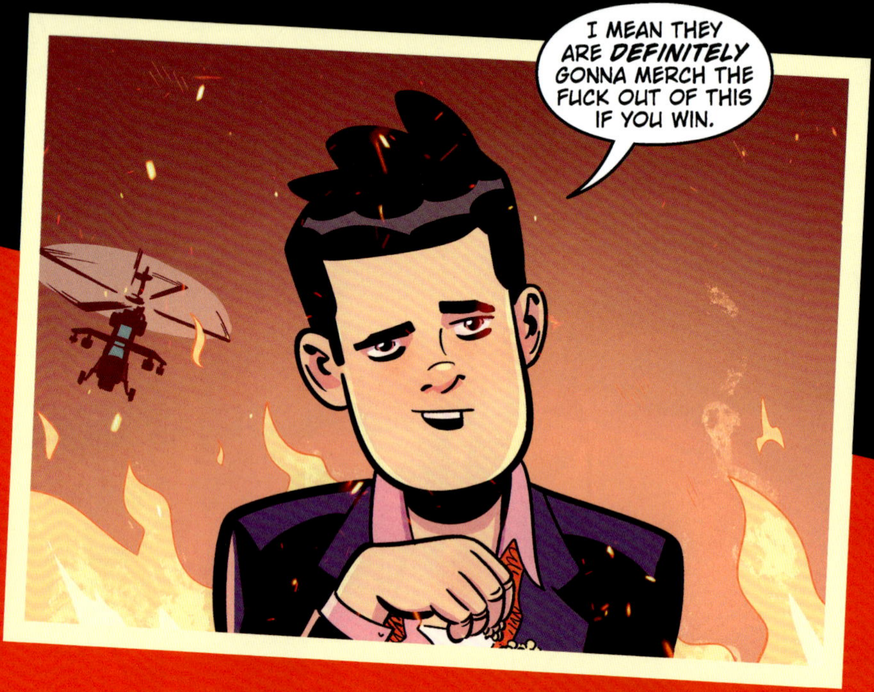
I MEAN THEY ARE *DEFINITELY* GONNA MERCH THE FUCK OUT OF THIS IF YOU WIN.

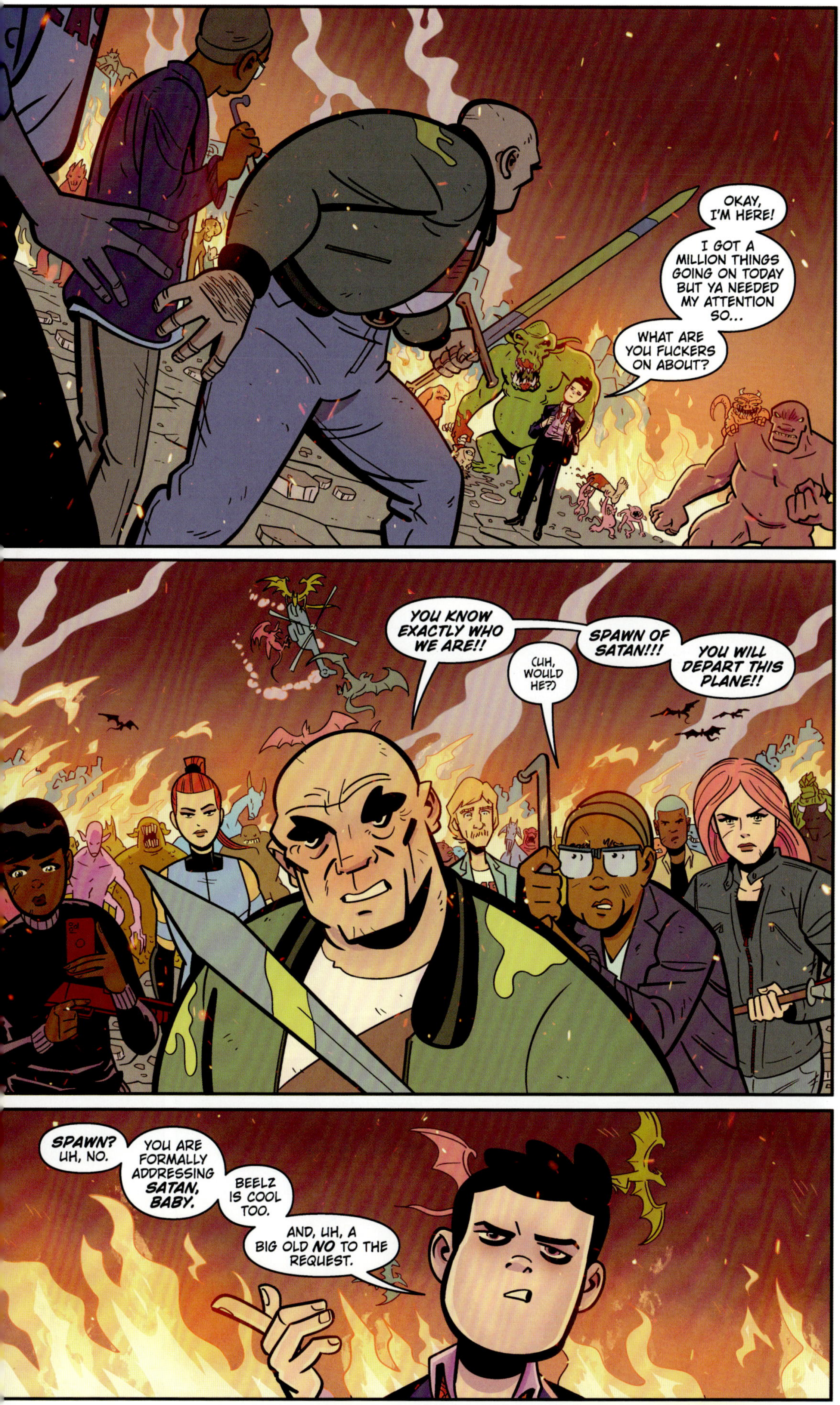
OKAY, I'M HERE!
I GOT A MILLION THINGS GOING ON TODAY BUT YA NEEDED MY ATTENTION SO...
WHAT ARE YOU FUCKERS ON ABOUT?
YOU KNOW EXACTLY WHO WE ARE!!
SPAWN OF SATAN!!!
YOU WILL DEPART THIS PLANE!!
(UH, WOULD HE?)
SPAWN? UH, NO.
YOU ARE FORMALLY ADDRESSING SATAN, BABY.
BEELZ IS COOL TOO.
AND, UH, A BIG OLD NO TO THE REQUEST.

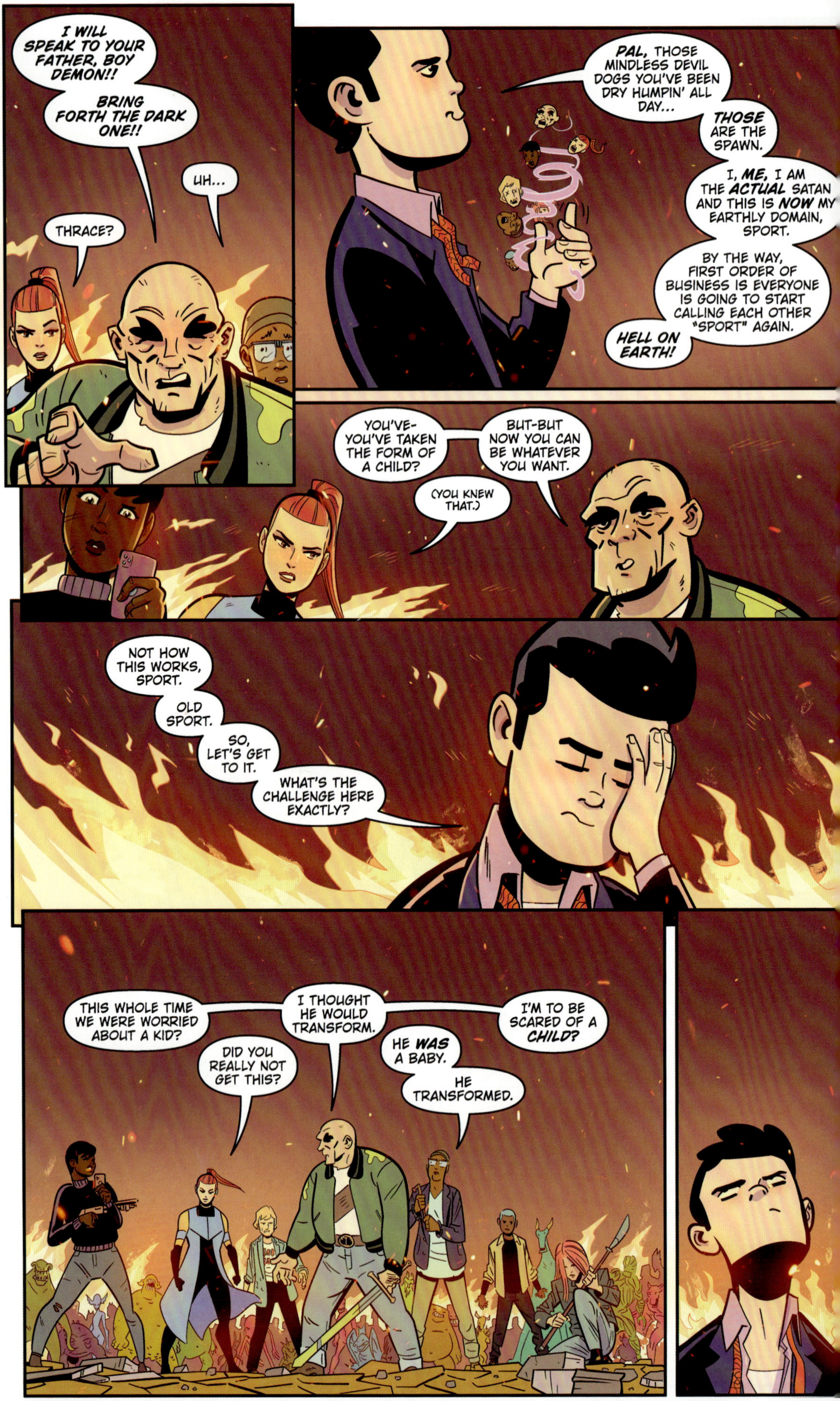
I WILL SPEAK TO YOUR FATHER, BOY DEMON!!
BRING FORTH THE DARK ONE!!
UH...
THRACE?
PAL, THOSE MINDLESS DEVIL DOGS YOU'VE BEEN DRY HUMPIN' ALL DAY...
THOSE ARE THE SPAWN.
I, ME, I AM THE ACTUAL SATAN AND THIS IS NOW MY EARTHLY DOMAIN, SPORT.
BY THE WAY, FIRST ORDER OF BUSINESS IS EVERYONE IS GOING TO START CALLING EACH OTHER "SPORT" AGAIN.
HELL ON EARTH!
YOU'VE- YOU'VE TAKEN THE FORM OF A CHILD?
BUT-BUT NOW YOU CAN BE WHATEVER YOU WANT.
(YOU KNEW THAT.)
NOT HOW THIS WORKS, SPORT.
OLD SPORT.
SO, LET'S GET TO IT.
WHAT'S THE CHALLENGE HERE EXACTLY?
THIS WHOLE TIME WE WERE WORRIED ABOUT A KID?
I THOUGHT HE WOULD TRANSFORM.
I'M TO BE SCARED OF A CHILD?
DID YOU REALLY NOT GET THIS?
HE WAS A BABY.
HE TRANSFORMED.

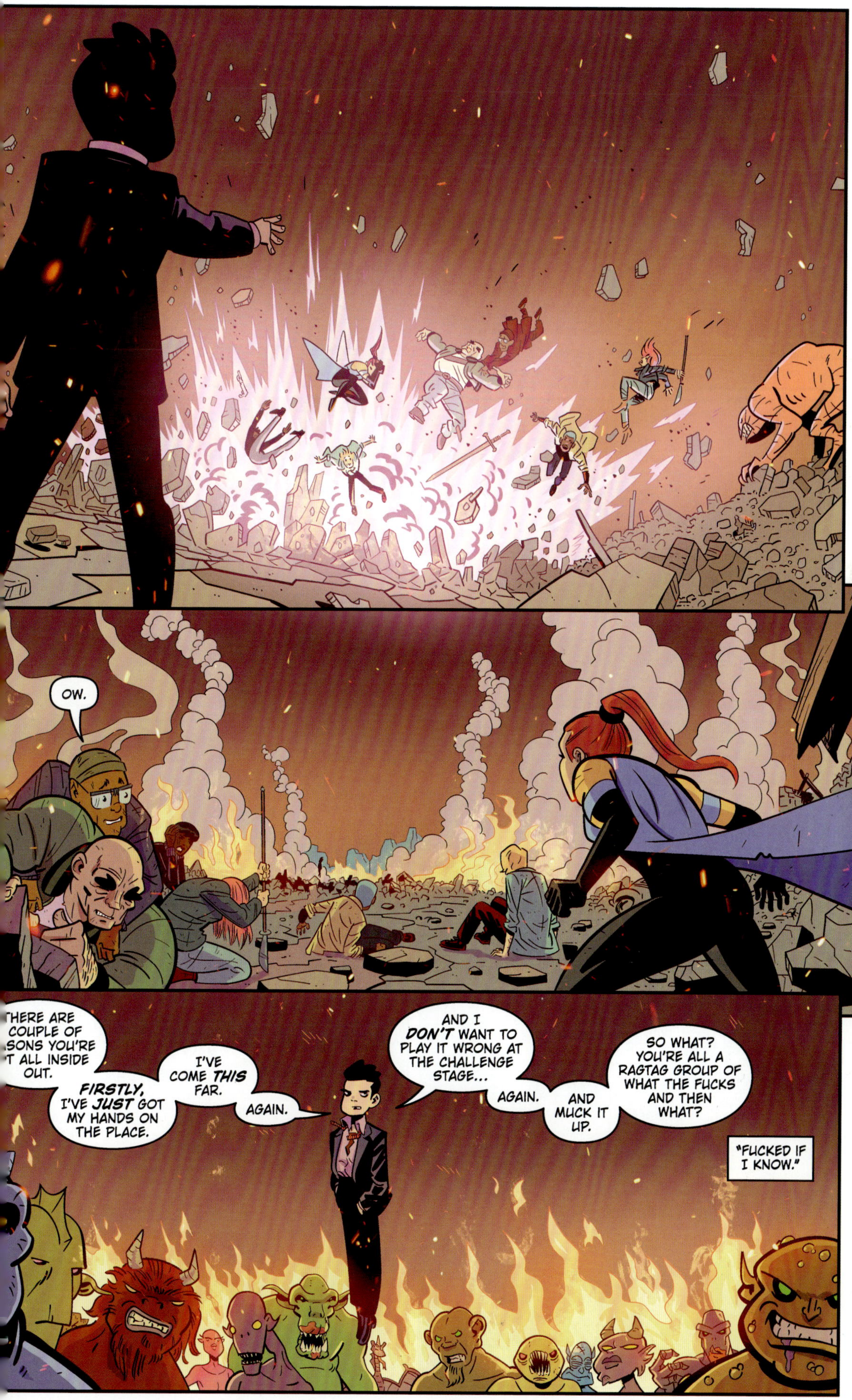
OW.
HERE ARE COUPLE OF SONS YOU'RE T ALL INSIDE OUT.
FIRSTLY, I'VE JUST GOT MY HANDS ON THE PLACE.
I'VE COME THIS FAR.
AGAIN.
AND I DON'T WANT TO PLAY IT WRONG AT THE CHALLENGE STAGE...
AGAIN.
AND MUCK IT UP.
SO WHAT? YOU'RE ALL A RAGTAG GROUP OF WHAT THE FUCKS AND THEN WHAT?
"FUCKED IF I KNOW."

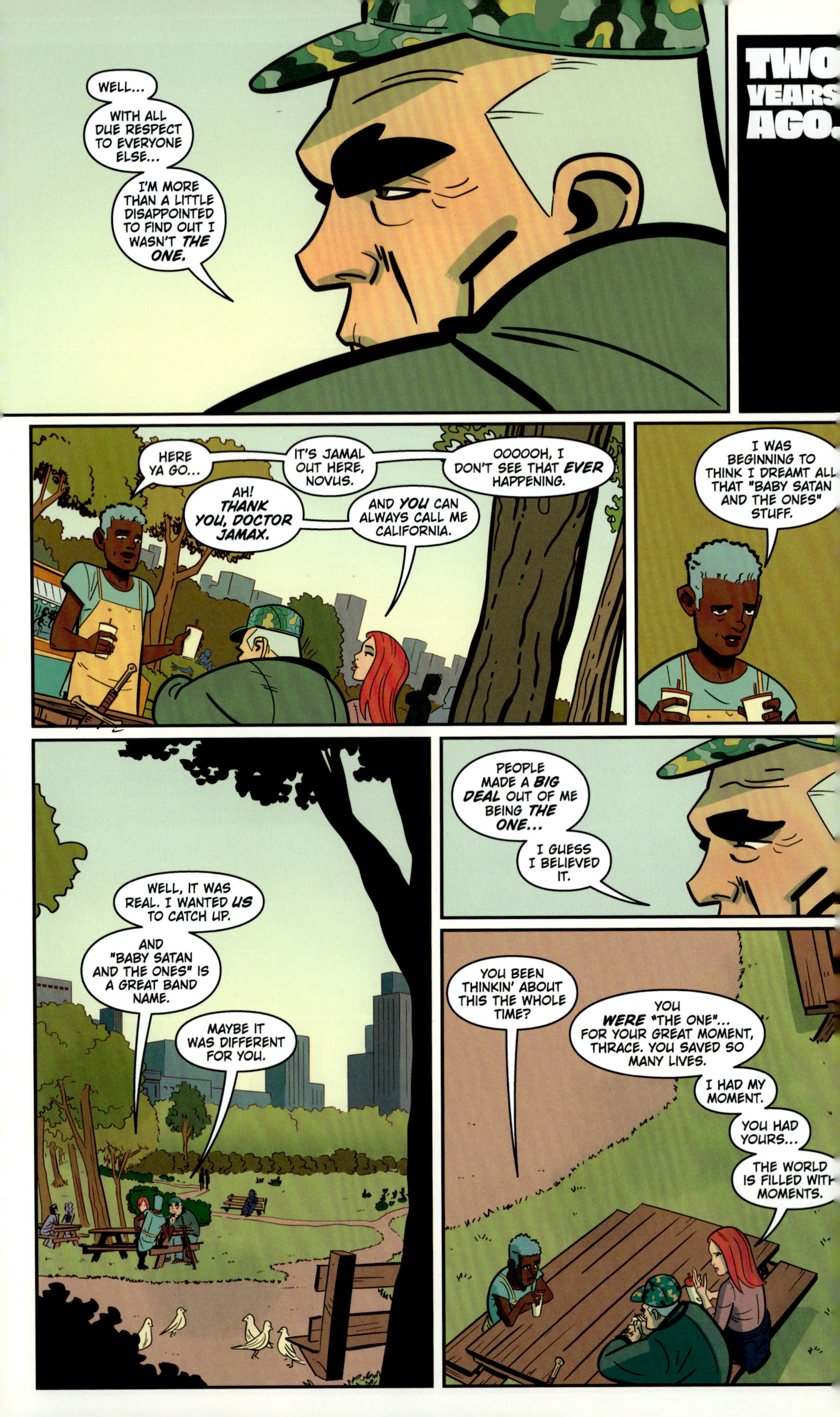

WELL...
WITH ALL DUE RESPECT TO EVERYONE ELSE...
I'M MORE THAN A LITTLE DISAPPOINTED TO FIND OUT I WASN'T *THE ONE.*
TWO YEARS AGO.
HERE YA GO...
AH! *THANK YOU, DOCTOR JAMAX.*
IT'S JAMAL OUT HERE, NOVUS.
AND *YOU* CAN ALWAYS CALL ME CALIFORNIA.
OOOOOH, I DON'T SEE THAT *EVER* HAPPENING.
I WAS BEGINNING TO THINK I DREAMT ALL THAT "BABY SATAN AND THE ONES" STUFF.
WELL, IT WAS REAL. I WANTED *US* TO CATCH UP.
AND "BABY SATAN AND THE ONES" IS A GREAT BAND NAME.
MAYBE IT WAS DIFFERENT FOR YOU.
PEOPLE MADE A *BIG DEAL* OUT OF ME BEING *THE ONE...*
I GUESS I BELIEVED IT.
YOU BEEN THINKIN' ABOUT THIS THE WHOLE TIME?
YOU *WERE* "THE ONE"... FOR YOUR GREAT MOMENT, THRACE. YOU SAVED SO MANY LIVES.
I HAD MY MOMENT.
YOU HAD YOURS...
THE WORLD IS FILLED WITH MOMENTS.

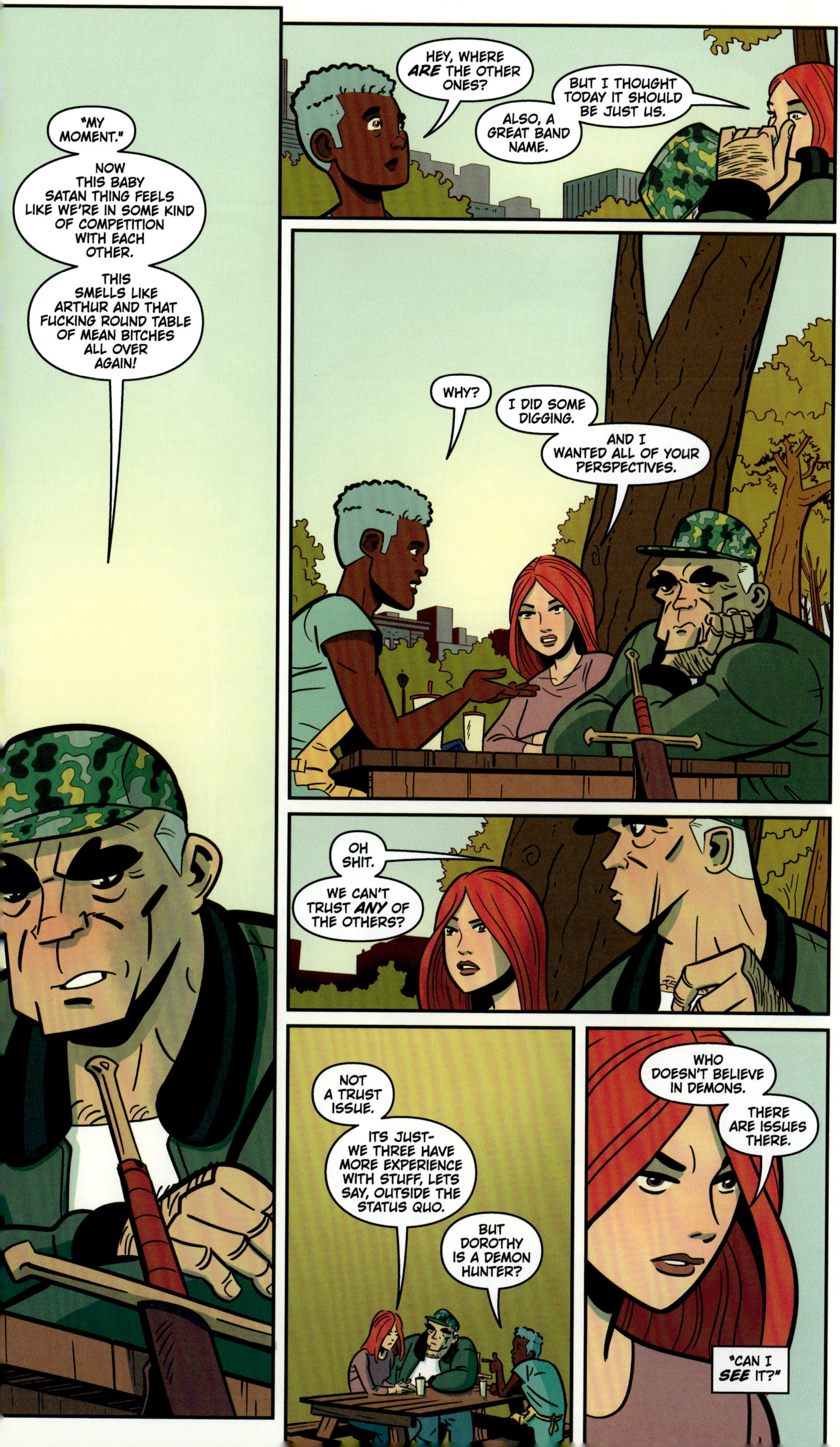
"MY MOMENT."
NOW THIS BABY SATAN THING FEELS LIKE WE'RE IN SOME KIND OF COMPETITION WITH EACH OTHER.
THIS SMELLS LIKE ARTHUR AND THAT FUCKING ROUND TABLE OF MEAN BITCHES ALL OVER AGAIN!
HEY, WHERE ARE THE OTHER ONES?
ALSO, A GREAT BAND NAME.
BUT I THOUGHT TODAY IT SHOULD BE JUST US.
WHY?
I DID SOME DIGGING.
AND I WANTED ALL OF YOUR PERSPECTIVES.
OH SHIT.
WE CAN'T TRUST ANY OF THE OTHERS?
NOT A TRUST ISSUE.
ITS JUST- WE THREE HAVE MORE EXPERIENCE WITH STUFF, LETS SAY, OUTSIDE THE STATUS QUO.
BUT DOROTHY IS A DEMON HUNTER?
WHO DOESN'T BELIEVE IN DEMONS.
THERE ARE ISSUES THERE.
"CAN I SEE IT?"

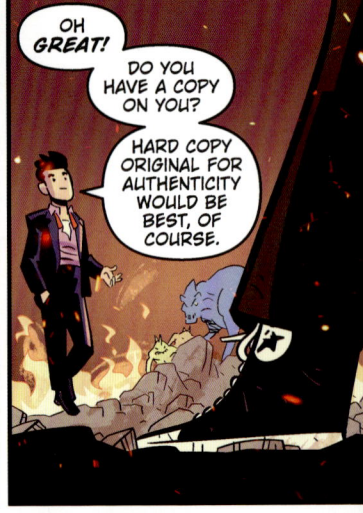

This prophecy of yours. "The Ones versus Satan." Can I read it?

I uh-- I am *Wilson*. The-the Keeper of the Prophecy.

Oh *great*! Do you have a copy on you? Hard copy original for authenticity would be best, of course.

I-I-I didn't bring it here.

It's a sacred text.

It's not a warrant, Chester.

It's not a cease and desist.

You could have brought a copy.

It *kind* of is.

So you don't actually *have* the paperwork?

Do we?

Guys! It's not a *paperwork* thing! It's the apocalypse.

But--

He's *fucking* with you!!

Ha! You Earth dummies thin— everything i— about paperwo—

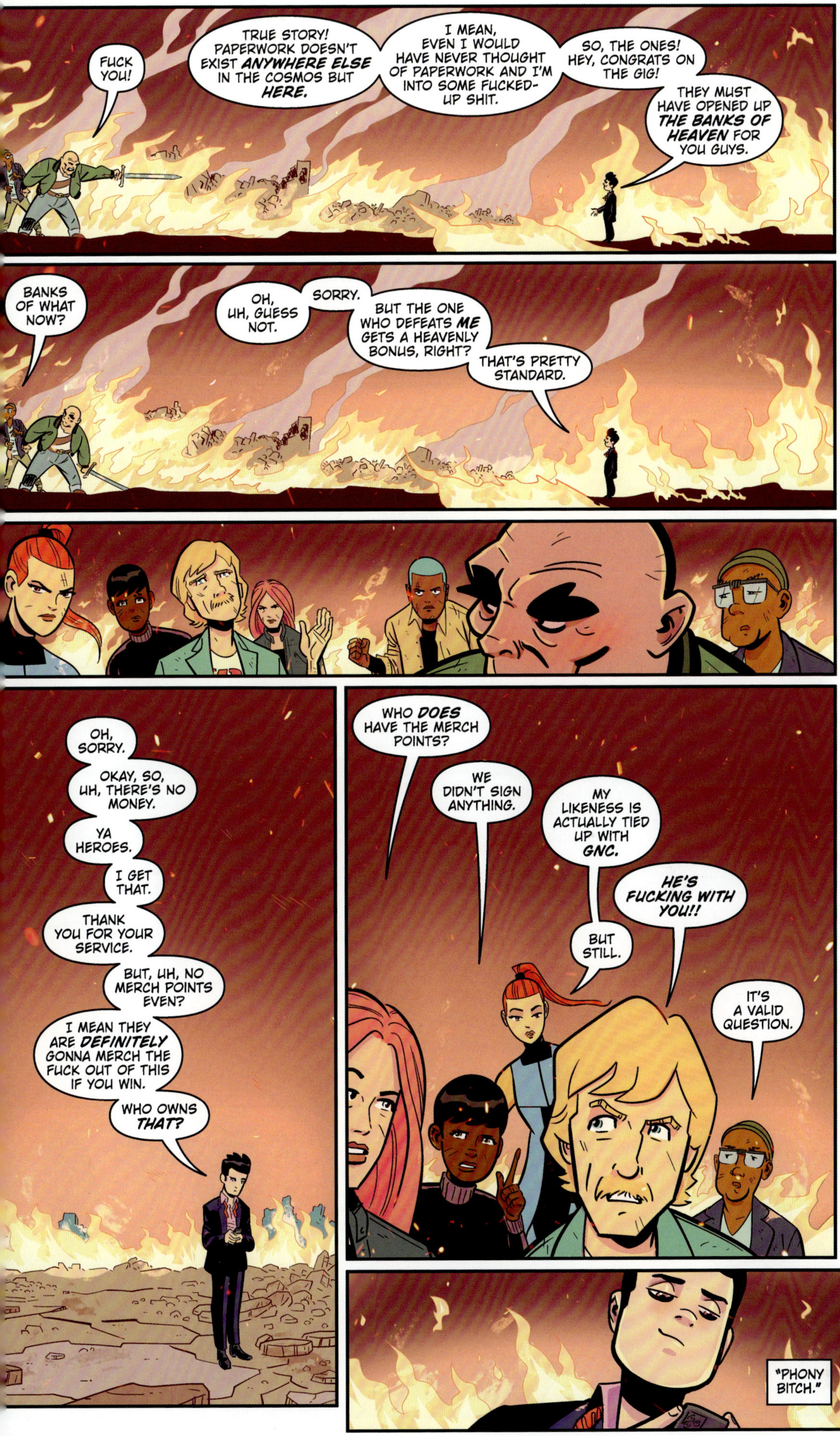

FUCK YOU!
TRUE STORY! PAPERWORK DOESN'T EXIST ANYWHERE ELSE IN THE COSMOS BUT HERE.
I MEAN, EVEN I WOULD HAVE NEVER THOUGHT OF PAPERWORK AND I'M INTO SOME FUCKED-UP SHIT.
SO, THE ONES! HEY, CONGRATS ON THE GIG!
THEY MUST HAVE OPENED UP THE BANKS OF HEAVEN FOR YOU GUYS.
BANKS OF WHAT NOW?
OH, UH, GUESS NOT.
SORRY.
BUT THE ONE WHO DEFEATS ME GETS A HEAVENLY BONUS, RIGHT?
THAT'S PRETTY STANDARD.
OH, SORRY.
OKAY, SO, UH, THERE'S NO MONEY.
YA HEROES.
I GET THAT.
THANK YOU FOR YOUR SERVICE.
BUT, UH, NO MERCH POINTS EVEN?
I MEAN THEY ARE DEFINITELY GONNA MERCH THE FUCK OUT OF THIS IF YOU WIN.
WHO OWNS THAT?
WHO DOES HAVE THE MERCH POINTS?
WE DIDN'T SIGN ANYTHING.
MY LIKENESS IS ACTUALLY TIED UP WITH GNC.
HE'S FUCKING WITH YOU!!
BUT STILL.
IT'S A VALID QUESTION.
"PHONY BITCH."

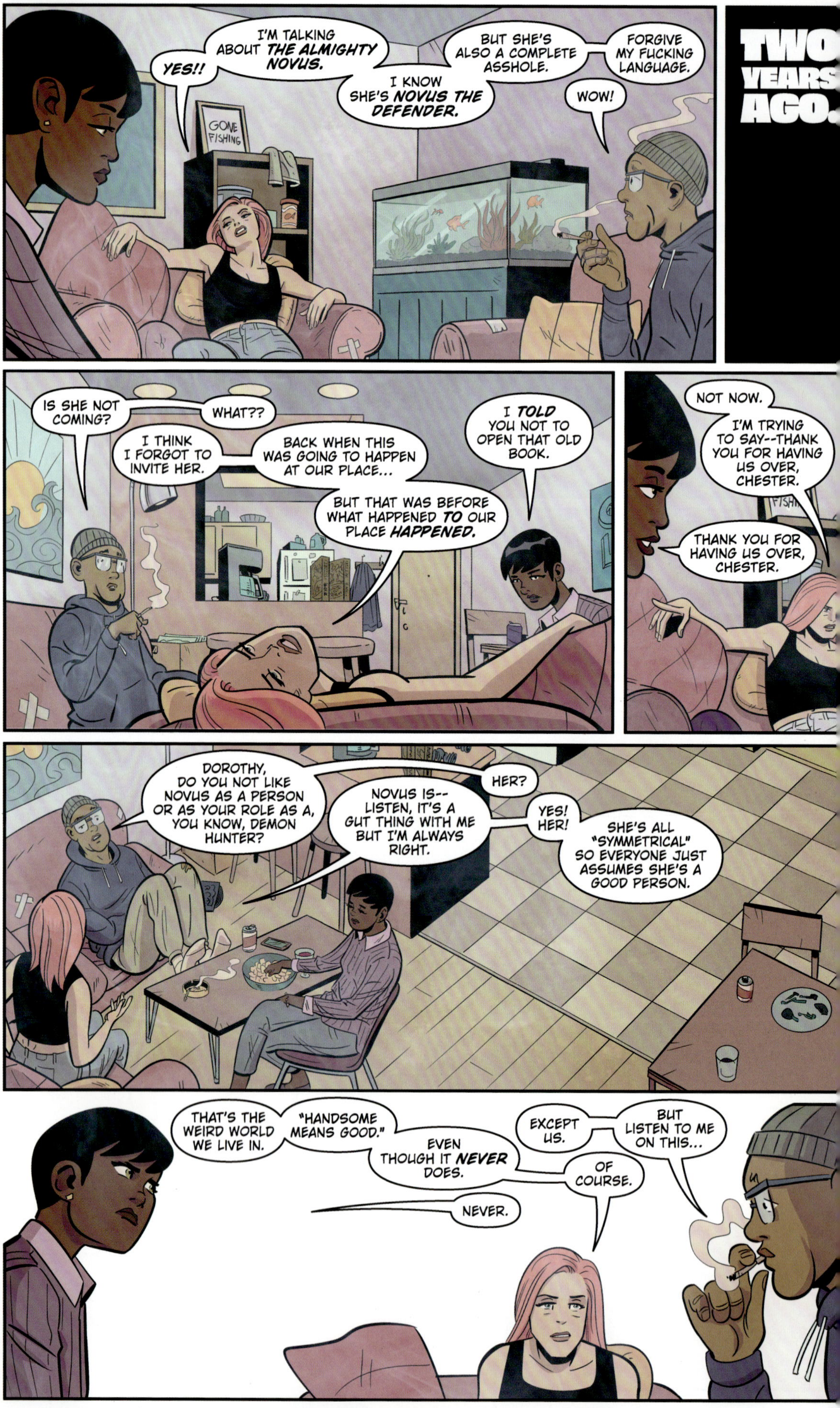
YES!!
I'M TALKING ABOUT THE ALMIGHTY NOVUS.
I KNOW SHE'S NOVUS THE DEFENDER.
BUT SHE'S ALSO A COMPLETE ASSHOLE.
FORGIVE MY FUCKING LANGUAGE.
WOW!
GONE FISHING
TWO YEARS AGO.
IS SHE NOT COMING?
WHAT??
I THINK I FORGOT TO INVITE HER.
BACK WHEN THIS WAS GOING TO HAPPEN AT OUR PLACE...
BUT THAT WAS BEFORE WHAT HAPPENED TO OUR PLACE HAPPENED.
I TOLD YOU NOT TO OPEN THAT OLD BOOK.
NOT NOW.
I'M TRYING TO SAY--THANK YOU FOR HAVING US OVER, CHESTER.
THANK YOU FOR HAVING US OVER, CHESTER.
DOROTHY, DO YOU NOT LIKE NOVUS AS A PERSON OR AS YOUR ROLE AS A, YOU KNOW, DEMON HUNTER?
HER?
NOVUS IS-- LISTEN, IT'S A GUT THING WITH ME BUT I'M ALWAYS RIGHT.
YES! HER!
SHE'S ALL "SYMMETRICAL" SO EVERYONE JUST ASSUMES SHE'S A GOOD PERSON.
THAT'S THE WEIRD WORLD WE LIVE IN.
"HANDSOME MEANS GOOD."
EVEN THOUGH IT NEVER DOES.
EXCEPT US.
BUT LISTEN TO ME ON THIS...
OF COURSE.
NEVER.

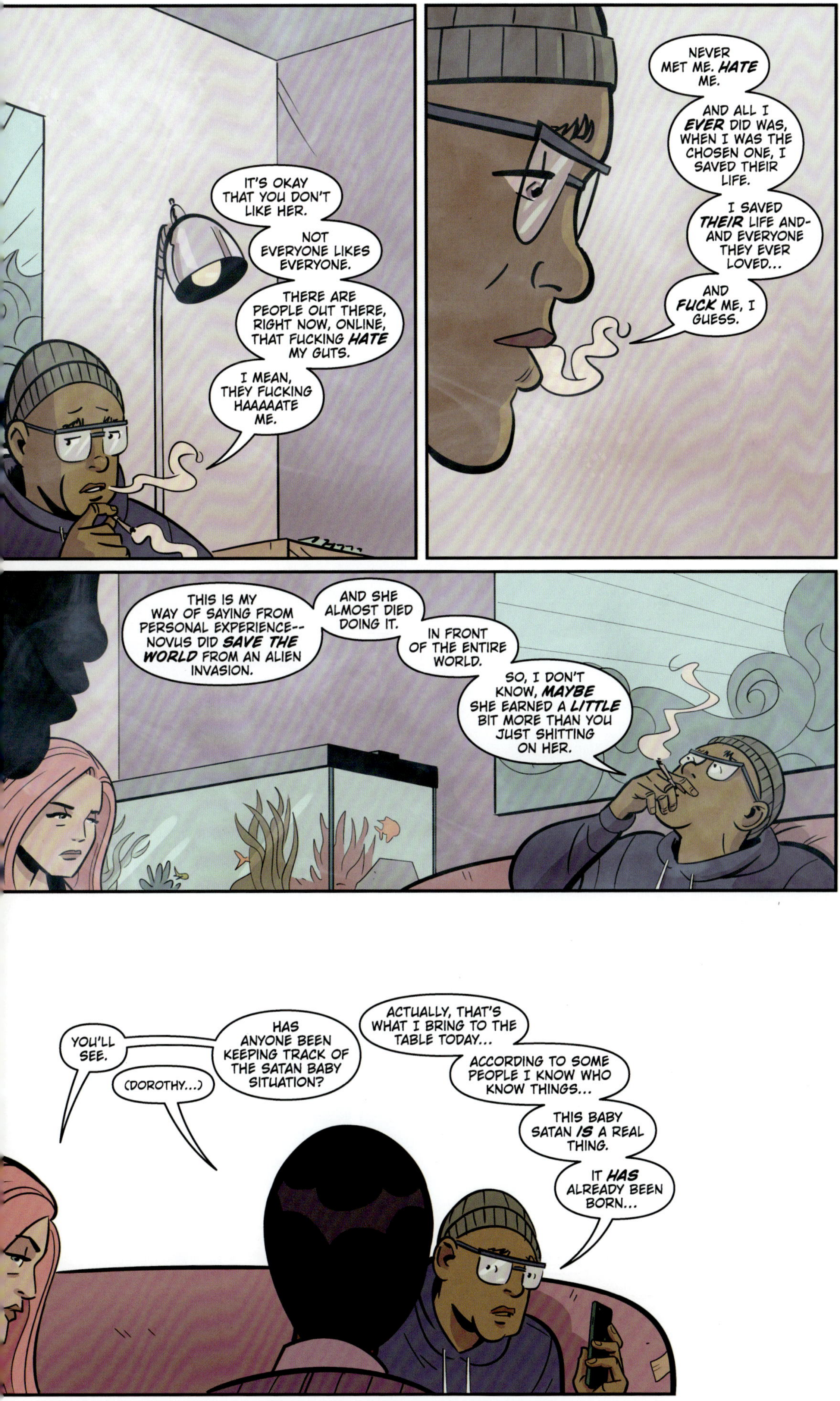
IT'S OKAY THAT YOU DON'T LIKE HER.
NOT EVERYONE LIKES EVERYONE.
THERE ARE PEOPLE OUT THERE, RIGHT NOW, ONLINE, THAT FUCKING HATE MY GUTS.
I MEAN, THEY FUCKING HAAAAATE ME.
NEVER MET ME. HATE ME.
AND ALL I EVER DID WAS, WHEN I WAS THE CHOSEN ONE, I SAVED THEIR LIFE.
I SAVED THEIR LIFE AND-AND EVERYONE THEY EVER LOVED...
AND FUCK ME, I GUESS.
THIS IS MY WAY OF SAYING FROM PERSONAL EXPERIENCE--NOVUS DID SAVE THE WORLD FROM AN ALIEN INVASION.
AND SHE ALMOST DIED DOING IT.
IN FRONT OF THE ENTIRE WORLD.
SO, I DON'T KNOW, MAYBE SHE EARNED A LITTLE BIT MORE THAN YOU JUST SHITTING ON HER.
YOU'LL SEE.
(DOROTHY...)
HAS ANYONE BEEN KEEPING TRACK OF THE SATAN BABY SITUATION?
ACTUALLY, THAT'S WHAT I BRING TO THE TABLE TODAY...
ACCORDING TO SOME PEOPLE I KNOW WHO KNOW THINGS...
THIS BABY SATAN IS A REAL THING.
IT HAS ALREADY BEEN BORN...

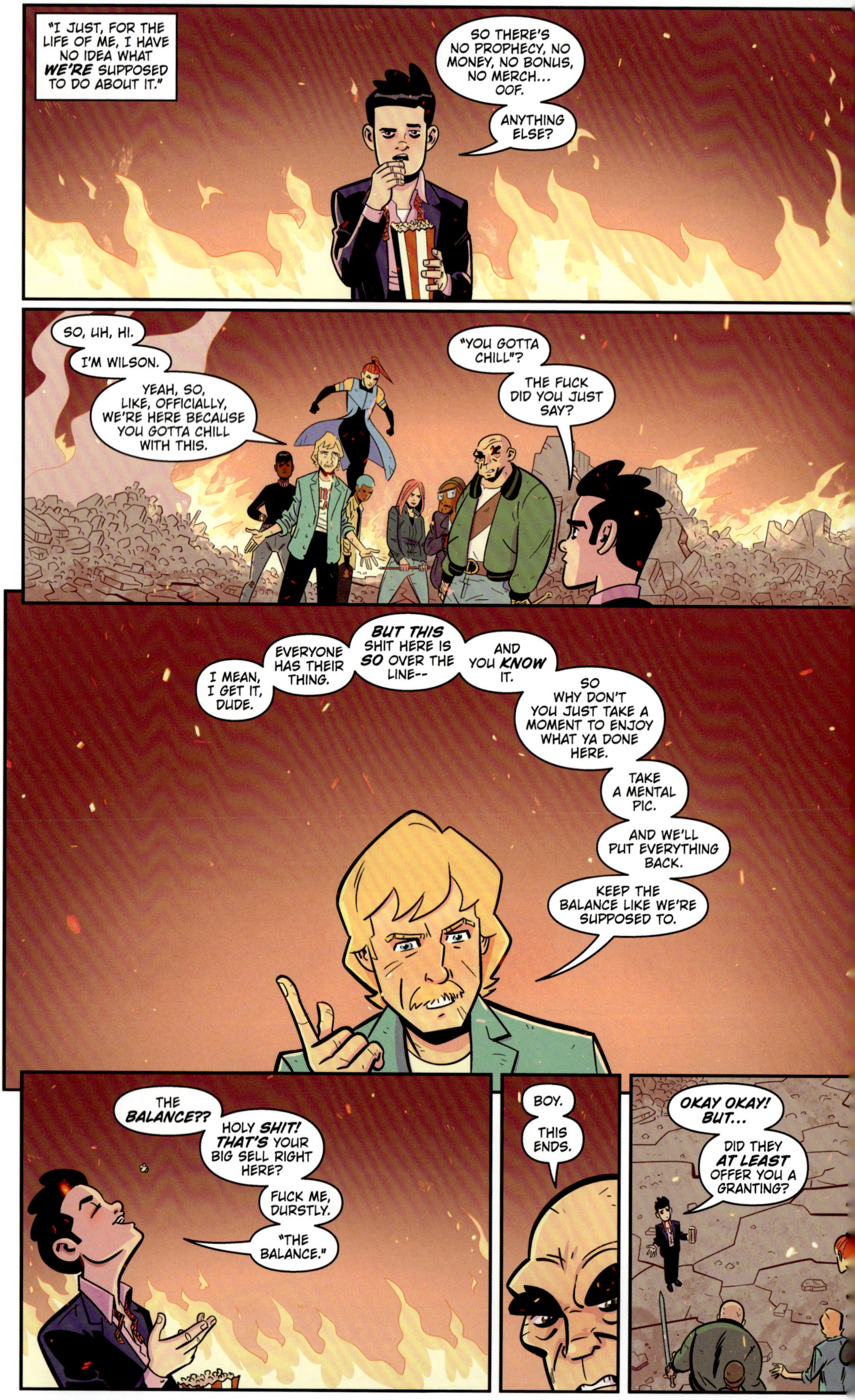
"I JUST, FOR THE LIFE OF ME, I HAVE NO IDEA WHAT ***WE'RE*** SUPPOSED TO DO ABOUT IT."
SO THERE'S NO PROPHECY, NO MONEY, NO BONUS, NO MERCH... OOF.
ANYTHING ELSE?
SO, UH, HI.
I'M WILSON.
YEAH, SO, LIKE, OFFICIALLY, WE'RE HERE BECAUSE YOU GOTTA CHILL WITH THIS.
"YOU GOTTA CHILL"?
THE FUCK DID YOU JUST SAY?
I MEAN, I GET IT, DUDE.
EVERYONE HAS THEIR THING.
BUT THIS SHIT HERE IS ***SO*** OVER THE LINE--
AND YOU ***KNOW*** IT.
SO WHY DON'T YOU JUST TAKE A MOMENT TO ENJOY WHAT YA DONE HERE.
TAKE A MENTAL PIC.
AND WE'LL PUT EVERYTHING BACK.
KEEP THE BALANCE LIKE WE'RE SUPPOSED TO.
THE ***BALANCE??***
HOLY ***SHIT! THAT'S*** YOUR BIG SELL RIGHT HERE?
FUCK ME, DURSTLY.
"THE BALANCE."
BOY.
THIS ENDS.
OKAY OKAY! BUT...
DID THEY ***AT LEAST*** OFFER YOU A GRANTING?

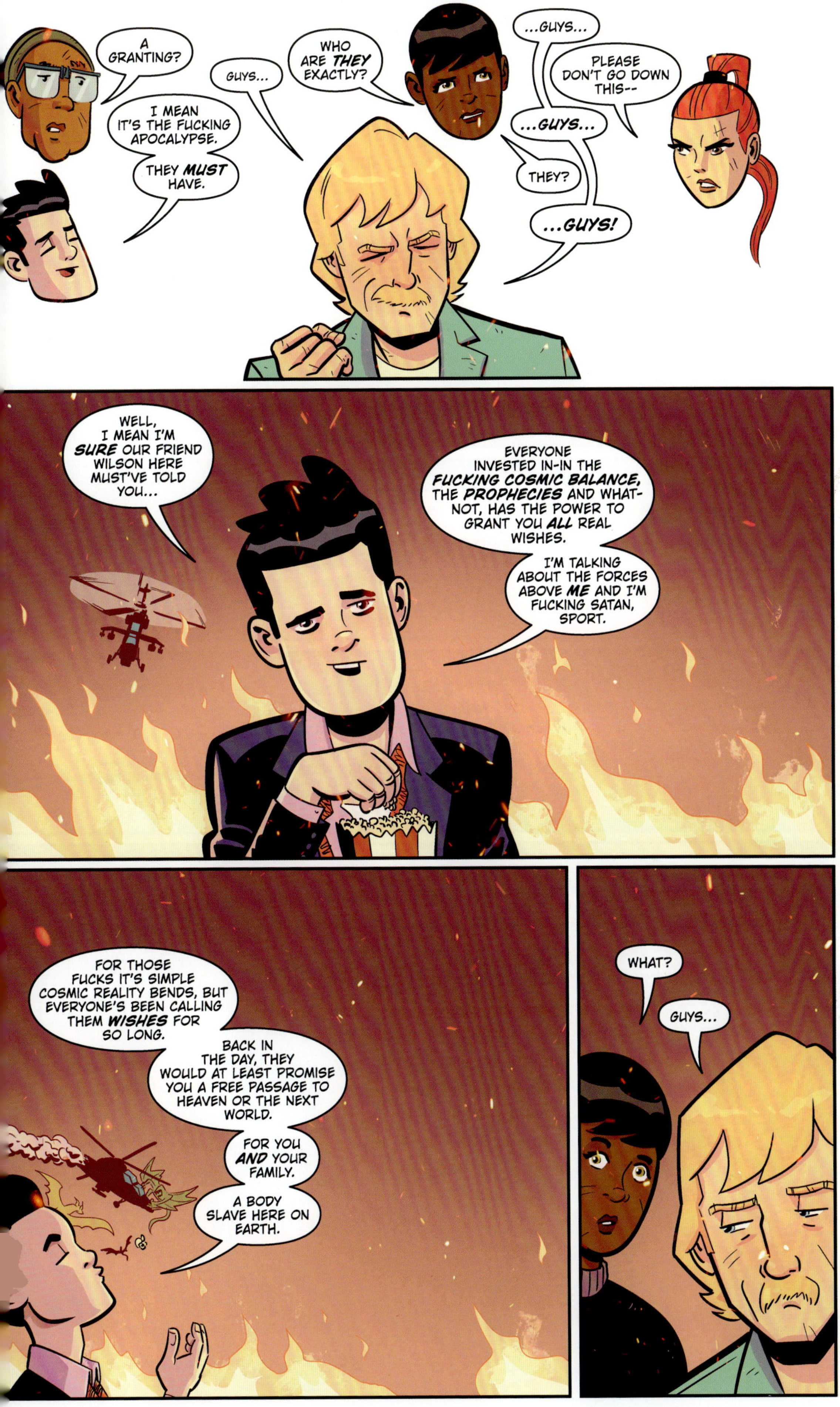
A GRANTING?
I MEAN IT'S THE FUCKING APOCALYPSE.
THEY MUST HAVE.
GUYS...
WHO ARE THEY EXACTLY?
...GUYS...
PLEASE DON'T GO DOWN THIS--
...GUYS...
THEY?
...GUYS!
WELL, I MEAN I'M SURE OUR FRIEND WILSON HERE MUST'VE TOLD YOU...
EVERYONE INVESTED IN-IN THE FUCKING COSMIC BALANCE, THE PROPHECIES AND WHAT-NOT, HAS THE POWER TO GRANT YOU ALL REAL WISHES.
I'M TALKING ABOUT THE FORCES ABOVE ME AND I'M FUCKING SATAN, SPORT.
FOR THOSE FUCKS IT'S SIMPLE COSMIC REALITY BENDS, BUT EVERYONE'S BEEN CALLING THEM WISHES FOR SO LONG.
BACK IN THE DAY, THEY WOULD AT LEAST PROMISE YOU A FREE PASSAGE TO HEAVEN OR THE NEXT WORLD.
FOR YOU AND YOUR FAMILY.
A BODY SLAVE HERE ON EARTH.
WHAT?
GUYS...

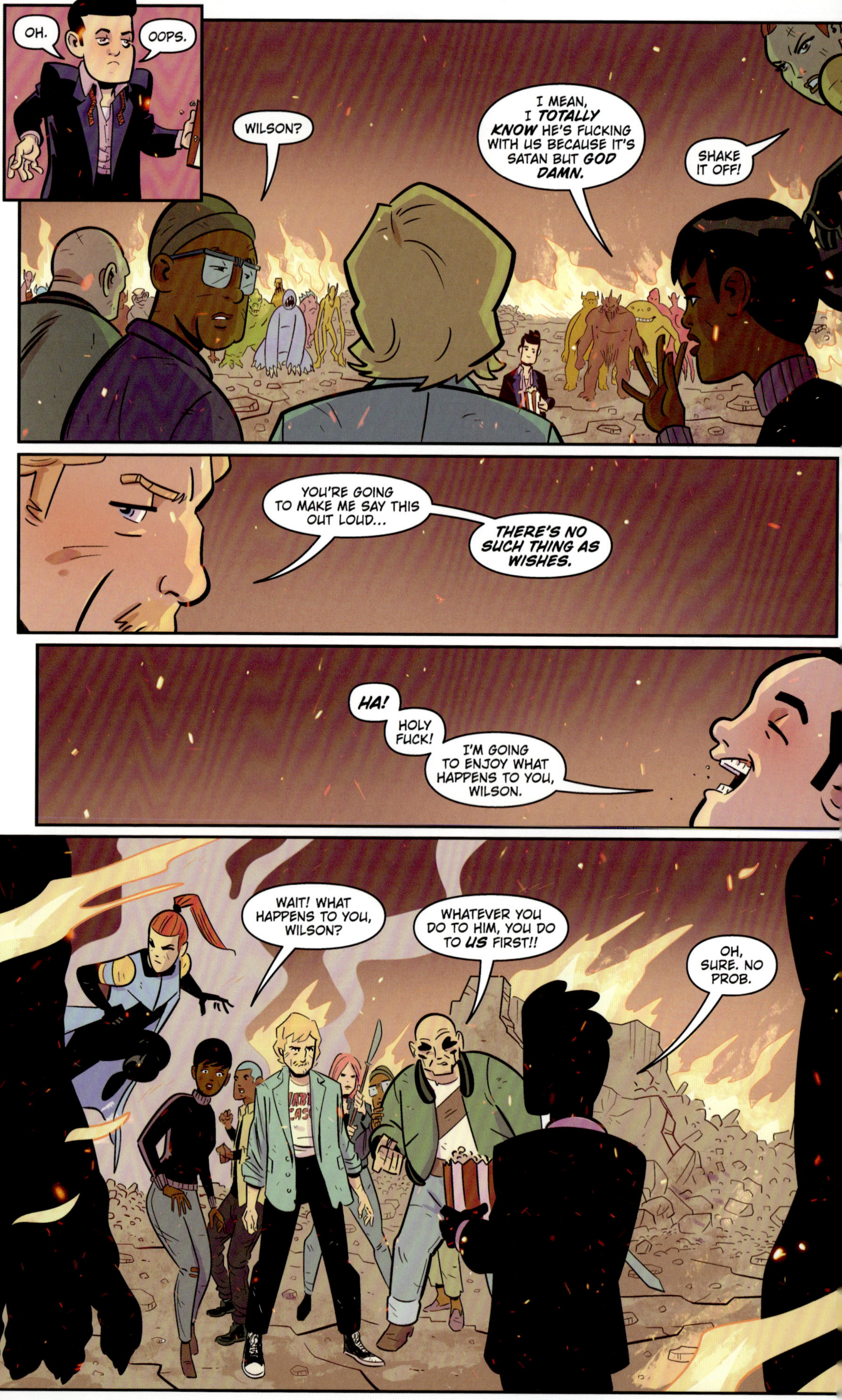
OH.
OOPS.
WILSON?
I MEAN, I TOTALLY KNOW HE'S FUCKING WITH US BECAUSE IT'S SATAN BUT GOD DAMN.
SHAKE IT OFF!
YOU'RE GOING TO MAKE ME SAY THIS OUT LOUD...
THERE'S NO SUCH THING AS WISHES.
HA!
HOLY FUCK!
I'M GOING TO ENJOY WHAT HAPPENS TO YOU, WILSON.
WAIT! WHAT HAPPENS TO YOU, WILSON?
WHATEVER YOU DO TO HIM, YOU DO TO US FIRST!!
OH, SURE. NO PROB.

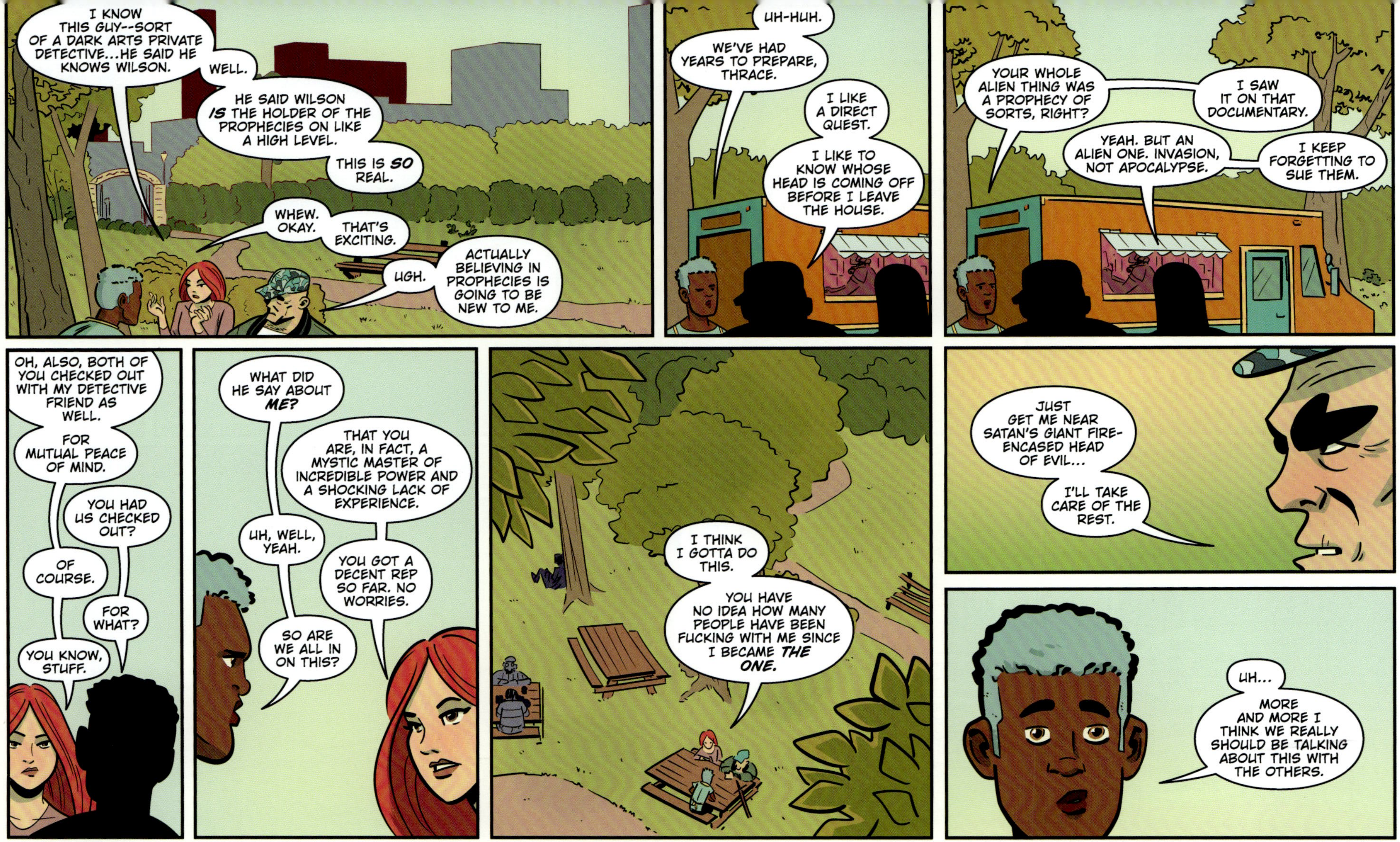
I KNOW THIS GUY--SORT OF A DARK ARTS PRIVATE DETECTIVE...HE SAID HE KNOWS WILSON.
WELL.
HE SAID WILSON *IS* THE HOLDER OF THE PROPHECIES ON LIKE A HIGH LEVEL.
THIS IS *SO* REAL.
WHEW. OKAY.
THAT'S EXCITING.
UGH.
ACTUALLY BELIEVING IN PROPHECIES IS GOING TO BE NEW TO ME.
UH-HUH.
WE'VE HAD YEARS TO PREPARE, THRACE.
I LIKE A DIRECT QUEST.
I LIKE TO KNOW WHOSE HEAD IS COMING OFF BEFORE I LEAVE THE HOUSE.
YOUR WHOLE ALIEN THING WAS A PROPHECY OF SORTS, RIGHT?
I SAW IT ON THAT DOCUMENTARY.
YEAH. BUT AN ALIEN ONE. INVASION, NOT APOCALYPSE.
I KEEP FORGETTING TO SUE THEM.
OH, ALSO, BOTH OF YOU CHECKED OUT WITH MY DETECTIVE FRIEND AS WELL.
FOR MUTUAL PEACE OF MIND.
YOU HAD US CHECKED OUT?
OF COURSE.
FOR WHAT?
YOU KNOW, STUFF.
WHAT DID HE SAY ABOUT *ME?*
THAT YOU ARE, IN FACT, A MYSTIC MASTER OF INCREDIBLE POWER AND A SHOCKING LACK OF EXPERIENCE.
UH, WELL, YEAH.
YOU GOT A DECENT REP SO FAR. NO WORRIES.
SO ARE WE ALL IN ON THIS?
I THINK I GOTTA DO THIS.
YOU HAVE NO IDEA HOW MANY PEOPLE HAVE BEEN FUCKING WITH ME SINCE I BECAME *THE ONE.*
JUST GET ME NEAR SATAN'S GIANT FIRE-ENCASED HEAD OF EVIL...
I'LL TAKE CARE OF THE REST.
UH...
MORE AND MORE I THINK WE REALLY SHOULD BE TALKING ABOUT THIS WITH THE OTHERS.

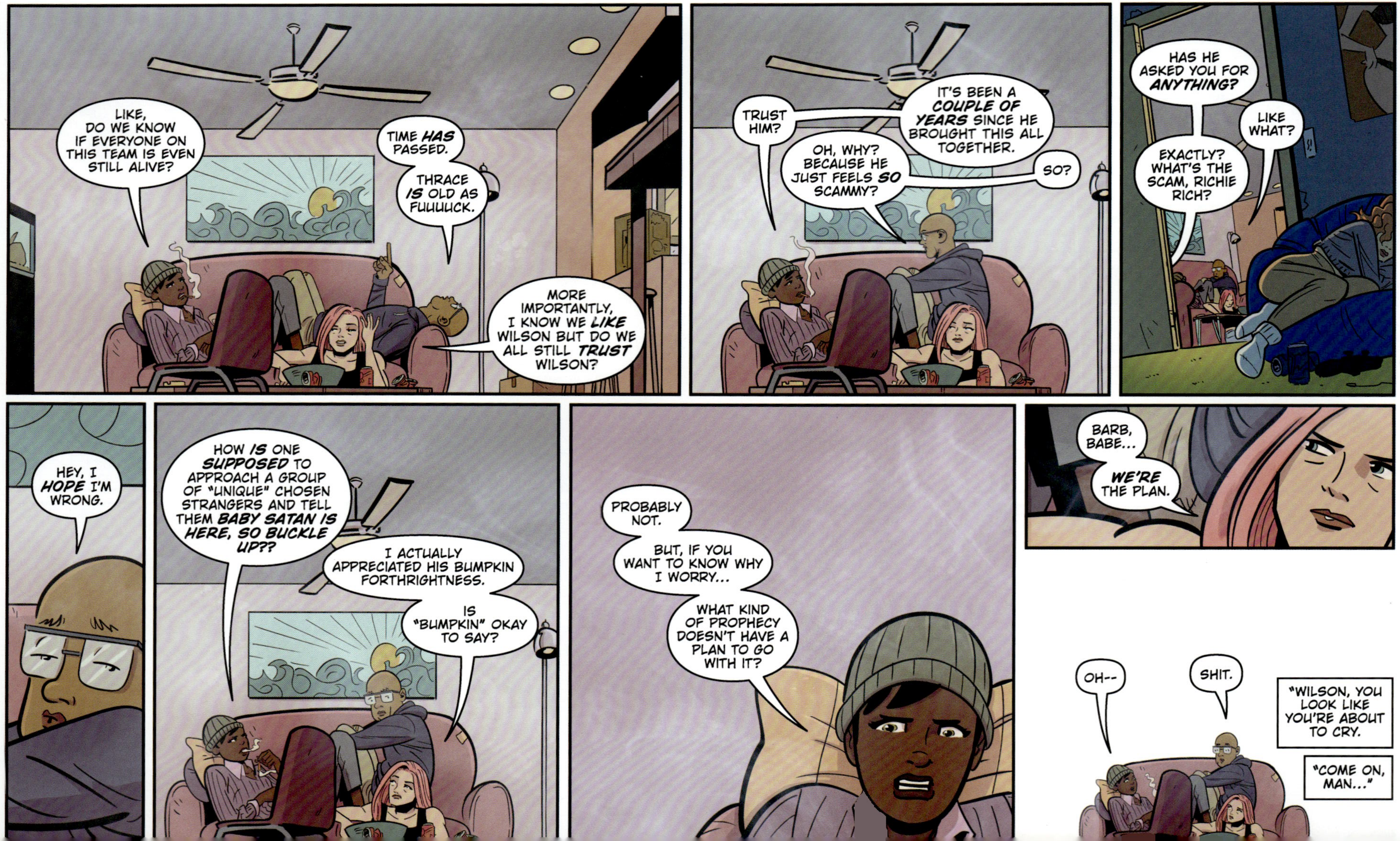

LIKE, DO WE KNOW IF EVERYONE ON THIS TEAM IS EVEN STILL ALIVE?
TIME *HAS* PASSED.
THRACE *IS* OLD AS FUUUUCK.
MORE IMPORTANTLY, I KNOW WE *LIKE* WILSON BUT DO WE ALL STILL *TRUST* WILSON?
TRUST HIM?
IT'S BEEN A *COUPLE OF YEARS* SINCE HE BROUGHT THIS ALL TOGETHER.
OH, WHY? BECAUSE HE JUST FEELS *SO* SCAMMY?
SO?
HAS HE ASKED YOU FOR *ANYTHING?*
LIKE WHAT?
EXACTLY? WHAT'S THE SCAM, RICHIE RICH?
HEY, I *HOPE* I'M WRONG.
HOW *IS* ONE *SUPPOSED* TO APPROACH A GROUP OF "UNIQUE" CHOSEN STRANGERS AND TELL THEM *BABY SATAN IS HERE, SO BUCKLE UP??*
I ACTUALLY APPRECIATED HIS BUMPKIN FORTHRIGHTNESS.
IS "BUMPKIN" OKAY TO SAY?
PROBABLY NOT.
BUT, IF YOU WANT TO KNOW WHY I WORRY...
WHAT KIND OF PROPHECY DOESN'T HAVE A PLAN TO GO WITH IT?
BARB, BABE...
WE'RE THE PLAN.
OH--
SHIT.
"WILSON, YOU LOOK LIKE YOU'RE ABOUT TO CRY.
"COME ON, MAN..."

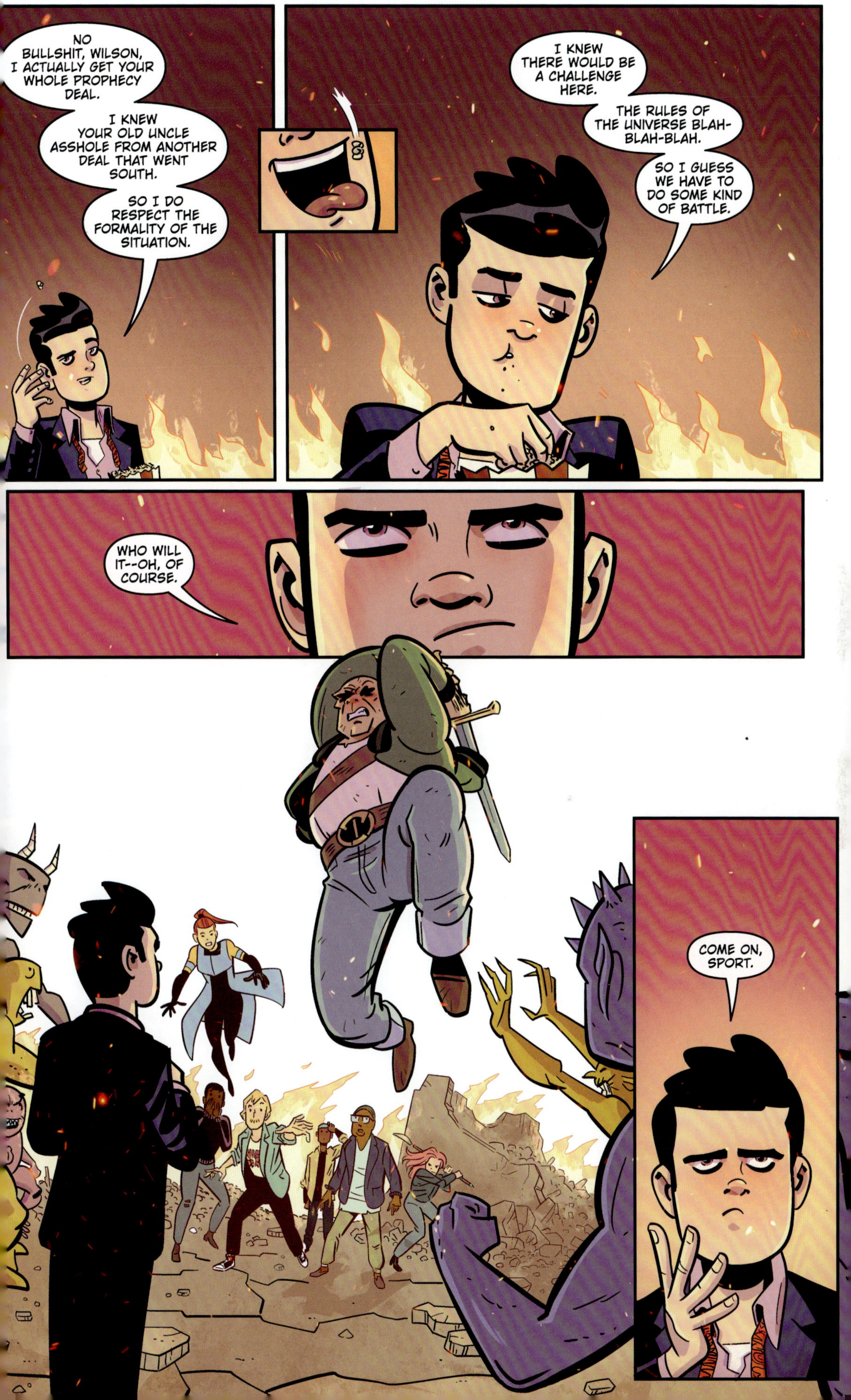
NO BULLSHIT, WILSON, I ACTUALLY GET YOUR WHOLE PROPHECY DEAL.
I KNEW YOUR OLD UNCLE ASSHOLE FROM ANOTHER DEAL THAT WENT SOUTH.
SO I DO RESPECT THE FORMALITY OF THE SITUATION.
I KNEW THERE WOULD BE A CHALLENGE HERE.
THE RULES OF THE UNIVERSE BLAH-BLAH-BLAH.
SO I GUESS WE HAVE TO DO SOME KIND OF BATTLE.
WHO WILL IT--OH, OF COURSE.
COME ON, SPORT.

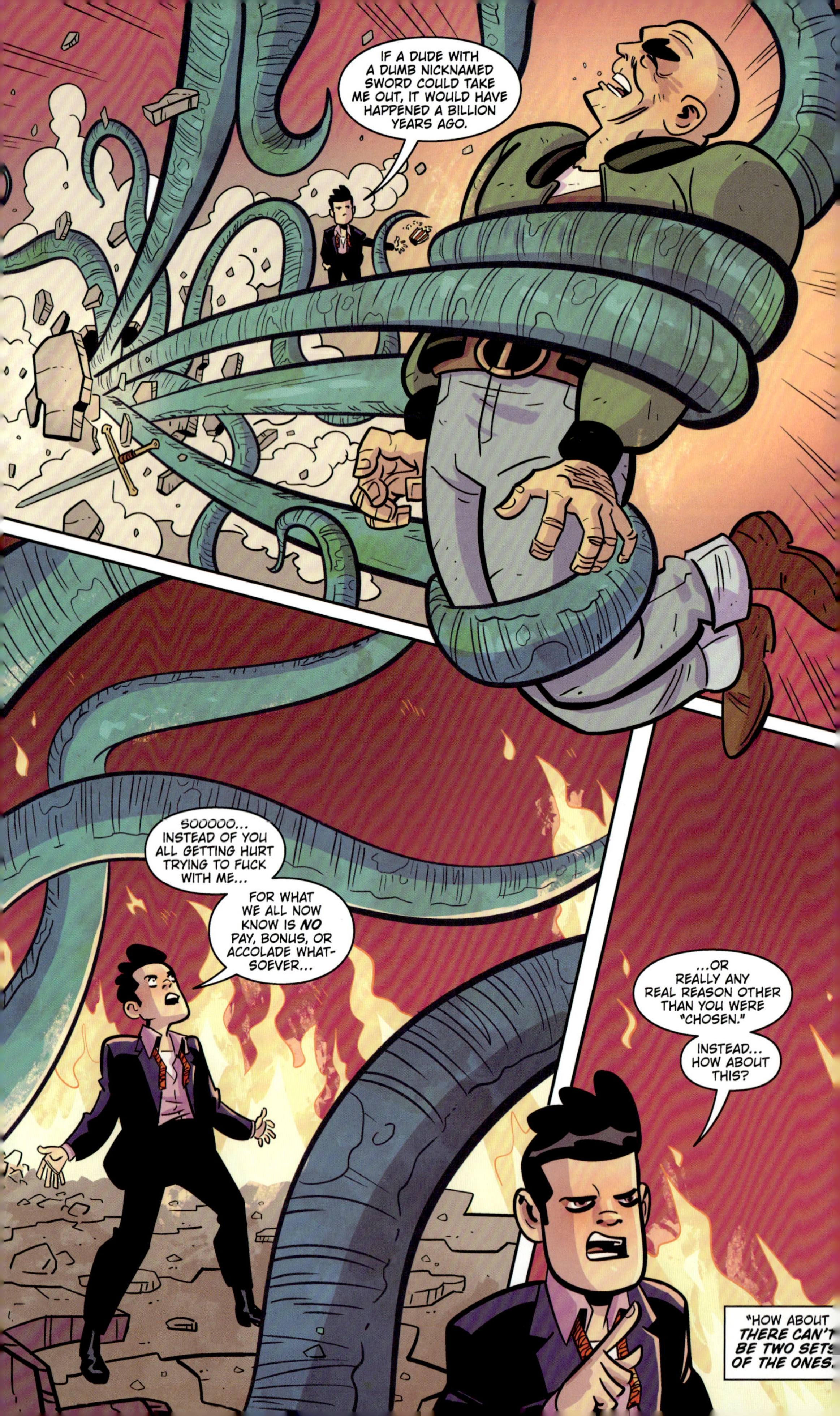
IF A DUDE WITH A DUMB NICKNAMED SWORD COULD TAKE ME OUT, IT WOULD HAVE HAPPENED A BILLION YEARS AGO.
SOOOOO... INSTEAD OF YOU ALL GETTING HURT TRYING TO FUCK WITH ME...
FOR WHAT WE ALL NOW KNOW IS ***NO*** PAY, BONUS, OR ACCOLADE WHAT-SOEVER...
...OR REALLY ANY REAL REASON OTHER THAN YOU WERE "CHOSEN."
INSTEAD... HOW ABOUT THIS?
"HOW ABOUT ***THERE CAN'T BE TWO SETS OF THE ONES.***

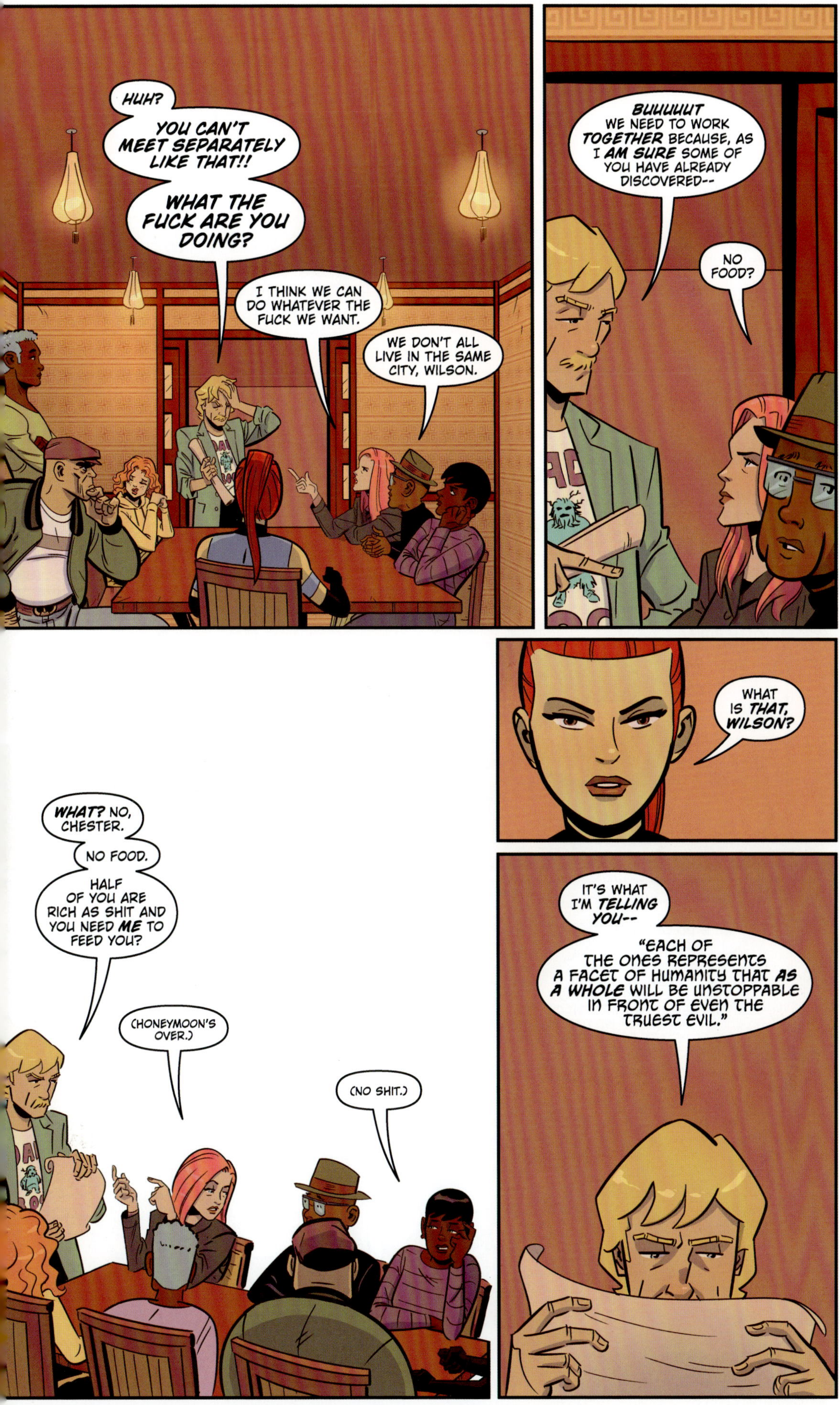
HUH?
YOU CAN'T MEET SEPARATELY LIKE THAT!!
WHAT THE FUCK ARE YOU DOING?
I THINK WE CAN DO WHATEVER THE FUCK WE WANT.
WE DON'T ALL LIVE IN THE SAME CITY, WILSON.
BUUUUUT WE NEED TO WORK TOGETHER BECAUSE, AS I AM SURE SOME OF YOU HAVE ALREADY DISCOVERED--
NO FOOD?
WHAT IS THAT, WILSON?
WHAT? NO, CHESTER.
NO FOOD.
HALF OF YOU ARE RICH AS SHIT AND YOU NEED ME TO FEED YOU?
(HONEYMOON'S OVER.)
(NO SHIT.)
IT'S WHAT I'M TELLING YOU--
"EACH OF THE ONES REPRESENTS A FACET OF HUMANITY THAT AS A WHOLE WILL BE UNSTOPPABLE IN FRONT OF EVEN THE TRUEST EVIL."

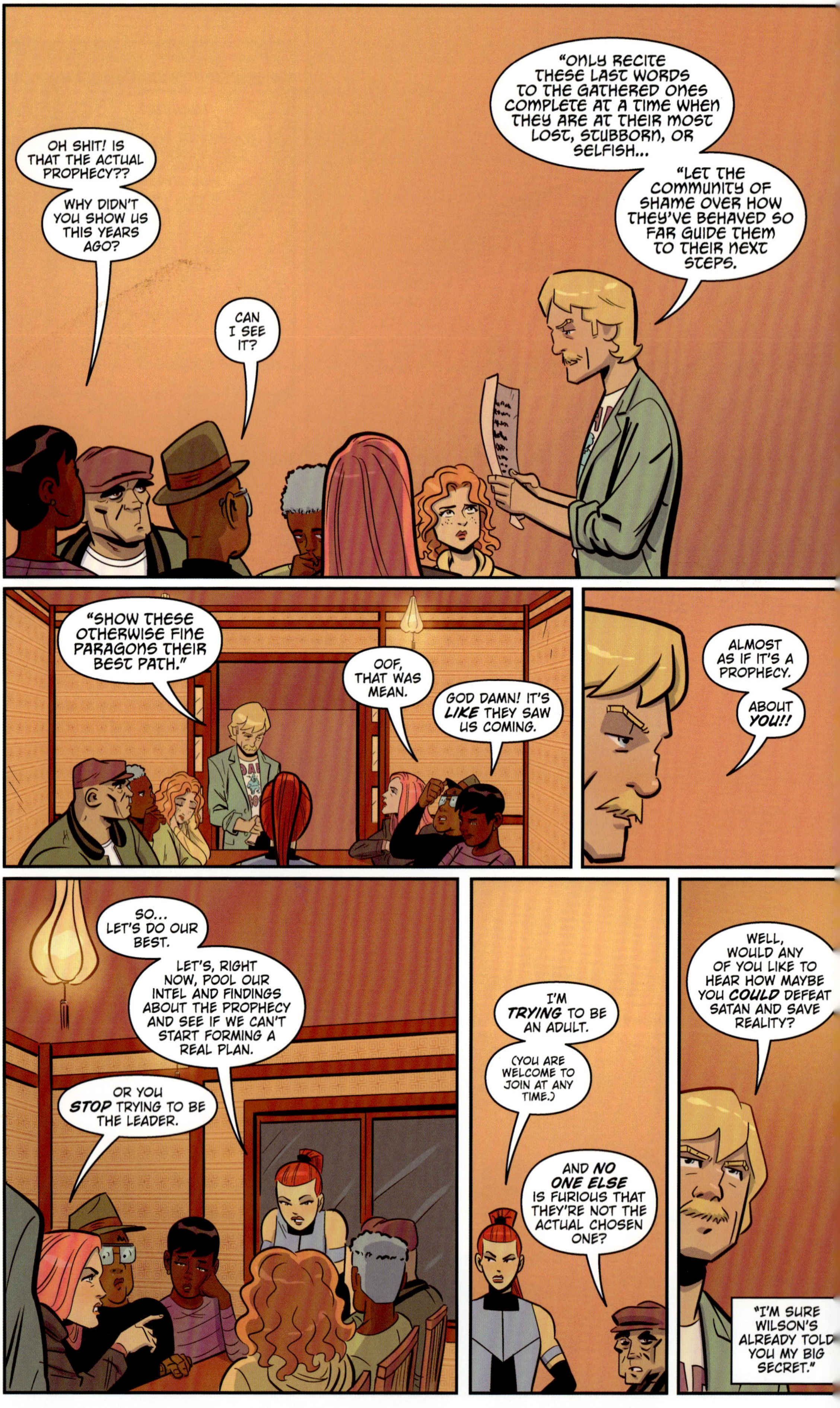
"ONLY RECITE THESE LAST WORDS TO THE GATHERED ONES COMPLETE AT A TIME WHEN THEY ARE AT THEIR MOST LOST, STUBBORN, OR SELFISH...
"LET THE COMMUNITY OF SHAME OVER HOW THEY'VE BEHAVED SO FAR GUIDE THEM TO THEIR NEXT STEPS.
OH SHIT! IS THAT THE ACTUAL PROPHECY??
WHY DIDN'T YOU SHOW US THIS YEARS AGO?
CAN I SEE IT?
"SHOW THESE OTHERWISE FINE PARAGONS THEIR BEST PATH."
OOF, THAT WAS MEAN.
GOD DAMN! IT'S LIKE THEY SAW US COMING.
ALMOST AS IF IT'S A PROPHECY.
ABOUT YOU!!
SO... LET'S DO OUR BEST.
LET'S, RIGHT NOW, POOL OUR INTEL AND FINDINGS ABOUT THE PROPHECY AND SEE IF WE CAN'T START FORMING A REAL PLAN.
OR YOU STOP TRYING TO BE THE LEADER.
I'M TRYING TO BE AN ADULT.
(YOU ARE WELCOME TO JOIN AT ANY TIME.)
AND NO ONE ELSE IS FURIOUS THAT THEY'RE NOT THE ACTUAL CHOSEN ONE?
WELL, WOULD ANY OF YOU LIKE TO HEAR HOW MAYBE YOU COULD DEFEAT SATAN AND SAVE REALITY?
"I'M SURE WILSON'S ALREADY TOLD YOU MY BIG SECRET."

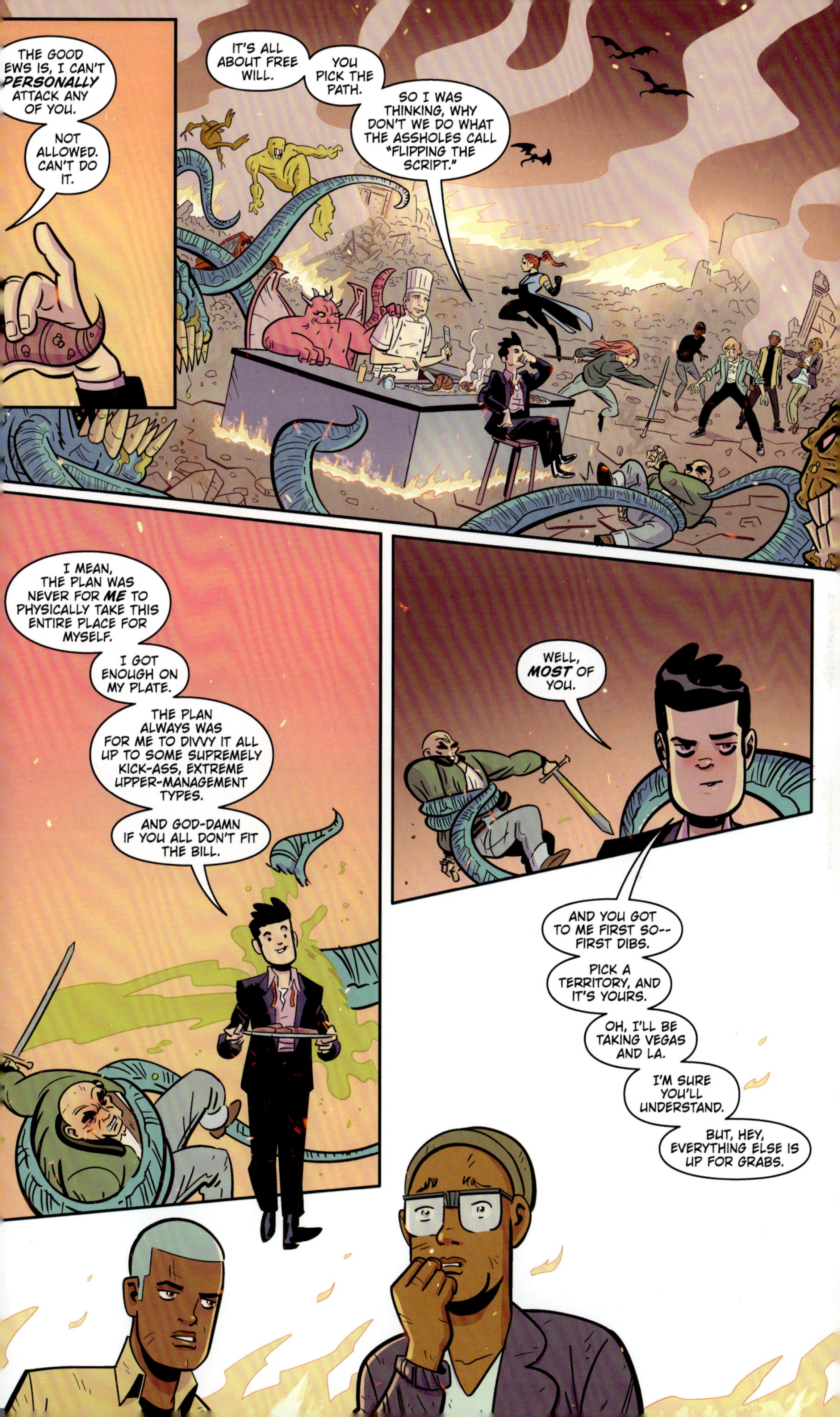
THE GOOD
EWS IS, I CAN'T **PERSONALLY** ATTACK ANY OF YOU.
NOT ALLOWED. CAN'T DO IT.
IT'S ALL ABOUT FREE WILL.
YOU PICK THE PATH.
SO I WAS THINKING, WHY DON'T WE DO WHAT THE ASSHOLES CALL "FLIPPING THE SCRIPT."
I MEAN, THE PLAN WAS NEVER FOR **ME** TO PHYSICALLY TAKE THIS ENTIRE PLACE FOR MYSELF.
I GOT ENOUGH ON MY PLATE.
THE PLAN ALWAYS WAS FOR ME TO DIVVY IT ALL UP TO SOME SUPREMELY KICK-ASS, EXTREME UPPER-MANAGEMENT TYPES.
AND GOD-DAMN IF YOU ALL DON'T FIT THE BILL.
WELL, **MOST** OF YOU.
AND YOU GOT TO ME FIRST SO-- FIRST DIBS.
PICK A TERRITORY, AND IT'S YOURS.
OH, I'LL BE TAKING VEGAS AND LA.
I'M SURE YOU'LL UNDERSTAND.
BUT, HEY, EVERYTHING ELSE IS UP FOR GRABS.

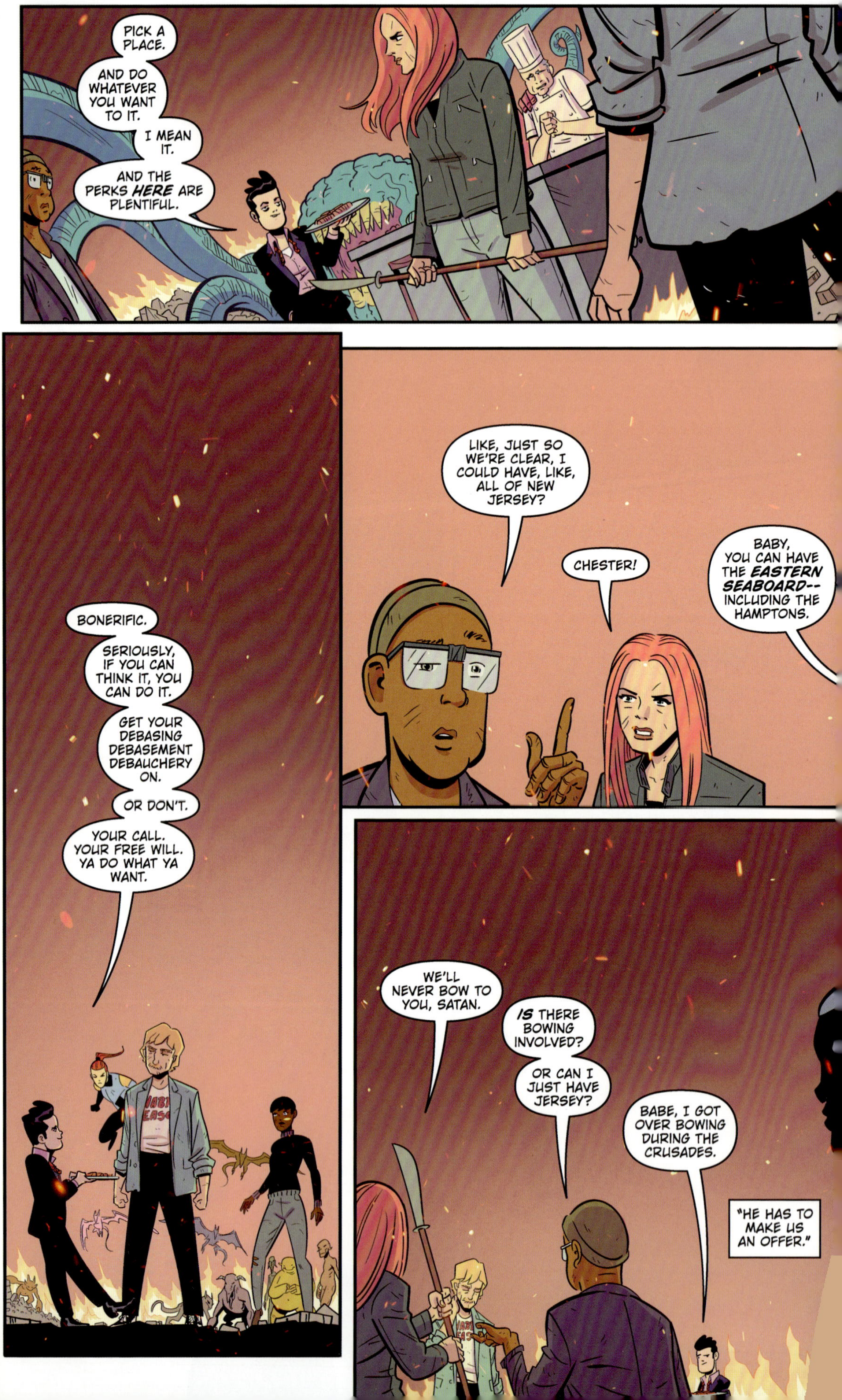
PICK A PLACE.
AND DO WHATEVER YOU WANT TO IT.
I MEAN IT.
AND THE PERKS *HERE* ARE PLENTIFUL.
BONERIFIC.
SERIOUSLY, IF YOU CAN THINK IT, YOU CAN DO IT.
GET YOUR DEBASING DEBASEMENT DEBAUCHERY ON.
OR DON'T.
YOUR CALL. YOUR FREE WILL. YA DO WHAT YA WANT.
LIKE, JUST SO WE'RE CLEAR, I COULD HAVE, LIKE, ALL OF NEW JERSEY?
CHESTER!
BABY, YOU CAN HAVE THE *EASTERN SEABOARD--* INCLUDING THE HAMPTONS.
WE'LL NEVER BOW TO YOU, SATAN.
IS THERE BOWING INVOLVED?
OR CAN I JUST HAVE JERSEY?
BABE, I GOT OVER BOWING DURING THE CRUSADES.
"HE HAS TO MAKE US AN OFFER."

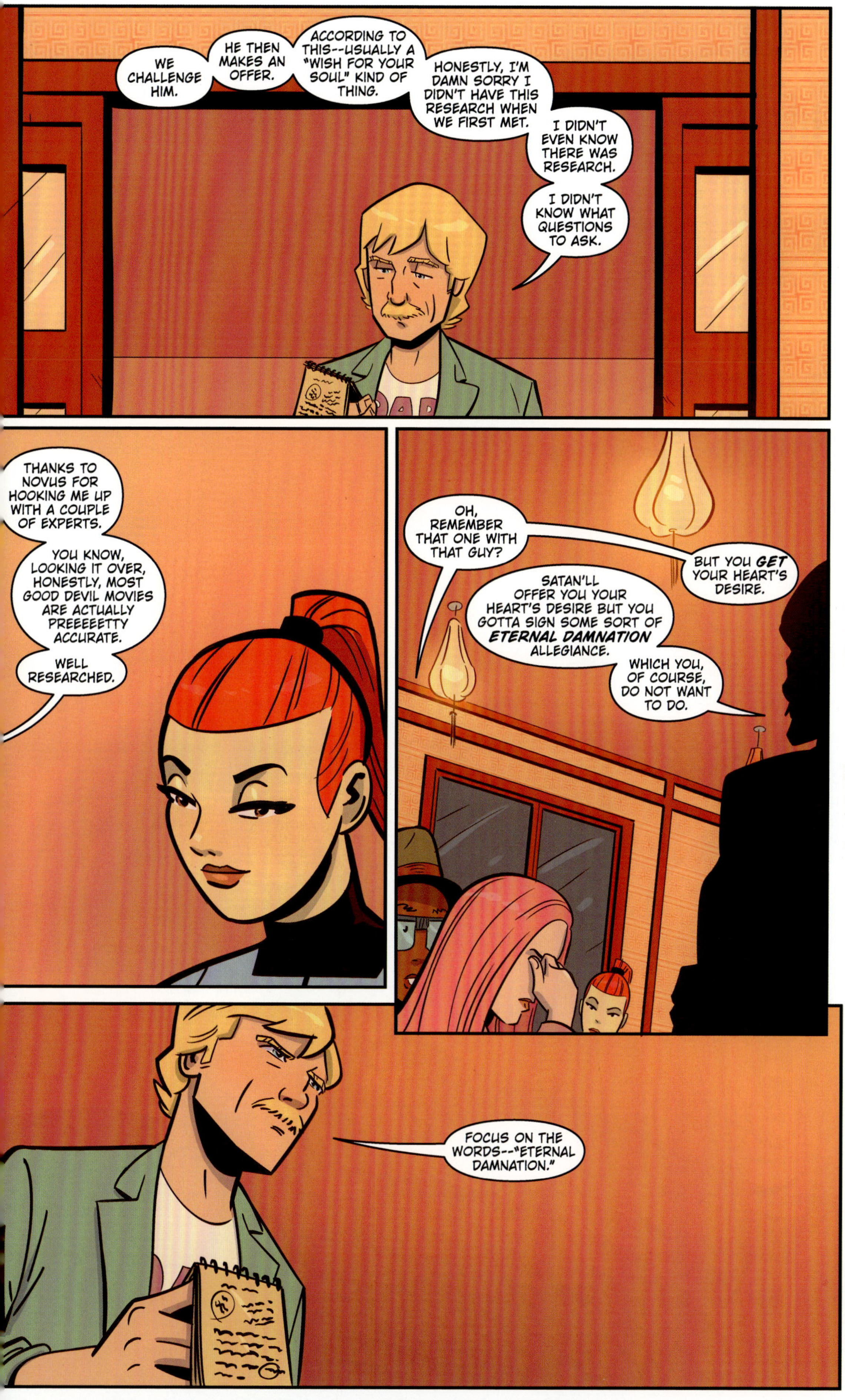
WE CHALLENGE HIM.
HE THEN MAKES AN OFFER.
ACCORDING TO THIS--USUALLY A "WISH FOR YOUR SOUL" KIND OF THING.
HONESTLY, I'M DAMN SORRY I DIDN'T HAVE THIS RESEARCH WHEN WE FIRST MET.
I DIDN'T EVEN KNOW THERE WAS RESEARCH.
I DIDN'T KNOW WHAT QUESTIONS TO ASK.
THANKS TO NOVUS FOR HOOKING ME UP WITH A COUPLE OF EXPERTS.
YOU KNOW, LOOKING IT OVER, HONESTLY, MOST GOOD DEVIL MOVIES ARE ACTUALLY PREEEEETTY ACCURATE.
WELL RESEARCHED.
OH, REMEMBER THAT ONE WITH THAT GUY?
BUT YOU **GET** YOUR HEART'S DESIRE.
SATAN'LL OFFER YOU YOUR HEART'S DESIRE BUT YOU GOTTA SIGN SOME SORT OF ***ETERNAL DAMNATION*** ALLEGIANCE.
WHICH YOU, OF COURSE, DO NOT WANT TO DO.
FOCUS ON THE WORDS--"ETERNAL DAMNATION."

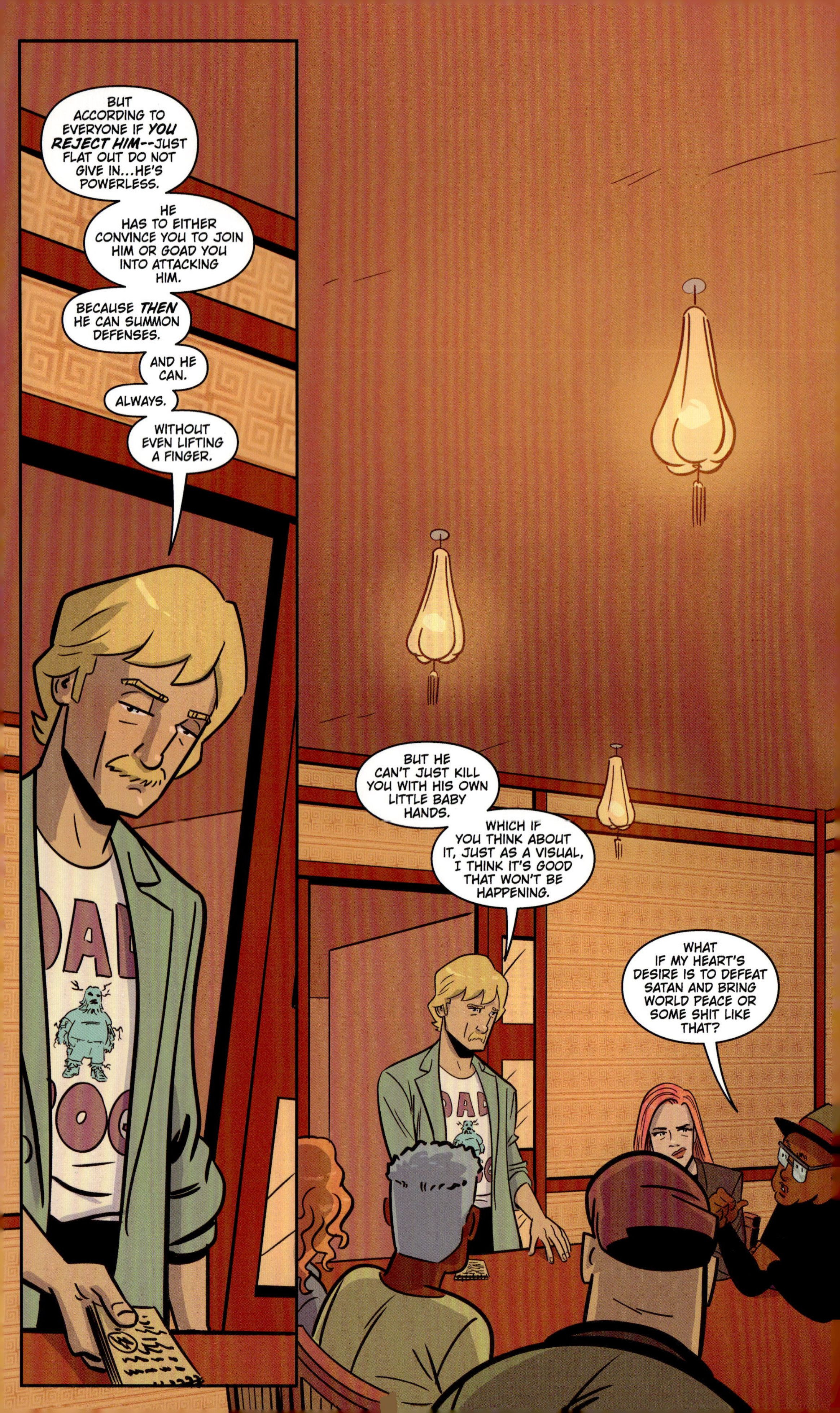
BUT ACCORDING TO EVERYONE IF *YOU REJECT HIM*--JUST FLAT OUT DO NOT GIVE IN...HE'S POWERLESS.
HE HAS TO EITHER CONVINCE YOU TO JOIN HIM OR GOAD YOU INTO ATTACKING HIM.
BECAUSE *THEN* HE CAN SUMMON DEFENSES.
AND HE CAN.
ALWAYS.
WITHOUT EVEN LIFTING A FINGER.
BUT HE CAN'T JUST KILL YOU WITH HIS OWN LITTLE BABY HANDS.
WHICH IF YOU THINK ABOUT IT, JUST AS A VISUAL, I THINK IT'S GOOD THAT WON'T BE HAPPENING.
WHAT IF MY HEART'S DESIRE IS TO DEFEAT SATAN AND BRING WORLD PEACE OR SOME SHIT LIKE THAT?

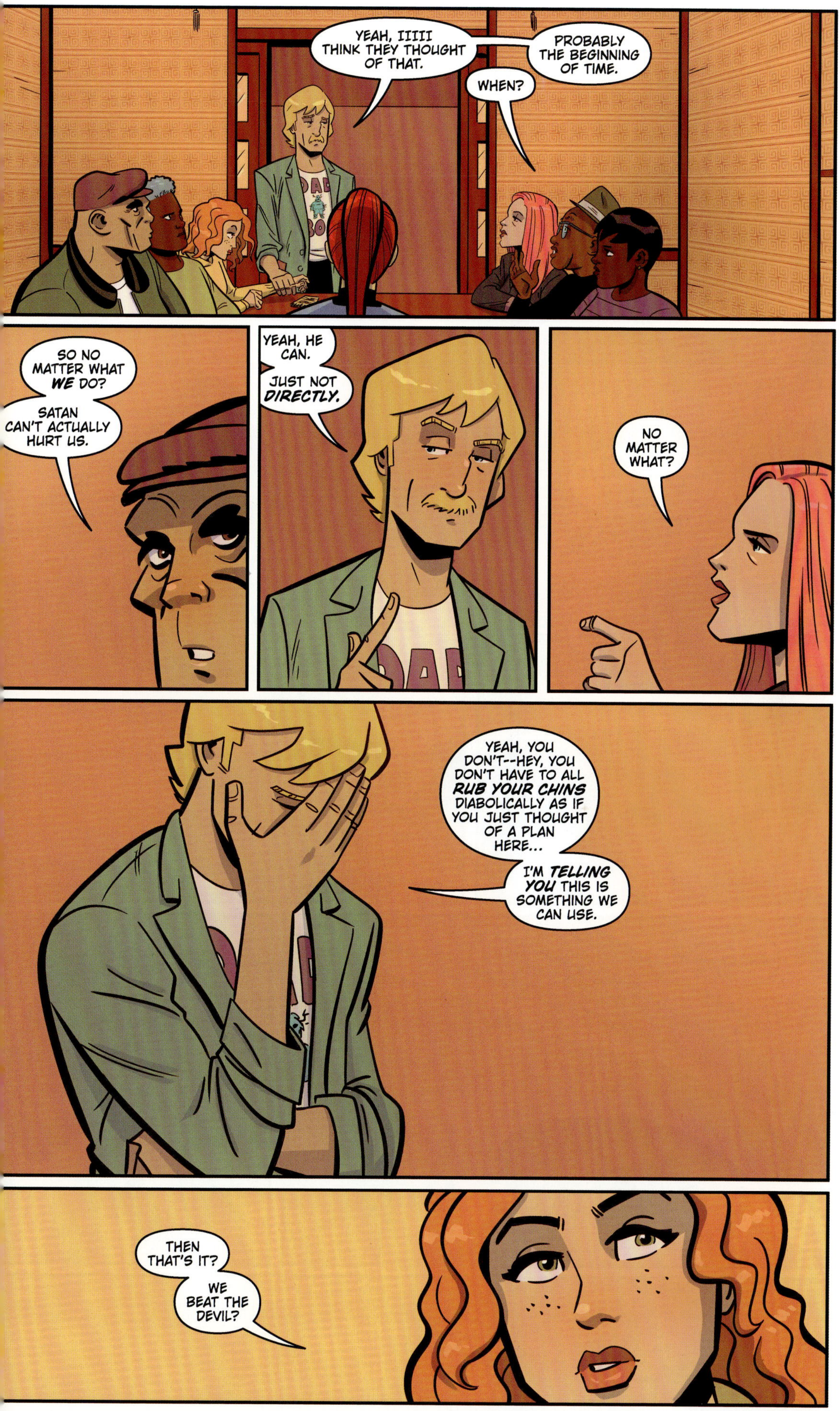
YEAH, IIIII THINK THEY THOUGHT OF THAT.
WHEN?
PROBABLY THE BEGINNING OF TIME.
SO NO MATTER WHAT **WE** DO?
SATAN CAN'T ACTUALLY HURT US.
YEAH, HE CAN.
JUST NOT **DIRECTLY.**
NO MATTER WHAT?
YEAH, YOU DON'T--HEY, YOU DON'T HAVE TO ALL **RUB YOUR CHINS** DIABOLICALLY AS IF YOU JUST THOUGHT OF A PLAN HERE...
I'M **TELLING YOU** THIS IS SOMETHING WE CAN USE.
THEN THAT'S IT?
WE BEAT THE DEVIL?

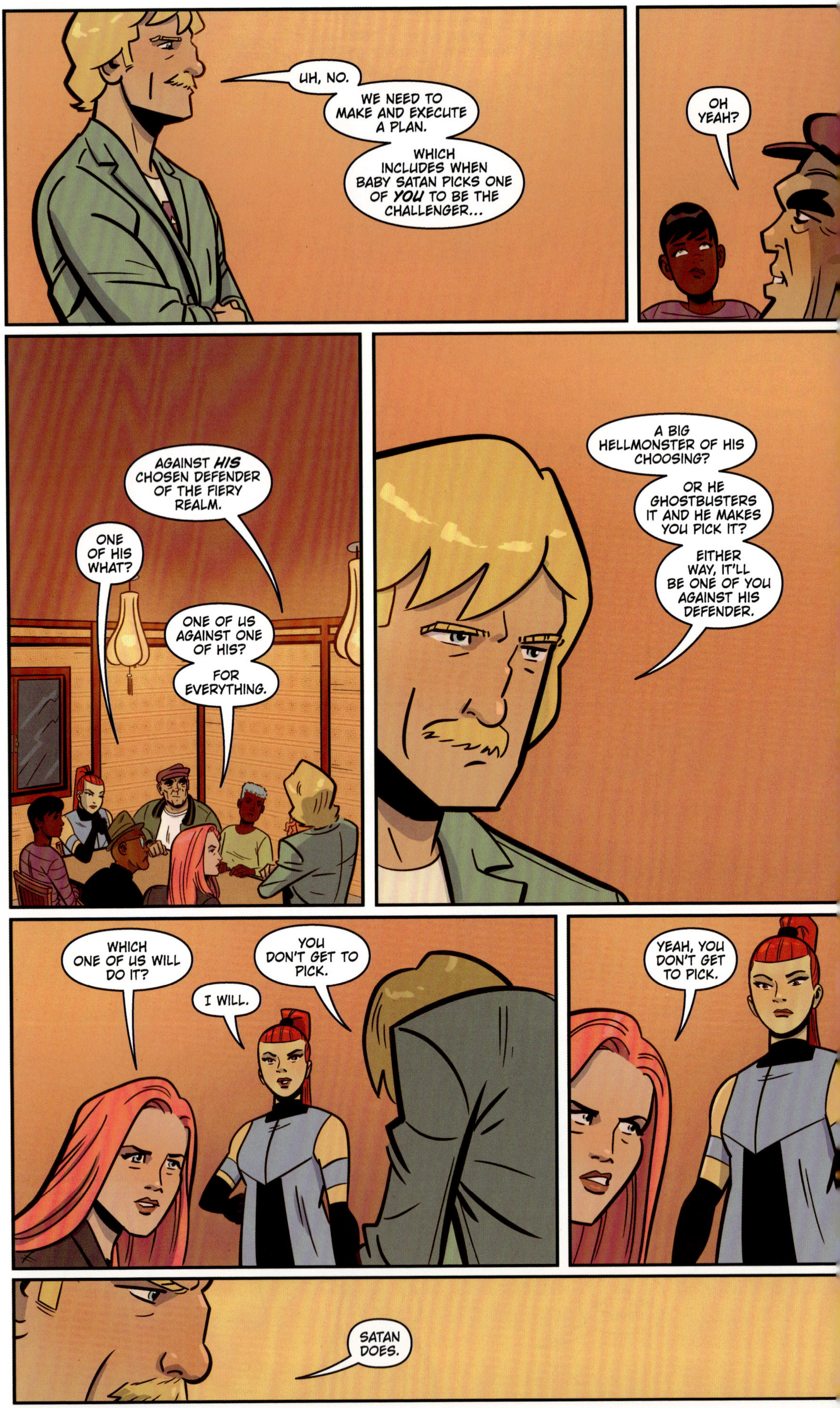
UH, NO.
WE NEED TO MAKE AND EXECUTE A PLAN.
WHICH INCLUDES WHEN BABY SATAN PICKS ONE OF *YOU* TO BE THE CHALLENGER...
OH YEAH?
AGAINST *HIS* CHOSEN DEFENDER OF THE FIERY REALM.
ONE OF HIS WHAT?
ONE OF US AGAINST ONE OF HIS?
FOR EVERYTHING.
A BIG HELLMONSTER OF HIS CHOOSING?
OR HE GHOSTBUSTERS IT AND HE MAKES YOU PICK IT?
EITHER WAY, IT'LL BE ONE OF YOU AGAINST HIS DEFENDER.
WHICH ONE OF US WILL DO IT?
I WILL.
YOU DON'T GET TO PICK.
YEAH, YOU DON'T GET TO PICK.
SATAN DOES.

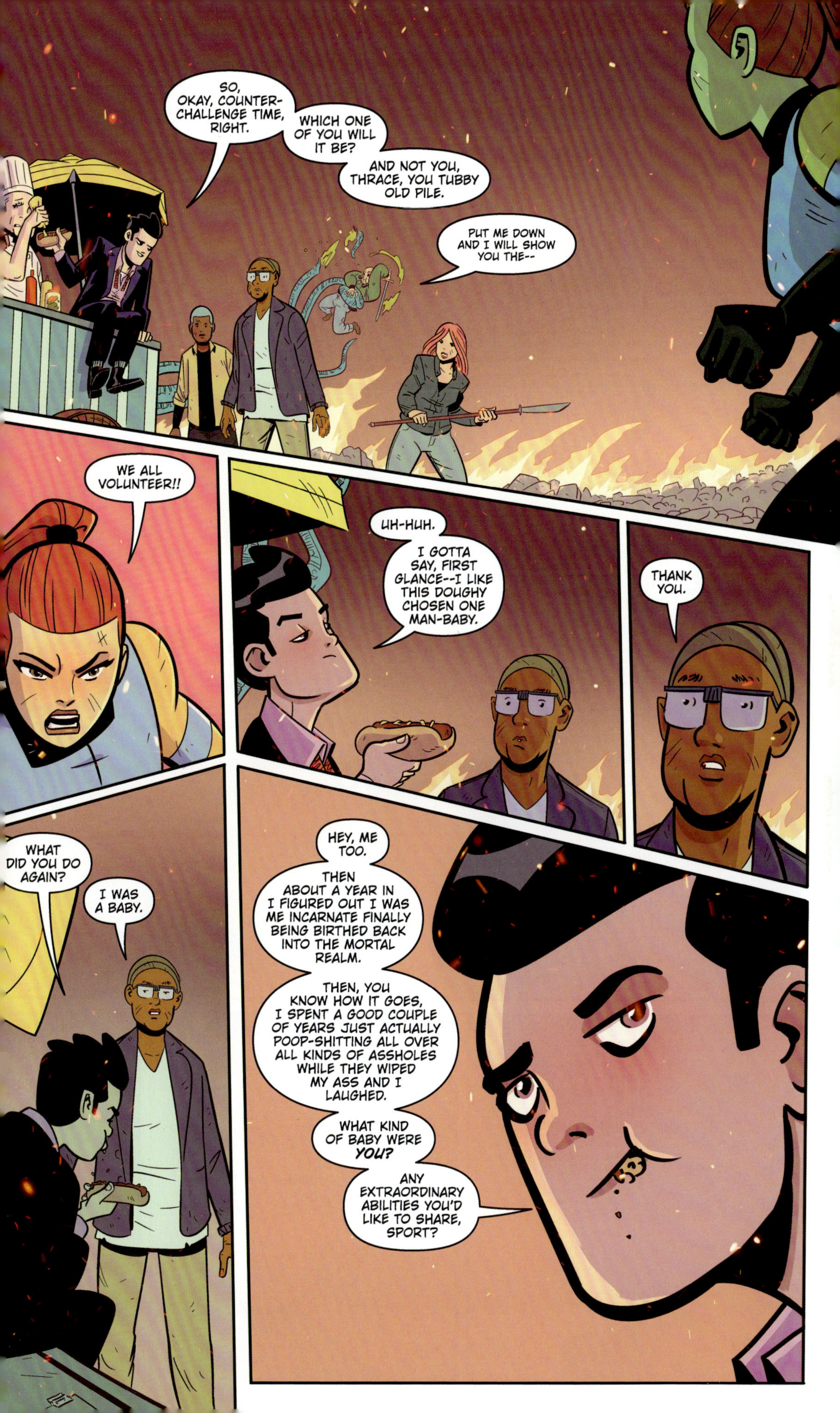

SO, OKAY, COUNTER-CHALLENGE TIME, RIGHT.
WHICH ONE OF YOU WILL IT BE?
AND NOT YOU, THRACE, YOU TUBBY OLD PILE.
PUT ME DOWN AND I WILL SHOW YOU THE--
WE ALL VOLUNTEER!!
UH-HUH.
I GOTTA SAY, FIRST GLANCE--I LIKE THIS DOUGHY CHOSEN ONE MAN-BABY.
THANK YOU.
WHAT DID YOU DO AGAIN?
I WAS A BABY.
HEY, ME TOO.
THEN ABOUT A YEAR IN I FIGURED OUT I WAS ME INCARNATE FINALLY BEING BIRTHED BACK INTO THE MORTAL REALM.
THEN, YOU KNOW HOW IT GOES, I SPENT A GOOD COUPLE OF YEARS JUST ACTUALLY POOP-SHITTING ALL OVER ALL KINDS OF ASSHOLES WHILE THEY WIPED MY ASS AND I LAUGHED.
WHAT KIND OF BABY WERE *YOU?*
ANY EXTRAORDINARY ABILITIES YOU'D LIKE TO SHARE, SPORT?

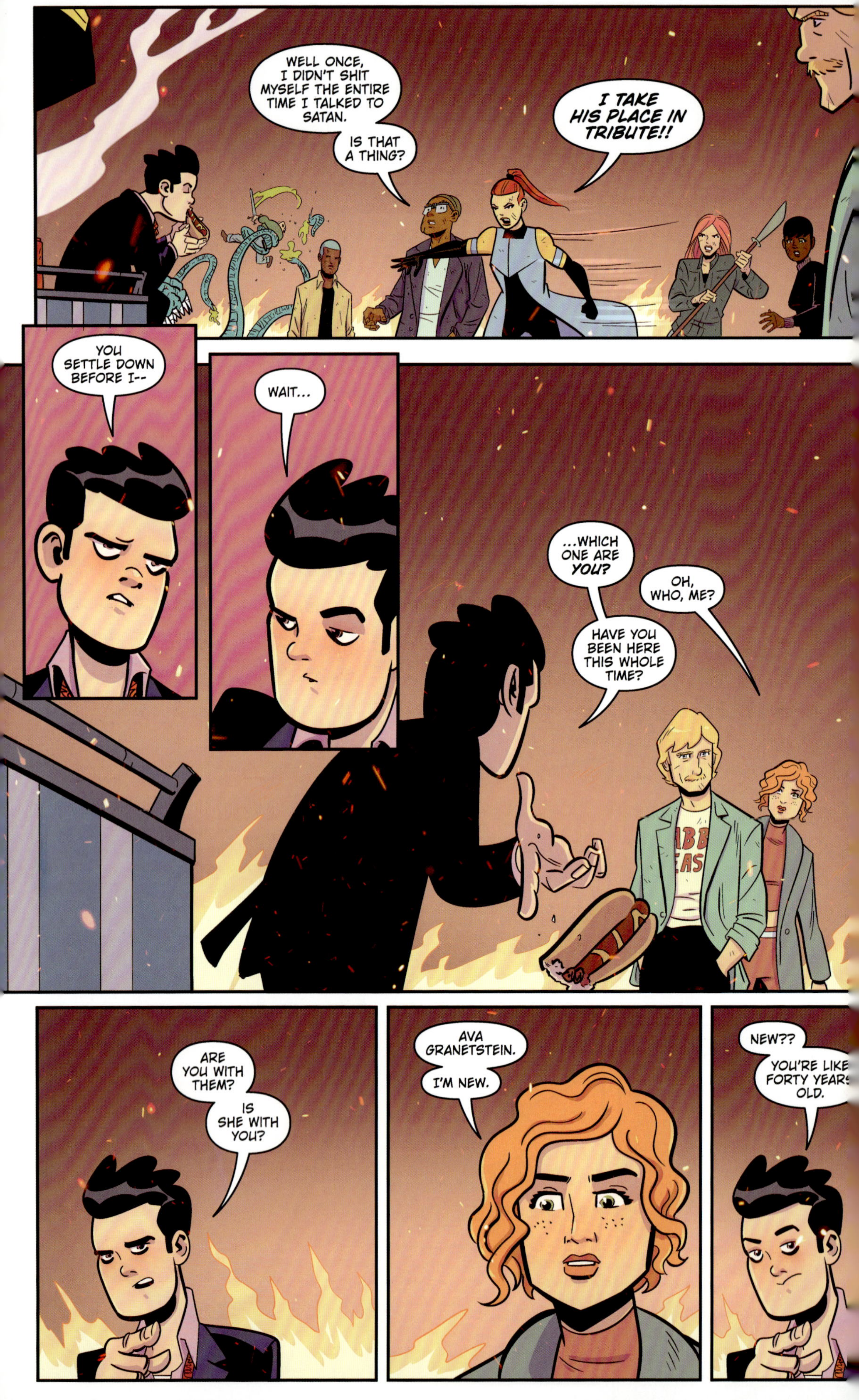
WELL ONCE, I DIDN'T SHIT MYSELF THE ENTIRE TIME I TALKED TO SATAN.
IS THAT A THING?
I TAKE HIS PLACE IN TRIBUTE!!
YOU SETTLE DOWN BEFORE I--
WAIT...
...WHICH ONE ARE YOU?
HAVE YOU BEEN HERE THIS WHOLE TIME?
OH, WHO, ME?
ARE YOU WITH THEM?
IS SHE WITH YOU?
AVA GRANETSTEIN.
I'M NEW.
NEW??
YOU'RE LIKE FORTY YEARS OLD.

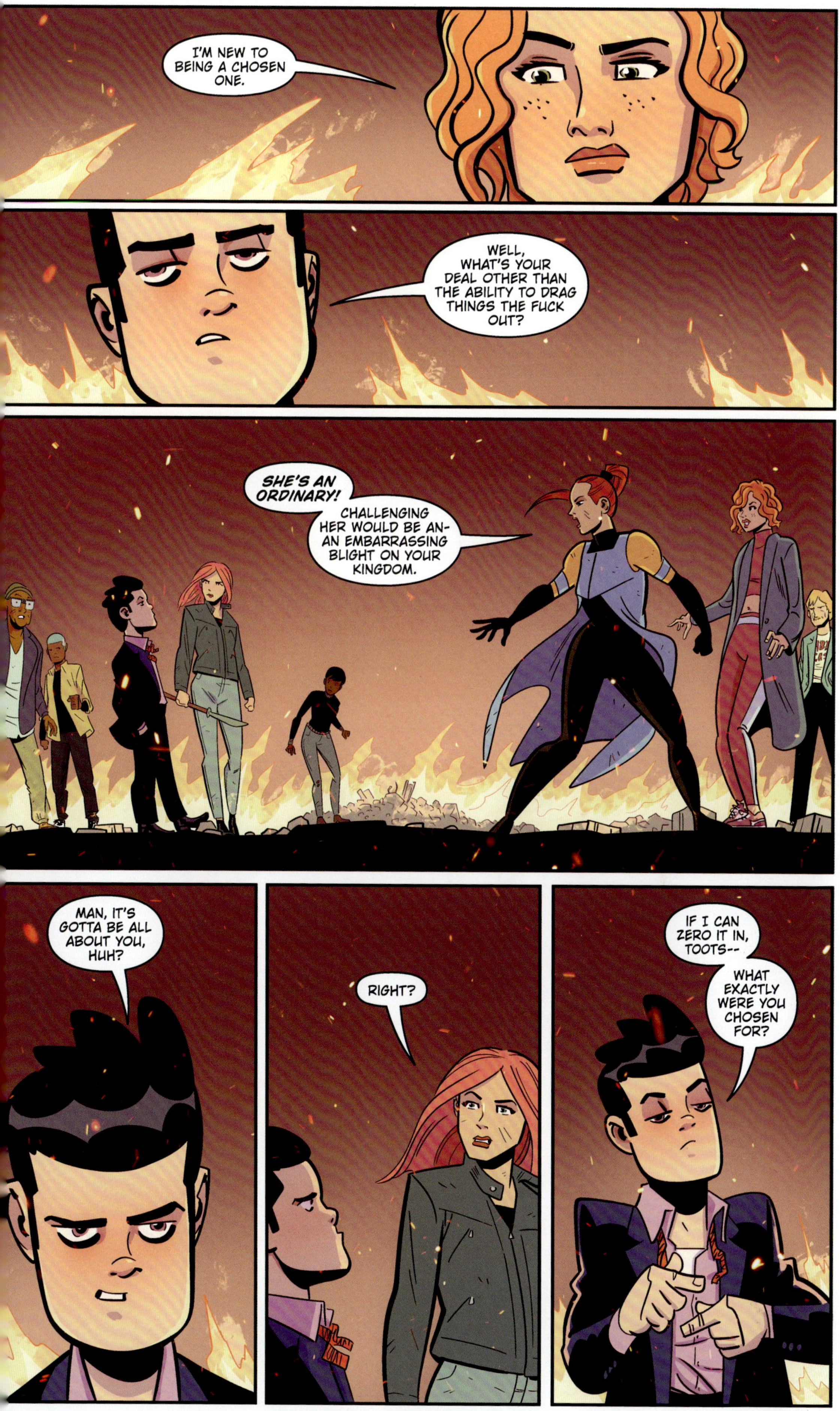
I'M NEW TO BEING A CHOSEN ONE.
WELL, WHAT'S YOUR DEAL OTHER THAN THE ABILITY TO DRAG THINGS THE FUCK OUT?
SHE'S AN ORDINARY!
CHALLENGING HER WOULD BE AN-AN EMBARRASSING BLIGHT ON YOUR KINGDOM.
MAN, IT'S GOTTA BE ALL ABOUT YOU, HUH?
RIGHT?
IF I CAN ZERO IT IN, TOOTS--
WHAT EXACTLY WERE YOU CHOSEN FOR?

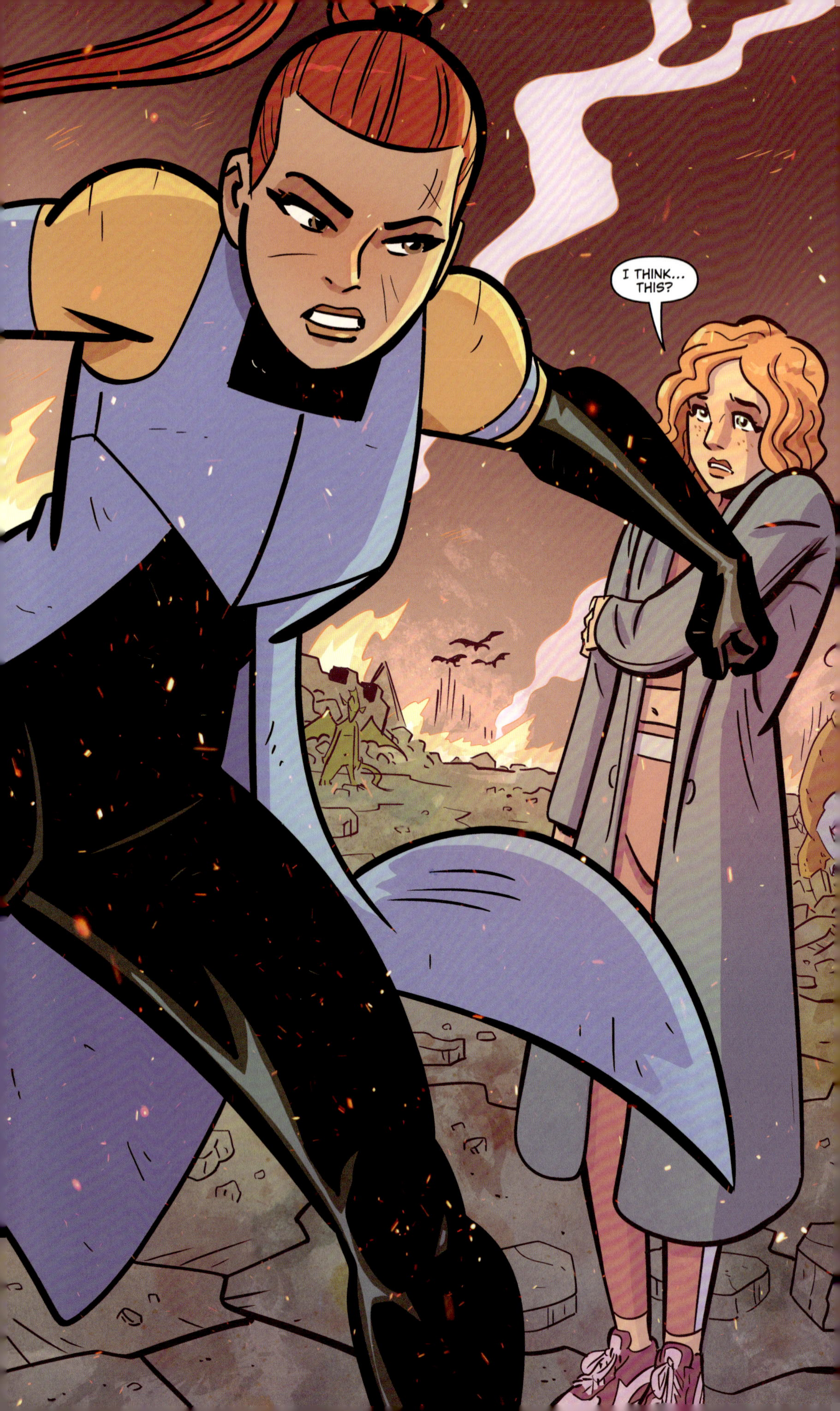
I THINK... THIS?

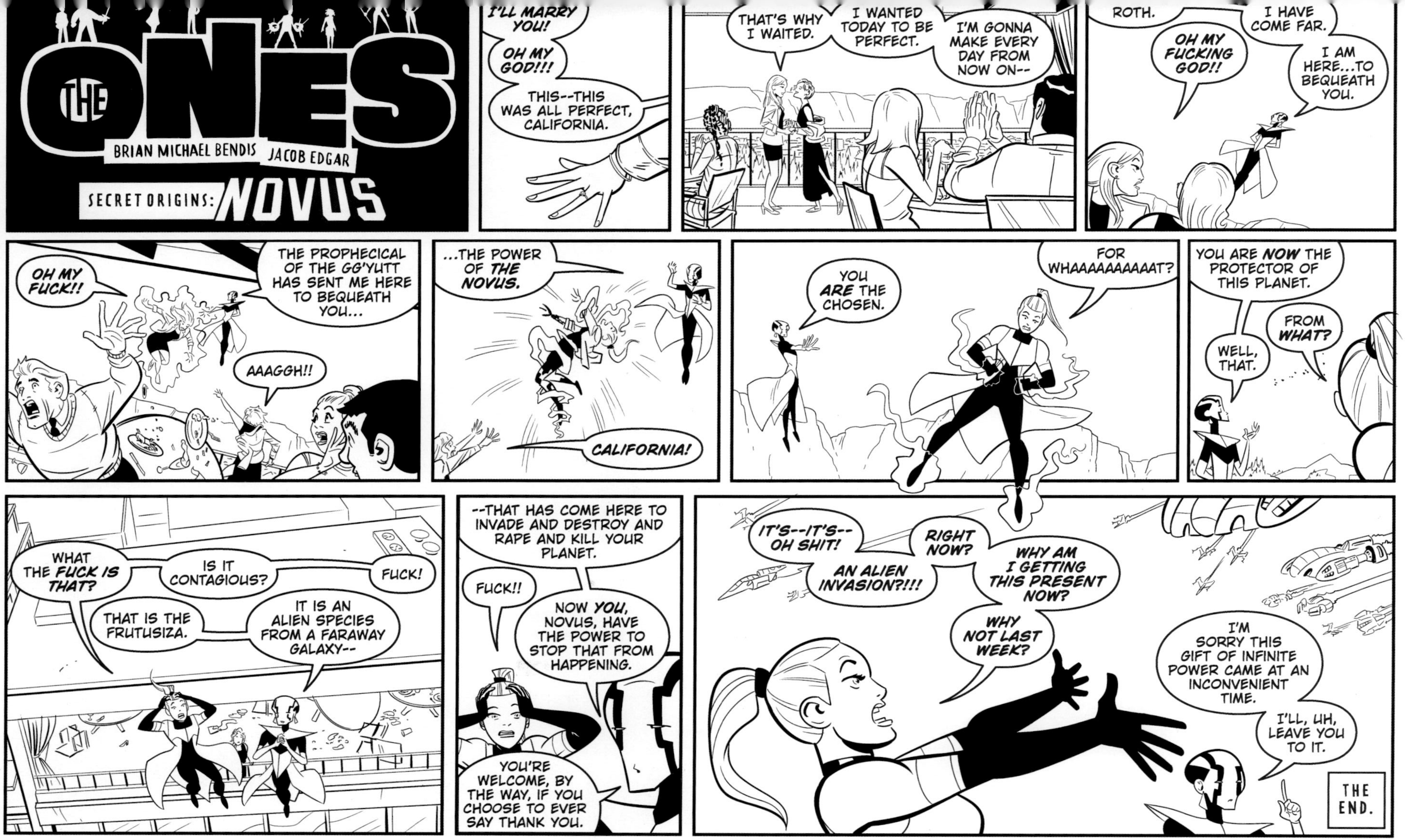
THE ONES
BRIAN MICHAEL BENDIS
JACOB EDGAR
SECRET ORIGINS: NOVUS
I'LL MARRY YOU!
OH MY GOD!!!
THIS--THIS WAS ALL PERFECT, CALIFORNIA.
THAT'S WHY I WAITED.
I WANTED TODAY TO BE PERFECT.
I'M GONNA MAKE EVERY DAY FROM NOW ON--
ROTH.
OH MY FUCKING GOD!!
I HAVE COME FAR.
I AM HERE...TO BEQUEATH YOU.
OH MY FUCK!!
THE PROPHECICAL OF THE GG'YUTT HAS SENT ME HERE TO BEQUEATH YOU...
AAAGGH!!
...THE POWER OF THE NOVUS.
CALIFORNIA!
YOU ARE THE CHOSEN.
FOR WHAAAAAAAAAAT?
YOU ARE NOW THE PROTECTOR OF THIS PLANET.
FROM WHAT?
WELL, THAT.
WHAT THE FUCK IS THAT?
IS IT CONTAGIOUS?
FUCK!
THAT IS THE FRUTUSIZA.
IT IS AN ALIEN SPECIES FROM A FARAWAY GALAXY--
--THAT HAS COME HERE TO INVADE AND DESTROY AND RAPE AND KILL YOUR PLANET.
FUCK!!
NOW YOU, NOVUS, HAVE THE POWER TO STOP THAT FROM HAPPENING.
YOU'RE WELCOME, BY THE WAY, IF YOU CHOOSE TO EVER SAY THANK YOU.
IT'S--IT'S--OH SHIT!
AN ALIEN INVASION?!!!
RIGHT NOW?
WHY AM I GETTING THIS PRESENT NOW?
WHY NOT LAST WEEK?
I'M SORRY THIS GIFT OF INFINITE POWER CAME AT AN INCONVENIENT TIME.
I'LL, UH, LEAVE YOU TO IT.
THE END.

FOUR

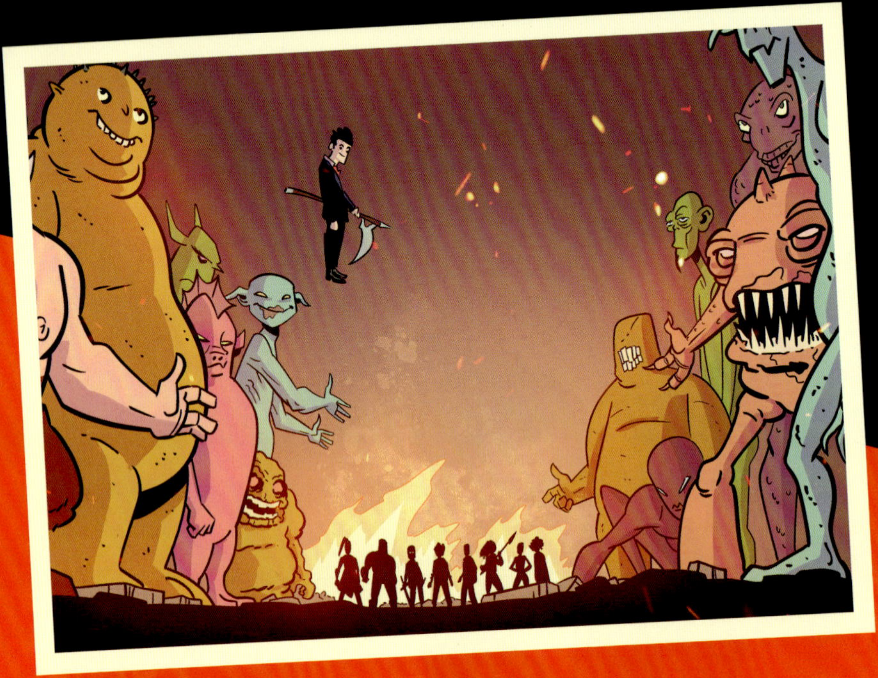

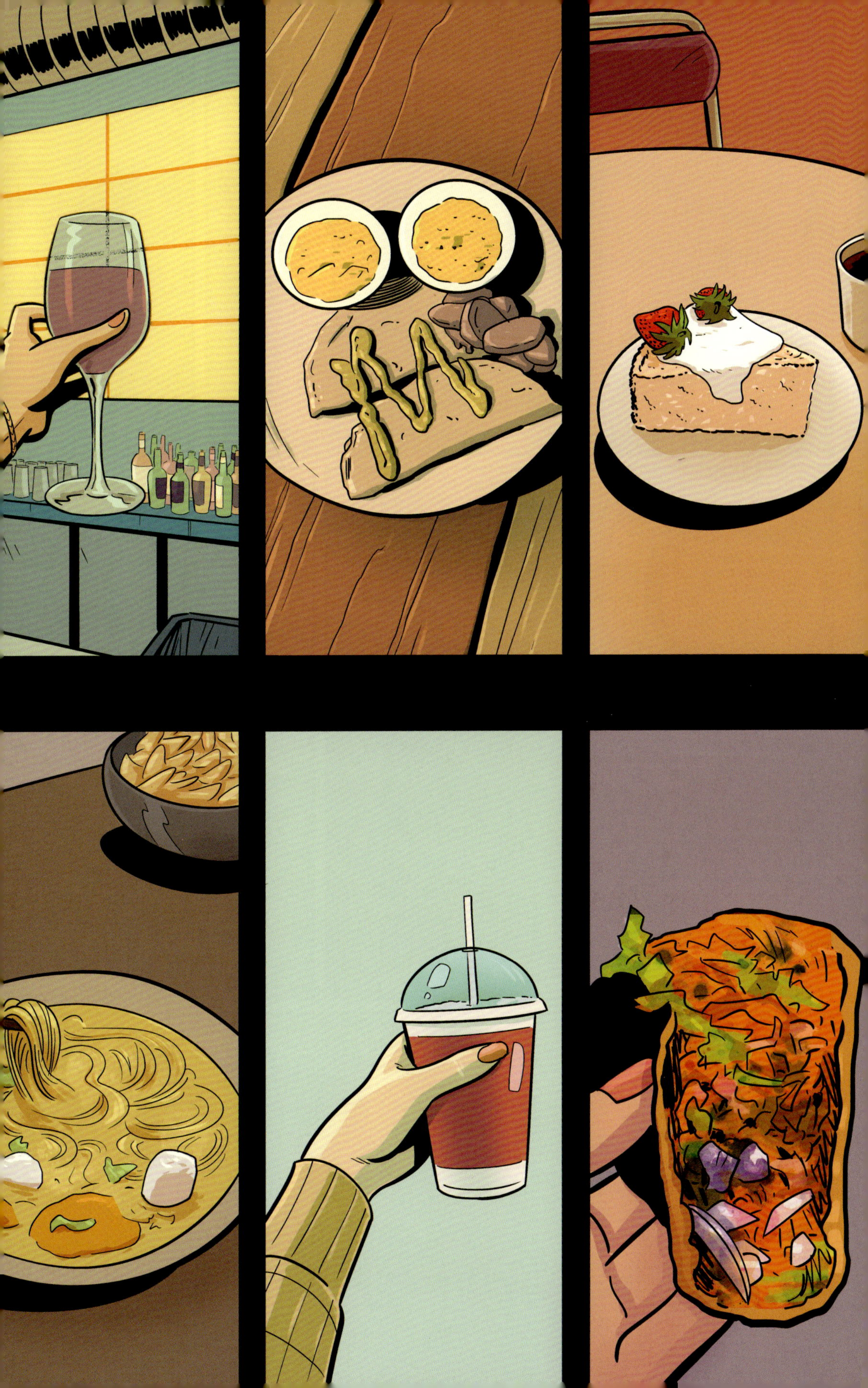

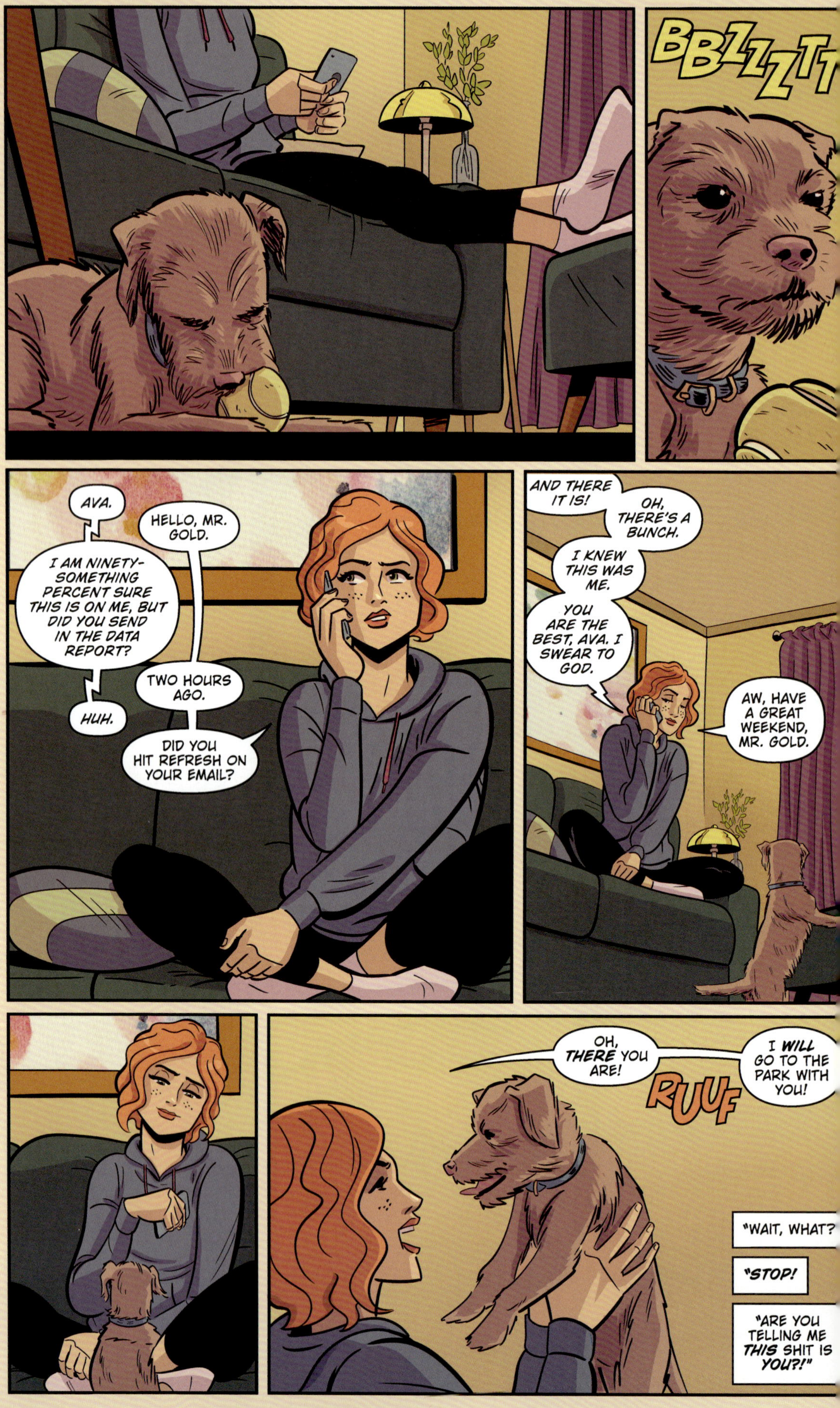
BBZZZTT
AVA.
HELLO, MR. GOLD.
I AM NINETY-SOMETHING PERCENT SURE THIS IS ON ME, BUT DID YOU SEND IN THE DATA REPORT?
TWO HOURS AGO.
HUH.
DID YOU HIT REFRESH ON YOUR EMAIL?
AND THERE IT IS!
OH, THERE'S A BUNCH.
I KNEW THIS WAS ME.
YOU ARE THE BEST, AVA. I SWEAR TO GOD.
AW, HAVE A GREAT WEEKEND, MR. GOLD.
OH, *THERE* YOU ARE!
RUUF
I *WILL* GO TO THE PARK WITH YOU!
"WAIT, WHAT?
"*STOP!*
"ARE YOU TELLING ME *THIS* SHIT IS *YOU?!*"

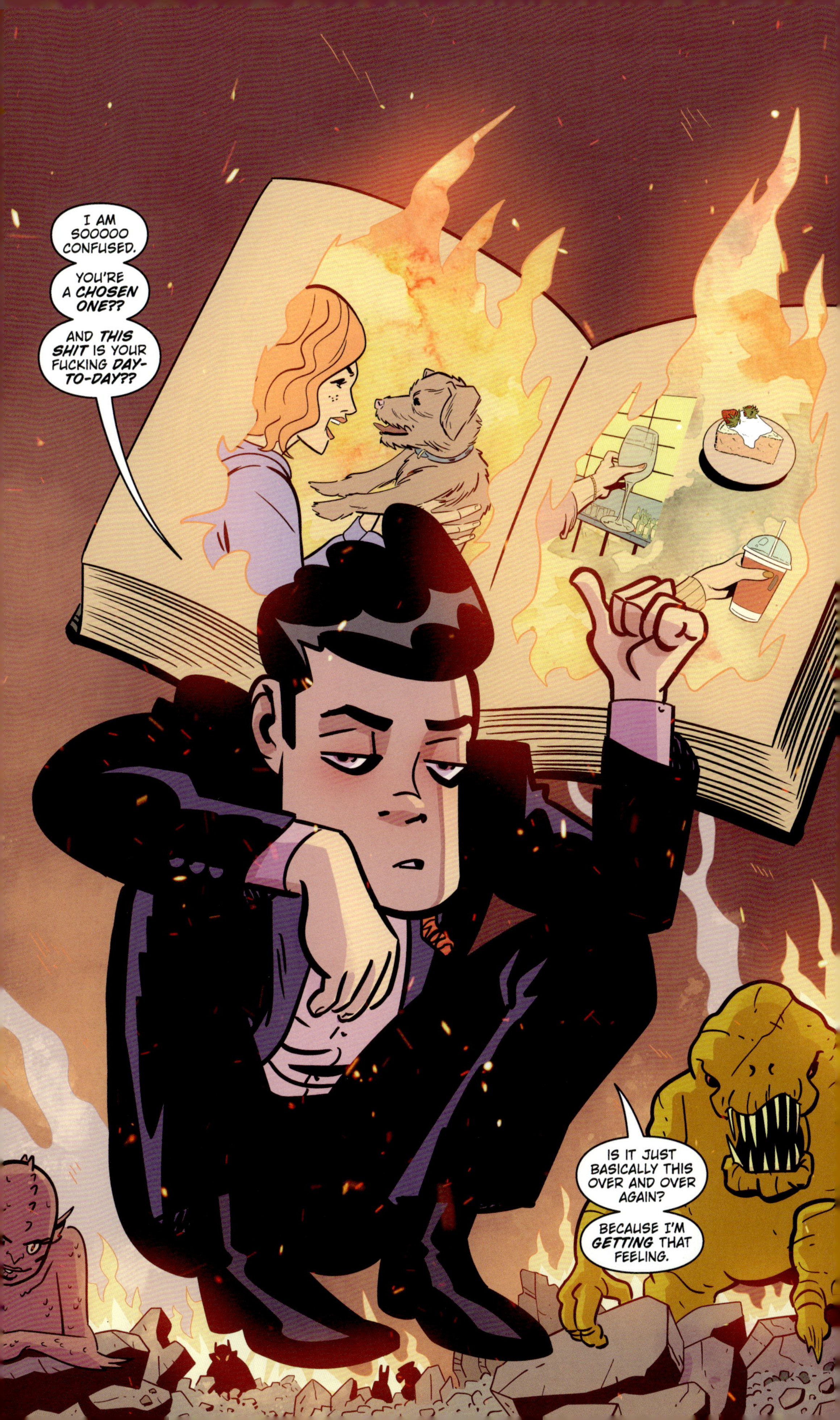
I AM SOOOOO CONFUSED.
YOU'RE A **CHOSEN ONE??**
AND **THIS SHIT** IS YOUR FUCKING **DAY-TO-DAY??**
IS IT JUST BASICALLY THIS OVER AND OVER AGAIN?
BECAUSE I'M **GETTING** THAT FEELING.

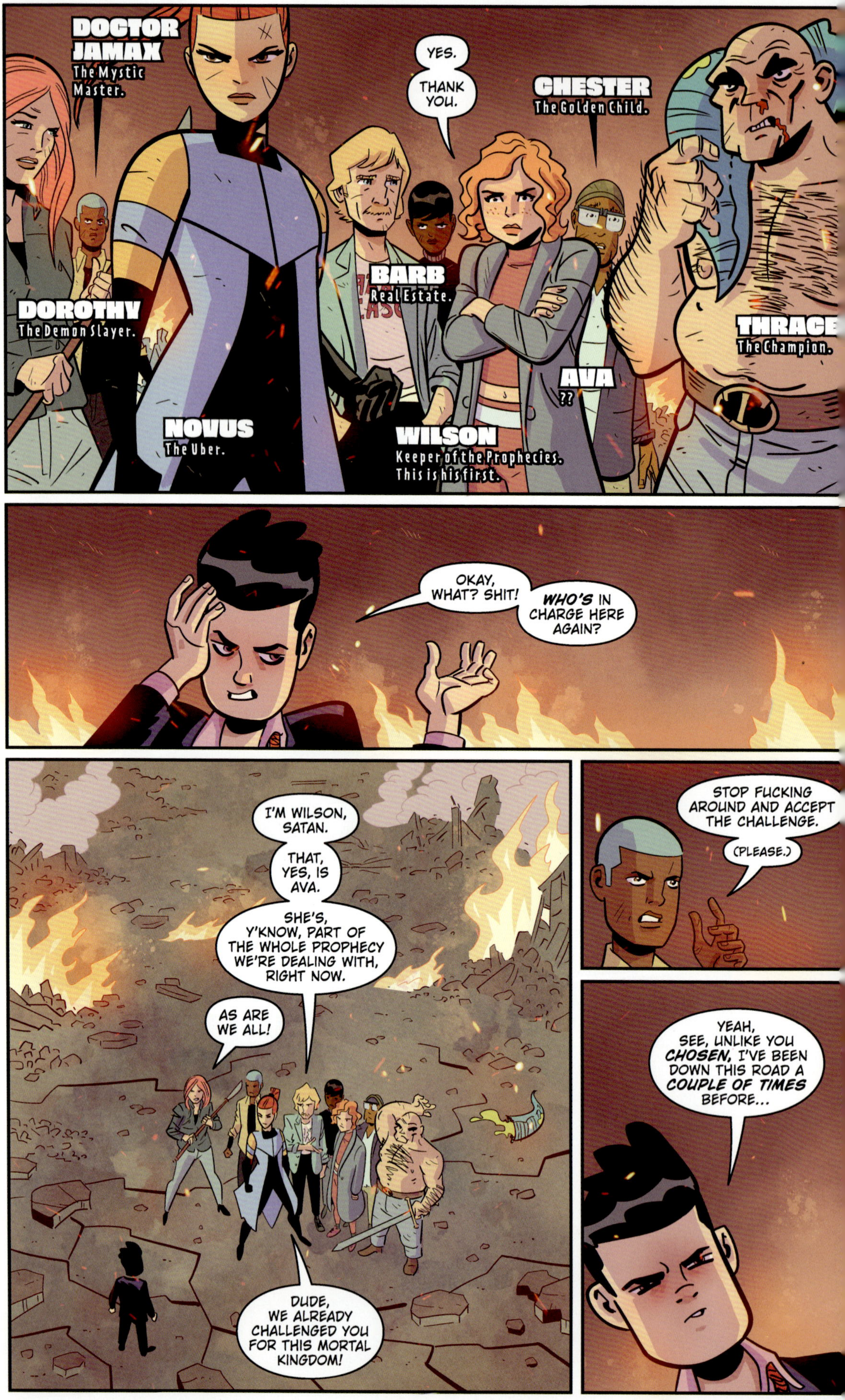
DOCTOR JAMAX
The Mystic Master.
YES.
THANK YOU.
CHESTER
The Golden Child.
DOROTHY
The Demon Slayer.
BARB
Real Estate.
THRACE
The Champion.
AVA
??
NOVUS
The Uber.
WILSON
Keeper of the Prophecies. This is his first.
OKAY, WHAT? SHIT!
WHO'S IN CHARGE HERE AGAIN?
I'M WILSON, SATAN.
THAT, YES, IS AVA.
SHE'S, Y'KNOW, PART OF THE WHOLE PROPHECY WE'RE DEALING WITH, RIGHT NOW.
AS ARE WE ALL!
DUDE, WE ALREADY CHALLENGED YOU FOR THIS MORTAL KINGDOM!
STOP FUCKING AROUND AND ACCEPT THE CHALLENGE.
(PLEASE.)
YEAH, SEE, UNLIKE YOU CHOSEN, I'VE BEEN DOWN THIS ROAD A COUPLE OF TIMES BEFORE...

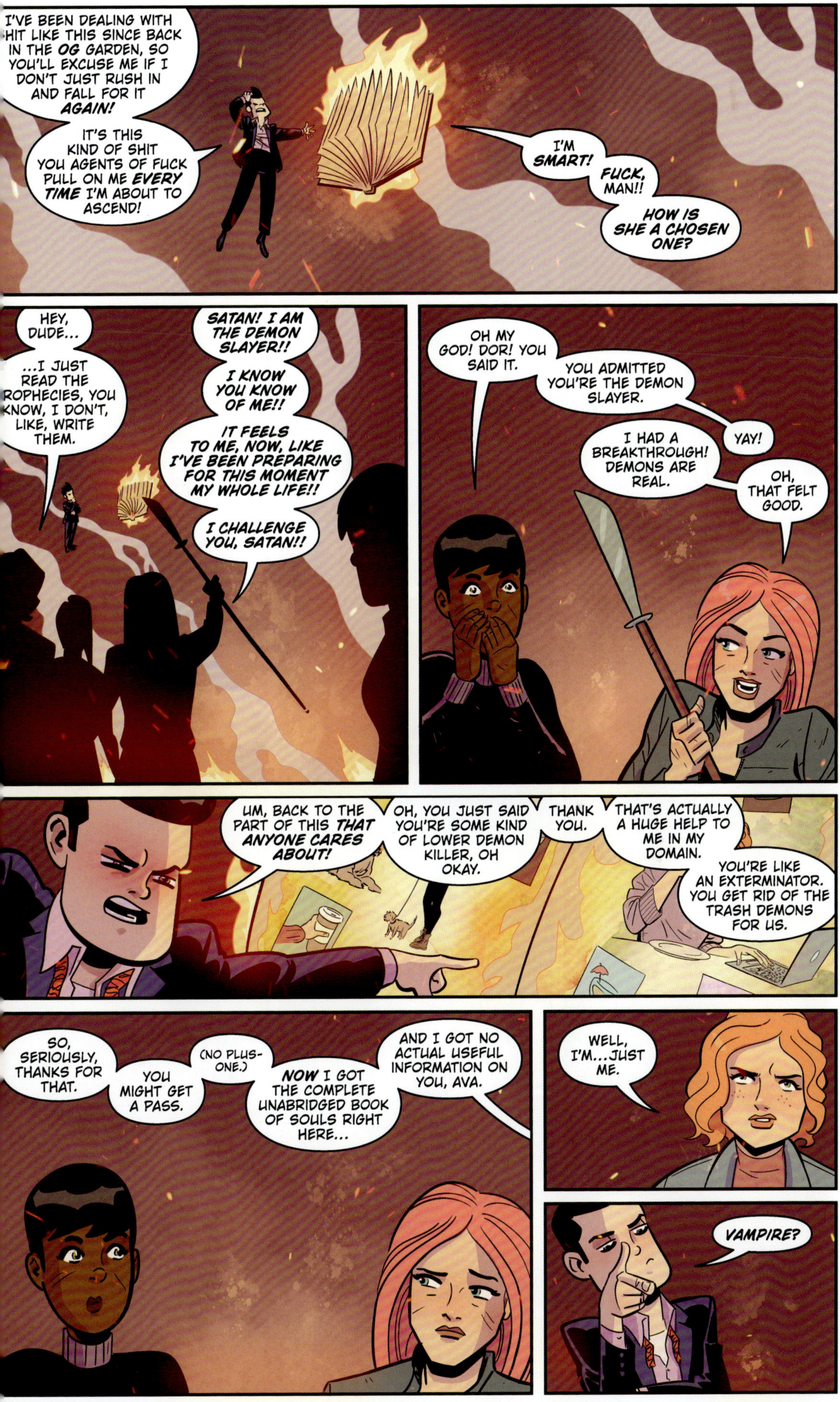

I'VE BEEN DEALING WITH SHIT LIKE THIS SINCE BACK IN THE OG GARDEN, SO YOU'LL EXCUSE ME IF I DON'T JUST RUSH IN AND FALL FOR IT AGAIN!
IT'S THIS KIND OF SHIT YOU AGENTS OF FUCK PULL ON ME EVERY TIME I'M ABOUT TO ASCEND!
I'M SMART!
FUCK, MAN!!
HOW IS SHE A CHOSEN ONE?
HEY, DUDE...
...I JUST READ THE PROPHECIES, YOU KNOW, I DON'T, LIKE, WRITE THEM.
SATAN! I AM THE DEMON SLAYER!!
I KNOW YOU KNOW OF ME!!
IT FEELS TO ME, NOW, LIKE I'VE BEEN PREPARING FOR THIS MOMENT MY WHOLE LIFE!!
I CHALLENGE YOU, SATAN!!
OH MY GOD! DOR! YOU SAID IT.
YOU ADMITTED YOU'RE THE DEMON SLAYER.
YAY!
I HAD A BREAKTHROUGH! DEMONS ARE REAL.
OH, THAT FELT GOOD.
UM, BACK TO THE PART OF THIS THAT ANYONE CARES ABOUT!
OH, YOU JUST SAID YOU'RE SOME KIND OF LOWER DEMON KILLER, OH OKAY.
THANK YOU.
THAT'S ACTUALLY A HUGE HELP TO ME IN MY DOMAIN.
YOU'RE LIKE AN EXTERMINATOR. YOU GET RID OF THE TRASH DEMONS FOR US.
SO, SERIOUSLY, THANKS FOR THAT.
YOU MIGHT GET A PASS.
(NO PLUS-ONE.)
NOW I GOT THE COMPLETE UNABRIDGED BOOK OF SOULS RIGHT HERE...
AND I GOT NO ACTUAL USEFUL INFORMATION ON YOU, AVA.
WELL, I'M...JUST ME.
VAMPIRE?

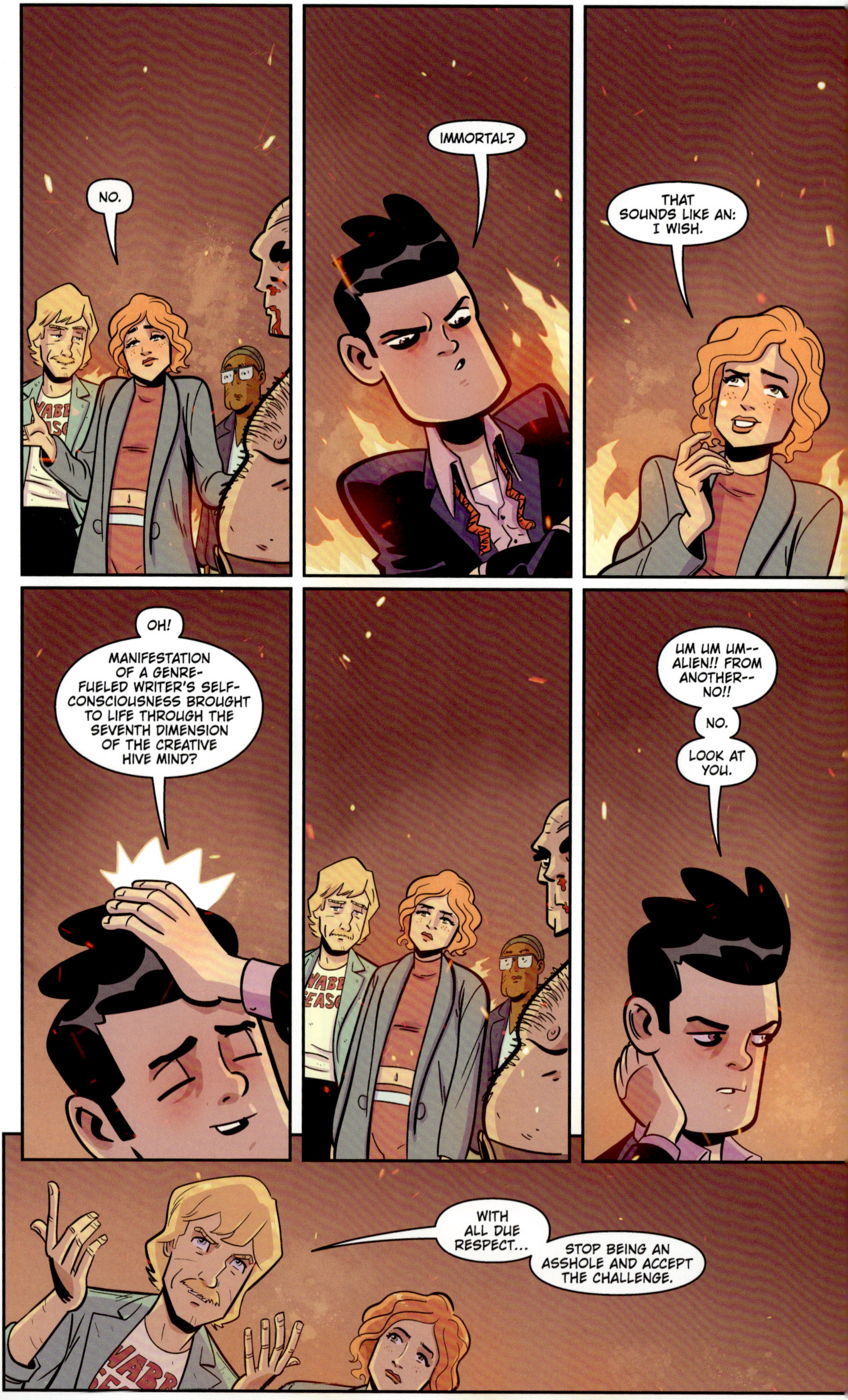
NO.
IMMORTAL?
THAT SOUNDS LIKE AN: I WISH.
OH!
MANIFESTATION OF A GENRE-FUELED WRITER'S SELF-CONSCIOUSNESS BROUGHT TO LIFE THROUGH THE SEVENTH DIMENSION OF THE CREATIVE HIVE MIND?
UM UM UM-- ALIEN!! FROM ANOTHER-- NO!!
NO.
LOOK AT YOU.
WITH ALL DUE RESPECT...
STOP BEING AN ASSHOLE AND ACCEPT THE CHALLENGE.

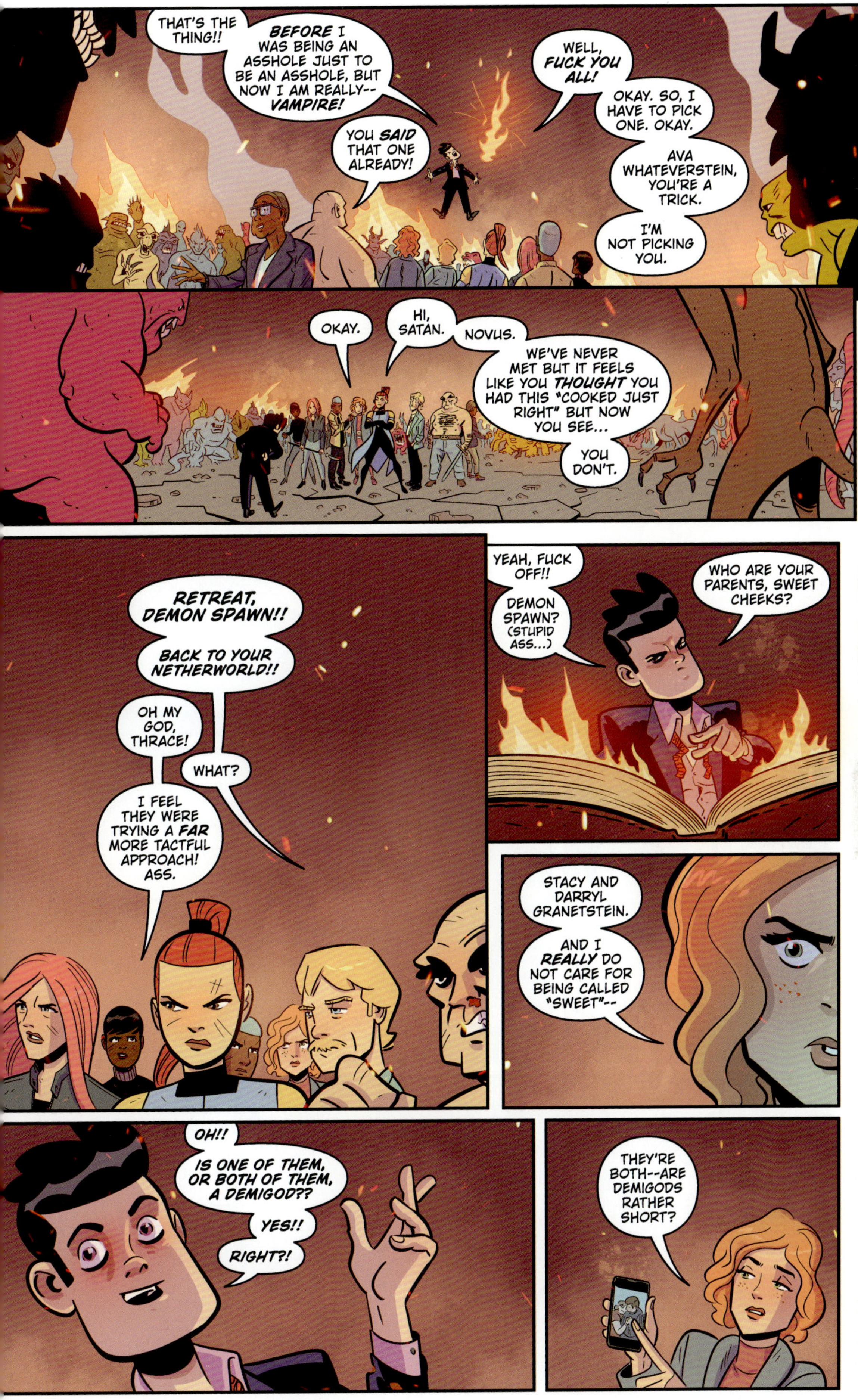

THAT'S THE THING!!
BEFORE I WAS BEING AN ASSHOLE JUST TO BE AN ASSHOLE, BUT NOW I AM REALLY-- VAMPIRE!
YOU SAID THAT ONE ALREADY!
WELL, FUCK YOU ALL!
OKAY. SO, I HAVE TO PICK ONE. OKAY.
AVA WHATEVERSTEIN, YOU'RE A TRICK.
I'M NOT PICKING YOU.
OKAY.
HI, SATAN.
NOVUS.
WE'VE NEVER MET BUT IT FEELS LIKE YOU THOUGHT YOU HAD THIS "COOKED JUST RIGHT" BUT NOW YOU SEE...
YOU DON'T.
RETREAT, DEMON SPAWN!!
BACK TO YOUR NETHERWORLD!!
OH MY GOD, THRACE!
WHAT?
I FEEL THEY WERE TRYING A FAR MORE TACTFUL APPROACH! ASS.
YEAH, FUCK OFF!!
DEMON SPAWN? (STUPID ASS...)
WHO ARE YOUR PARENTS, SWEET CHEEKS?
STACY AND DARRYL GRANETSTEIN.
AND I REALLY DO NOT CARE FOR BEING CALLED "SWEET"--
OH!!
IS ONE OF THEM, OR BOTH OF THEM, A DEMIGOD??
YES!!
RIGHT?!
THEY'RE BOTH--ARE DEMIGODS RATHER SHORT?

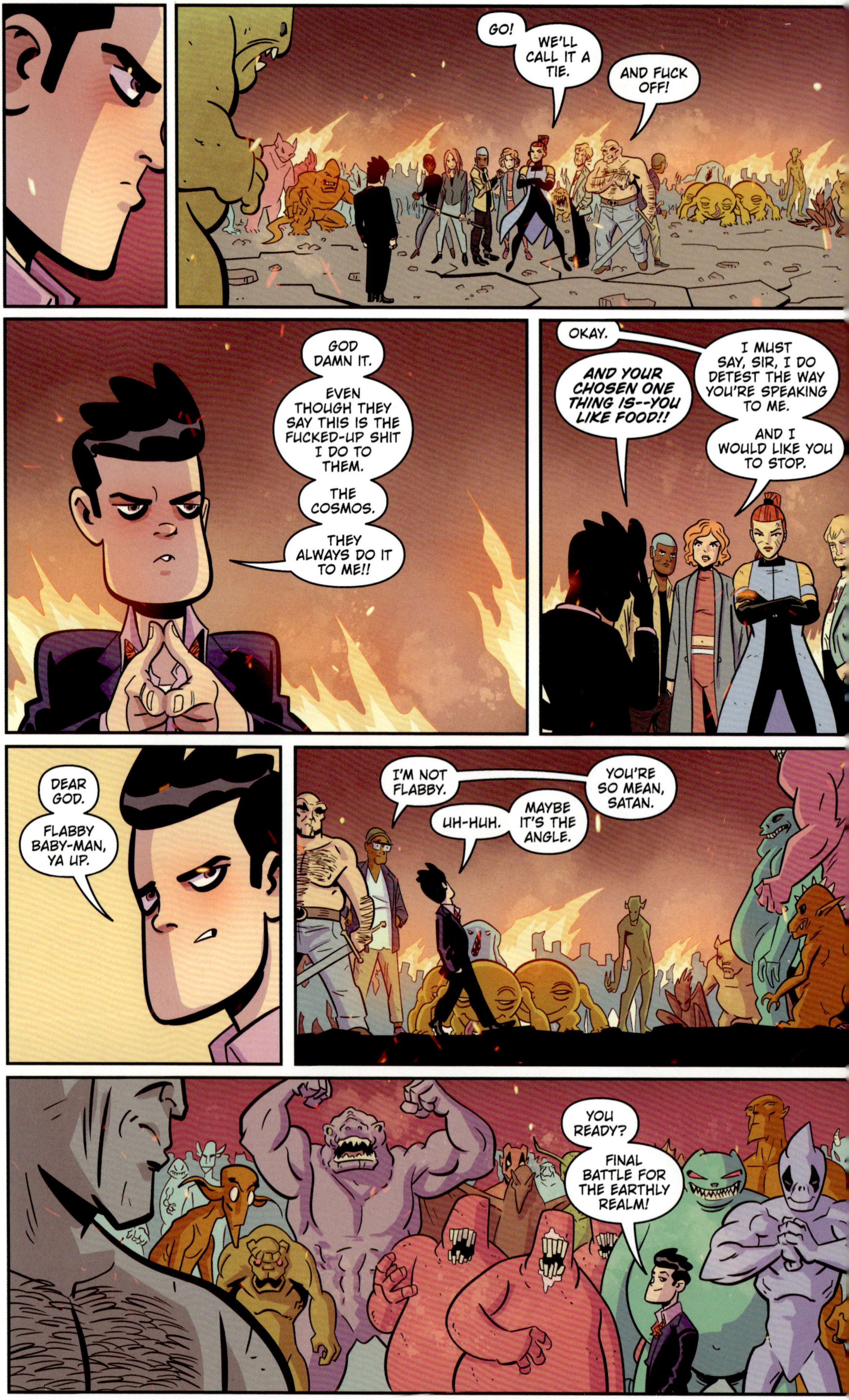
GO!
WE'LL CALL IT A TIE.
AND FUCK OFF!
GOD DAMN IT.
EVEN THOUGH THEY SAY THIS IS THE FUCKED-UP SHIT I DO TO THEM.
THE COSMOS.
THEY ALWAYS DO IT TO ME!!
OKAY.
I MUST SAY, SIR, I DO DETEST THE WAY YOU'RE SPEAKING TO ME.
AND YOUR CHOSEN ONE THING IS--YOU LIKE FOOD!!
AND I WOULD LIKE YOU TO STOP.
DEAR GOD.
FLABBY BABY-MAN, YA UP.
I'M NOT FLABBY.
YOU'RE SO MEAN, SATAN.
UH-HUH.
MAYBE IT'S THE ANGLE.
YOU READY?
FINAL BATTLE FOR THE EARTHLY REALM!

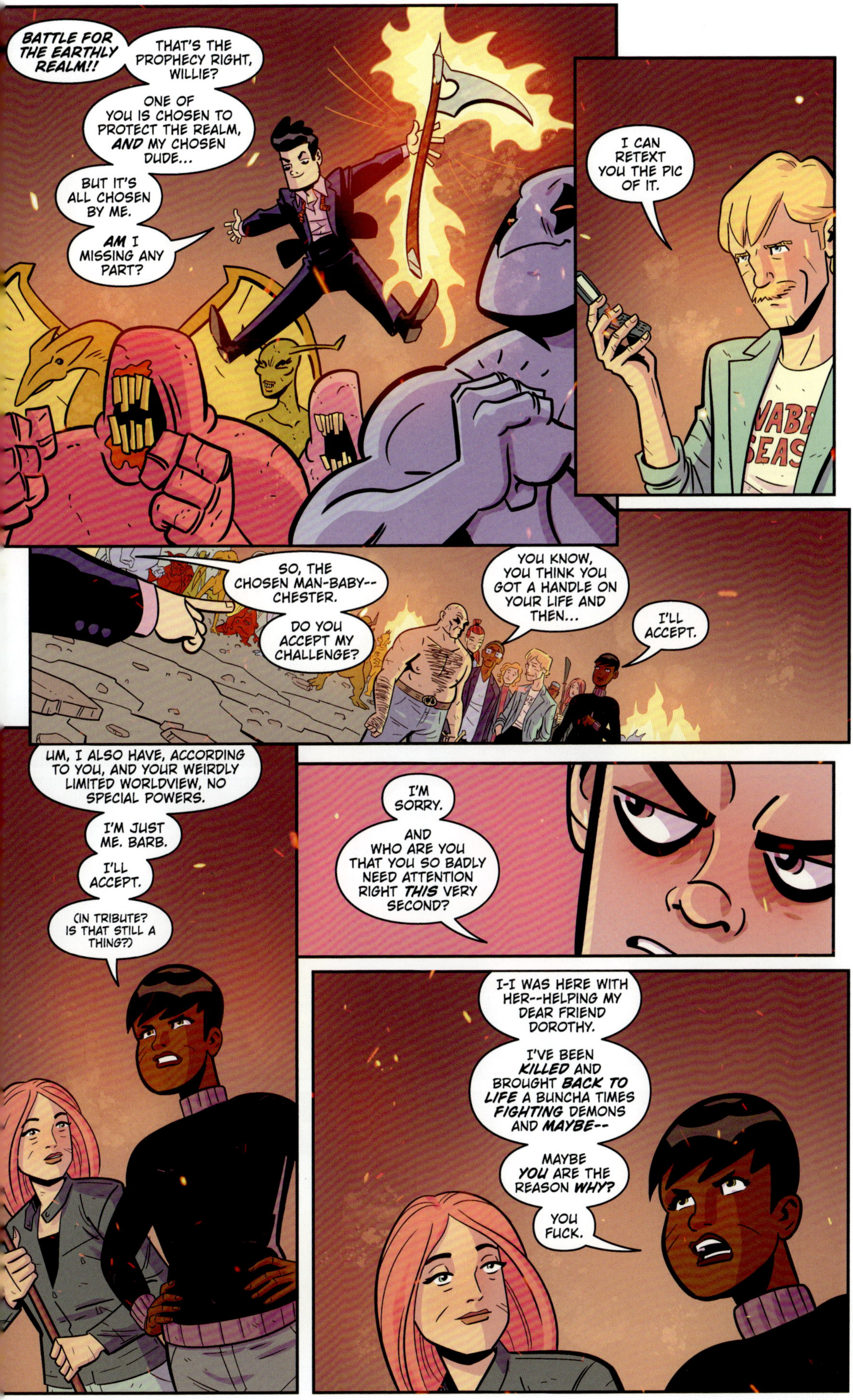

BATTLE FOR THE EARTHLY REALM!!
THAT'S THE PROPHECY RIGHT, WILLIE?
ONE OF YOU IS CHOSEN TO PROTECT THE REALM, AND MY CHOSEN DUDE...
BUT IT'S ALL CHOSEN BY ME.
AM I MISSING ANY PART?
I CAN RETEXT YOU THE PIC OF IT.
SO, THE CHOSEN MAN-BABY--CHESTER.
DO YOU ACCEPT MY CHALLENGE?
YOU KNOW, YOU THINK YOU GOT A HANDLE ON YOUR LIFE AND THEN...
I'LL ACCEPT.
UM, I ALSO HAVE, ACCORDING TO YOU, AND YOUR WEIRDLY LIMITED WORLDVIEW, NO SPECIAL POWERS.
I'M JUST ME. BARB.
I'LL ACCEPT.
(IN TRIBUTE? IS THAT STILL A THING?)
I'M SORRY.
AND WHO ARE YOU THAT YOU SO BADLY NEED ATTENTION RIGHT THIS VERY SECOND?
I-I WAS HERE WITH HER--HELPING MY DEAR FRIEND DOROTHY.
I'VE BEEN KILLED AND BROUGHT BACK TO LIFE A BUNCHA TIMES FIGHTING DEMONS AND MAYBE--
MAYBE YOU ARE THE REASON WHY?
YOU FUCK.

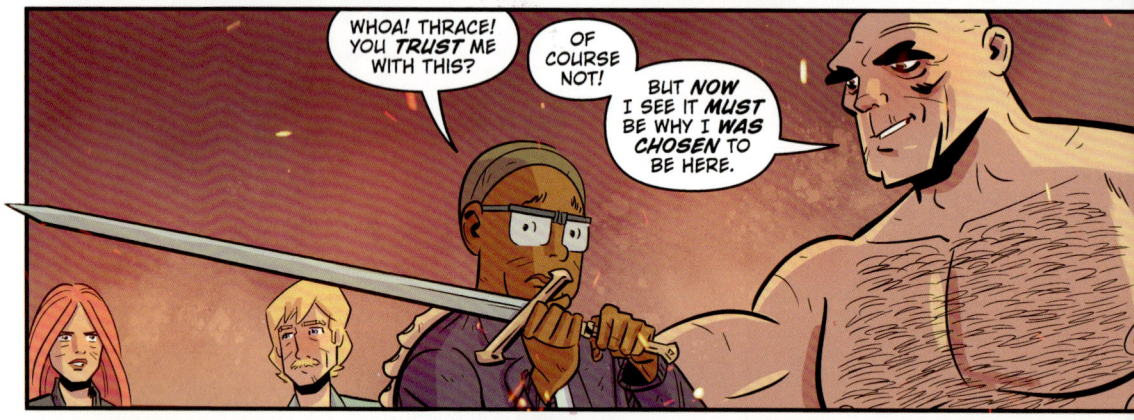

ANYWAY, CHESTER, I CHALLENGE YOU FOR THE EARTHLY REALM.

I ACCEPT. (YOU FUCK.)

WELL, PREPARE HIM FOR BATTLE WHILE I PICK MY WARRIOR.

YOUNG WARRIOR, I OFFER YOU MY PRIZED WEAPON.

MY TRUE RIGHT ARM!

THE ANCIENT AND ALL-POWERFUL BLOODSPILLER.

WHOA! THRACE! YOU TRUST ME WITH THIS?

OF COURSE NOT! BUT NOW I SEE IT MUST BE WHY I WAS CHOSEN TO BE HERE.

AND TAKE THIS TOO-- THE NECRO BLADE.

THE TRUE DEMON KILLER.

IT HAS TASTED DEMON BLOOD FOR CENTURIES.

IT WILL GUIDE YOUR HAND.

UH, THANKS.

DID YOU HAVE THIS THE ENTIRE TIME?

HMM? YEAH. UH-HUH.

OH YEAH, THE WHOLE TIME.

YOU DID? I NEVER SAW IT.

HEY, CHESTER, MAN, THIS IS THE AMULET OF TUQATONG.

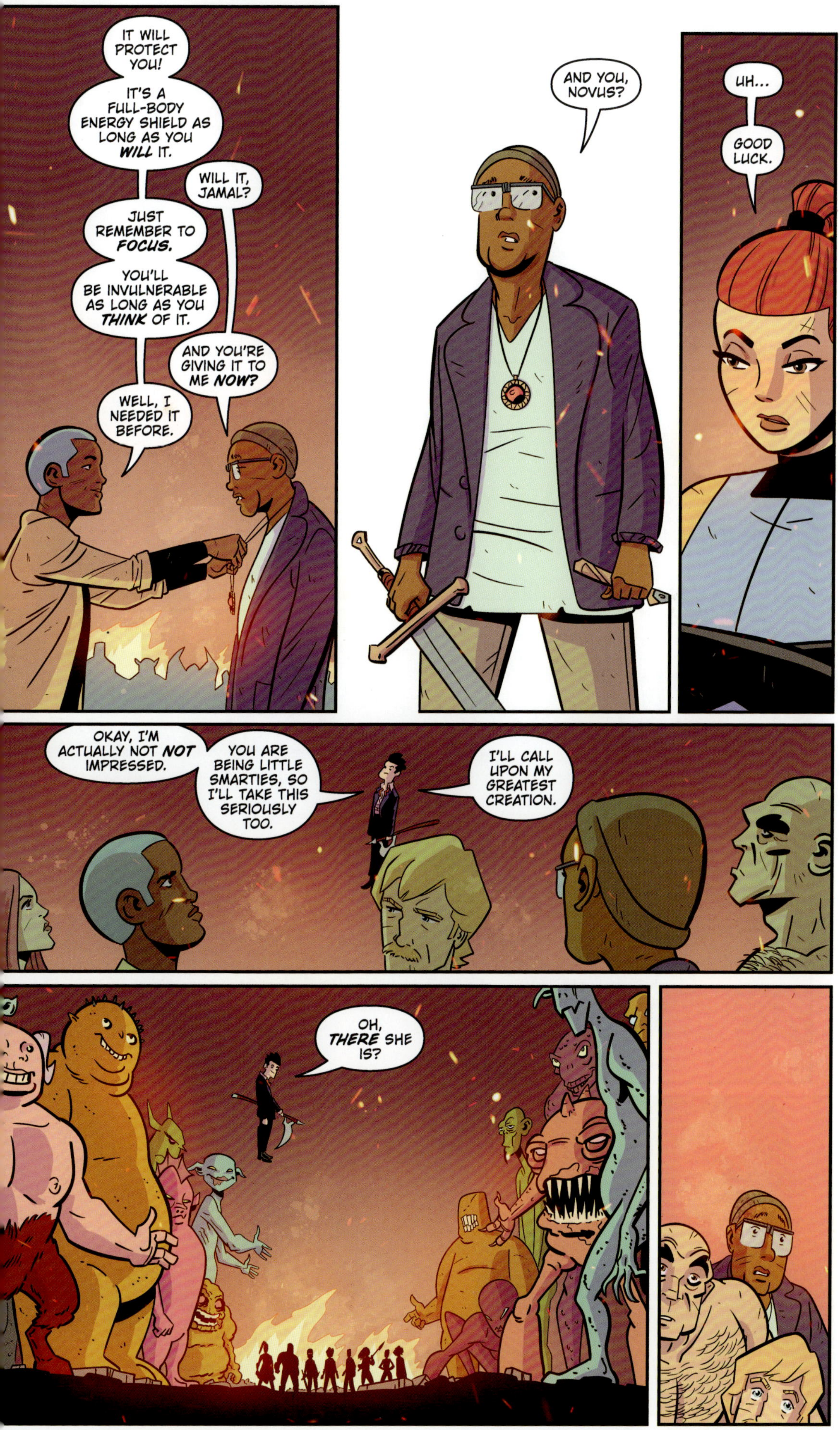
IT WILL PROTECT YOU!
IT'S A FULL-BODY ENERGY SHIELD AS LONG AS YOU WILL IT.
WILL IT, JAMAL?
JUST REMEMBER TO FOCUS.
YOU'LL BE INVULNERABLE AS LONG AS YOU THINK OF IT.
AND YOU'RE GIVING IT TO ME NOW?
WELL, I NEEDED IT BEFORE.
AND YOU, NOVUS?
UH...
GOOD LUCK.
OKAY, I'M ACTUALLY NOT NOT IMPRESSED.
YOU ARE BEING LITTLE SMARTIES, SO I'LL TAKE THIS SERIOUSLY TOO.
I'LL CALL UPON MY GREATEST CREATION.
OH, THERE SHE IS?

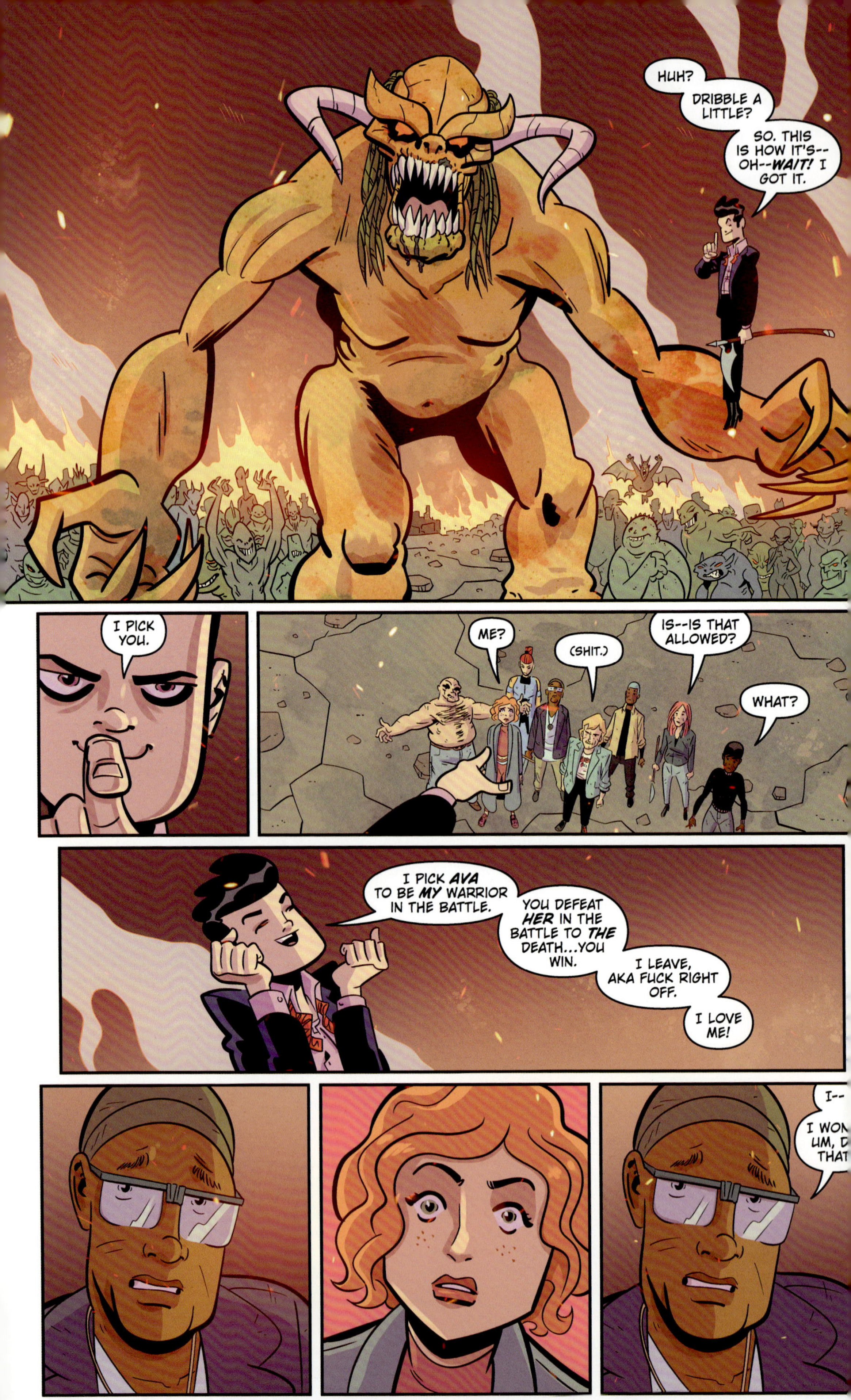

HUH?
DRIBBLE A LITTLE?
SO. THIS IS HOW IT'S-- OH--*WAIT!* I GOT IT.
I PICK YOU.
ME?
(SHIT.)
IS--IS THAT ALLOWED?
WHAT?
I PICK *AVA* TO BE *MY* WARRIOR IN THE BATTLE.
YOU DEFEAT *HER* IN THE BATTLE TO *THE* DEATH...YOU WIN.
I LEAVE, AKA FUCK RIGHT OFF.
I LOVE ME!
I--

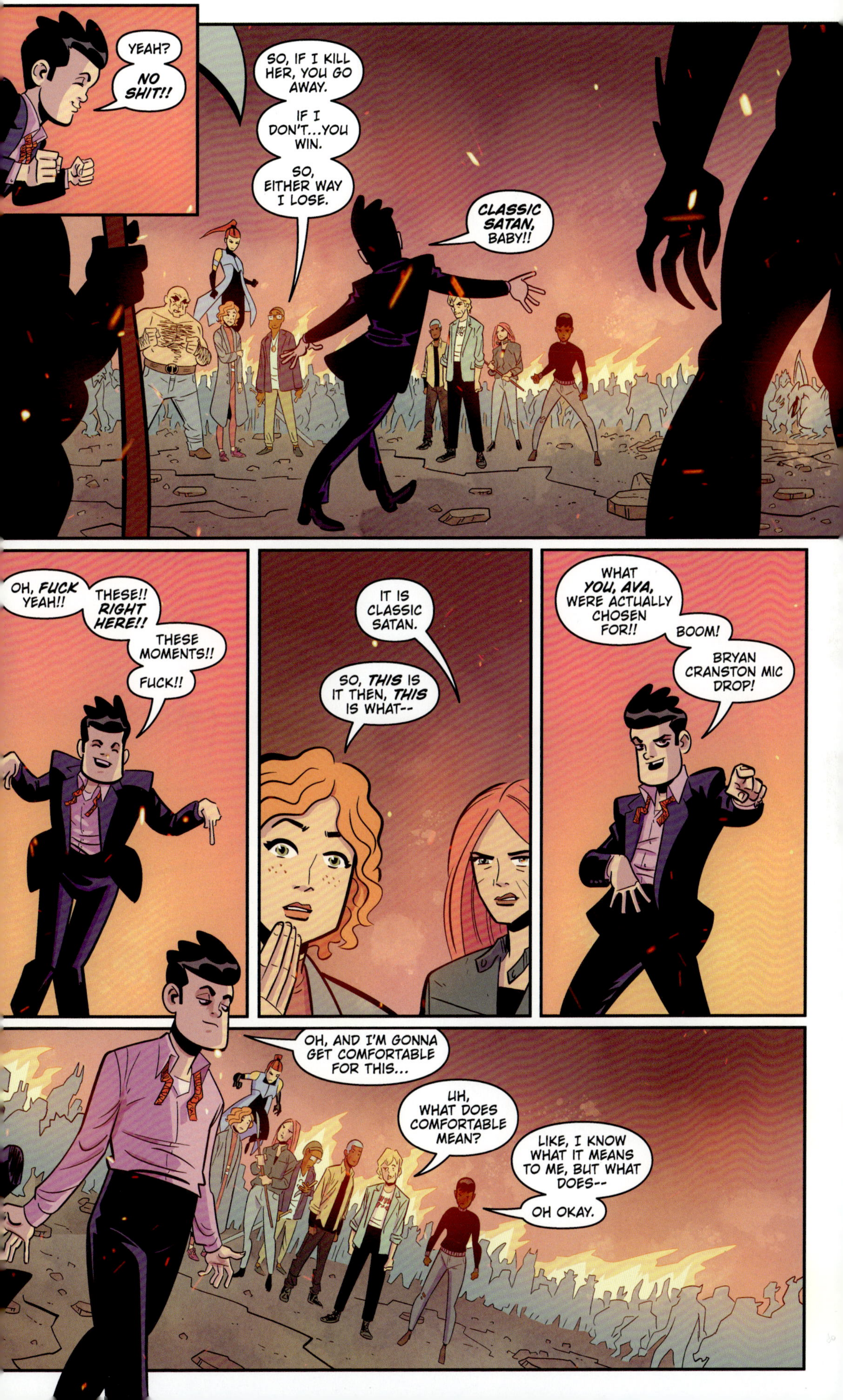
YEAH? NO SHIT!!
SO, IF I KILL HER, YOU GO AWAY.
IF I DON'T...YOU WIN.
SO, EITHER WAY I LOSE.
CLASSIC SATAN, BABY!!
OH, FUCK YEAH!!
THESE!! RIGHT HERE!!
THESE MOMENTS!!
FUCK!!
IT IS CLASSIC SATAN.
SO, THIS IS IT THEN, THIS IS WHAT--
WHAT YOU, AVA, WERE ACTUALLY CHOSEN FOR!!
BOOM!
BRYAN CRANSTON MIC DROP!
OH, AND I'M GONNA GET COMFORTABLE FOR THIS...
UH, WHAT DOES COMFORTABLE MEAN?
LIKE, I KNOW WHAT IT MEANS TO ME, BUT WHAT DOES--
OH OKAY.

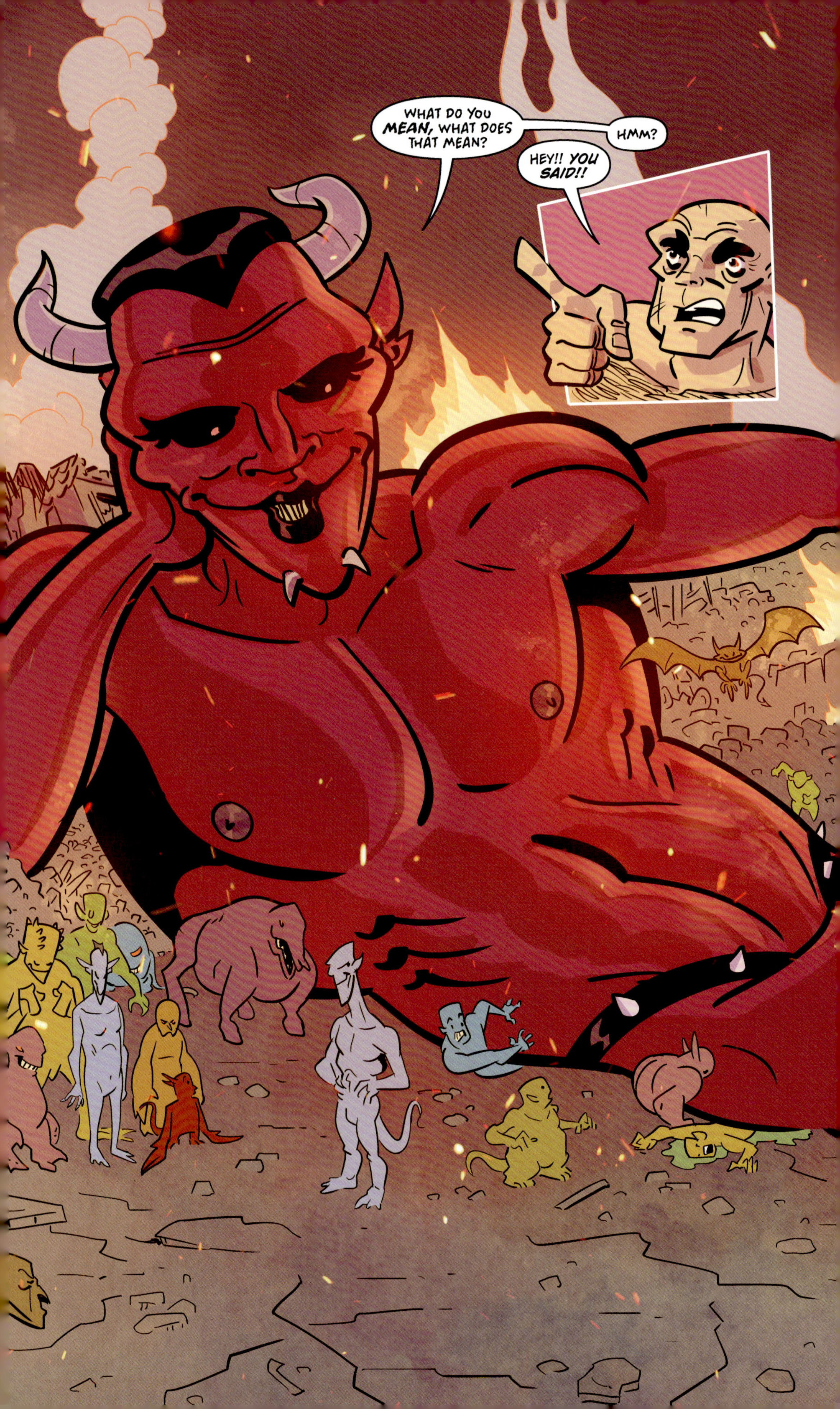
WHAT DO YOU MEAN, WHAT DOES THAT MEAN?
HMM?
HEY!! YOU SAID!!

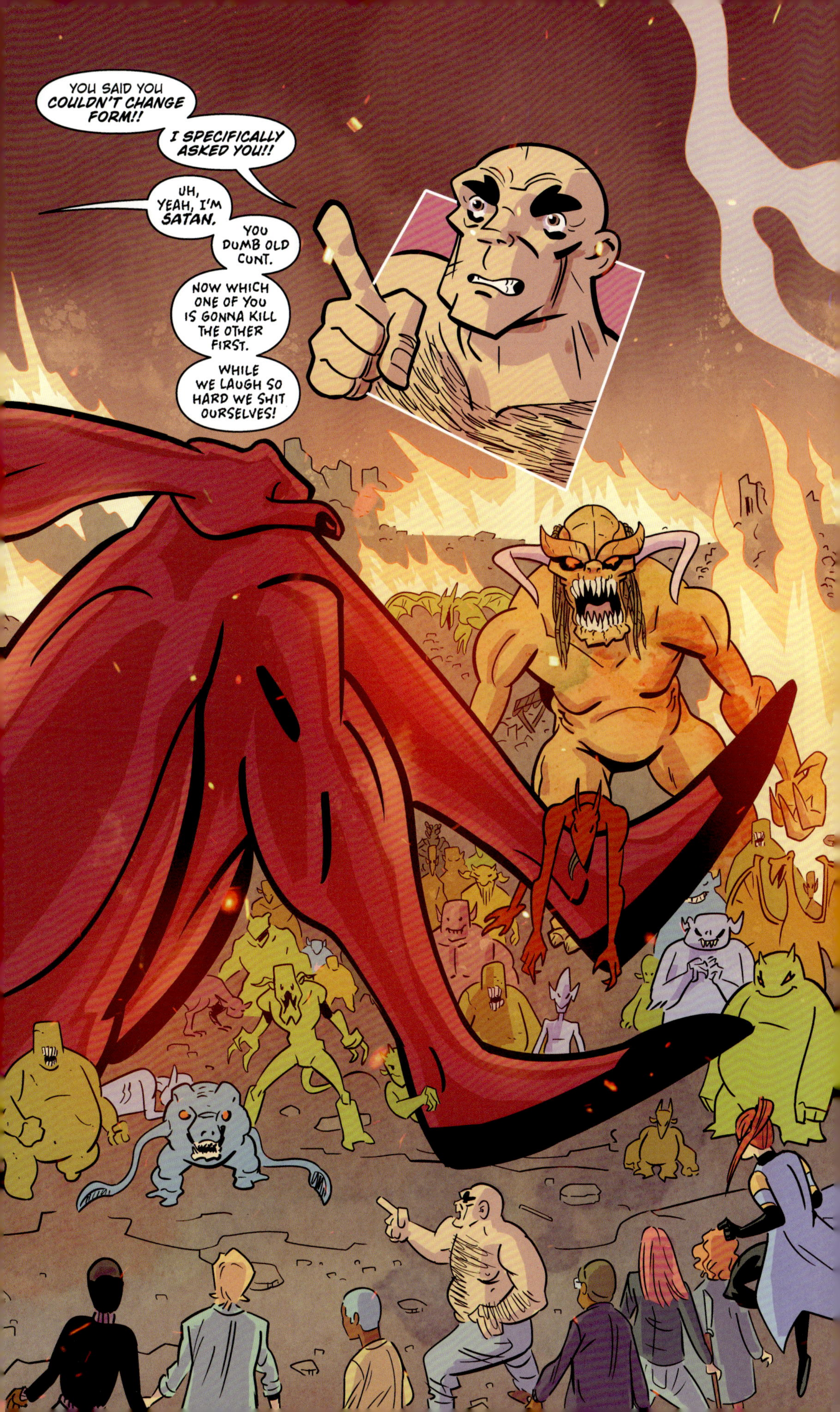
YOU SAID YOU COULDN'T CHANGE FORM!!
I SPECIFICALLY ASKED YOU!!
UH, YEAH, I'M SATAN.
YOU DUMB OLD CUNT.
NOW WHICH ONE OF YOU IS GONNA KILL THE OTHER FIRST.
WHILE WE LAUGH SO HARD WE SHIT OURSELVES!

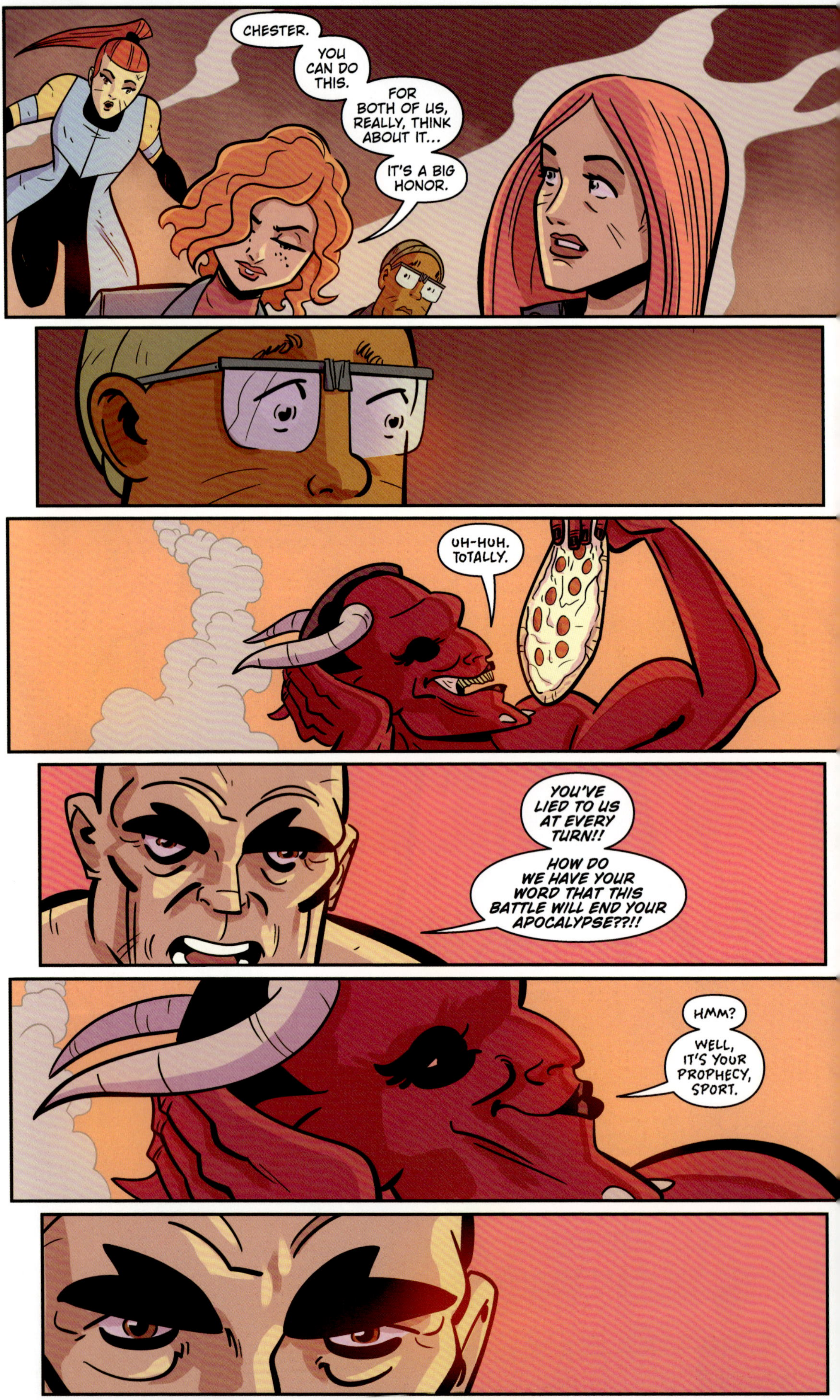

CHESTER.
YOU CAN DO THIS.
FOR BOTH OF US, REALLY, THINK ABOUT IT...
IT'S A BIG HONOR.
UH-HUH. TOTALLY.
YOU'VE LIED TO US AT EVERY TURN!!
HOW DO WE HAVE YOUR WORD THAT THIS BATTLE WILL END YOUR APOCALYPSE??!!
HMM?
WELL, IT'S YOUR PROPHECY, SPORT.

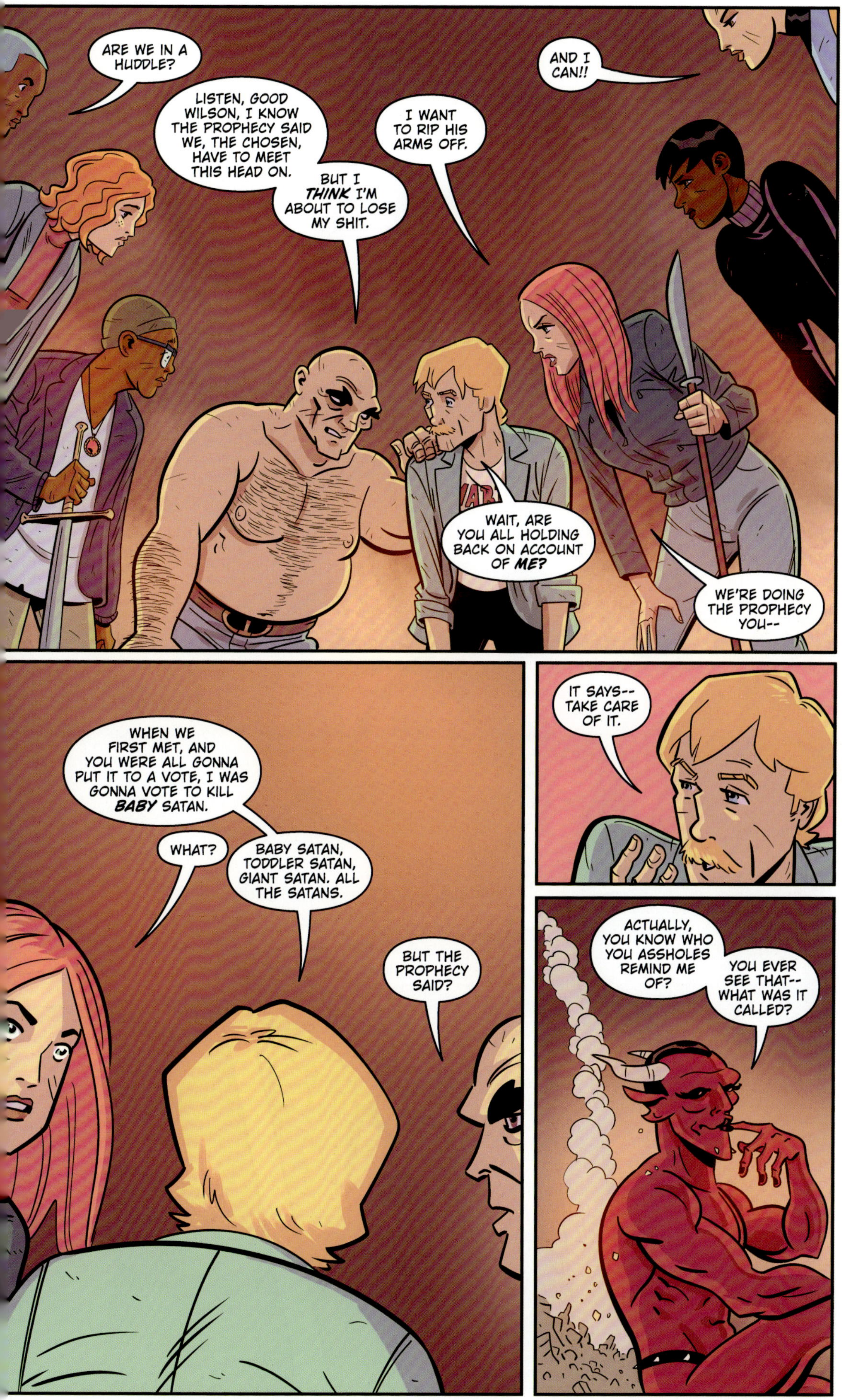
ARE WE IN A HUDDLE?
LISTEN, GOOD WILSON, I KNOW THE PROPHECY SAID WE, THE CHOSEN, HAVE TO MEET THIS HEAD ON.
BUT I *THINK* I'M ABOUT TO LOSE MY SHIT.
I WANT TO RIP HIS ARMS OFF.
AND I CAN!!
WAIT, ARE YOU ALL HOLDING BACK ON ACCOUNT OF *ME?*
WE'RE DOING THE PROPHECY YOU--
IT SAYS--TAKE CARE OF IT.
WHEN WE FIRST MET, AND YOU WERE ALL GONNA PUT IT TO A VOTE, I WAS GONNA VOTE TO KILL *BABY* SATAN.
WHAT?
BABY SATAN, TODDLER SATAN, GIANT SATAN. ALL THE SATANS.
BUT THE PROPHECY SAID?
ACTUALLY, YOU KNOW WHO YOU ASSHOLES REMIND ME OF?
YOU EVER SEE THAT--WHAT WAS IT CALLED?

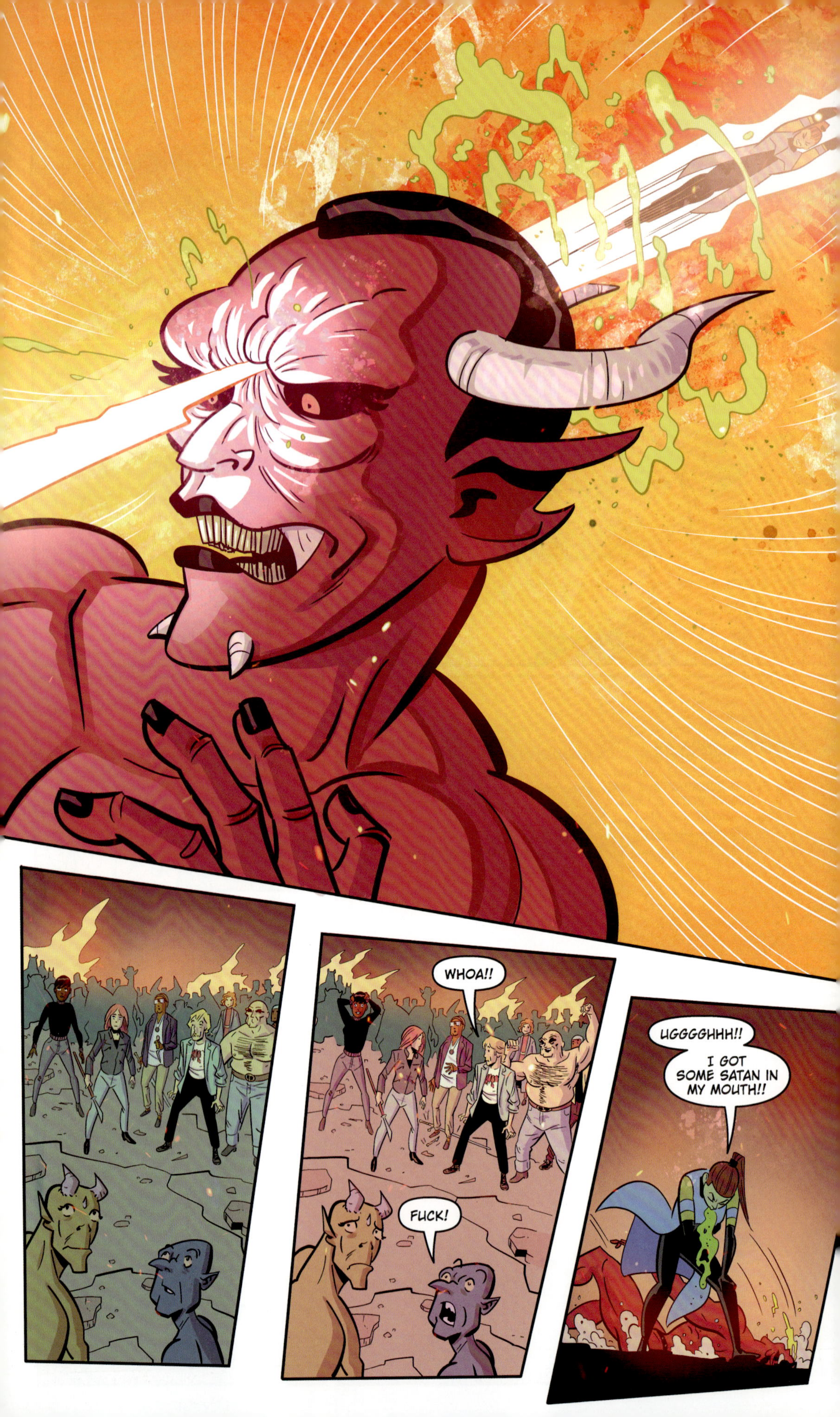
WHOA!!
FUCK!
UGGGGHHH!!
I GOT SOME SATAN IN MY MOUTH!!

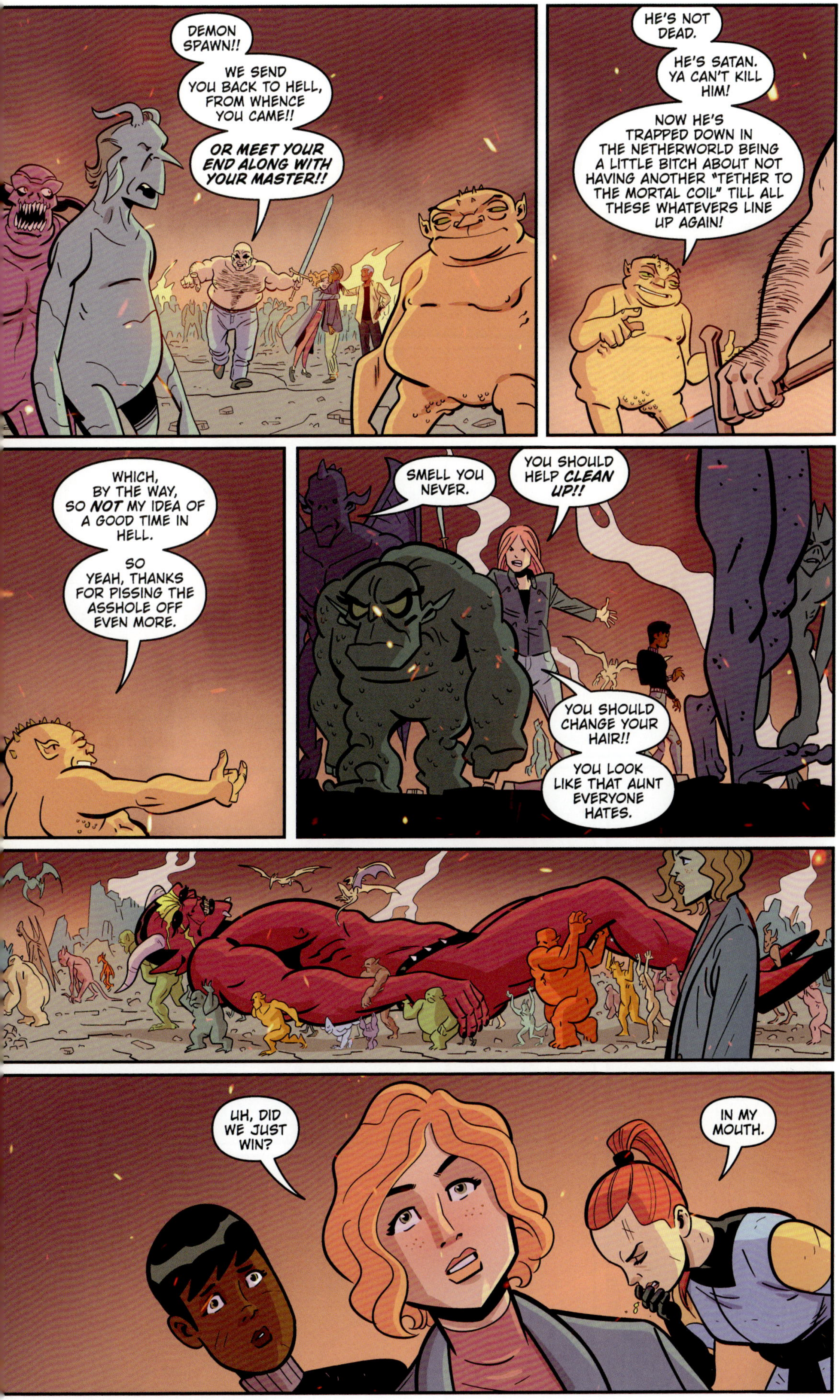
DEMON SPAWN!!
WE SEND YOU BACK TO HELL, FROM WHENCE YOU CAME!!
OR MEET YOUR END ALONG WITH YOUR MASTER!!
HE'S NOT DEAD.
HE'S SATAN. YA CAN'T KILL HIM!
NOW HE'S TRAPPED DOWN IN THE NETHERWORLD BEING A LITTLE BITCH ABOUT NOT HAVING ANOTHER "TETHER TO THE MORTAL COIL" TILL ALL THESE WHATEVERS LINE UP AGAIN!
WHICH, BY THE WAY, SO NOT MY IDEA OF A GOOD TIME IN HELL.
SO YEAH, THANKS FOR PISSING THE ASSHOLE OFF EVEN MORE.
SMELL YOU NEVER.
YOU SHOULD HELP CLEAN UP!!
YOU SHOULD CHANGE YOUR HAIR!!
YOU LOOK LIKE THAT AUNT EVERYONE HATES.
UH, DID WE JUST WIN?
IN MY MOUTH.

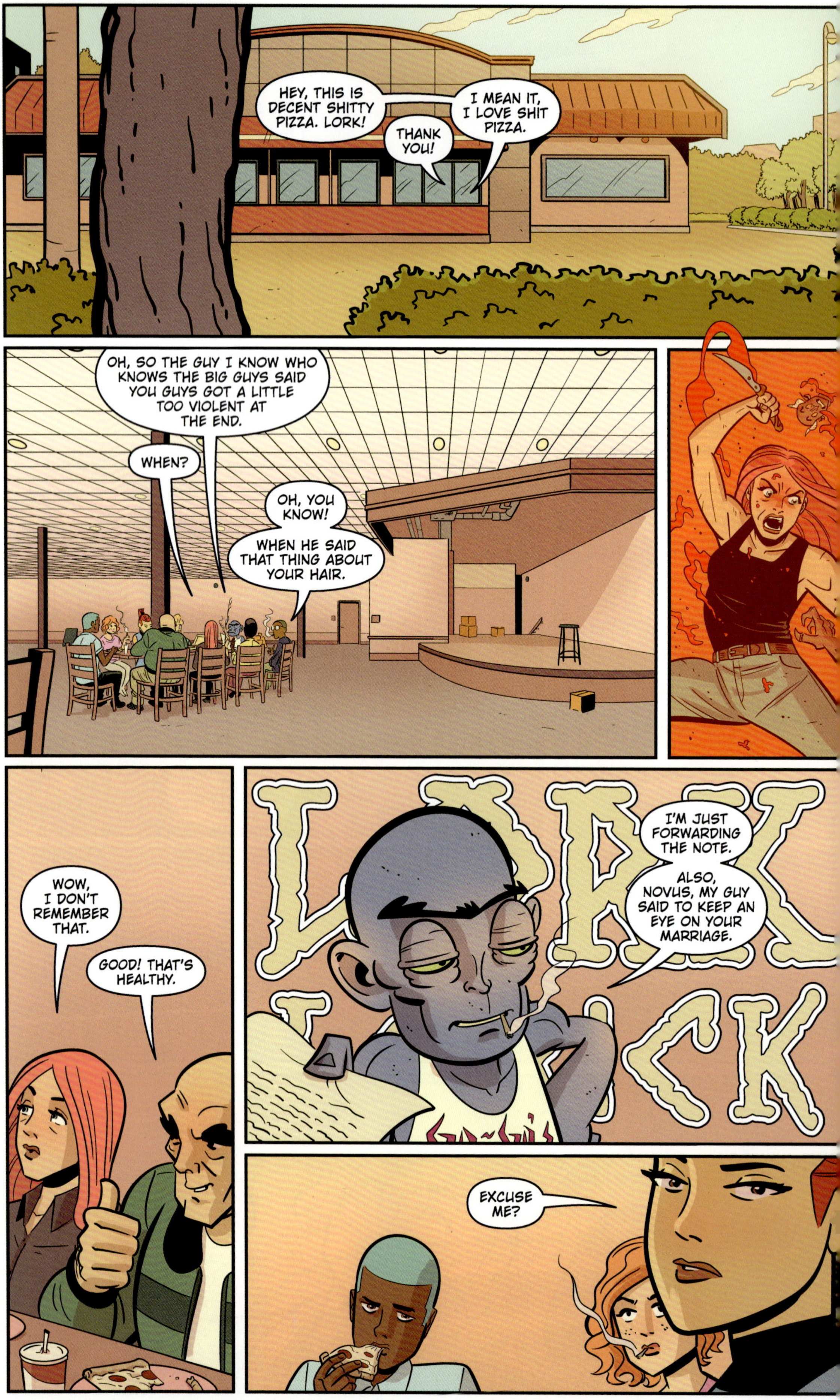
HEY, THIS IS DECENT SHITTY PIZZA. LORK!
I MEAN IT, I LOVE SHIT PIZZA.
THANK YOU!
OH, SO THE GUY I KNOW WHO KNOWS THE BIG GUYS SAID YOU GUYS GOT A LITTLE TOO VIOLENT AT THE END.
WHEN?
OH, YOU KNOW!
WHEN HE SAID THAT THING ABOUT YOUR HAIR.
WOW, I DON'T REMEMBER THAT.
GOOD! THAT'S HEALTHY.
I'M JUST FORWARDING THE NOTE.
ALSO, NOVUS, MY GUY SAID TO KEEP AN EYE ON YOUR MARRIAGE.
EXCUSE ME?

"SUPPOSABLY, SATAN HAS, LIKE, THIS THING, IF SHIT GETS PERSONAL, WHICH I GUESS YOU MADE IT...

HE LIKES TO GO AFTER PEOPLE'S MARRIAGES.

I KNOW YOU SAID YOU LIKE YOURS."

"WHAT?"

"LIKE IF, LET'S SAY, YOUR AUNT GETS SICK.

HE'LL SHOW UP AND OFFER TO *SAVE YOUR AUNT* BUT IN TRADE HE'LL ERASE YOUR MARRIAGE... FROM REALITY."

"FROM REALITY??"

"WELL, *THIS* ONE. AT LEAST. I GUESS."

"WHY WOULD HE DO THAT?

IT'S TRUE *BTW*.

I READ THIS."

"SO, WHAT HAPPENS NOW?"

"I THINK THAT'S BASICALLY IT!

THAT WAS THE PROPHECY FULFILLED."

"THAT'S WHAT MY GUY SAID."

"WHO'S YOUR GUY?"

"HE'S MY GUY."

"HEY! I'M SO SURE I'M STILL IN SHOCK BUT-- I'M ALIVE.

YOU GOT US ALL OUT OF THERE ALIVE AND IN ONE PIECE.

SO, TO OUR POWERS PEOPLE, THANK YOU."

"I'M GLAD I CAN TAKE A MINUTE AND TOAST THIS--

AND SAY THANKS *AND WISH YOU*--

UH, IS THAT THE AC?"

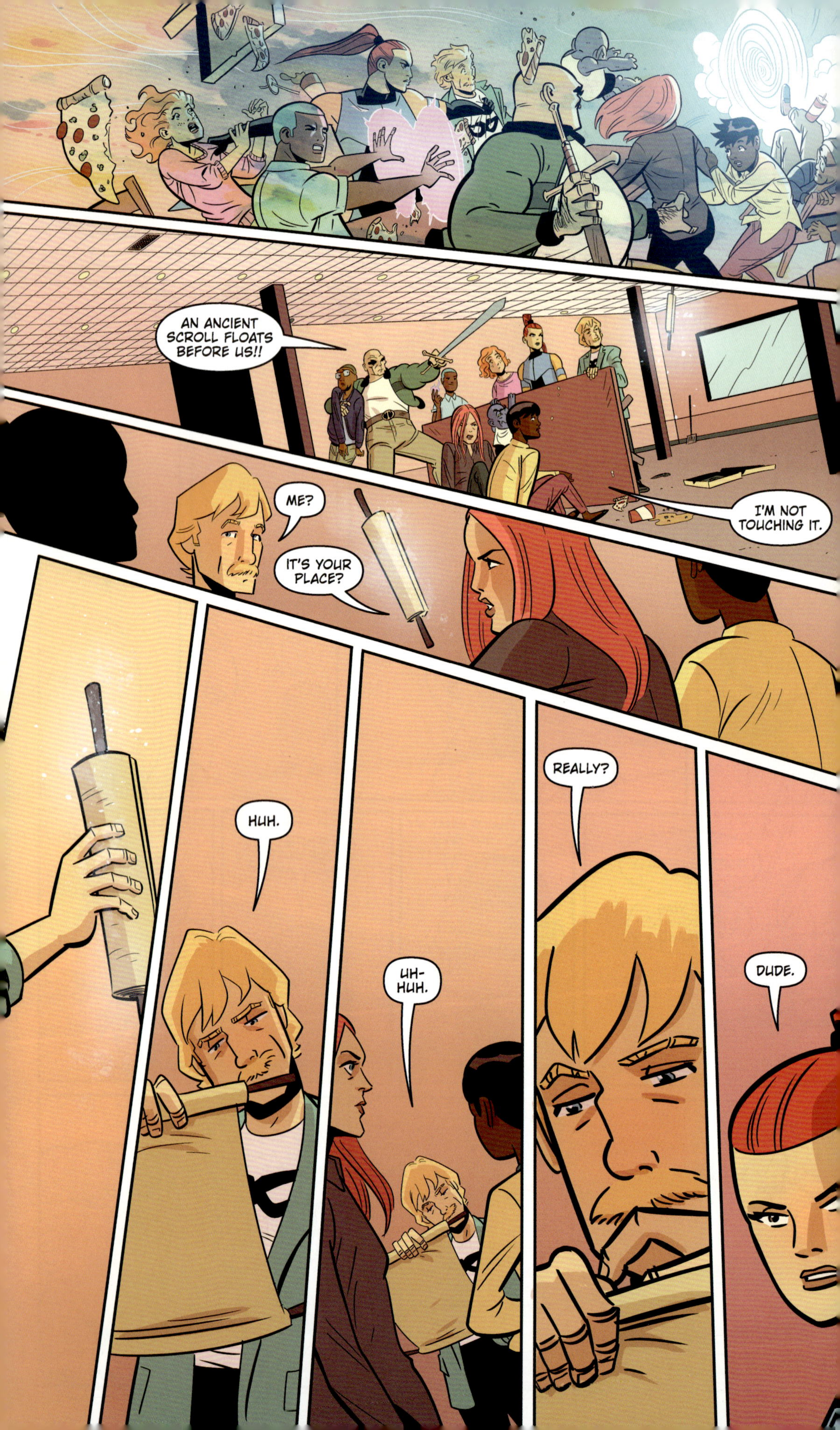
AN ANCIENT SCROLL FLOATS BEFORE US!!
I'M NOT TOUCHING IT.
ME?
IT'S YOUR PLACE?
HUH.
UH-HUH.
REALLY?
DUDE.

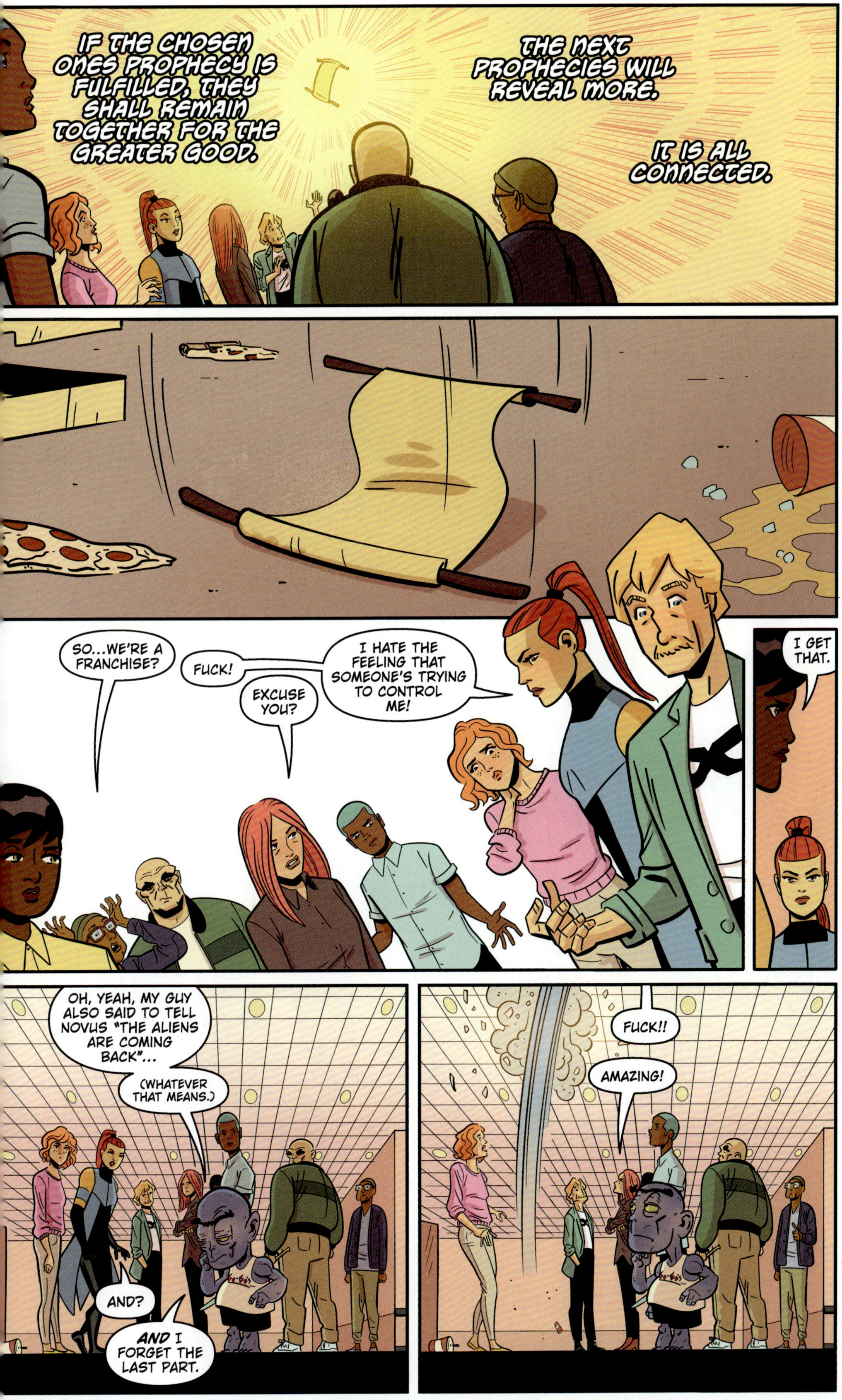
IF THE CHOSEN ONES PROPHECY IS FULFILLED, THEY SHALL REMAIN TOGETHER FOR THE GREATER GOOD.
THE NEXT PROPHECIES WILL REVEAL MORE.
IT IS ALL CONNECTED.
SO...WE'RE A FRANCHISE?
FUCK!
EXCUSE YOU?
I HATE THE FEELING THAT SOMEONE'S TRYING TO CONTROL ME!
I GET THAT.
OH, YEAH, MY GUY ALSO SAID TO TELL NOVUS "THE ALIENS ARE COMING BACK"...
(WHATEVER THAT MEANS.)
AND?
AND I FORGET THE LAST PART.
FUCK!!
AMAZING!

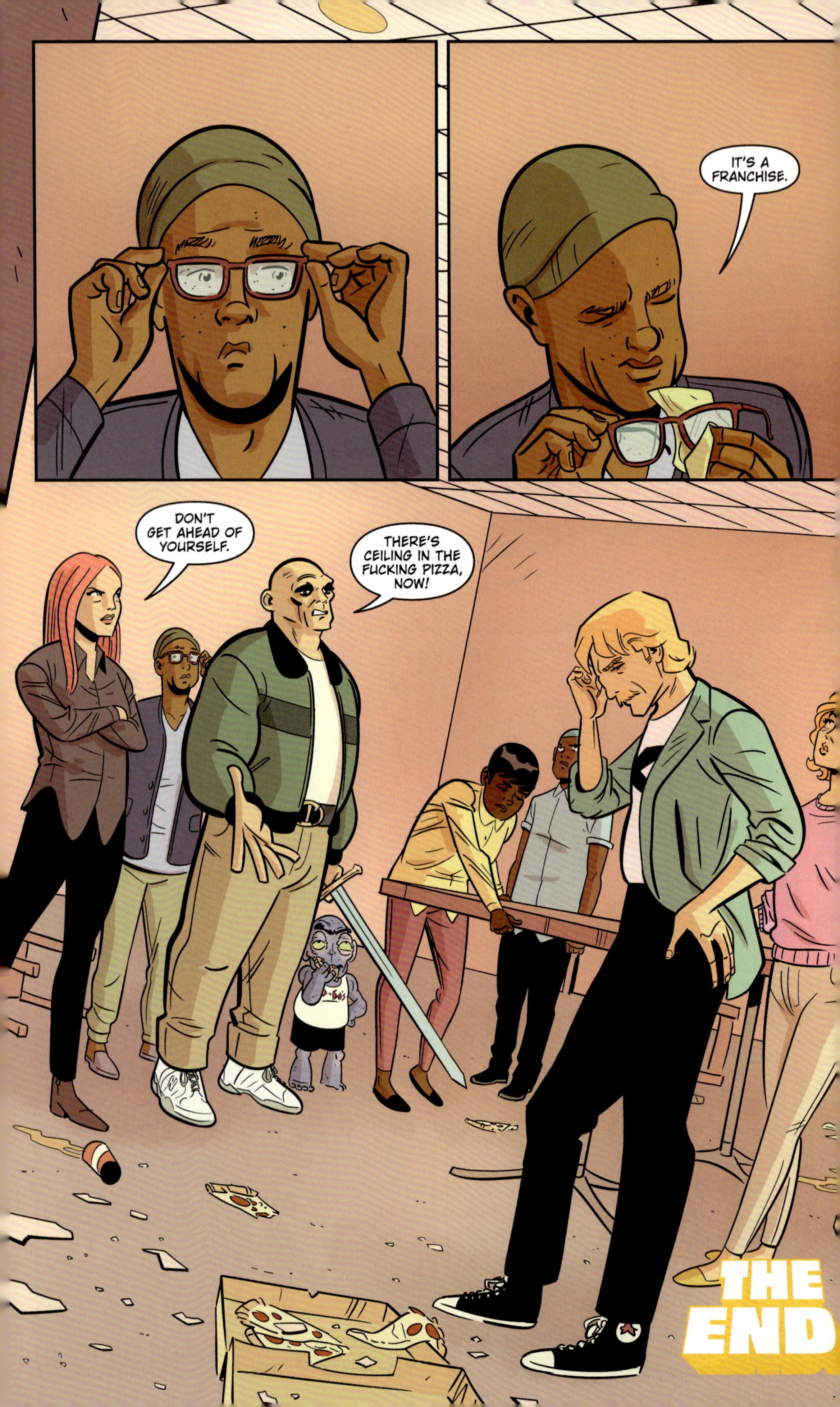
IT'S A FRANCHISE.
DON'T GET AHEAD OF YOURSELF.
THERE'S CEILING IN THE FUCKING PIZZA, NOW!
THE END

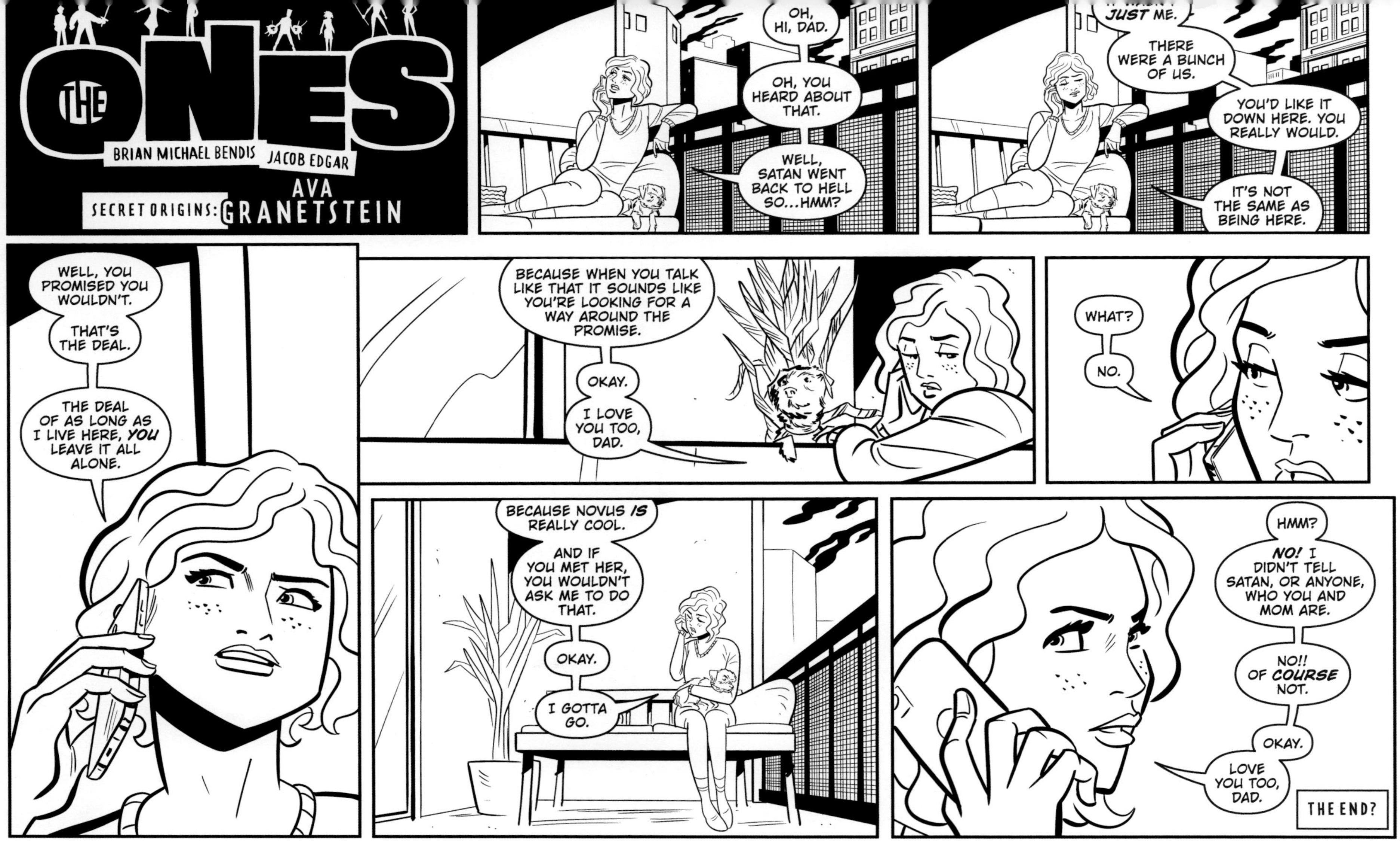
THE ONES
BRIAN MICHAEL BENDIS
JACOB EDGAR
SECRET ORIGINS: AVA GRANETSTEIN
OH, HI, DAD.
OH, YOU HEARD ABOUT THAT.
WELL, SATAN WENT BACK TO HELL SO...HMM?
JUST ME.
THERE WERE A BUNCH OF US.
YOU'D LIKE IT DOWN HERE. YOU REALLY WOULD.
IT'S NOT THE SAME AS BEING HERE.
WELL, YOU PROMISED YOU WOULDN'T.
THAT'S THE DEAL.
THE DEAL OF AS LONG AS I LIVE HERE, *YOU* LEAVE IT ALL ALONE.
BECAUSE WHEN YOU TALK LIKE THAT IT SOUNDS LIKE YOU'RE LOOKING FOR A WAY AROUND THE PROMISE.
OKAY.
I LOVE YOU TOO, DAD.
WHAT?
NO.
BECAUSE NOVUS *IS* REALLY COOL.
AND IF YOU MET HER, YOU WOULDN'T ASK ME TO DO THAT.
OKAY.
I GOTTA GO.
HMM?
NO! I DIDN'T TELL SATAN, OR ANYONE, WHO YOU AND MOM ARE.
NO!! OF *COURSE* NOT.
OKAY.
LOVE YOU TOO, DAD.
THE END?

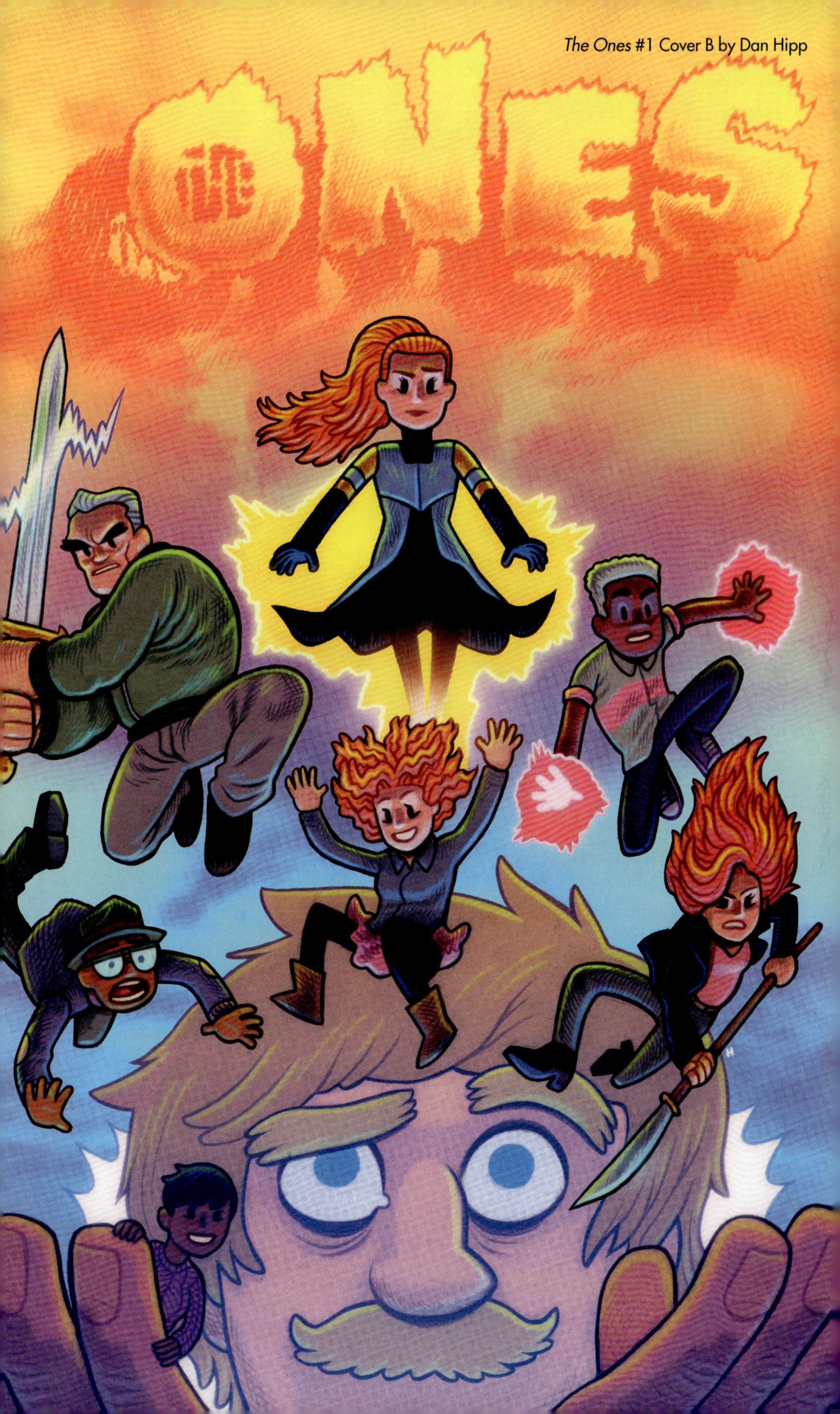
THE ONES

The Ones #1 Cover B by Dan Hipp

The Ones #1 Cover C by Yanick Paquette with K. J. Díaz

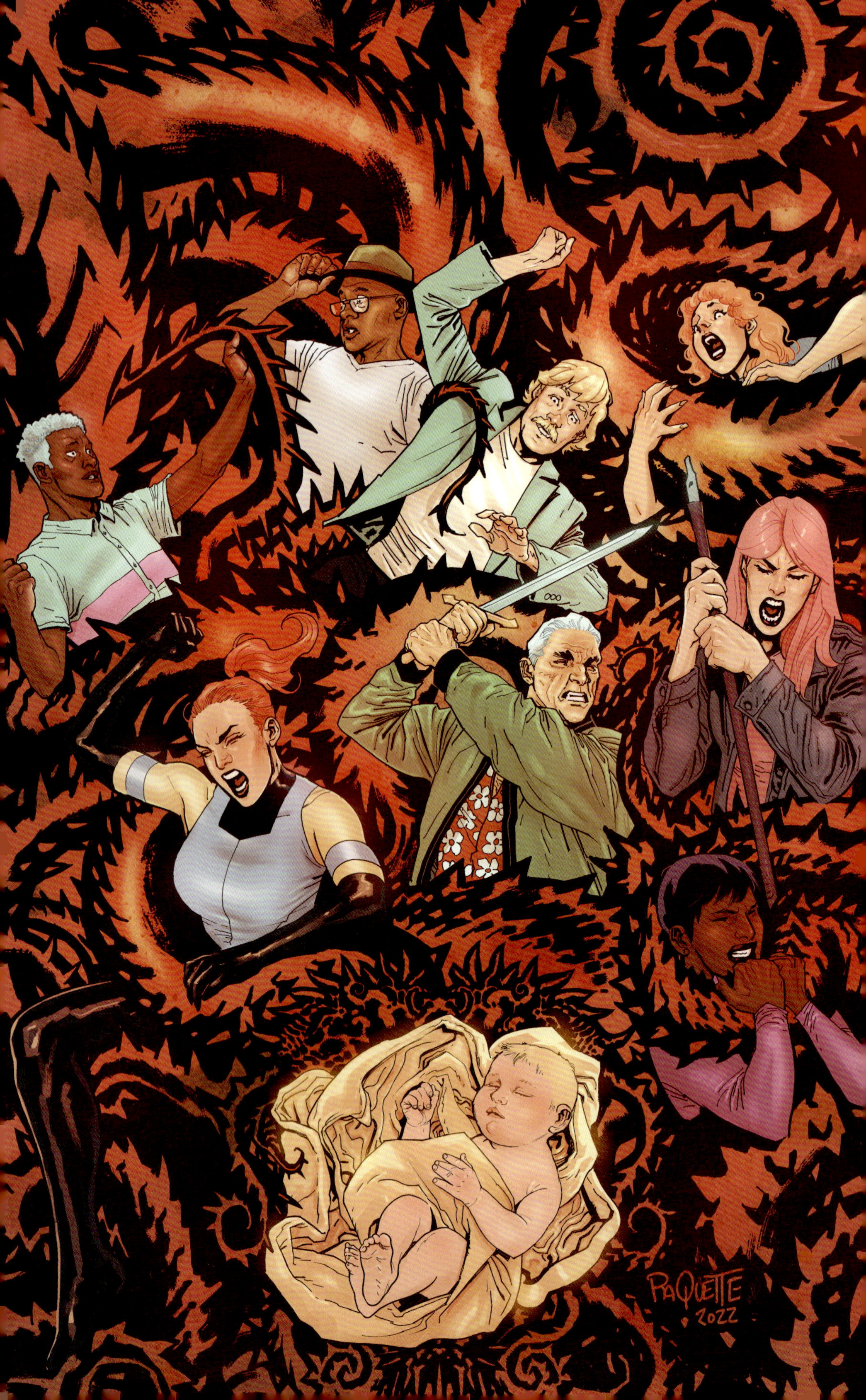
PAQUETTE
2022

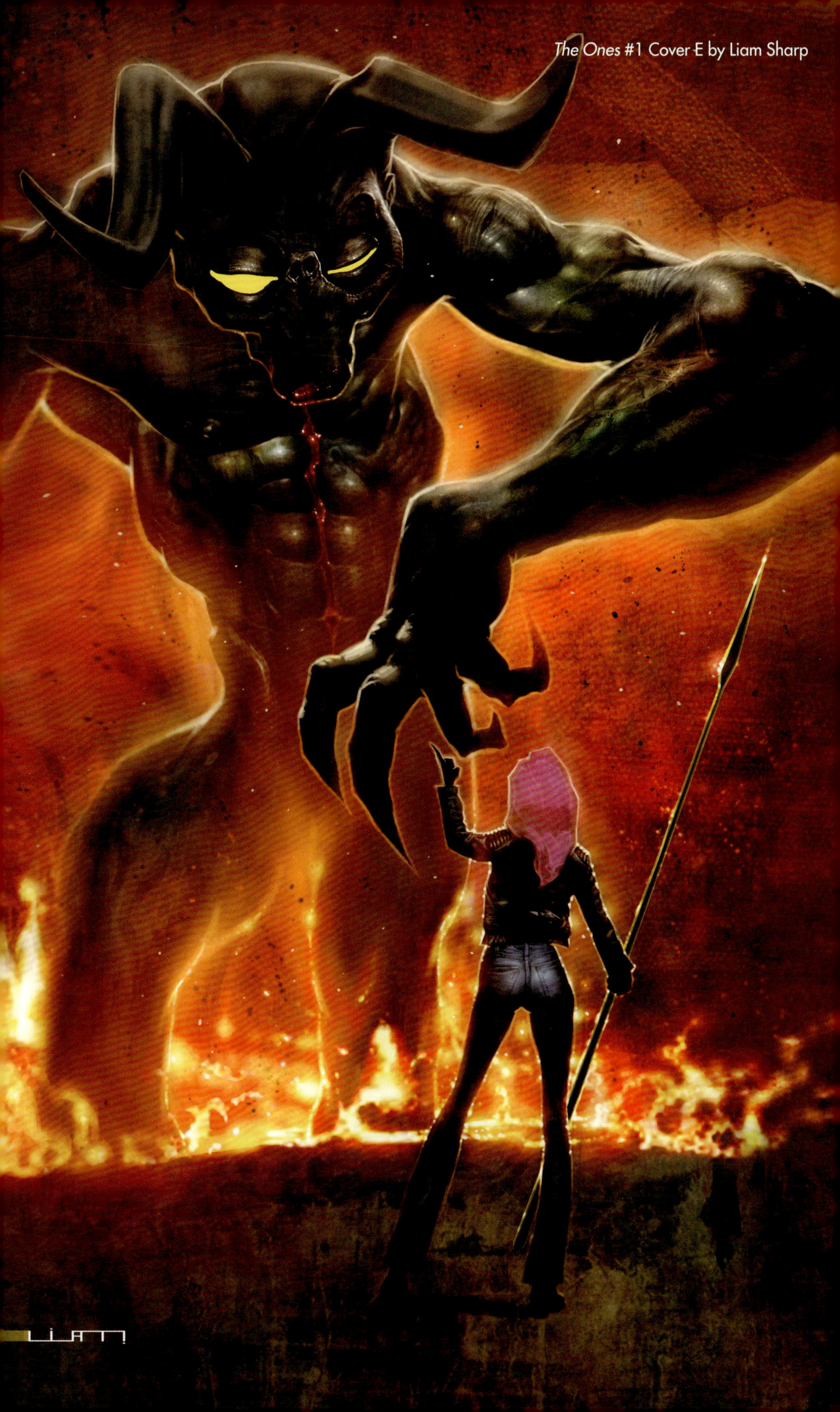
The Ones #1 Cover E by Liam Sharp

The Ones #2 Cover B by Tyler Boss

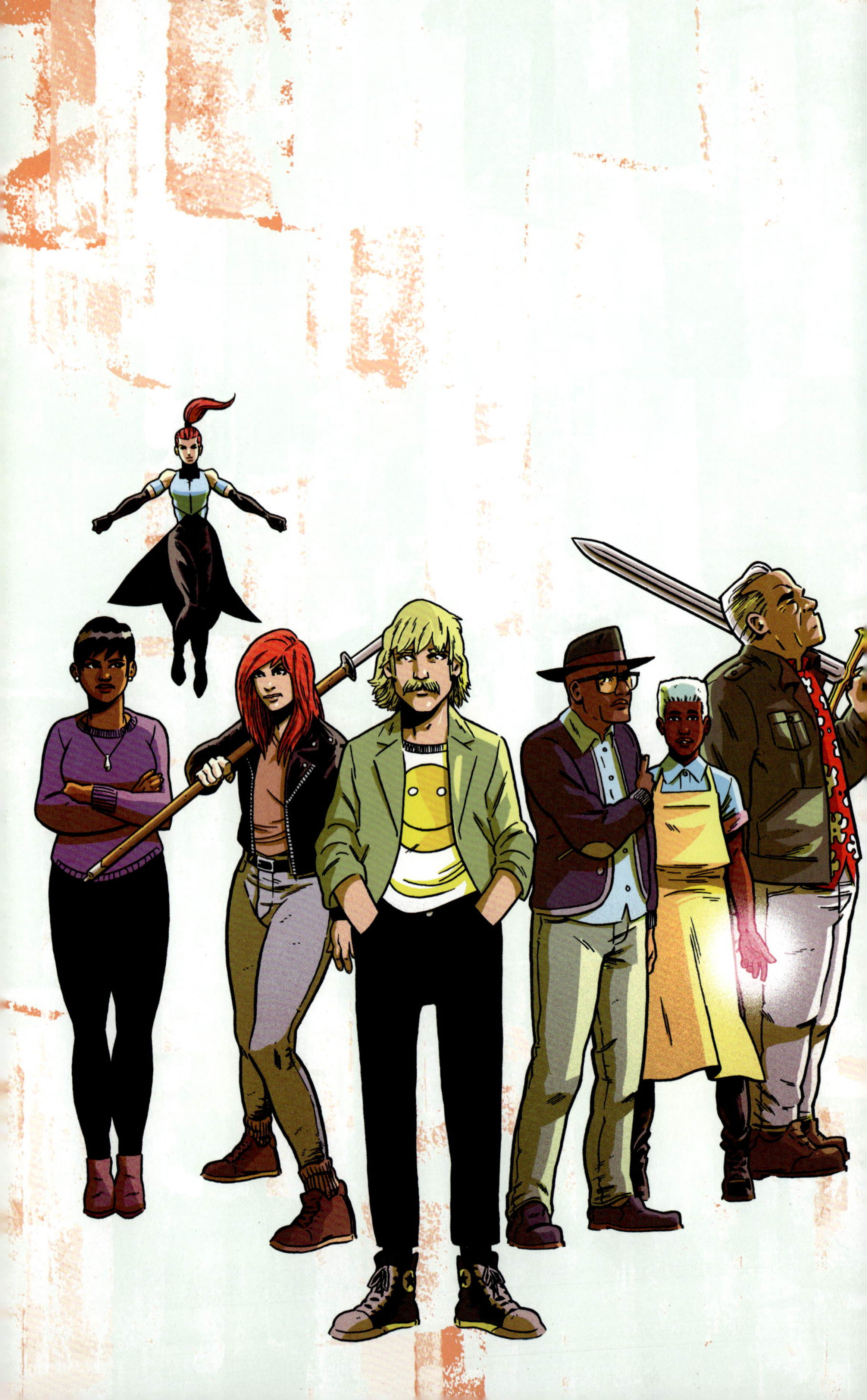

The Ones #3 Cover B by Michael Avon Oeming with Nick Filardi

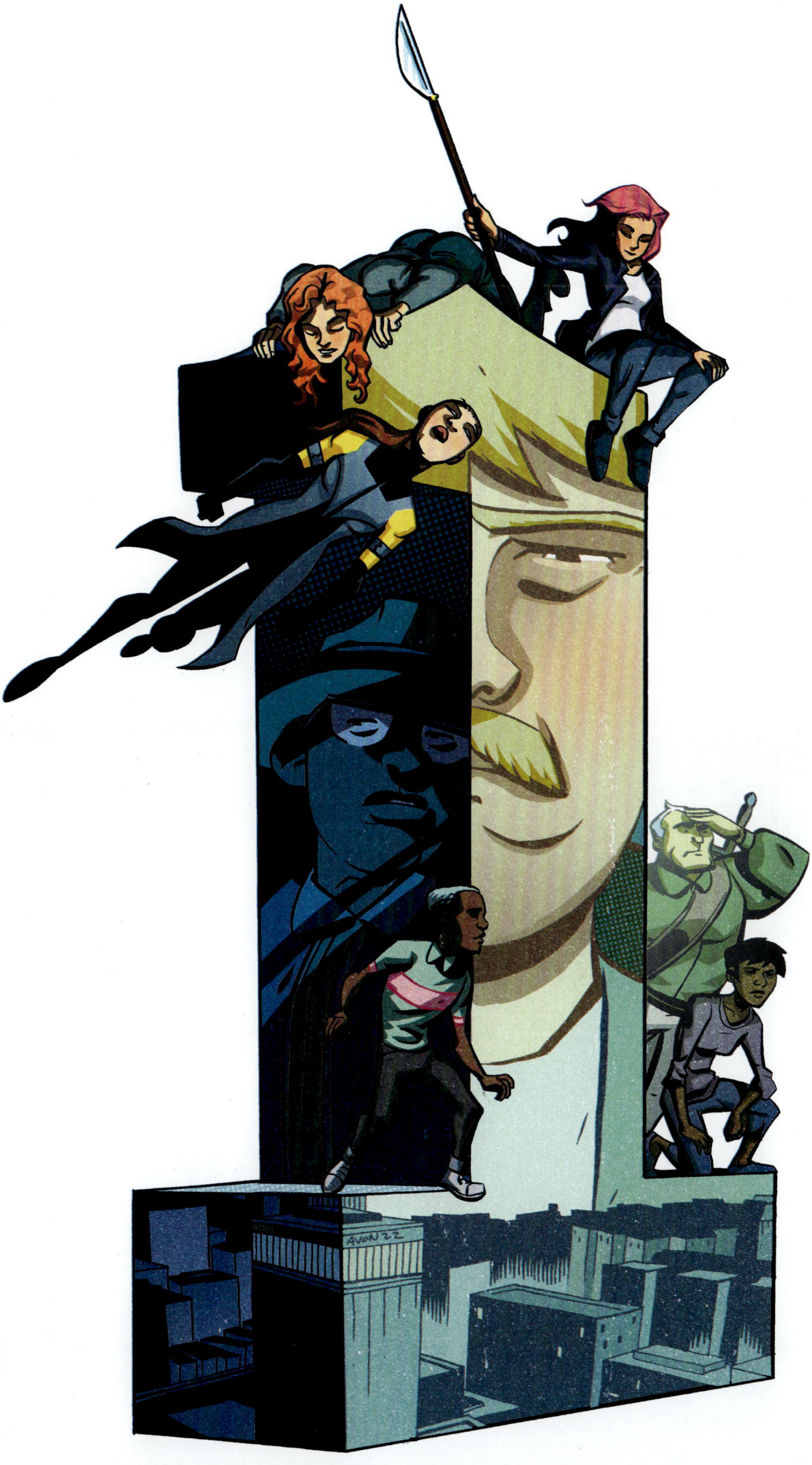

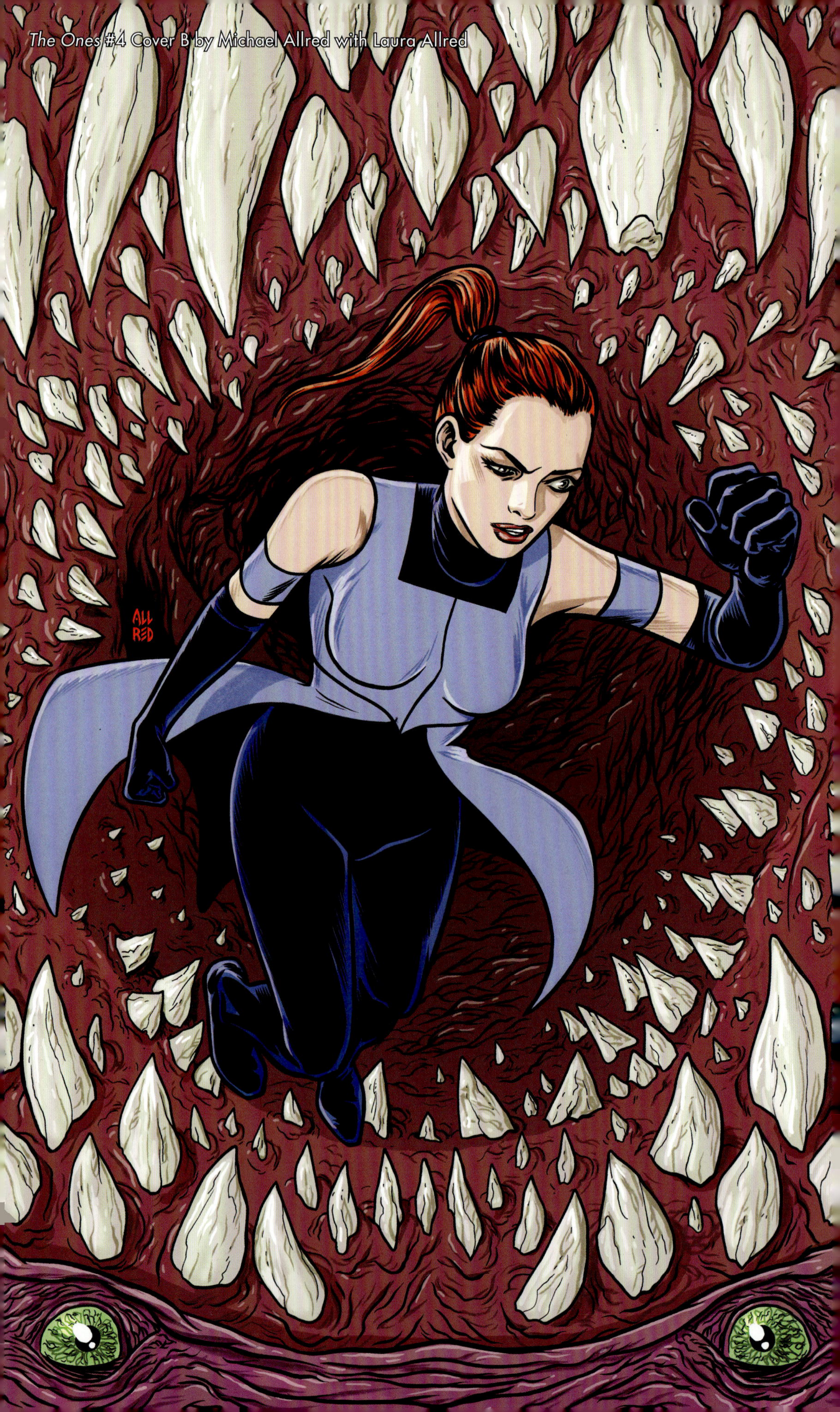
ALL
RED
The Ones #4 Cover B by Michael Allred with Laura Allred

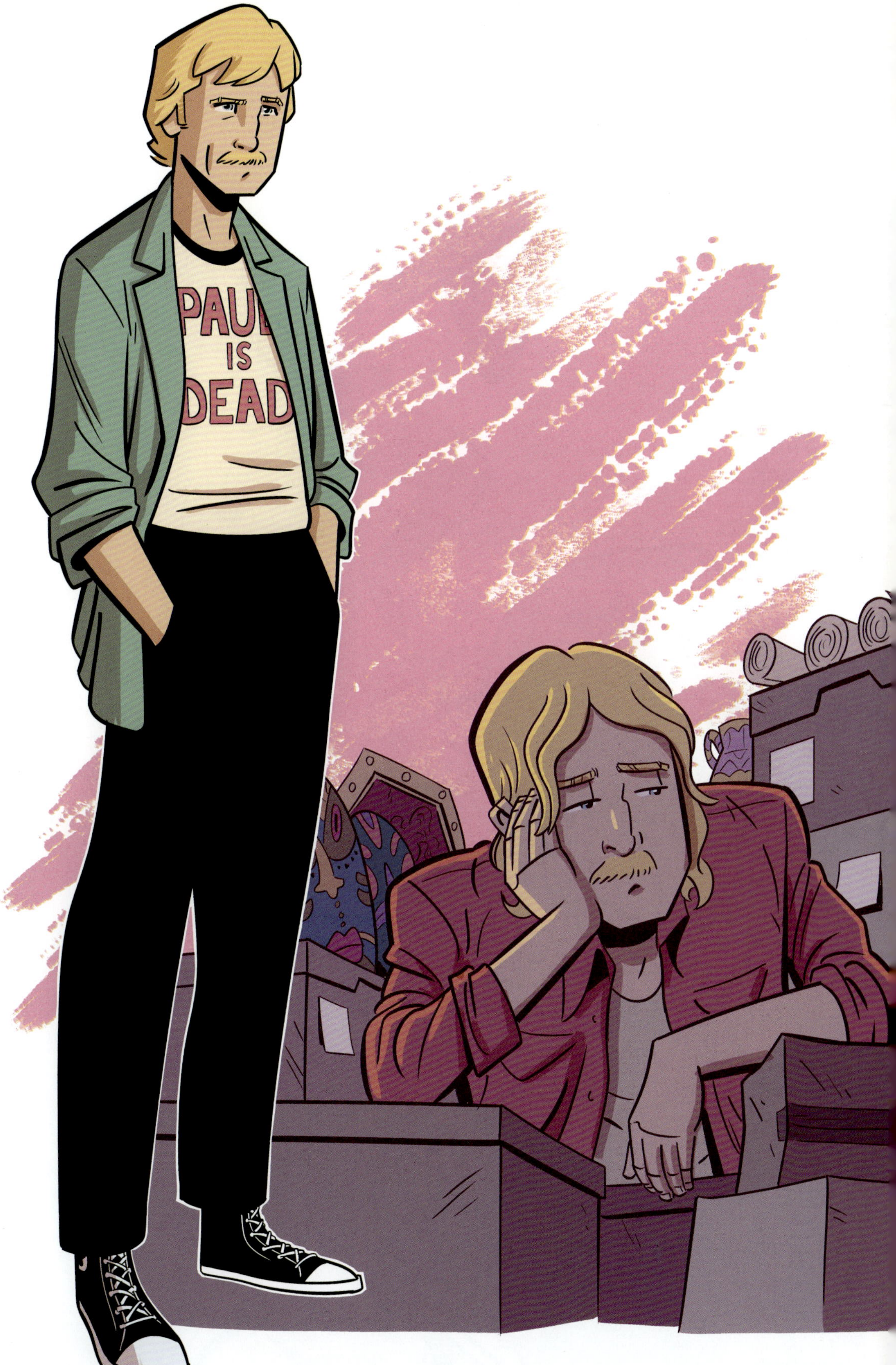
PAUL
IS
DEAD

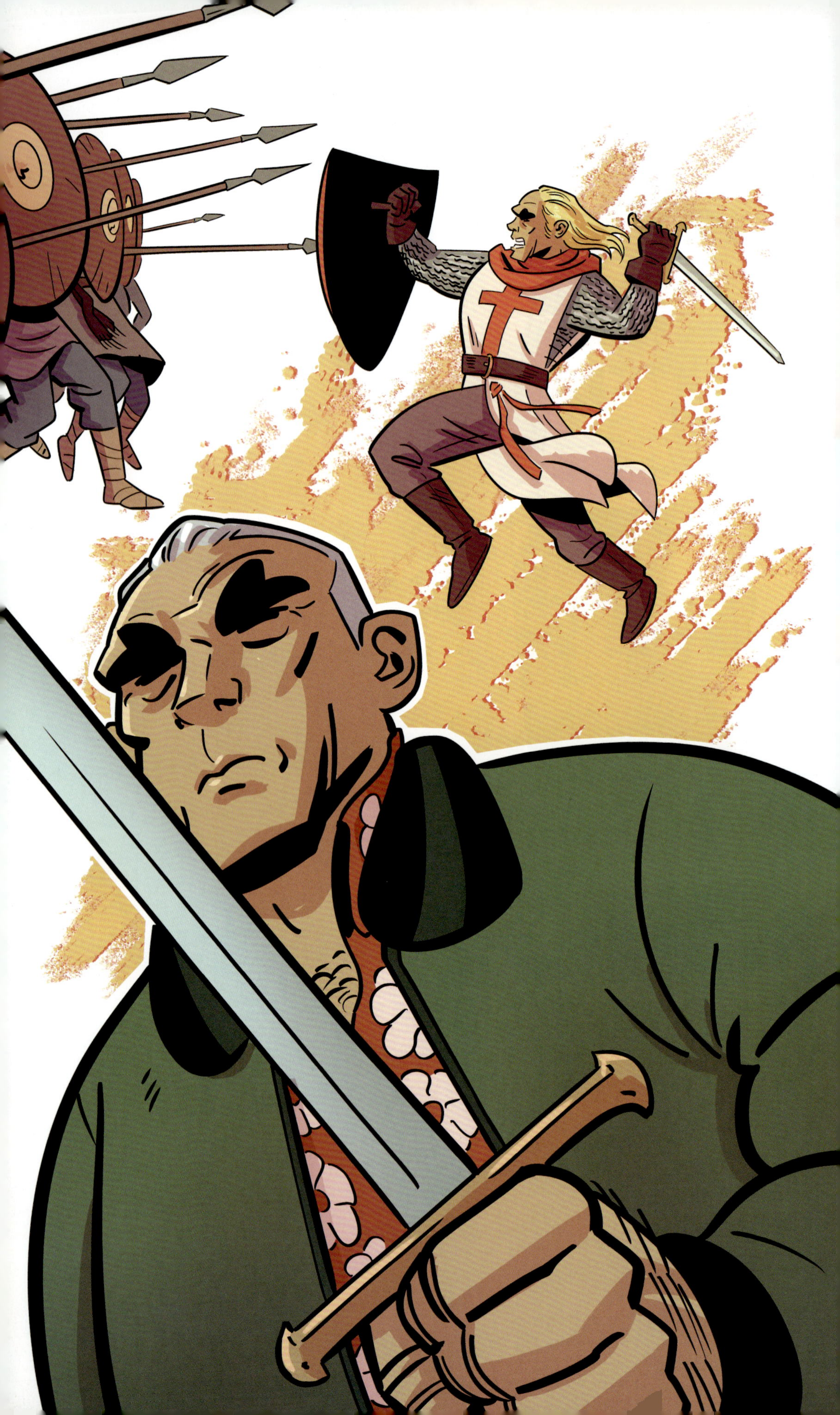

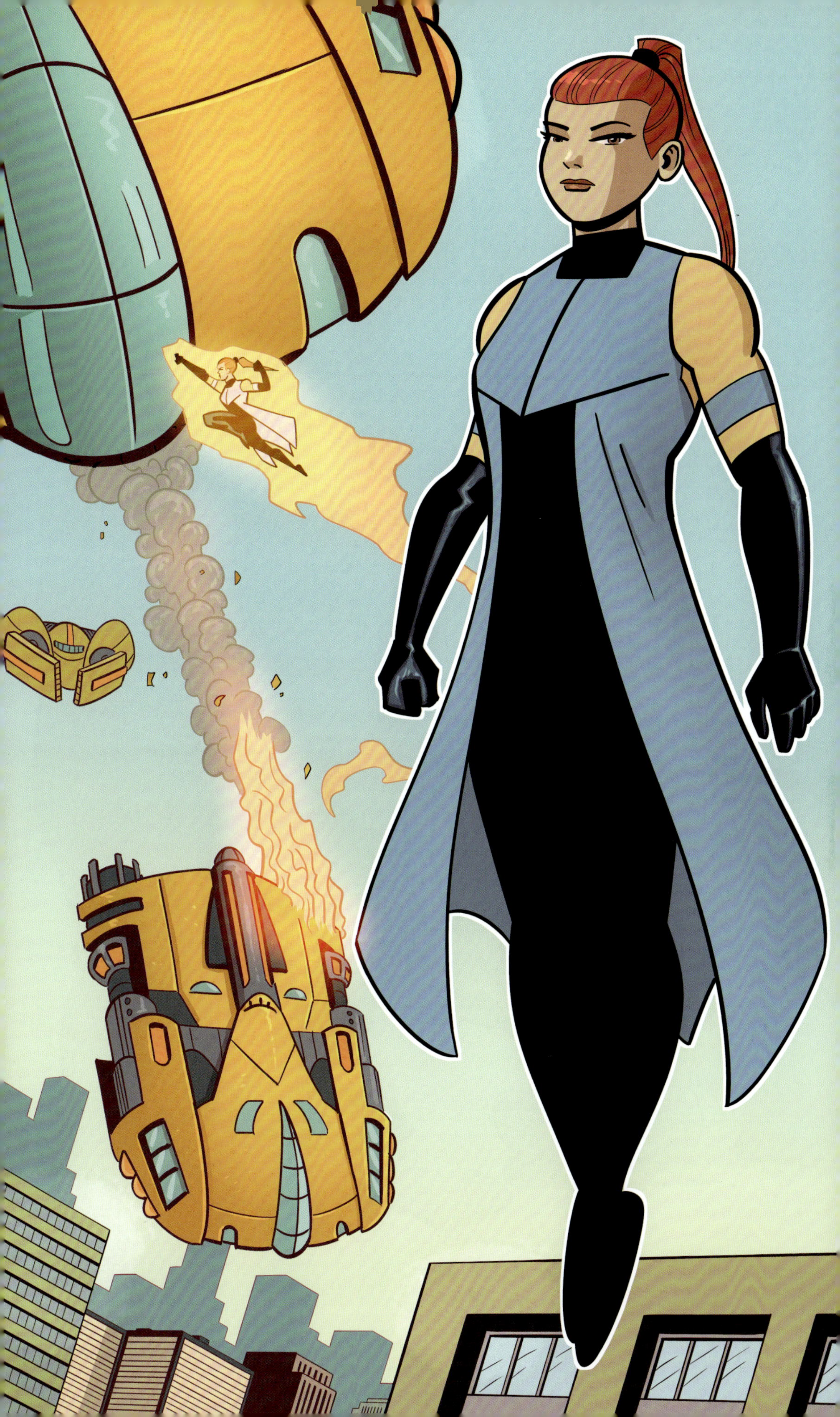

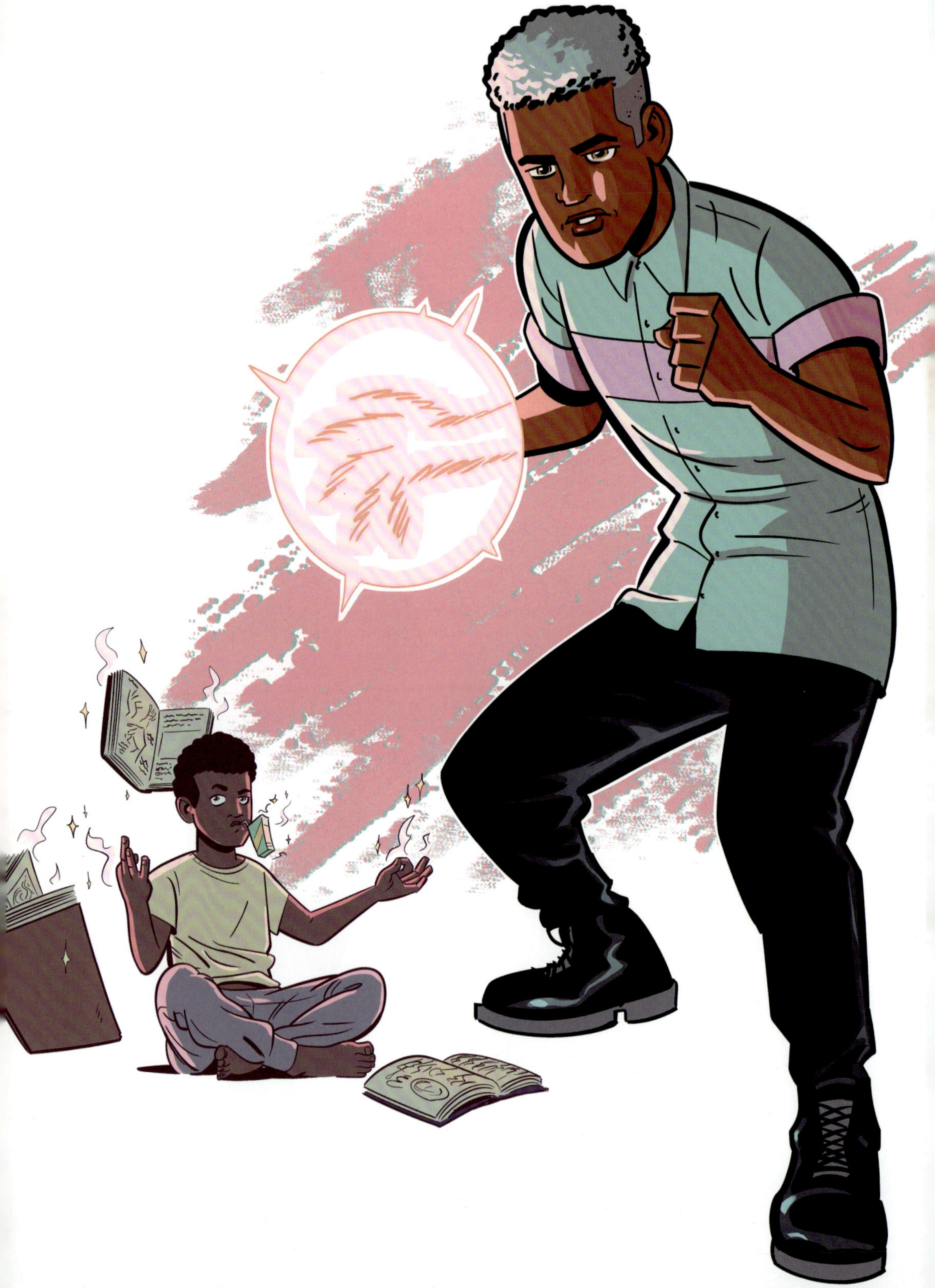

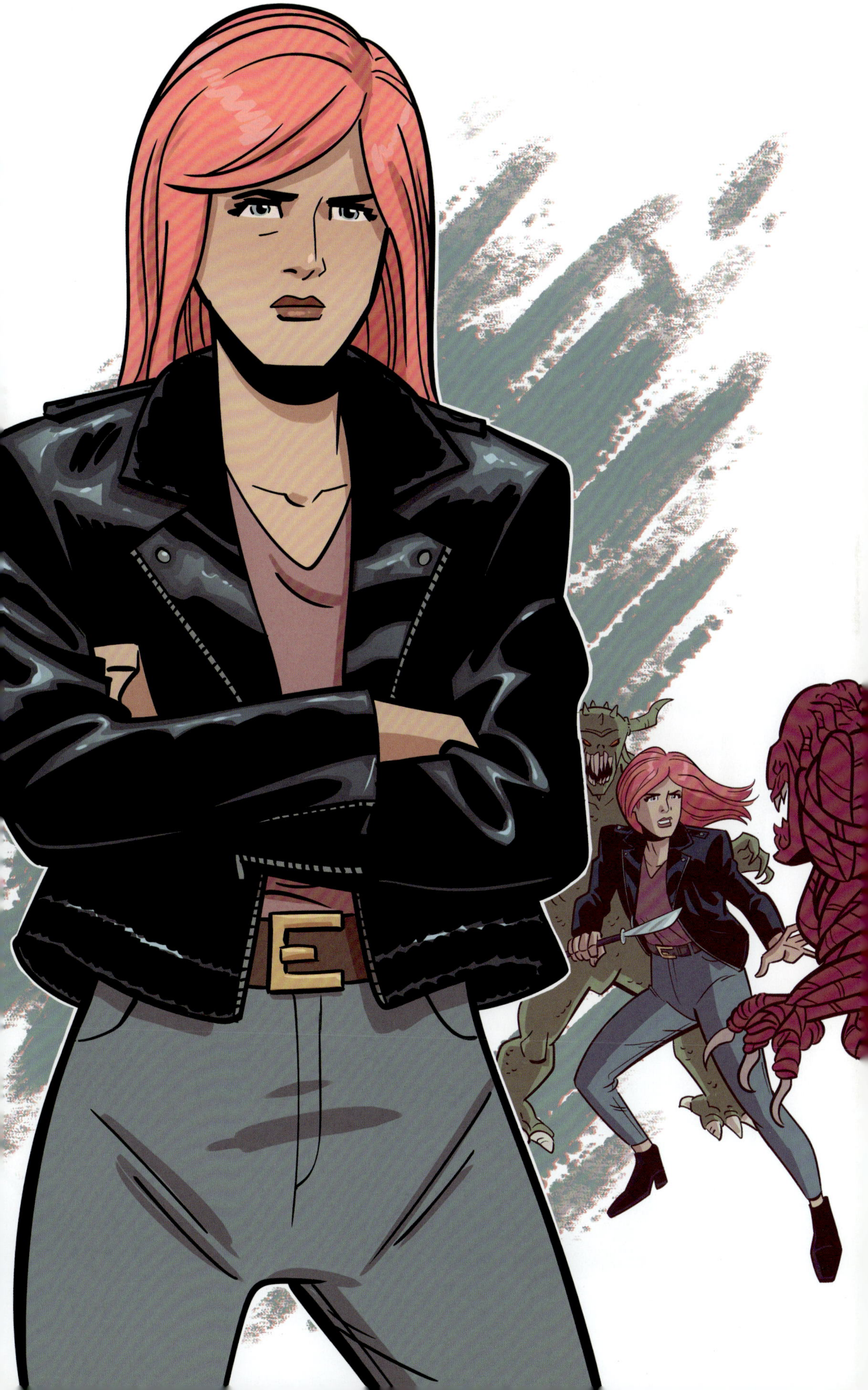

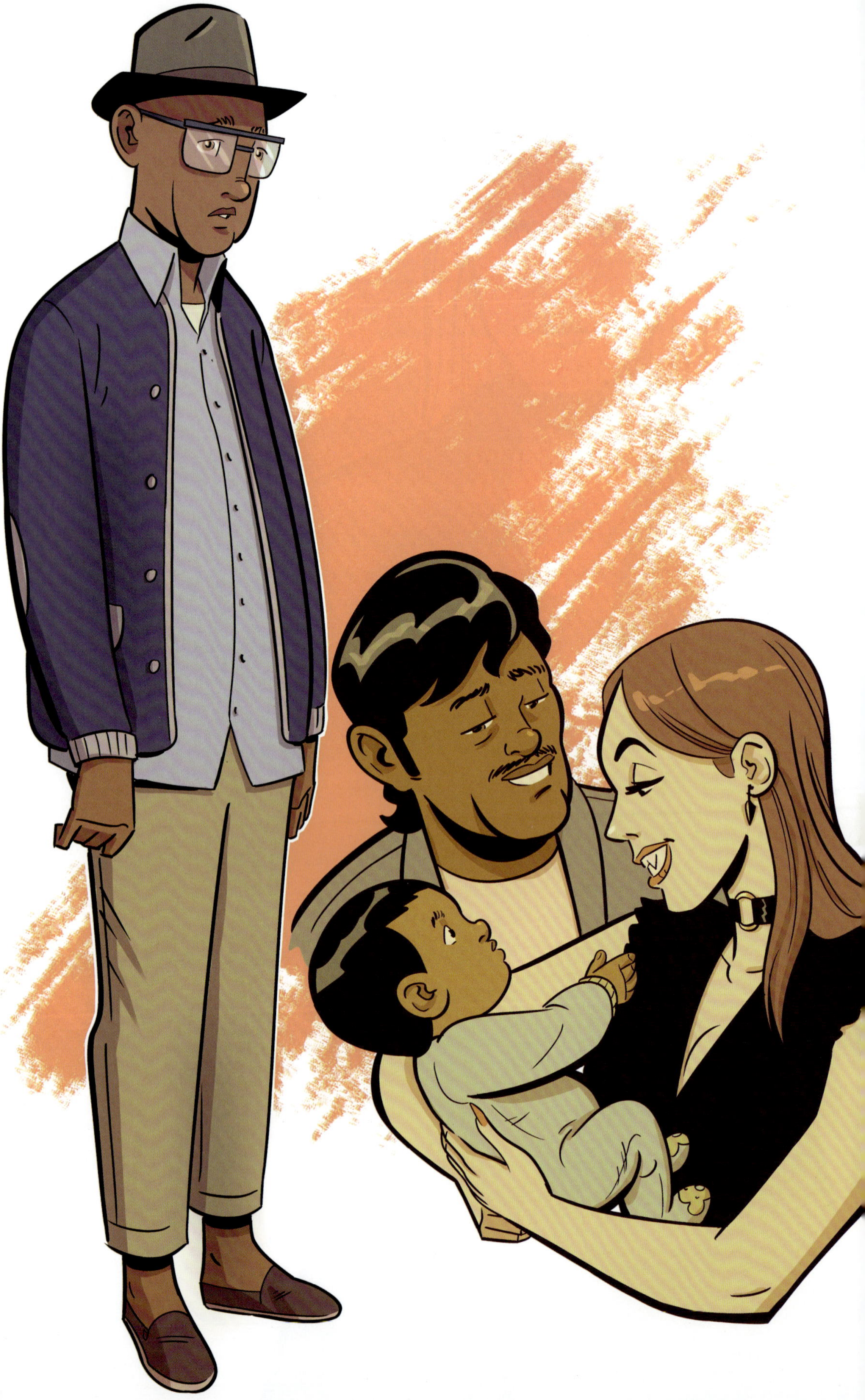

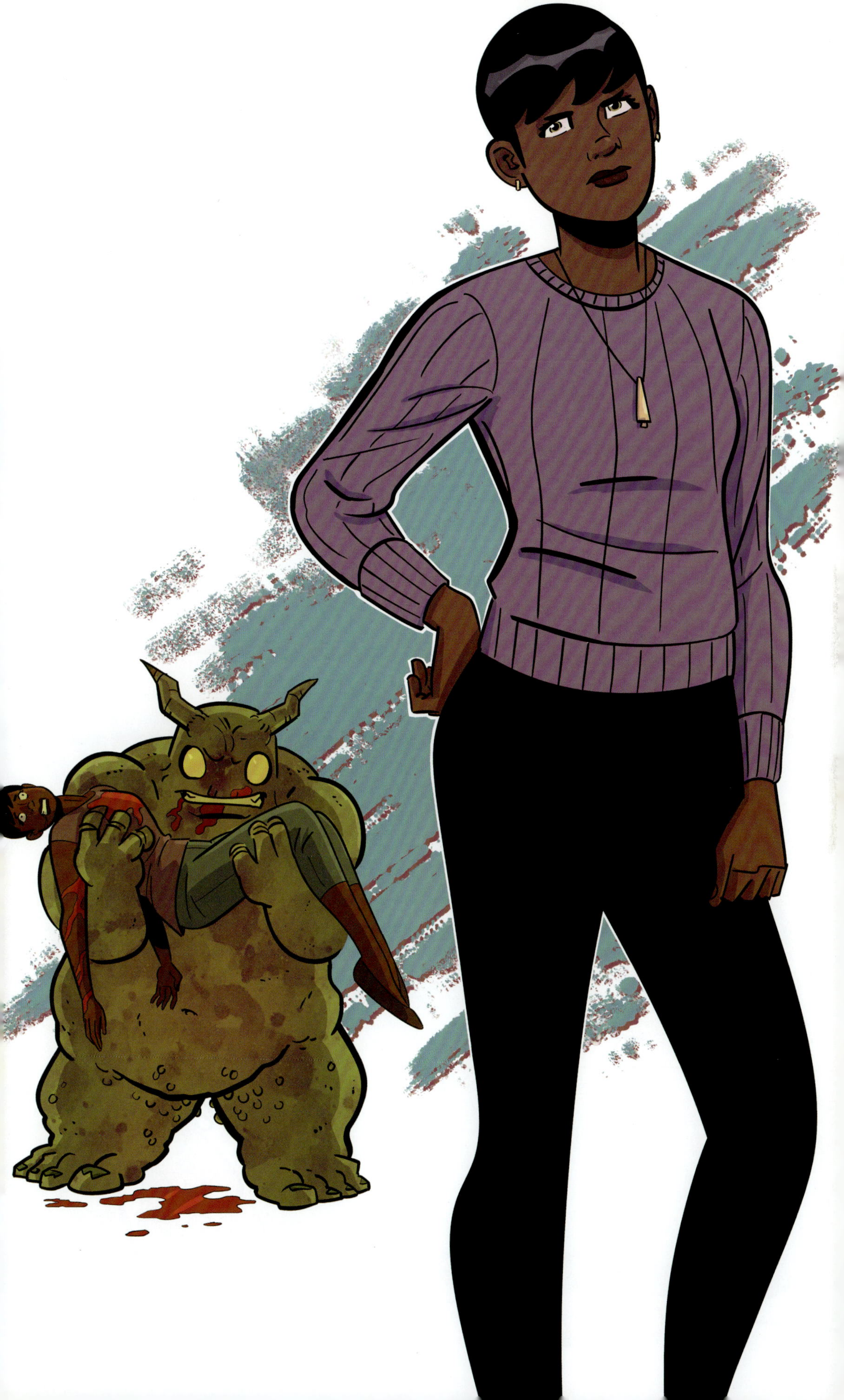

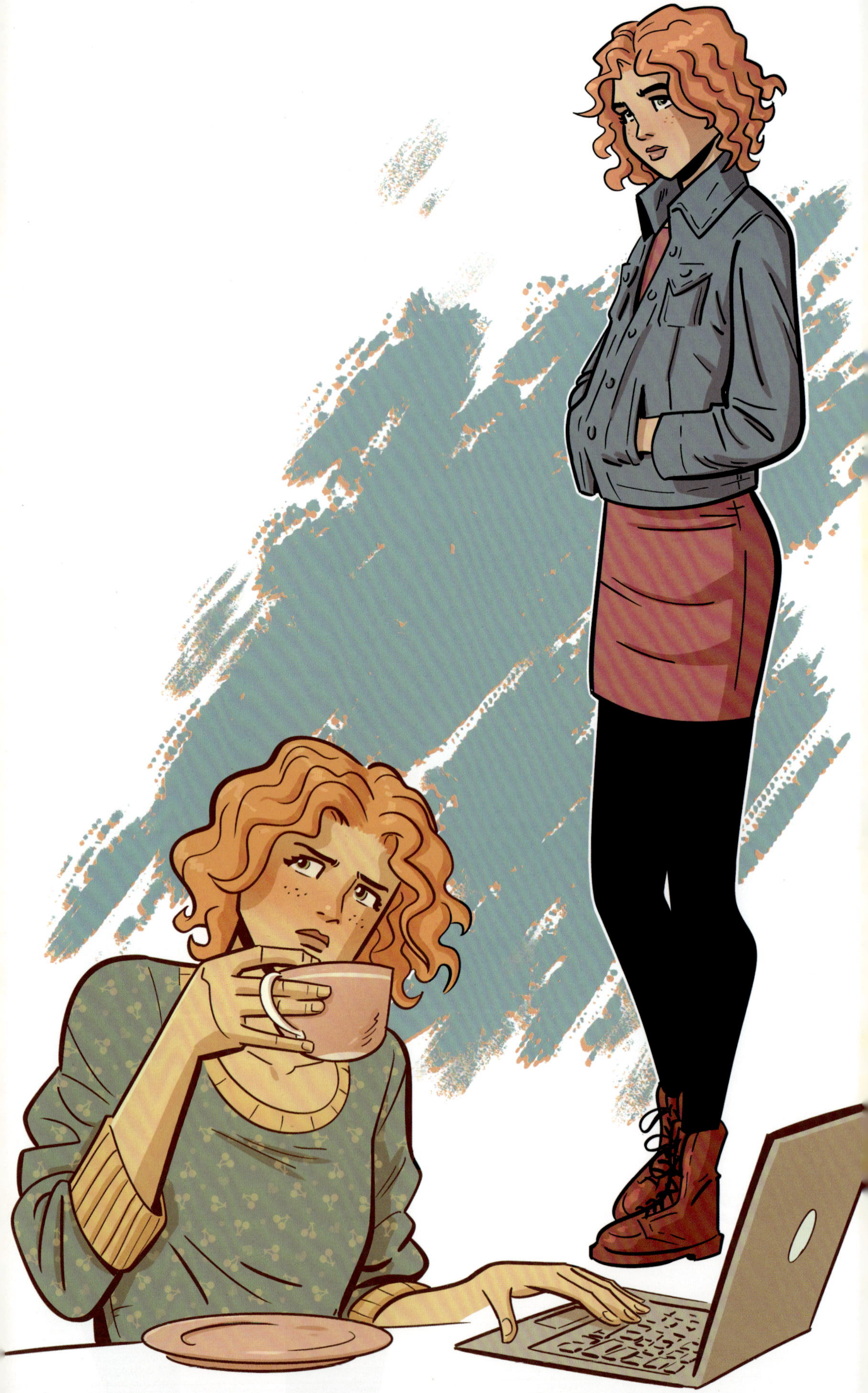

"CLEAN AND CLEAR"

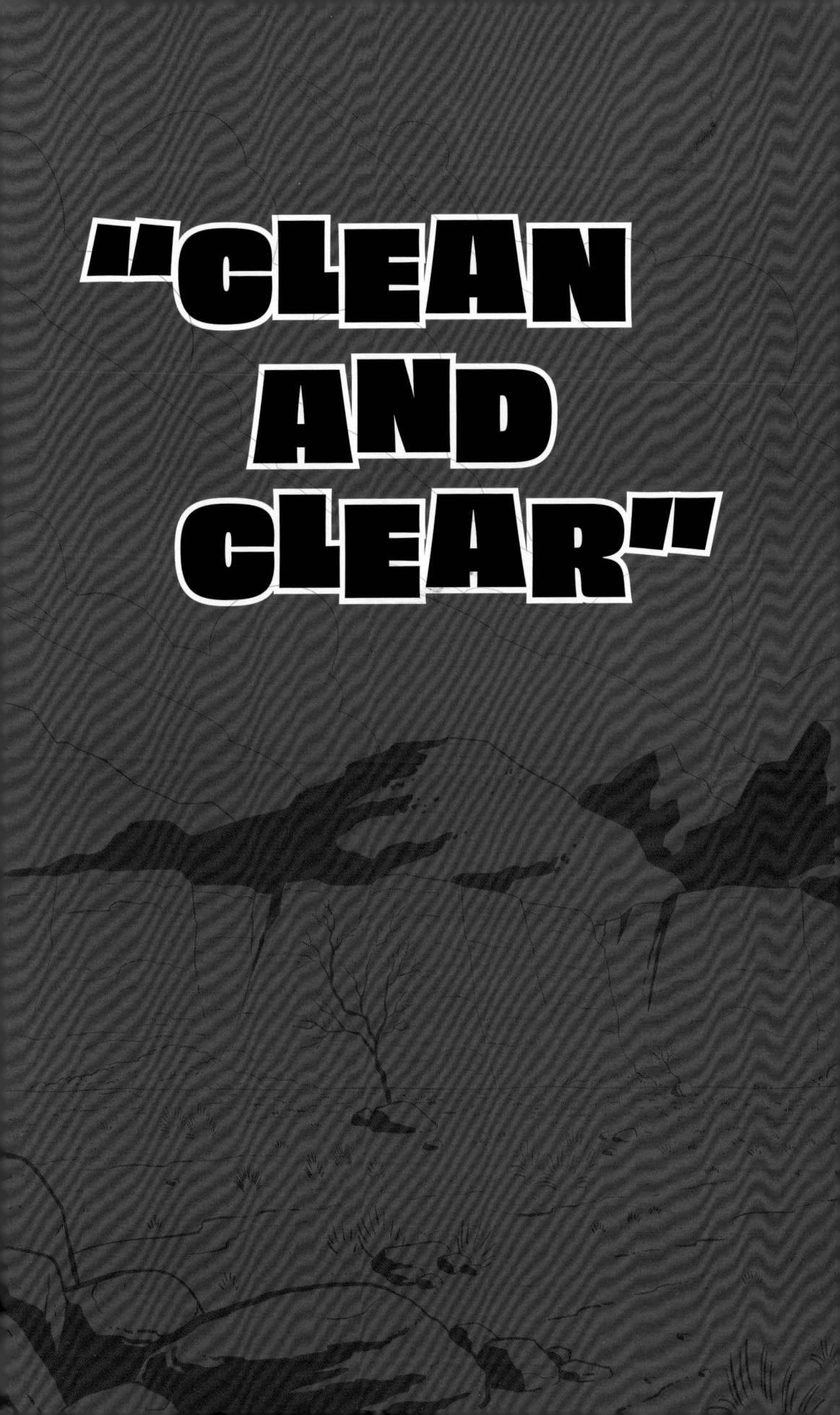

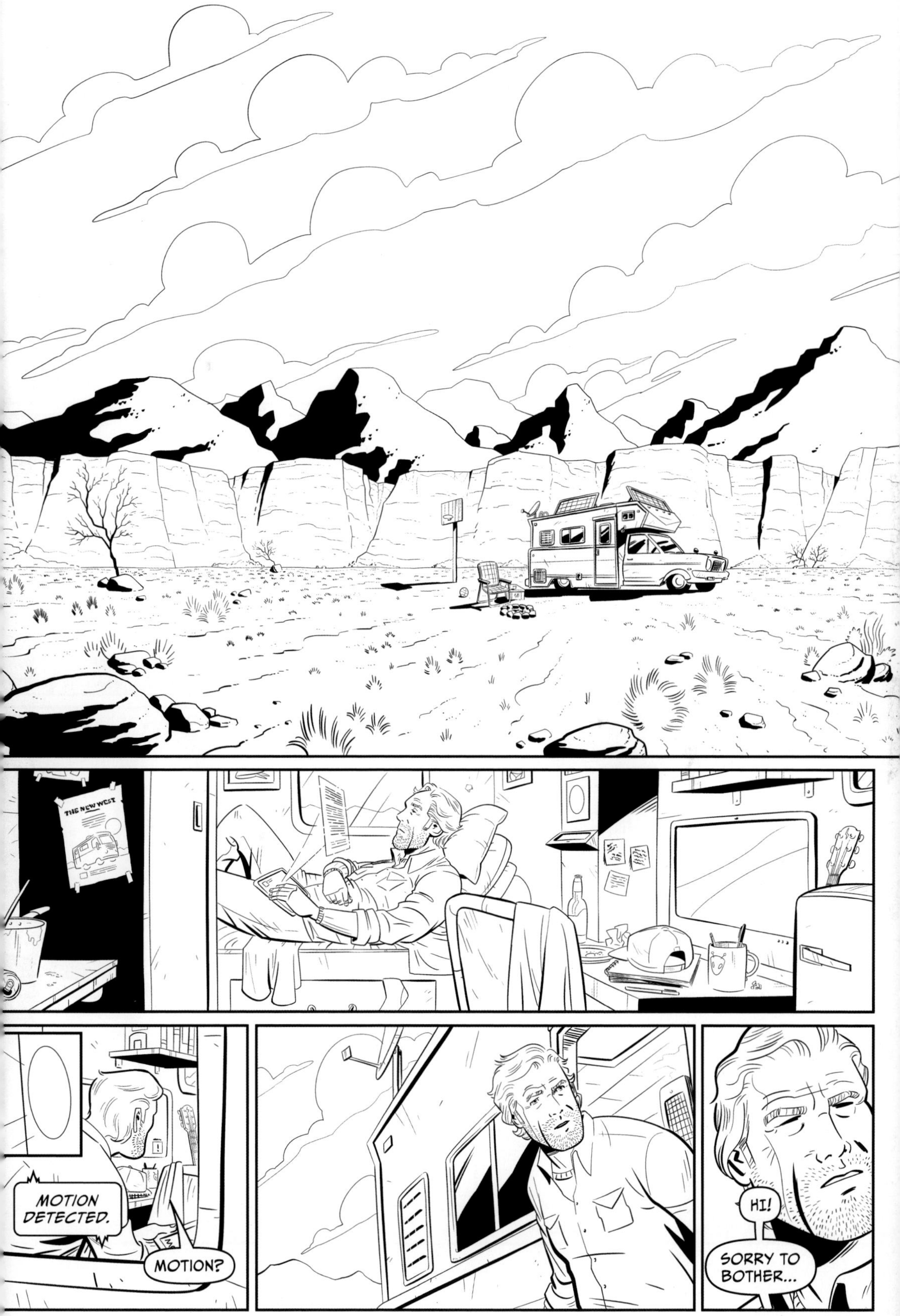
THE NEW WEST
MOTION DETECTED.
MOTION?
HI!
SORRY TO BOTHER...

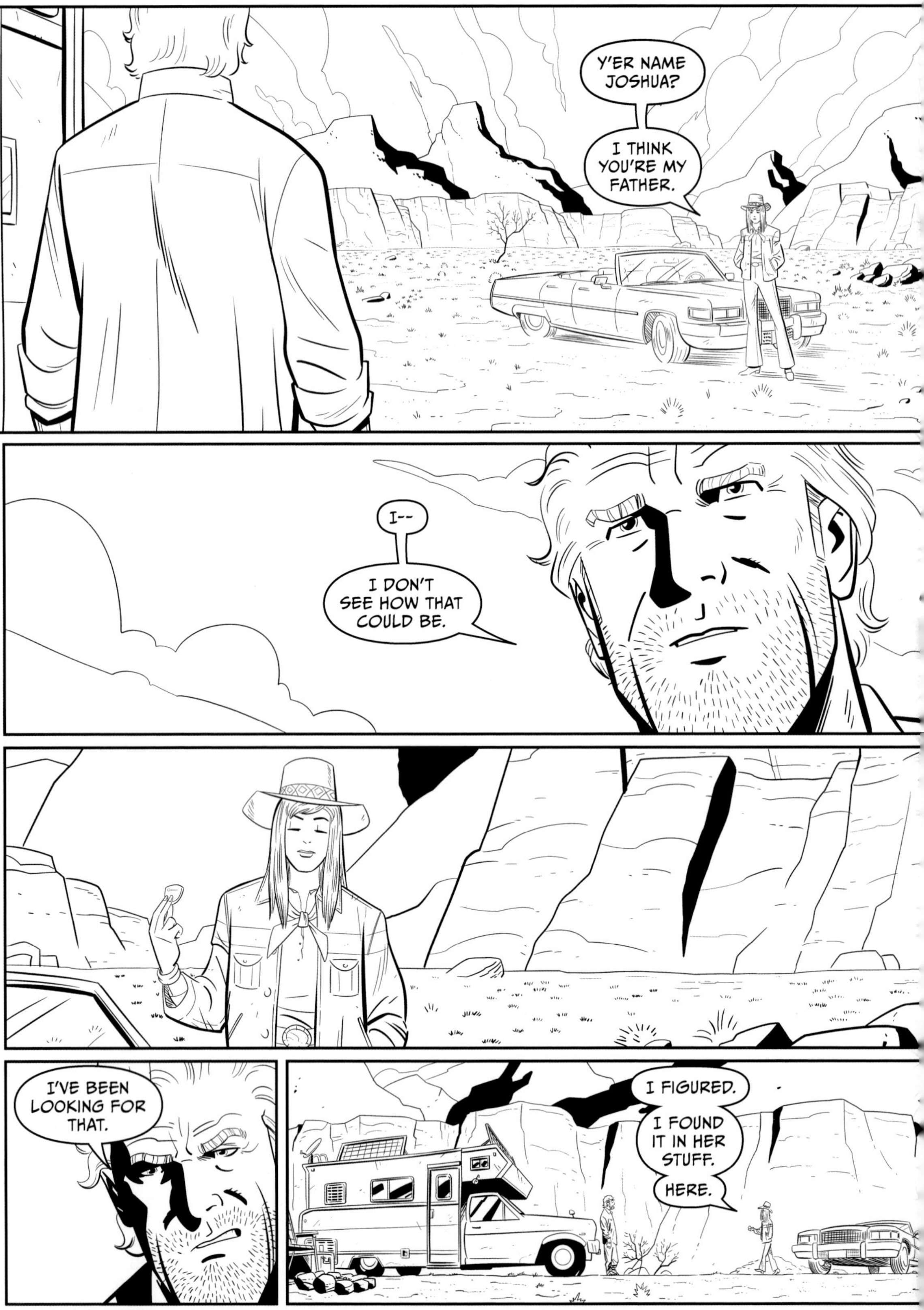

Y'ER NAME JOSHUA?
I THINK YOU'RE MY FATHER.
I--
I DON'T SEE HOW THAT COULD BE.
I'VE BEEN LOOKING FOR THAT.
I FIGURED.
I FOUND IT IN HER STUFF.
HERE.

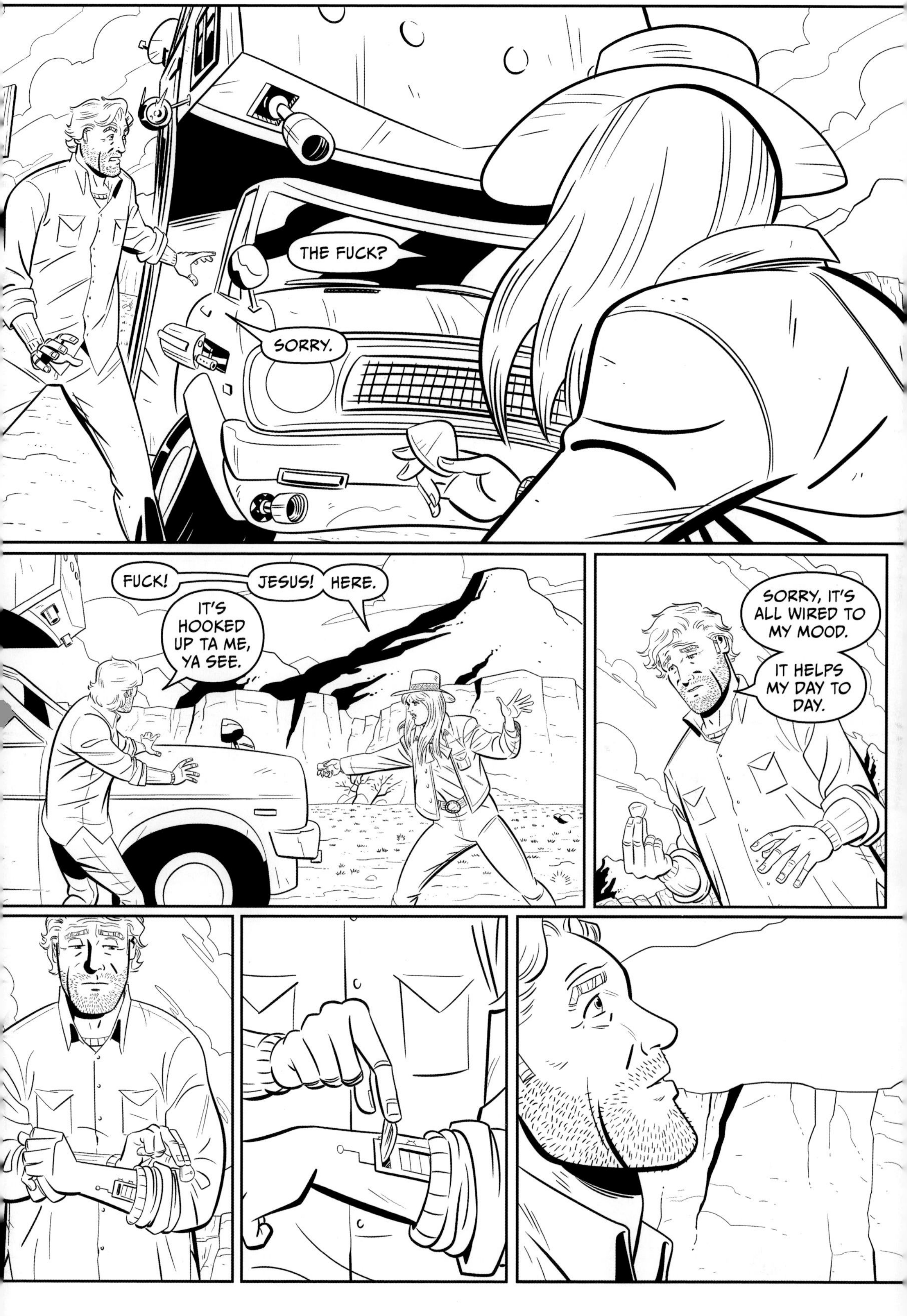
THE FUCK?
SORRY.
FUCK!
JESUS!
IT'S HOOKED UP TA ME, YA SEE.
HERE.
SORRY, IT'S ALL WIRED TO MY MOOD.
IT HELPS MY DAY TO DAY.

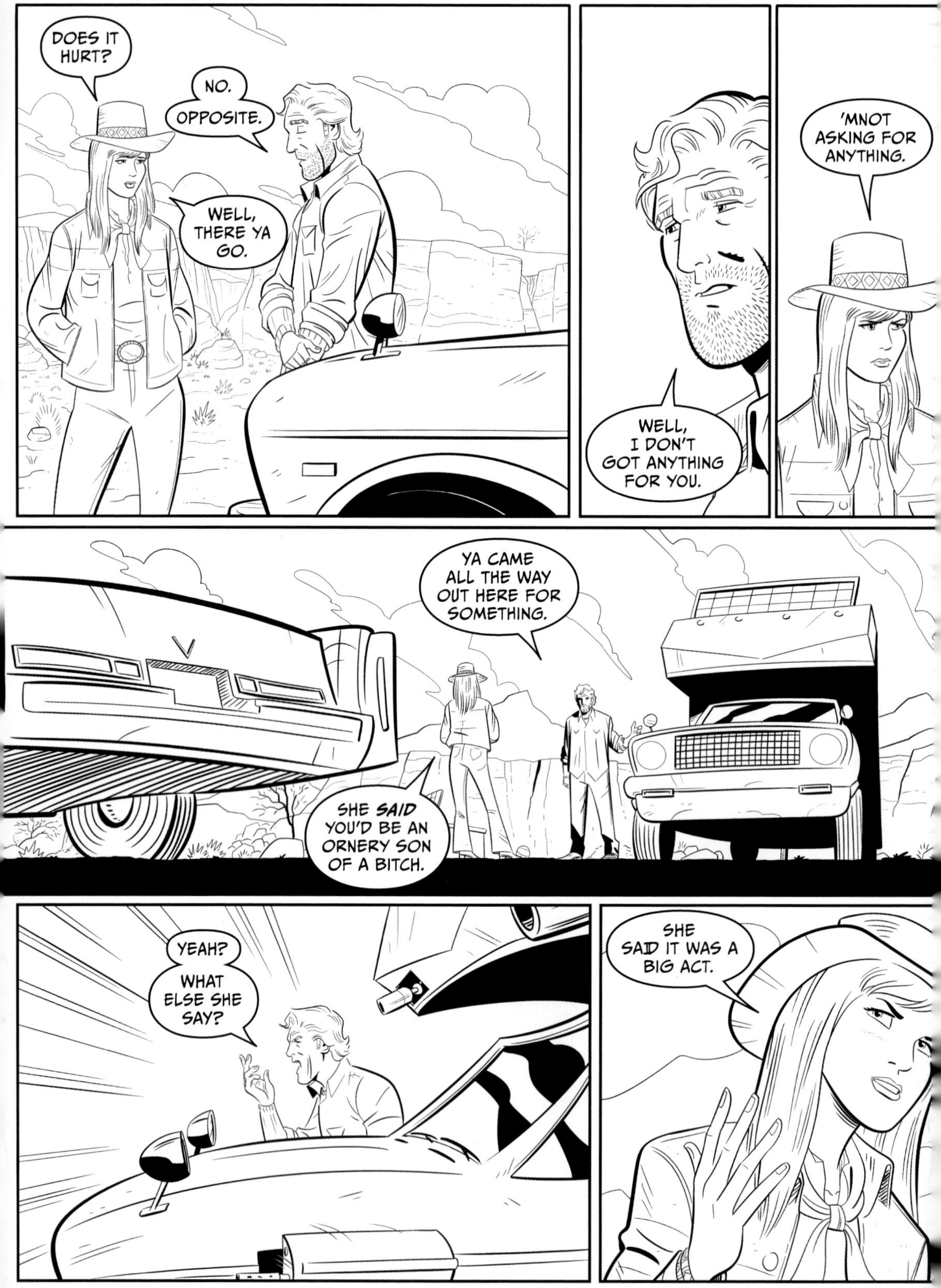
DOES IT HURT?
NO. OPPOSITE.
WELL, THERE YA GO.
WELL, I DON'T GOT ANYTHING FOR YOU.
'MNOT ASKING FOR ANYTHING.
YA CAME ALL THE WAY OUT HERE FOR SOMETHING.
SHE *SAID* YOU'D BE AN ORNERY SON OF A BITCH.
YEAH?
WHAT ELSE SHE SAY?
SHE SAID IT WAS A BIG ACT.

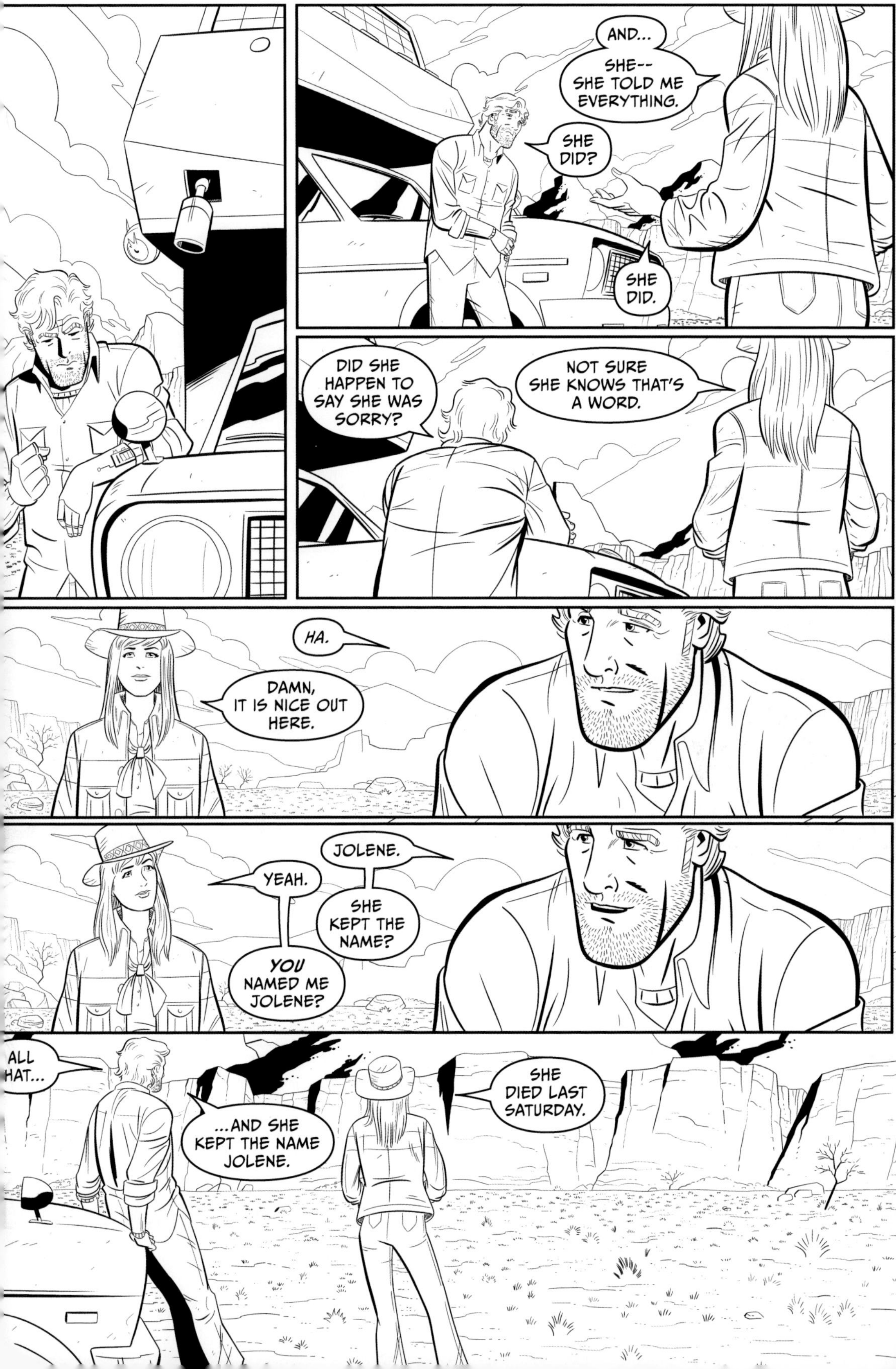
AND...
SHE-- SHE TOLD ME EVERYTHING.
SHE DID?
SHE DID.
DID SHE HAPPEN TO SAY SHE WAS SORRY?
NOT SURE SHE KNOWS THAT'S A WORD.
HA.
DAMN, IT IS NICE OUT HERE.
JOLENE.
YEAH.
SHE KEPT THE NAME?
YOU NAMED ME JOLENE?
ALL HAT...
...AND SHE KEPT THE NAME JOLENE.
SHE DIED LAST SATURDAY.

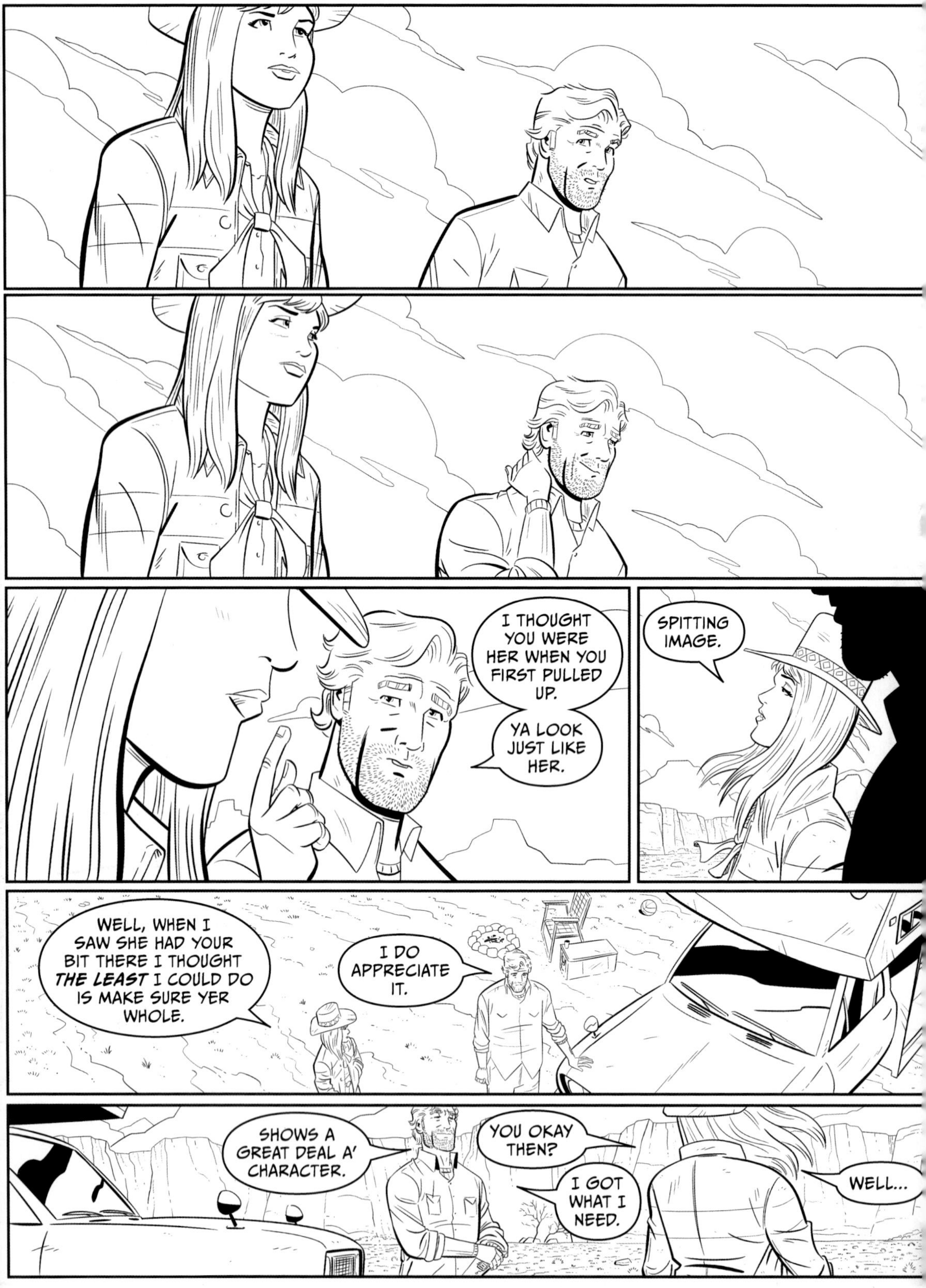
I THOUGHT YOU WERE HER WHEN YOU FIRST PULLED UP.
YA LOOK JUST LIKE HER.
SPITTING IMAGE.
WELL, WHEN I SAW SHE HAD YOUR BIT THERE I THOUGHT ***THE LEAST*** I COULD DO IS MAKE SURE YER WHOLE.
I DO APPRECIATE IT.
SHOWS A GREAT DEAL A' CHARACTER.
YOU OKAY THEN?
I GOT WHAT I NEED.
WELL...

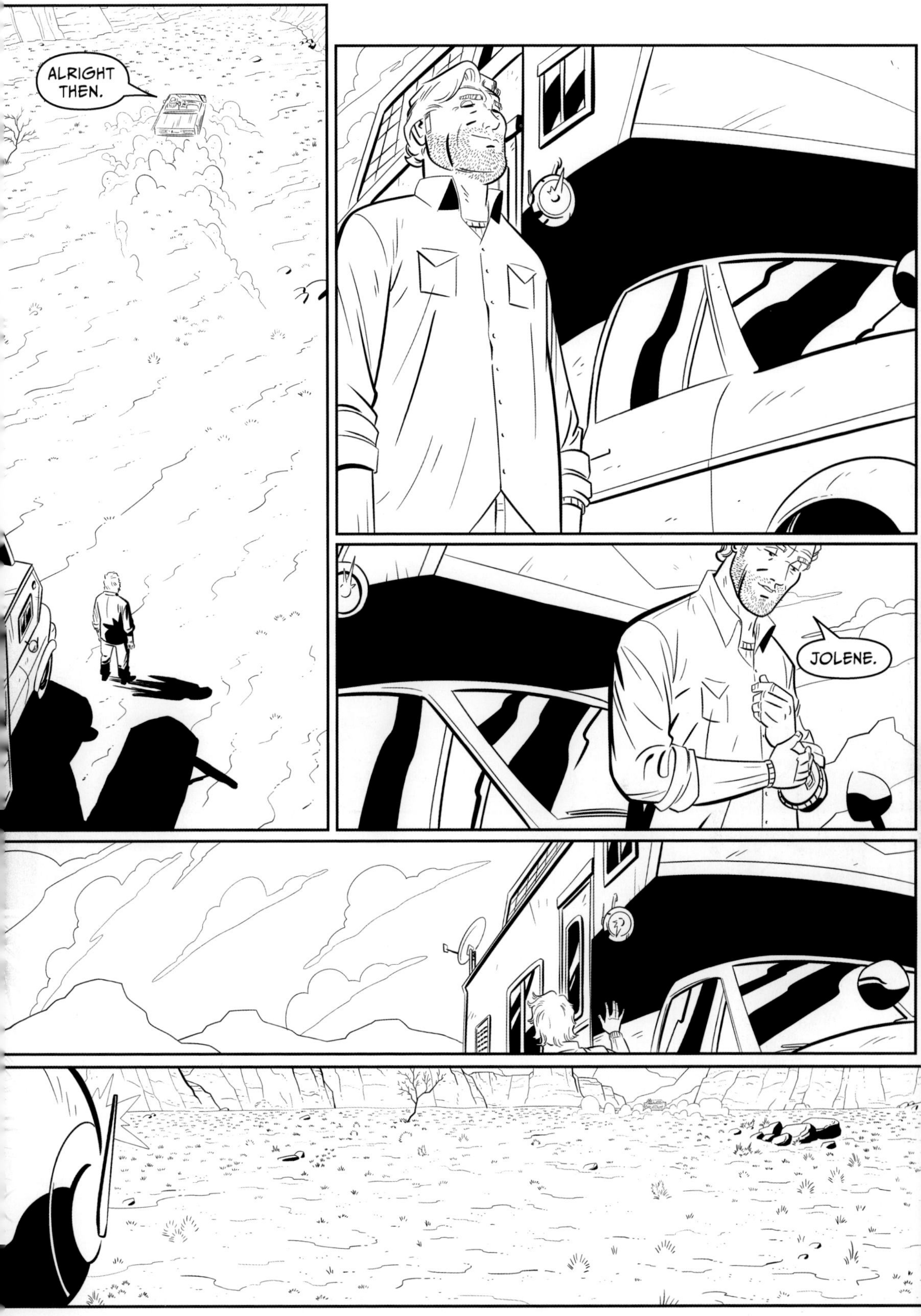
ALRIGHT THEN.
JOLENE.

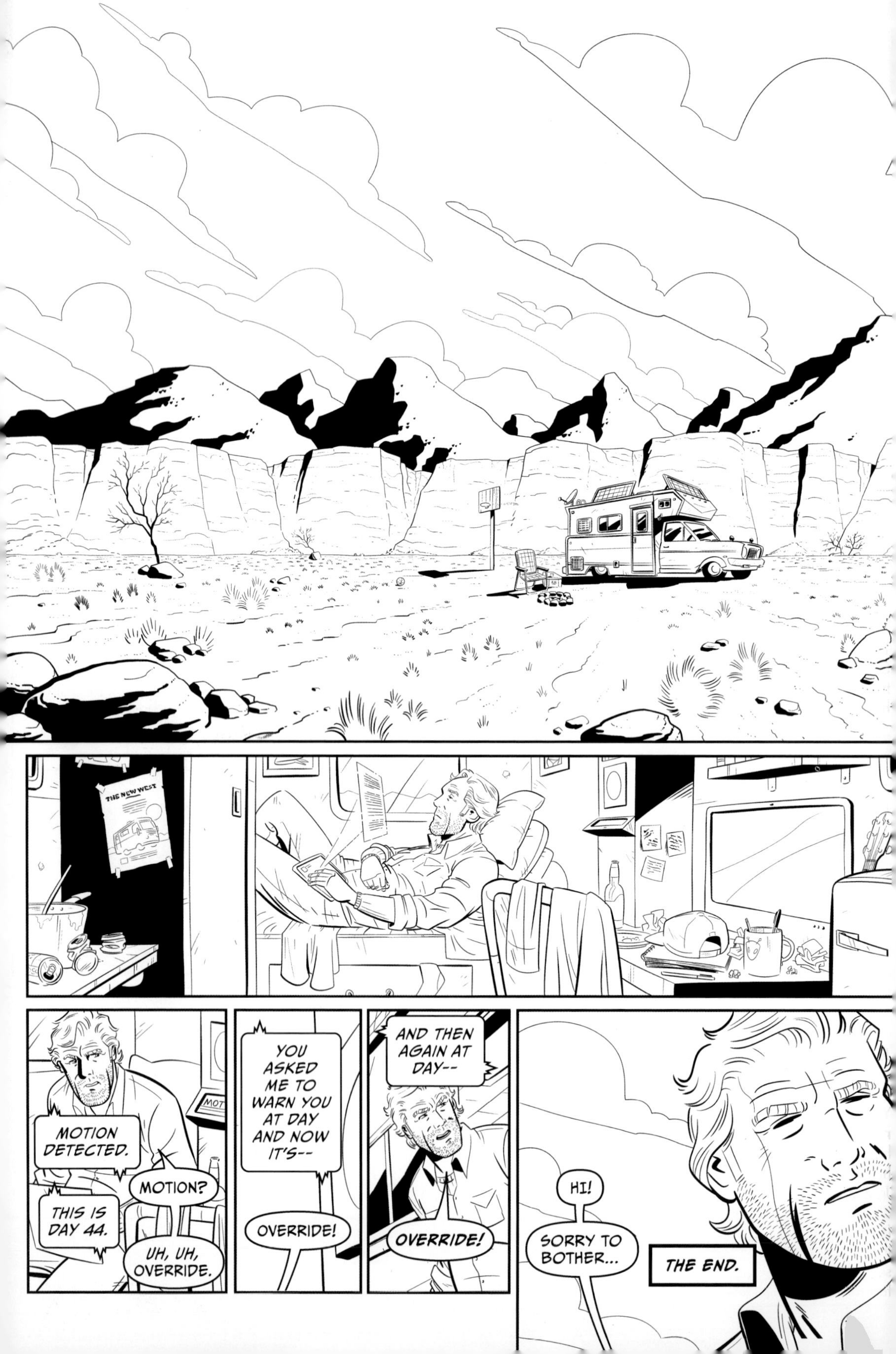
THE NEW WEST
MOTION DETECTED.
THIS IS DAY 44.
MOTION?
UH, UH, OVERRIDE.
YOU ASKED ME TO WARN YOU AT DAY AND NOW IT'S--
OVERRIDE!
AND THEN AGAIN AT DAY--
OVERRIDE!
HI!
SORRY TO BOTHER...
THE END.

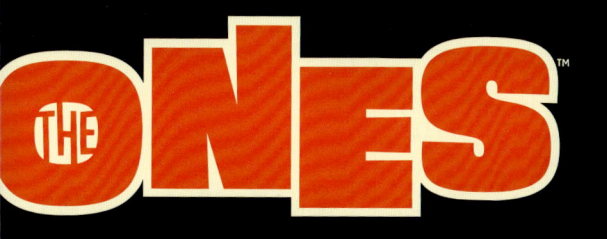

THE ONES™

SKETCHBOOK

NOTES BY JACOB EDGAR

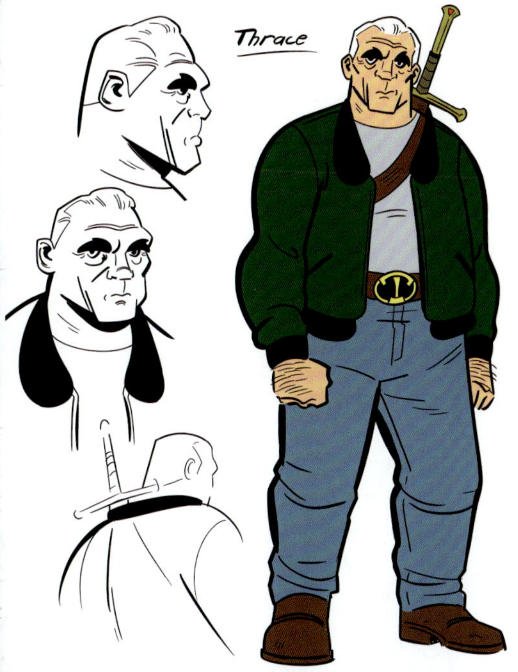

Thrace

Thrace is very inspired by my love of Jack Kirby and Tim Sale. Specifically, in his face and his blocky build, I tried to echo some of the things I admire in their work. And then later in the story when I chose to have Thrace lose his hair, I started to see a lot of Vinnie Jones in him.

Novus probably went through more tweaking than anyone; we even had a male version at one point. I wanted her costume to be clean and instantly recognizable in a way that classic Silver/Bronze Age superheroes were. She's the only one of our characters that I really think of as a "superhero."

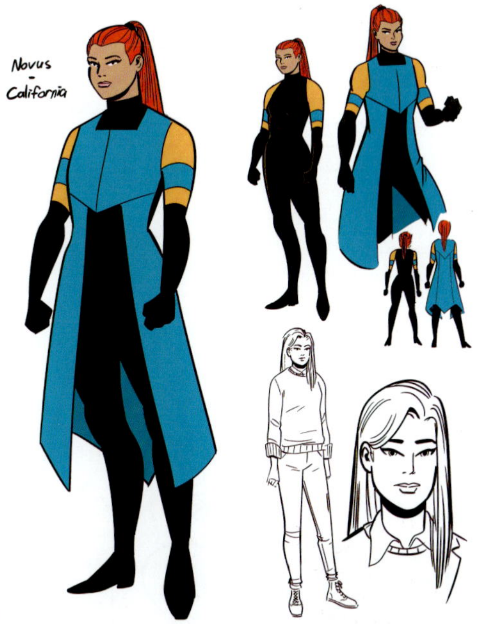

Novus
-
California

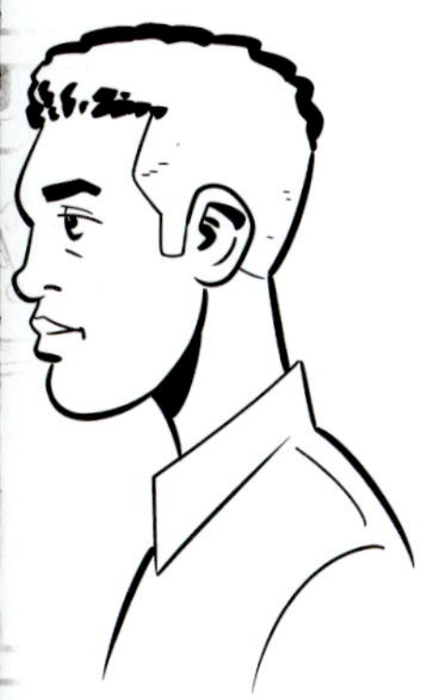

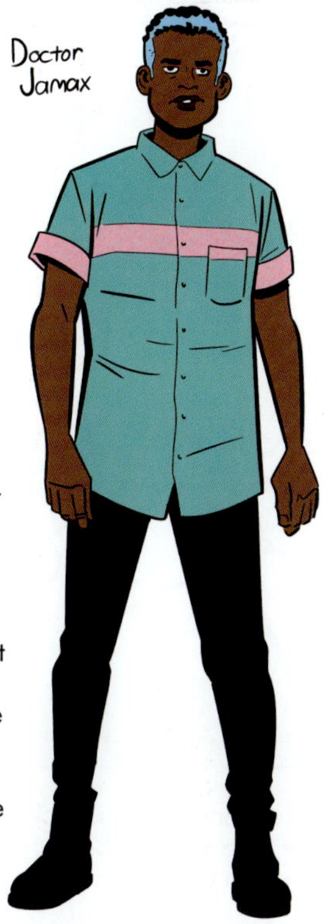

Doctor
Jamax

Jamax is the cool kid in your school that you realize you don't know anything about. You just see him across the room and think, "That guy has cool style, I wonder what his deal is?" Our original Jamax was female and more obviously "wizardesque" (trademarking this term) in the way they dressed, but we settled on a more discreet fashion sense.

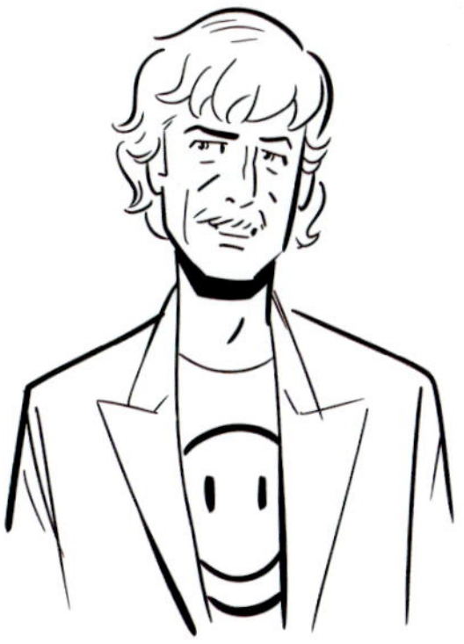

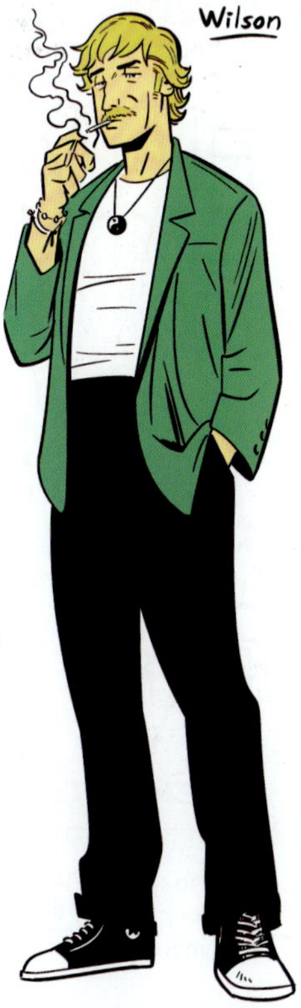

Wilson

Wilson came pretty easy. We talked a lot about actors for his inspiration. Jason Bateman, Owen Wilson, and Jason Sudeikis mainly. Obviously more of . . . Wilson comes through in the final. His fashion sense is a bit of Don Johnson from *Miami Vice* and a bit of '90s Johnny Depp and Robert Downey Jr. His rotation of joke T-shirts came to me randomly; I've got no real explanation for it other than it was fun for me. I originally imagined him as a constant smoker, but that faded away fairly quickly.

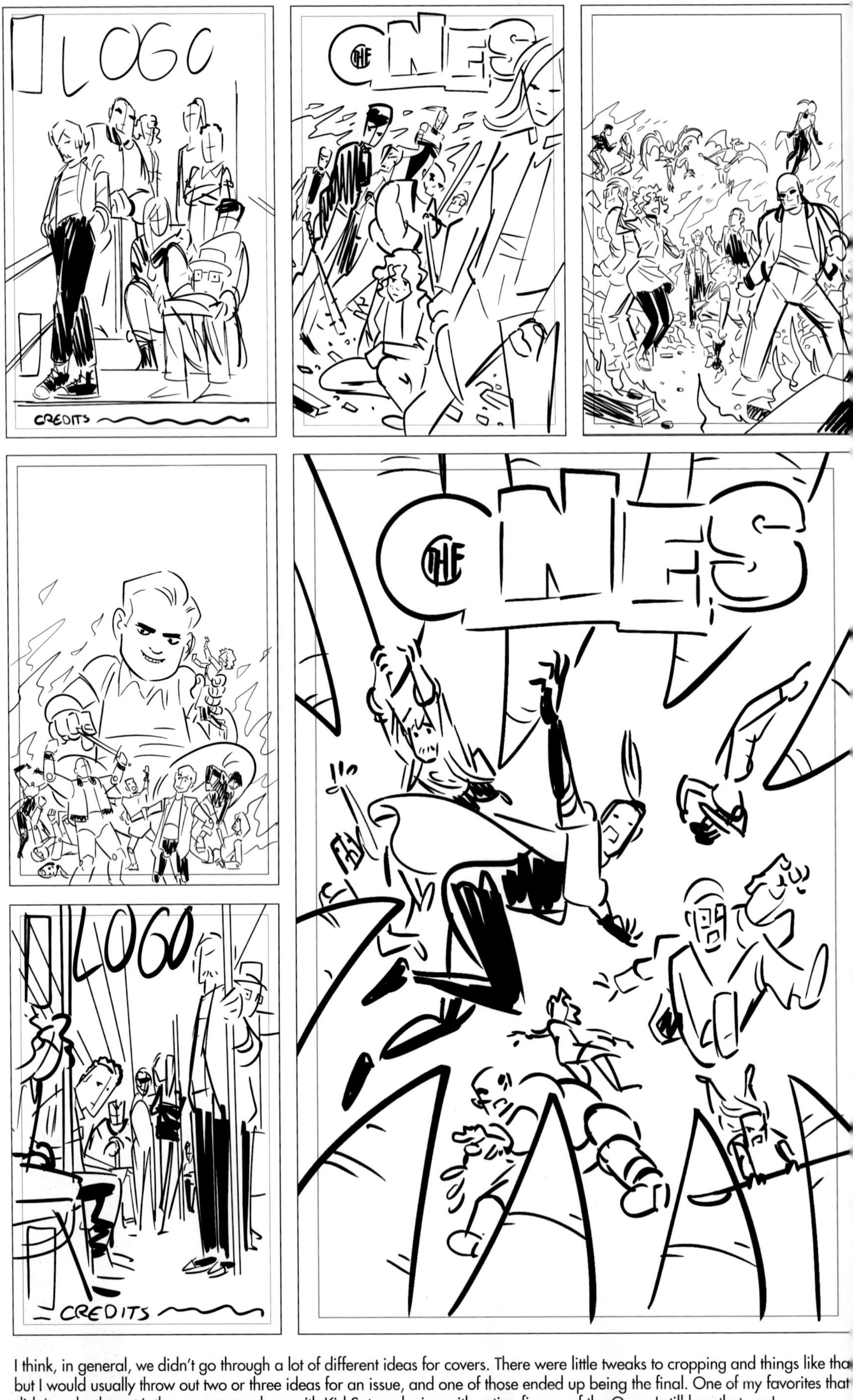
LOGO
CREDITS
THE ONES
THE ONES
LOGO
CREDITS

I think, in general, we didn't go through a lot of different ideas for covers. There were little tweaks to cropping and things like tha but I would usually throw out two or three ideas for an issue, and one of those ended up being the final. One of my favorites that didn't make the cut is the one you see here with Kid Satan playing with action figures of the Ones. I still love that one!

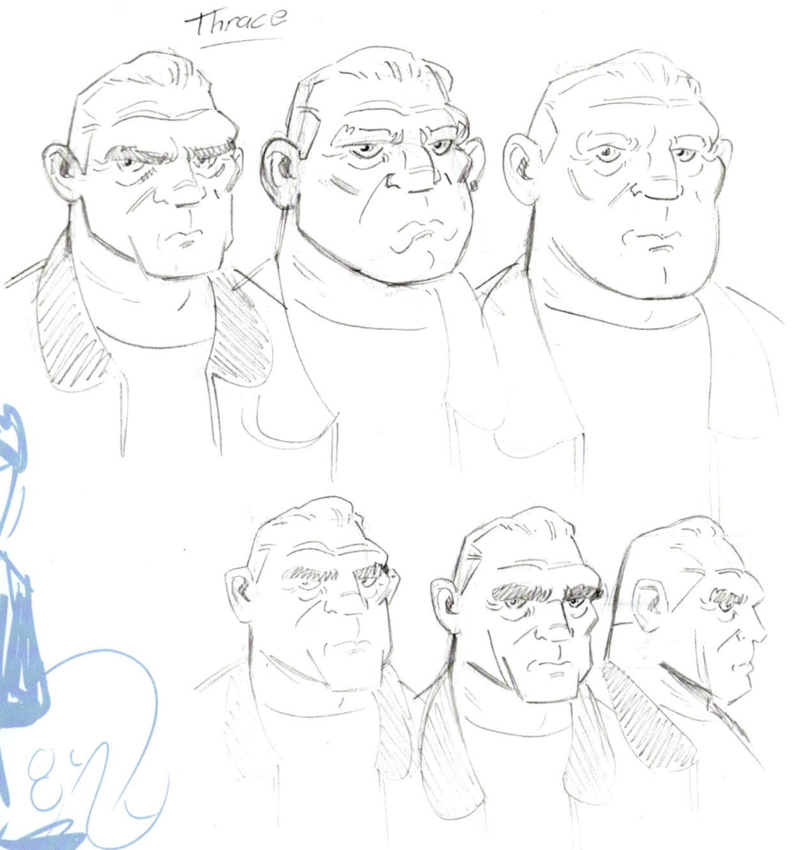
Thrace

became obvious with Thrace that e needed to have harsh, angular eatures. A rounded face didn't fit is character.

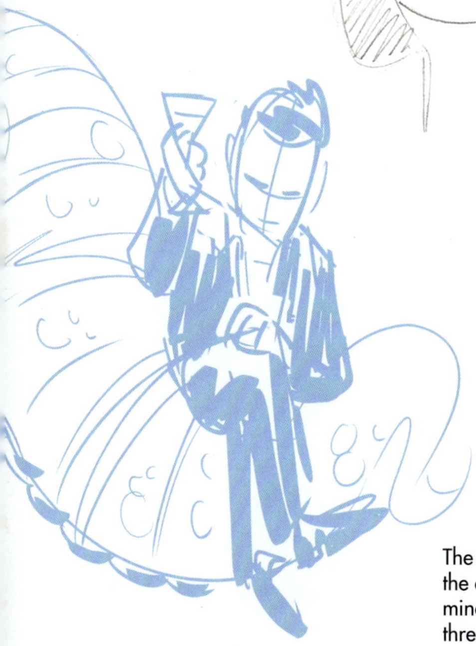

The cover for issue four came from Brian. I think this sketch may have been the only rough we did for it . . . but he had this one fully formed in his mind, including all of the negative space. It's so different from the other three and such a striking way to end the arc, I think.

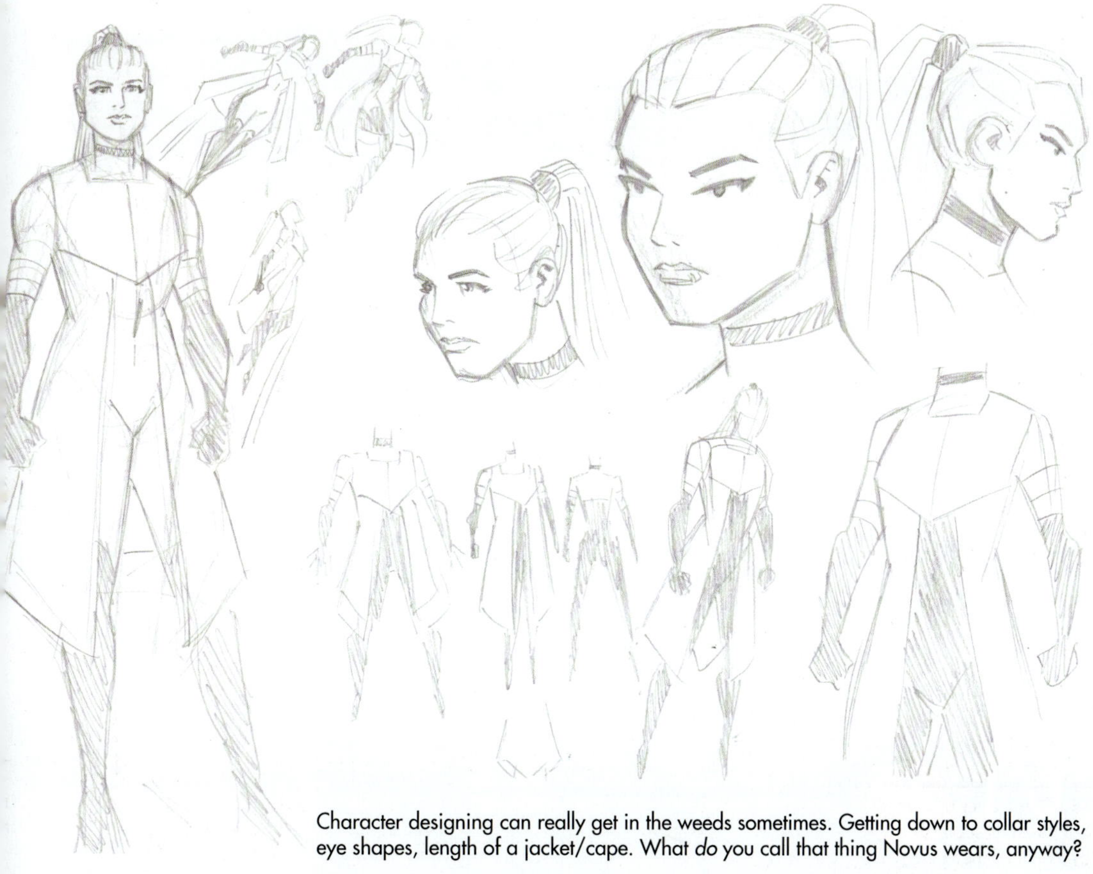

Character designing can really get in the weeds sometimes. Getting down to collar styles, eye shapes, length of a jacket/cape. What *do* you call that thing Novus wears, anyway?

[...]K OUT MORE BOOKS [...] THE *NEW YORK TIMES* BESTSELLING AND EISNER AWARD-WINNING

JINXWORLD LINE FROM DARK HORSE COMICS!

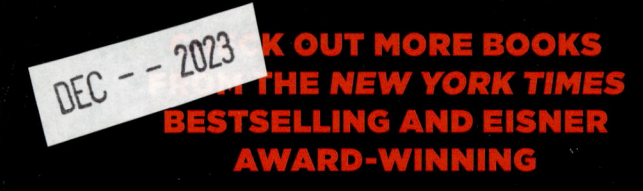

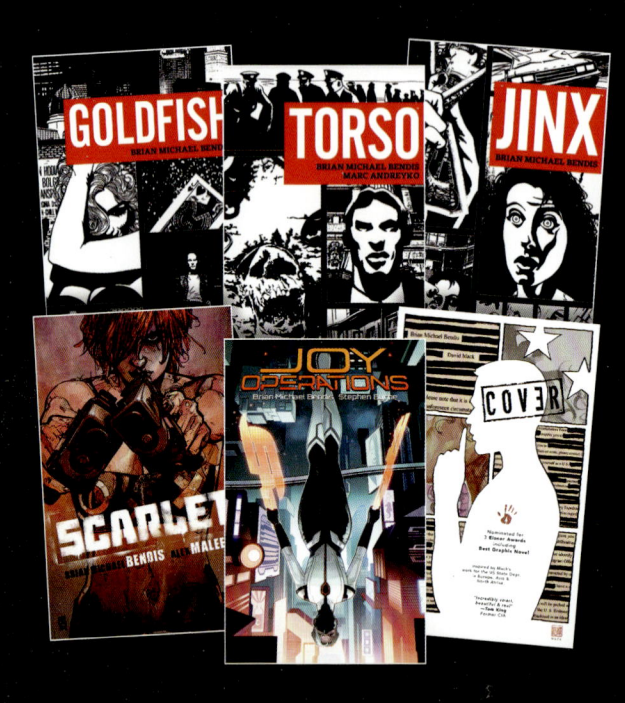

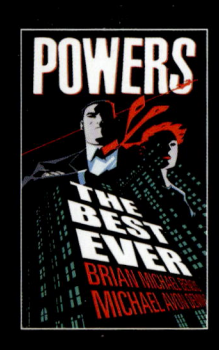

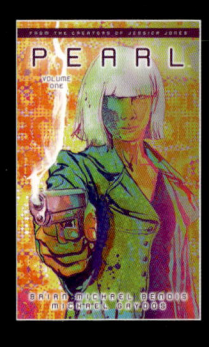

POWERS
THE BEST EVER
BRIAN MICHAEL BENDIS
MICHAEL AVON OEMING

PEARL
VOLUME ONE

POWERS: THE BEST EVER
ISBN 978-1-50673-016-5 | $29.99
Brian Michael Bendis, Michael Avon Oeming

POWERS VOLUME 1
ISBN 978-1-50673-017-2 | $29.99
Brian Michael Bendis, Michael Avon Oeming

POWERS VOLUME 2
ISBN 978-1-50673-018-9 | $29.99
Brian Michael Bendis, Michael Avon Oeming

POWERS VOLUME 3
ISBN 978-1-50673-019-6 | $29.99
Brian Michael Bendis, Michael Avon Oeming

POWERS VOLUME 4
ISBN 978-1-50673-020-2 | $29.99
Brian Michael Bendis, Michael Avon Oeming

PEARL VOLUME 1
ISBN 978-1-50672-932-9 | $19.99
Brian Michael Bendis, Alex Maleev

PEARL VOLUME 2
ISBN 978-1-50672-933-6 | $19.99
Brian Michael Bendis, Alex Maleev

PEARL VOLUME 3
ISBN 978-1-50672-934-3 | $24.99
Brian Michael Bendis, Alex Maleev

GOLDFISH
TORSO
BRIAN MICHAEL BENDIS
MARC ANDREYKO
JINX
BRIAN MICHAEL BENDIS
JOY OPERATIONS
SCARLET
COVER

GOLDFISH
ISBN 978-1-50673-014-1 | $19.99
Brian Michael Bendis

TORSO
ISBN 978-1-50673-025-7 | $19.99
Brian Michael Bendis

JINX
ISBN 978-1-50673-015-8 | $24.99
Brian Michael Bendis

SCARLET
ISBN 978-1-50673-024-0 | $29.99
Brian Michael Bendis, Alex Maleev

JOY OPERATIONS
ISBN 978-1-50672-946-6 | $24.99
Brian Michael Bendis, Stephen Byrne

COVER VOLUME 1
ISBN 978-1-50673-055-4 | $19.99
Brian Michael Bendis, David Mack

BRILLIANT
ISBN 978-1-50673-011-0 | $19.99
Brian Michael Bendis, Mike Bagley

THE ONES VOLUME 1
ISBN 978-1-50672-991-6 | $24.99
Brian Michael Bendis, Jacob Edgar

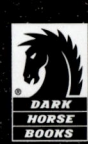

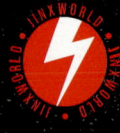

AVAILABLE AT YOUR LOCAL COMICS SHOP OR BOOKSTORE TO FIND A COMICS SHOP IN YOUR AREA, VISIT COMICSHOPLOCATOR.COM
For more information or to order direct, visit darkhorse.com

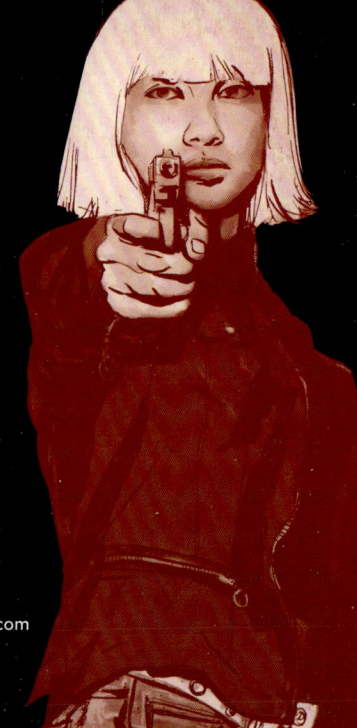